Population Zero: Rise of the Exosapiens

By L.N. Parsons

This is a work of fiction. Names, characters, businesses, places, events and incidents are either the products of the author's imagination or used in a fictitious manner. Any resemblance to actual persons, living or dead, or actual events is purely coincidental.

Copyright © 2016 by L.N. Parsons

All rights reserved.

Published in the United States of America by AREA 42.

ISBN (13): 978-0-692-71501-7

ISBN (10): 0-692-71501-0

Printed in the United States of America.

Cover image by NASA/JPL-Caltech.

Creative contributions by J.A. Swift.

All rights reserved.

DEDICATION

This volume one original is dedicated to TNT (my troops "T" and "T"). I stared evil in the face armed with my undying love for both of you. With timeless thoughts of you as my heart's armor, I stared down the ambassadors of darkness with contemptuous mockery. That subversive, endangered evil was powerless to do anything to extinguish my eternal love for you.

I would like to deliver my extreme thanks and undying gratitude to my eternal soul mate: The Captain. You are out of this world Quickdraw! I will protect your heart for all eternity in this multiverse.

For my families in the Doghouses: There is no end to your special relativity! I love you guys without time!

Preface

The prospect of settling Earth's species into other areas of space is no longer uncertain at this moment in time. The familiar arguments on both sides of the space colonization debate have strong points. But in 2025, the case for hastily leaving the planet *before* a species-ending situation could develop was by far one of the most predominant human imperatives of all. Even those who insisted on disagreeing with a premature mass exodus into the hostile void of space knew in their hearts that their argument of "get real and come back down to Earth" was failing.

If wars throughout history were supposed to have been fought about ideas, then the war to fight for living or dying is an *idea* about the preferred future of our race. This is the story of one small group of humans and their disagreement with the idea that humans should forego or postpone leaving planet Earth in this lifetime.

The war the humans were fighting in the early 21st century was a life and death fight against all evil, and was fought to firmly promulgate the *idea* that we all need to unite for a purpose that is greater than ourselves. To the people who believe humans will find answers on other worlds for some of the most vexing problems of human civilization: I salute you. You are one of the many manifestations of the light of hope in this life.

You, the explorers and settlers of space must continue your journey into the unknown with increasingly bold resolve as time continues marching on. You will not be alone out there in that timeless dark space. You are all leaders, and the number of your likeness must be allowed to thrive into the future. If you view space as a future home, then your greatest challenge here on Earth is training yourself to ignore the admonishment of those who think space is nothing but wholesale death and a collection of useless rocks.

Space is neither an empty void, nor is it destined to be the exclusive future domain of selfish dreamers and heartless profiteers. Home is best defined in the keen eyes of the beholder, and you are that beholder. Your great-great-grandchildren might turn out to be interplanetary salmon farmers and "off-planet" vehicle maintenance mechanics. I heard those jobs have good medical benefits, but I'd sure worry about those fish.

My decision to write this book was based on my long held belief that the human race is in unnecessary danger of becoming extinct. But people are people, and not everyone agrees about the absolute true level of danger. In fact, some people think that only something like outright mental illness could lead to such a hypothesis.

There are many humans willing to leave the planet right now, today. Not because we do not have the fortitude here on Earth to fight for what we believe in, or because we are "crazy", or any of that other garbage. It is because we know we are destined to have our "eggs" in more than one basket.

We humans collectively have a limited focus of the *meanings* of fortitude. Let us be strong and firm in our conviction to settle into other worlds. Yes, it will require fortitude. If you have ever been lost at sea, or stuck above the Arctic Circle wondering whether the world forgot about you, then you probably have a special appreciation for *that* kind of fortitude eh?

Biology teaches us that when two or more populations fall into conflict in the biosphere, the product of the resulting overlap is something unique, and largely unpredictable. We are all prone to become entirely different from the original uniform ingredients that went into the first human casserole. Species migrate to more conducive habitats. Humans migrate to other planets, and there is going to be a lot of those planets to choose from. We're running out of room and resources to fit everyone on this planet in a healthful way. And hey, most people aren't very happy about the possibility of having their sex lives controlled by the population enforcers. My thoughts on that have always been something like, "procure replacements for yourselves and focus on extending the longevity of those of us who are already here". In light of that sentiment, it seems like longevity would always lag procreation.

Let's get busy building robots and put humans out there in the solar system and beyond. Let us increase the probability that we will survive, and eliminate the "one-habitat-extinction" constant from future survival formulas. We need you to consider leaving the planet if you think you can survive it.

Rise now and go forward. Be one of the masters of this long foreseen plan. We are the Exosapiens. We will permanently preserve our culture at all cost. We hope you will choose exodus over extinction. We are headed for another world where the human population is presently zero. If we should encounter other life forms on our journey, we will exercise full planetary protection protocols and avoid uninformed contact. What follows thereafter will likely be stranger than fiction.

-Life without fear is the defeat of death. Death without fear is the defeat of doubt.

-Neve R. Luzanah

X-Tenuating Circumstances

California, USA
Contra Costa County
1972, 0933 HRS

"Congratulations Mrs. O'Conaill, it's a beautiful healthy baby". Those were the first words Marie O'Conaill remembered hearing from the nurse after waking up from an exhaustion-induced slumber. She was glad to be having a second child while she was still in her early twenties. She was filled with joy about having a family of her own, and was determined to take her family in a direction that led to happier, brighter places than the ones she and her younger sister were brought up in.

Marie felt almost guilty for her inability to ignore her unusual hunger from the grueling process of child birth. She was truly filled with emotion about her second child, but could not ignore the persistent visions she kept having of ham and cheese omelets, orange juice, and toast with blackberry jam. The nursing staff was glad to oblige Marie with the mechanisms of her craving, and reassured her that it was perfectly normal for child birth to evoke a powerful appetite. They reminded her that the only way the baby would thrive was if she kept herself healthy. But two bites into the omelet, Marie realized that she knew nothing about her newborn child.

"Here is your coffee Mrs. O'Conaill. Baby is sleeping comfortably. We just finished cleaning her up and checking her vitals."

"It's a girl? Are you serious?" All in an instant, Marie forgot about her breakfast entirely, and became nauseous and disgusted with herself for having placed her own needs before the needs of the child. At least, that's the punishment she inflicted upon herself. She couldn't help but think, *"Geez, what a shitty mom I am already...eating an omelet before I even knew the damn gender for crying out loud."* Her mouth began to water unchecked with her saliva, and her gag reflex was teetering on avalanche-breakdown. The veteran nurse immediately recognized the signs and placed the wastebasket under Marie's chin just in time for the short-notice vomit to flood out into the plastic liner. The nurse produced a clean, moist hand towel for her to wipe her mouth with, and reassured her again while she tried to collect her thoughts and redirect her mind.

"May I please hold her?" asked Marie.

"You most certainly can Mrs. O'Conaill. I'll bring her right in. Thank you for trying to eat. Baby needs that, and so does mama."

The nurse left the room and Mr. Clyde O'Conaill saw an opportunity to approach his honey and comfort her in her exhaustion.

"Hey you. Do you feel better after throwing up?" asked Clyde.

"No, I need to have her close to me. She's all alone surrounded by strangers."

"Here she is" said the nurse as she lowered the newborn into Marie's arms. "She's a healthy nine pound, fifteen and three-quarters-ounces baby girl."

"Isn't that unusually heavy nurse?" asked Clyde.

"Well, yes, it is a little on the heavy side. But we're running tests to make sure she's not in any danger. I wouldn't worry too much sir."

Marie stared at the face of her precious daughter and gently rubbed her fingertip across baby's cheek to check for the rooting reflex. Marie reached into the bottom of the little blanket-cocoon her new baby was wrapped in to feel for warmth on her feet. What she felt was strange enough to get her undivided attention. It felt like the feet of a ten-year old. Marie unfurled the bottom of the blanket and observed what could only have been described as the longest feet on a newborn she had ever seen. The second and third toes of both feet were so long that it looked unnatural. She quickly covered the feet back up and checked the hands. It was the same thing-extraordinarily long fingers for a newborn baby.

Marie kept these observations to herself and relaxed herself back into the recline of her hospital bed, nervously staring at the ceiling all night wondering whether Mr. O'Conaill was going to be able to handle the baby's abnormalities. She knew he had wanted a son, but she trusted that his heart was big enough to love both of his daughters with the same genuine affection as he would have bestowed upon a son. She trusted in his love, and allowed herself the privilege of falling asleep to that one vital thought.

12 April, 1981

Kahmay O'Conaill and her older sister Rebecca knew they would be in trouble if they were caught out of bed at 3:45 in the morning playing with the radio. But neither O'Conaill child could resist tuning back in to the station they had found on Kahmay's Hallicrafters S-120 two days earlier. The station was broadcasting live coverage of the first Space Shuttle launch. Kahmay found it quite by accident while slowly sweeping through each of the four bands of the radio. Such was her habit in the wee sleepless hours of her night owl life. She had the headphones plugged in so that nobody in the house could hear the copious static, which had to be suffered through in order to get to the brief signs of intelligent signal. Kahmay already had the patience necessary to persist at age eight.

The radio's band selector knob had a problem when switching between Bands 1, 2, and 3. So when Kahmay found the live broadcast from the Kennedy Space Center two days earlier, she wasn't sure whether it was coming through on 9.9 Megacycles, 3.78 Megacycles, or 1340 Kilocycles. It was exciting to Kahmay to be joined by her older sister for this momentous event. They were both happy that the original launch was scrubbed two days earlier. It allowed them the time to thoroughly premeditate their quiet launch party in Kahmay's room.

"We are joined live here at Launch Complex 39A to witness the next phase of human discovery into the uncharted regions of space, as the veteran Commander John Young will blast off here in about three minutes accompanied by Skylab expert and first time space flyer, Pilot Robert Crippen."

"I can't believe these fools are about to launch out into space" said Rebecca. "Can you imagine? What if they can't get back? Are they just supposed to drift off out into space and what...run out of air to breathe...and food to eat?"

      Kahmay thought about her sister's comments while the countdown audio from the launch pad was fed through the transmission. She could feel her stomach getting butterflies in empathetic imaginations of what it would really be like to be less than a minute away from blasting off into space at over 17,000 miles per hour. Once the countdown reached "10", it was like someone plugged her epidermis into a light socket. The anticipation of it caused Kahmay's neck and arm fuzz to stand up. Immediately after lift-off, the rumble of the rocket boosters and the play-by-play commentary from the radio announcer was better than any sports contest. The imagined vision of these two astronauts screaming toward the stars with their hair on fire burned itself into Kahmay's unnaturally keen long-term memory. It was her first major injection of the highly addictive substance known as "realistic imagination", and she desperately hoped she would not be forced into rehab over it. She knew it was real. She had to have it.

March, 1988
5th Period Calculus

The feeling of nausea, and the watery saliva of nervous energy, fear, and intimidation filled Kahmay's being as she waited patiently in the empty classroom after the formal class period was over. Today was the day she was to receive her personality judgement from the dreaded Mr. Jake Bumbaugh. The Vietnam veteran turned calculus teacher was glad to single out those students who were underachieving, because he knew just how to dig into their soul and "straighten them out". The world according to Bumbaugh was a world that did not care about what your personal hang-ups were, or what your latest excuse for underperforming on the exam was. All he cared about was slapping you into reality and getting you to focus on what was really important in life. His uninitiated junior trigonometry students were quick to discover that the shedding of childishness, the future of high-technology and engineering, and the "eleventh commandment" were his three most important teaching priorities. Although, everyone in the junior class was pretty sure he was *not* being serious when he suggested designating the identity "$Sin^2\theta + Cos^2\theta = 1$" as the eleventh commandment of God.

Kahmay swore he was intentionally prolonging the wait to increase the stress her mind would have to endure before he tore her apart. His mob-boss style entrance into the classroom only exacerbated the tension, as he closed the door and sat quietly for a minute while pulling the cigars from his inner coat pocket and lighting one up. It was time.

"Do you have any idea why I would even bother wasting my time talking to someone like you?" asked Bumbaugh, exhaling a thick cloud of late-eighties indifference into the air immediately in front of Kahmay.

"No sir, I don't".

"It's because you make me sick...students like you. You waltz in here with your little hippie outfits and your jokes, and you couldn't care less about the impact this course will have on your life in the future". Bumbaugh allowed several moments of uncomfortable silence to pass while he puffed his stogie and strained to keep the intimidating look on his face long enough to transition into his next talking point. "The only reason why you haven't been completely eliminated from the advanced placement program yet is because you're too damn smart for your own good. You think you can just coast and laugh your way through this indefinitely, staying just far enough above standards to avoid meetings like this? You are currently riding the academic line between average and good, while your dedicated classmates, who EAT, SLEEP, and BREATHE this material, are working their asses off to maintain a 'B'. You should be ashamed of yourself for pissing away a once in a lifetime opportunity like this. With your attitude, I don't see you progressing beyond this level. You're just not taking it seriously enough. You have the potential to be great at this, and to go on in your life and do great things in the future. But unless you start taking this seriously, I'm going to insist that you stop dragging the other students down and get out of my classroom."

Kahmay could feel herself starting to lose her self-control, and desperately wanted to get in his face to make him understand what kind of crap she had been through in her life. But playing the "I'd like to see you do as well as I have after walking a mile in my shoes" card was not going to fly with someone who flew through a wall of surface-to-air missiles, Triple-A fire, and rocket propelled grenades to go pick up his wounded and dying brothers in a foreign country. The recent death of Kahmay's father Clyde would probably have been laughable to him. Bumbaugh was a former combat pilot in the U.S. Army's Air Calvary from 1965 to 1972. Kahmay was going to have to live up to a higher standard and just take her verbal flogging with silence. *No problem*, she thought.

"Yes sir. Sorry it didn't work out."

"It didn't work out, because YOU haven't worked it out yet O'Conaill. Look me up again next year after you pull your head out of your ass! Get out of my sight, and don't come back until you can write out the antiderivative of the next incoming shit storm!"

Kahmay defiantly rose up out of her chair and made her rapid, door-slamming exit from the classroom. *FUCK him*, she thought. She walked with a purposeful, rapid pace toward the old 81' Mercury Cougar out in the high school parking lot. She had been driving it around town illegally for several weeks to get to school and run errands. She wanted to prove him wrong, and she wanted to prove to herself that he was not clairvoyant enough to determine her future with his words. She sped out of the parking lot past the truancy officers leaving a trail of black smoke and the stench of burnt motor oil in her wake. She was going to the library to check out some books and shut herself into a cocoon of painful metamorphosis and unnaturally fast-paced learning. *Fuck him*, she thought again. *Fuck him! Hippie outfit? He doesn't fuckin' know me! FUCK! HIM!*

Kaminari

Each time we look back into our history, we are somehow oddly perturbed by how crude and primitive our best efforts seem to us in the clarity of hindsight. Today's cutting edge razor of progress will surely appear more like a butter knife to our eyes in 50 years. In the future, seemingly mundane news of the present will be segregated into homogenous categories, then analyzed and scrutinized retrospectively for the ignorance of its contents. But in the present where we all exist right now, we carry on doing what we believe we *should* be doing.

We humans develop a sense of attachment to one another in our common plight to manage the inherently foul nature of our more challenging shared problems. With the most informed experts, we "move forward" into the future together. Sometimes we feel like we need to "move forward" knowing that the consequences of our actions could be even worse than death. What is this thing that drives us to push out of our familiar surroundings into the unknown? Does a salmon know that it will die for all of its hard work swimming to the spawning ground? We humans "swim upstream", and it seems like we intentionally invite pain into our lives. For what? Is it because we enjoy pain? Perhaps we are driven by something more obscured from our intuition; something more primitive maybe? Just how badly do you want to be that person who "goes forward", even when all the world seems to be telling you to turn back? Sometimes if you don't turn back, the world just wants you to disappear entirely.

    The people who dedicated their lives to Operation *Kibo* went to their deaths believing that their sacrifices would benefit every living thing on Earth. The benevolence of their actions made them a target for the kind of evil that seeks utter destruction on Earth. Because Team *Kibo* sacrificed for a benevolent higher purpose, and expected nothing more than validation from loved ones and countrymen, they were granted the rank of "eternal teachers". But the accumulation of ranks and prestigious-sounding titles were not their objectives. They simply wanted to feel good about their impact on the future of the human race...*in spite* of, and *despite* the haters.

    The people who would subsequently carry the spirit of *Kibo's* purpose into the next chapter of living human history were students of the old ways and masters. All available human knowledge and experience would need to be mustered in the endeavor to overcome the problem of evil in the immediate. In the wake of *Kibo*, the terrorist filth that destroyed the physical heroes did not succeed in extinguishing the ideology of hope and faith. Instead, the champions of the light were made stronger by the tragedy of *Kibo*. Another attempt to resettle the humans would be required. It was time to "get back on the horse" and ignore the voices of discouragement.

The second attempt to colonize interplanetary and interstellar space by the Earth humans would come quite a bit sooner than most expected it would. Operation *Kaminari*, as it was called, was meant to distribute the general human and economic damage from any future mission failures across a wide variety of risk-absorbing special organizational entities. *Kaminari* was the natural response of the Deep Space Expeditionary Command Council (DSECC) after the tragic failure of Operation *Kibo*. The Command Council sought to continue the doctrine of *Kibo* through the use of an improved plan. Really, it was rather like an improved way of *thinking* about the problem of Earth's increasingly uncertain future. The members of the council still wanted to create a safe haven for Earth as before. This time though, they only made themselves accountable for the vetting of personnel and for part of the funding processes. They could not afford for the last remaining remnants of public trust in them to evaporate. The council also knew that if the home government lost any more of the community's faith, chaos and anarchy would creep deeper into all of the countless cracks and crevices of society. Our worst enemies would use an environment of confusion to strike us while we were lost in the clutches of divided self-destruction.

Independent teams of trained individuals began springing up across all sectors of Earth, each with their own separate plans and procedures for complying with the primary mission objectives of *Kaminari*. The way it worked was that each participating team would need to make their own unique mission plan available to Headquarters Deep Space Expeditionary Forces (HQ/DSEF). Once all plans were submitted, DSECC had the last say for regulatory approval and launch window reservations. If the initial DSECC evaluation of a given ops-plan was favorable, the unique plan would then be sent to the special budgetary appropriations committee for an in-depth review and grant-ranking survey. The more merits a plan had in the eyes of the appropriations committee, the more likely it was that a plan would qualify for special non-commercial grants in accordance with the "interest(s) of the governmental body and/or citizenry" clause in the committee's revised mission assessment instructions. Optionally, each team with a completed DSECC-conforming mission plan would be allowed to pitch their plan to a number of commercial enterprises, who had all expressed advanced willingness to DSEF to invest in the projects of their choosing. Once certain favorable business concessions were made to the participating companies, and the team(s) had complied with all of the compulsory DSECC objectives outlined by *Kaminari*, the assumption was that the team(s) would then fulfill their contractual obligations to their corporate sponsors as applicable. The teams were hindered by nothing more than the limitations of their own ignorance and imaginations as to how to do this, and would still be allowed to launch from Earth regardless of whether extra funding was obtained or not. But a team without funding would never realistically be expected to get underway without something more than their own meager private financial resources. In the respective contractual agreement(s) between companies and mission teams, some contracts were worded in ways that put enormous legal pressure on groups that were strapped for resources. But humans were well accustomed to working and earning a living, and for the most part were not afraid of sweat and tears.

Undoubtedly there would be problems. Contract breach, accidents, and unforeseen outcomes were just a few of the likely obstacles for most teams. Ideally the participating teams would seek maximum advantage from wherever they could find it, and maintain honorable values in the process. Ideas like ethics, morals, and integrity were still valued by humanity in the early 21st century, but they were in danger of evaporating without some great positive breakthrough that all of the world would feel shared ownership of.

The collective effort of an individual team would guide it through the prevailing bureaucratic and technical obstacle courses, and then one day the team would just vanish into space. Not all departing teams would make it back to Earth, nor would all teams even have the *goal* of making it back to Earth.

Interstellar space would be the most hostile and unforgiving environment humans had yet encountered to the best of their own knowledge. But humans were not intimidated by this prospect. Large numbers of humans considered the hostile environs of space to be a calming alternative to the pervasive evil that had taken over Earth by the early 21st century. Space was really looking like the next logical move for humankind. In the spirit of *Carpe Diem,* some were more than ready for "tomorrow" to become "today".

By this time in history, most people did not care what the spin masters of global power said to ridicule the institution of hope. Over time, as the average human became increasingly more technologically empowered, the leaders of the global oligarchy tried their hardest to use subversive social engineering to stave off their loss of control. But humanity had gradually come to think of venturing into deep interstellar space as being significantly less dangerous than the risk of starvation, and *undeniably* less dangerous than 20th century terrestrial norms. People of Earth were not going to sit by and wait for the momentum to shift back to the old tired ways of wasting one's life just trying not to drown in rules, restrictions, or character assassinations. For the first time in known Earth history, the intersection of wisdom, experience, knowledge, technology, and scant resources had successfully germinated the seed of a mass exodus into space. Operation *Kaminari* was the economical choice. The collective conscience of people seemed to shift away from the conflicted moral arguments of the past. Patriots who were painted as traitors no longer cared what *this* world thought of them. Sure, the religions of the Earth each had their own various views on the moral questions of leaving Earth. But those who had resolved in their hearts to go into the beyond had no real moral questions. They felt compelled by their own higher powers to seek another world. They felt a duty to seek a solution to the problem of Earth having all of her "eggs in one basket".

The future was just too threatening to the human and non-human species of Earth to be forever ignored. Passive tolerance of the worsening odds gave way to decisive action. Regardless of beliefs, people from all sectors of Earth knew that everyone would surely perish if plans for a systematic evacuation were not formed and executed. The grim-looking predicted future had the ring of universal truth to nearly all of the communities of Earth across every part of the wealth and health spectra. Once this phenomenon of "common sense trumps chaos" gained a certain critical inertia, there was no turning back.

Massive evacuations would need to be planned well in advance of a problem that might be too big for us humans to handle with standard crisis response tactics. At the turn of the 21st century, there were no *real* response contingencies for the many Earthly scenarios that seemed most likely to end humanity. How could a response contingency be formed for every probable scenario? How many petaflops and exabytes would be required to think everything through? Preemptively moving ourselves to another world in large numbers would be practical and necessary irrespective of the many unanswered questions.

In the years leading up to the *Kibo* disaster, more and more young people knew the difference between stalactites and stalagmites. Most twelve-year-olds across the land knew the variable mathematical relationships that were used to calculate stable circular orbits, even if they could not yet get the math exactly right quite as often as an experienced engineer in the pertinent field. In addition to the improvements in the quality of education for the human youngsters, elderly and middle-aged people had by now been dosed with enough DHA and regenerative therapies that they began to steal back their "mental mojo" from the chronic long-term cumulative effects of too much ambient toxicity in their work environments. The twentieth century had been brutal on the bodies of humans.

Science, technology, engineering, and mathematics (STEM) knowledge alone did not automatically mean we weren't all still foolish in many ways. After all, thus far in history we had repeatedly been foolish enough to think that everything was just going to be okay forever and ever. Ultimately, it became a widely held belief that the probability of maintaining an indefinite status quo of contentment and safety on Earth, or any other planet for that matter, was 0.000%. Everyone from the truck driver who lived next door, to the most eminent scientific minds of academia knew that humans were not even remotely prepared for the extinction level disasters that would surely be headed our way in the future. In fact, collectively, all the humans knew for certain was that life always seemed to have a cruel way of suddenly teaching all of us how the words "ignorant" and "blind" still firmly apply to our kind. But then, there's something to be said about "seek" and "find" now isn't there?

Urging the situation into fruition at the turn of the century was the "new war". The so-called "new war" (after the other "new war[s]") was not really a war at all in most places. The front lines of combat were now at the churches, supermarkets, and shopping malls. The vulnerable rear flank of humanity was in places where few had ever imagined attacks would occur; the libraries, wedding showers, and youth sports bake-sales of the world. Many speculated that the reasons for the soft-target attacks were due to large numbers of geographically separated, like-minded groups becoming electronically united. By strategically applying their synchronized anger in the form of car-bombs, cyberattacks, and psy-ops, they could all simultaneously sting the object of their hatred. They did not need expensive command and control mechanisms. Their thinking evolved to circumvent the need for expensive solutions entirely. Their targets could be anybody, anything, and anywhere...at any time. Those who were not like "them" in those certain specific ways that mattered were one of "us"; also known as "we".

The decentralization of deep space exploration had given birth to new purpose for several thousand operational and technical experts who had previously been part of the Deep Space Expeditionary Forces (DSEF). Those forces who survived the fatal devastation of Operation *Kibo* had been abruptly disenfranchised by the tragic terrorist attack aboard the *E.S.S. Earth 1*, and at the ground control stations. The accurately synchronized ground attacks at the command and control facilities in the Idaho, Texas, and Florida territories killed all but 4,252 of the entire DSEF rank and file. The injured survivors were given bio-regenerated limbs and organs at government expense, and were then honorably discharged without ceremony. But with state-of-the-art skill sets, and no clear mission objectives in life, the ranks of throw-away experts took to Operation *Kaminari* without hesitation. They were reborn.

The government spared no expense in the years preceding Operation *Kibo* to identify and indoctrinate these now-deactivated people into the belief that the proverbial "ends of the earth" just weren't a far enough "ends" for humanity anymore. Most of those original individuals from the post- *Kibo* era went on faithfully believing the lessons of the training they received. They would never abandon the original mission. No not ever.

The primary mission objective of the new and improved Operation *Kaminari* was simple in concept, and was the promise of the early 21st century governments to the people of Earth to find a new beginning for what finite life remained in Earth's original biosphere. Exhaustively-trained teams of humans from almost every nation-state on Earth were to travel from Earth-orbit toward exoplanet EDO-00010011. The planet was discovered to be orbiting Alpha Centauri B in an elliptical orbit that was observed to have an average distance from the star's core of about 72 million miles. Although gravitationally perturbed in its own orbit around B by the binary counterpart-star Alpha Centauri A, the planet was proven to be firmly in the gravitational grasp of Alpha Centauri B, and not close enough to A to be stripped away from its habitable zone by the gravitational pull of A. Early findings were confirmed and validated by the European Space Observatory (ESO) and by the James Webb Space Telescope.

In the early 21st century, improved methods for confirming the habitability of exoplanets were still moderately inadequate for use in the justification of costly interstellar expeditions. Throughout the peak of the DSEF era, only the comparatively shorter-range inter*planetary* journeys passed the public litmus test. But the two problems of human suffering and long-term survival of the human race were still going to be addressed simultaneously by *Kaminari*.

The heavily admonished outcast members of society that made up the old pre-*Kibo* DSEF guard were eager to leave the planet, and would do whatever was necessary to see that the original *Kibo* mission objectives were carried out. They viewed *Kaminari* as a long-overdue expeditionary opportunity, and a unique chance to do something good for all the people who so intensely loathed DSEF and everything it stood for.

Once onsite at Edo, humans were to establish a base camp *on* or *under* the planet's surface and make comprehensive repairs to their organic personnel and capital equipment. The fullest possible level of bio-regeneration and mission capability would be needed for any teams bound by commercial contract to return to Earth. It was mandated and codified by DSEF into the conditions of any commercial contracts that a return phase would be complied with in a "timely" manner using the equipment and any personnel remaining alive and available for duty by the time the mission was ready to commence. Crews travelling without commercial legal constraints would have the choice to either remain on Edo-00010011, or attempt a return to Earth. The thought of crew desertion never entered into the minds of the participating corporations because, as they were so fond of saying, "only fools would condemn themselves to a life of being stranded in space with no ride home." Of course, it was usually said with nervous laughter, if at all. Deep down they knew that if the crew(s) were ever to get the impression that they were all expendable, they would surely choose to survive by any means necessary. Some might even choose to utilize non-terrestrial resources and make a go of it without any materiel support from Earth.

Participating ships were to utilize standard Class-B nuclear propulsion systems that had been designed and mass produced for use by DSEF on interstellar supercruisers. There were 30 Class-B propulsion systems remaining, but all of the supercruisers that had been built thus far were different from one another. Each chassis had a different set of challenges associated with retrofitting the propulsion systems into the chassis frames.

The coupling of the first supercruiser chassis to the B-class propulsion system aboard the *E.S.S. Earth 1* was believed to be a fool-proof recipe for the ultimate success of Operation *Kibo*. The engineers and technical teams on the vehicular part of Operation *Kibo* were so certain that they had designed a flawless masterpiece, that they began conducting their lives around the assumption that *Kibo* was *guaranteed* to be successful. By the time the first supercruiser had been green-lighted for *Kibo*, there were no observable human indications of doubt, and almost no human reservations about whether or not the ship would handle interplanetary space. The assistance of a practical Earth-based command and control mechanism for the first-of-its-kind *E.S.S. Earth 1* would only be partially helpful. Isolated and outside the human habitation zone, there would be impossible challenges if anything went wrong. Years were spent at the drawing board and in testing facilities applying redundant safeguards to the *Earth 1*'s life support systems and autonomous safe return systems.

After *Earth 1* left port from orbital dry dock, the entire world was celebrating what was considered at the time to be humankind's most daring venture into deep space with a human crew since the days of Apollo, Soyuz, Columbia, and Red Dragon. The Earth, in all of its vast uniqueness, was collectively filled with hope about the possibility of the likeness of Earth and everything in it being preserved, rediscovered, and/or regenerated if necessary on another world. But when hopes were destroyed overnight by the sudden failure of Operation *Kibo*, the new reality on Earth was one of utter human hopelessness and skepticism. Those disenfranchised DSEF survivors became the pariahs of their generation in the developed world. Each time one of the old DSEF guard was recognized in public, they felt the stewing anger of those who carried the most disappointment.

The world believed the surviving members of DSEF were a ridiculous example of the hubris of humankind. This sociological phenomenon had the effect of bringing the rogue DSEF elements *together*. They formed familial bonds in the knowledge that they would only be able to rely on *each other* in the future. The rebirth of their shared purpose was a watershed event, because they had found new happiness in a way that made them impervious to the ostracism of the rest of the planet. They knew the Universe was an infinitely large place. They knew somewhere out there in the darkness they would find the light again, and they were willing to sacrifice everything to get there. That was what they were all trained to do. If humanity benefitted in some way, so be it. But if humanity was content to choose the bliss of fated, scripted futures, then so be it. Operation *Kaminari* was now inevitable. The first several volumes of human exodus into space had already been painstakingly written by the many brave pioneers of the 20th century, and now it was time to leave the planet. The vanguard of a grand-scale human exodus was prepped for launch.

Rapid-Assist Distributed Emergency Response Squadron (RADERS)

EARTH
Sector JP-0019
May 15, 2021 C.E.
Saturday
1716 HRS

Yet another beautiful spring evening was taking shape on the east coast of Sector JP-0019 as dusk approached. The Blue Forest region of this part of the Japan territory really began coming to life at this time of year. Farmers were preparing their rice paddies for planting long before the last of the snow was melted, and merchants throughout the villages could be seen throughout the day primping and culling the hardy ornamental evergreen shrubbery along their storefronts. The entire region was engaged in preparatory activities for the increasing number of people who would surely come to frequent the shops in the approaching warm weather seasons. The ocean beaches to the east of the rice paddy grids were situated high above the break water, and offered rare vantages of the waves. Even on a calm day, one could observe an eternally angry surf beating against the steep sandy incline leading up to the high water level. To bear witness to the tidal patterns in this area was to observe one of the greatest natural power sources on planet Earth. But when Staff Sergeant Kahmay O'Conaill frequented this particular beach, she was primarily interested in the large numbers of intact sand dollars to be found. Ten years ago she would have been imagining all of the ways to harvest the kinetic energy from the waves. But the influence of the moon on the Earth's oceans, and all of the potential energy efficiency it offered to Earth was a classic example of an idea that initially seemed novel, but was later seen to be an idea that thousands of people had already thought of but were unable to put into applied reality. Back in the day, Kahmay would spend hours and hours with her uncle talking about all those fantastic unrealized ideas. But these days the weekends were her chance to get her mind off of work for a while.

  Kahmay despised taking time away from her duties, and preferred the heightened focus that the solitude of graveyard shift afforded her. From time to time, it was spiritually helpful for her to gaze out across the vast Pacific Ocean during daylight hours. After a long period of being inside of an underground bunker with no windows, any change of scenery provided a disproportionately high amount of relief and recuperative value. Crowds of people in the villages tended to make her uneasy. But the sounds of the surf and the great busy silence of nature *healed* the wounds of her anxious spirit.

It was a particularly meaningful experience for Kahmay to come to this *exact* beach. It was there, at her closest terrestrial approach to her biological family back home, that she could quietly remind herself of life's most important commandments. Her people were out there many thousands of kilometers away, and were privately *willing her* to come home. She could feel their daily sacrifices by tapping into her spiritually intuitive connection to them. She sometimes challenged herself to attempt the sending of telepathic messages to all of them. If they had their spiritual ears open, they would surely hear her calls. It was a purely faith-based exercise to trust that they would not forget her, and she believed they wanted to remain connected through time and distance just as she did.

The experience of being so far away from the collective strength of the home support network was a terribly hard and lonely path. Many within the organization had become barking mad thinking that their families had cast them into oblivion. Despite the challenging variables and formidable isolation, Kahmay and many others within DSEF embraced the hardship with the spiritual fortitude of warriors. In her own mind, every tough thing Sergeant Kahmay encountered was something to be absorbed, repolarized, and transformed into an even more determined resolve to stay the present course. It was truly important to her that her family be proud of her, and in what she was doing there so far away.

Kahmay met and exceeded the standards of her present organization so thoroughly that she was now setting new standards and leading a new generation into the future. She had to believe that her commitment to the greater cause of training a human force for the future would be enough to dull any sorrows in the hearts of her family. Her knowledge of the tribe's approval was one of the only things keeping her going when times were toughest. She would never give up on the oath she swore so many years back, nor would she ever choose the easy way out by forgetting about the folks at home. *Better to feel the stinging pain of whatever hell than to feel the guilt and regret of being a garden-variety quitter of some kind*, she thought.

The latitude of this part of sector JP-0019 was nearly identical to that of Kahmay's homeland, so she enjoyed thinking about how in theory, a direct easterly course could take her precisely to the shores of sector OR-42. She thought about human issues that were not part of the regular routines of her current assignment. She knew that all the technical training in the world could not teach a person how to truly be there for a loved one, or how to care for the sick with a human touch. With drones and artificially intelligent computers as co-workers, one struggled to polish the nuanced capacity to feel a sense of belonging with the rest of humanity. The duties she performed were terribly detached from raw humanity. But it was a reality she could live with.

One weekend after another, Kahmay methodically paced the long beach with her eyes focused on the hard-packed wet sand, and with her mind focused on the future. But today something felt different to the graveyard shift Non-Commissioned Officer in Charge (NCOIC) of Integrated Systems Element, Detachment IV, 35th Rapid-Assist Distributed Emergency Response Squadron (RADERS), Deep Space Expeditionary Forces (DSEF).

One of the Sergeant's gifts was her ability to somehow *feel* when something was wrong or otherwise "off" in some way. It was not strictly a function of feelings but rather, something more like a hybrid sensory concept that combined commensurate situational facts with human intuition to form an accurate, instinctive, informed reflex. Her mind could not ignore the present on this day, and went into a state of alert as she thought to herself, *What is going on out here today? What on Earth am I sensing? Why does the water seem so calm? Where are all the gulls? It's too quiet...the animals know something! What the...?"*

Just after Kahmay's heart began responding physiologically to her more elusive sensory inputs, she looked back to the west just in time to hear it. BOOM!!! It was the sickening sound of the region's characteristically loud earthquakes coming across the land, just as the mechanical shock of the s-waves began violently shaking the surrounding trees. Without hesitation Kahmay allowed her training to commandeer her thoughts and tore off into action. Concurrent mechanical energy through the earth's crust and audible sound waves meant the epicenter was right below the surface at her coordinates. She sprinted off the beach running full tilt, oblivious to the spilling of sand dollars from her hands onto the green blur of the dune grasses. The size of her little four-wheel drive Suzuki Nomade grew larger and larger as she raced toward it with furious urgency. Pulling her radio out of her jacket with her left hand and her car keys out of her pocket with her right hand, she wasted no time opening...the *passenger* door. Disgusted and embarrassed that she had again forgotten what country she was in, she verbalized a loud "ARRRRRG...JAPAN JAPAN JAPAN YUH IDIOT" as she ran to the other side of the vehicle. Without delay she began barking into the radio with controlled, rapid urgency.

"RADER 1, RADER 2 OVER...RADER 1, RADER 2 OVER..."

"RADER 1...THIS IS RADER 2, HOW COPY?!"

Hastily climbing into the tiny vehicle, she fired up the mighty 80 horsepower dune crawler and spun a burning reverse whip-around, casting a spray of sand from the edge of the skidding tire out into the dune grasses. Then, without thinking, she stomped down the clutch and slammed the manual shifter into 2nd gear. She knew the Nomade would have the torque necessary to make a fast enough insertion onto the beach trail if she just mashed the gas down and slipped the clutch a little. She needed the extra two seconds before redlining the tachometer in second gear to afford herself enough time to try the radio again and still be able to hold on to the steering wheel.

"RADER 1, RADER 2... COME IN!"

The little Nomade whined its way along the trail that ran parallel to the surf, as the abrupt shoulder-ledge of the main paved road approached. Kahmay glanced out to her left through the passenger window to observe the behavior of the ocean while keeping enough attention on the trail to safely get to the road. She noticed the surf quickly retreating to an increasingly more distant-appearing horizon, and then she saw it. Her stomach sank with a flip into numbness as the reality of what was about to occur was sinking in. In all likelihood, the punishment of Poseidon himself was coming. She could hear the auto-Japanese voice in the back of her mind shouting "ZETTAI DAHMAY! ZETTAI DAHMAY!" She tried to ignore the fact that she was still at the beach and still almost three kilometers away from the safety of entry hatch 55-B at the watertight underground bunker complex. The mocking laughter of the Tohoku demons were echoing in her head, taunting her for momentarily believing that life was just a stroll on the beach. Her thoughts were soon no longer divided between the radio, the bunker, and the other elements of the rapidly unfolding situation. Instead, she crammed the gas down and tuned out everything but the quickest route back to the hatch. She threw the radio over into the passenger's seat, gripped the steering wheel, and careened up onto the shoulder ledge of the main road. She maneuvered the little Suzuki into the middle of the paved road and brought the vehicle to maximum speed heading west away from the beach. With each successive gear shift and the accompanying high compression wind up, the engine whined in protest as it exhaled the gases of its explosions. She looked ahead for the road marker that she knew was precisely 2.4 klicks away from the bunker's Entry Control Point (ECP), and then punched the large red plunger on the dashboard that opened up the nitrous oxide jet into the throttle body.

"COME ON GIRL! HYAAAH! HYAAAAAAAH! COME ON, COME ON...MOVE! MOVE! MOVE!" she shouted aloud to an audience of tiny spiders that had colonized the vehicle interior. The stock 80 horses transformed into a lay person's 147 horsepower rally racing bullet. The whine of the engine transformed into something more like the miniature version of the airbrakes on a passenger bus. Downshifting into the tight curves of the coastal highway revealed the unmistakable sound of the turbo waste gate as the gears were slammed back into higher ratios to leverage a more responsive, useful short-term acceleration exiting the curves. Kahmay took no notice of the word "KUSO" that she had so meticulously decaled onto the red nitrous button a few months ago to add character to the vehicle interior. She madly honked her horn and shouted, "TSUNAMEEEEE...TSUNAMEEEE KURUUU!" out the window in the direction of the nearby farmhouses, as the vehicle screamed its way toward the gates of the ECP. There were no visible signs of any villagers, and there was absolutely no time to go out in search of anyone to rescue. She knew she had to complete the last few hundred meters to the ECP and take cover in the bunker immediately. It was to be her only hope of surviving the coming forces.

Recognizing Kahmay's vehicle through the dimming light of dusk, the two young security personnel on duty at the ECP began going through the motions of forcing themselves to treat the vehicle as if it were their first time ever seeing it. But they knew it was Kahmay and that she was in a hurry for something. They still had to wait until they made visual contact with her face in accordance with the day's procedural orders. She slowed the vehicle just enough to tell them in her most serious tone, "GET IN! GET IN! ...TSUNAMI INBOUND! TSUNAMI INBOUND!"

The two guards hurriedly raised the control boom and unshouldered their M-4Z Rifles. They looked at each other with a rare bit of mild surprise about not having questioned the situation more. They trusted the Staff Sergeant, and knew her well enough to see that she was dead serious. They were indeed two of the most situationally aware sentries you could ever run into, and they too felt the powerful shock of the quake. The two maneuvered themselves along with their weapons into the tiny rear passenger seats of Kahmay's Nomade while trying not to fall onto the pavement as the vehicle remained in motion. Instantaneously, after realizing both troops were safely inside, Kahmay again stomped on the throttle and headed toward entry hatch 55-B at the bunker complex. Somehow in the frantic interim, she expended at least three hundred milliseconds to involuntarily think about all of the people who would die in the coming minutes and hours. She couldn't help but think about how weird it was that this would happen on a day when she was *right there* at the beach.

Kahmay screeched to a halt just next to the hatch and got out to immediately look east. She needed to see if the wave could be seen coming yet, but the horizon appeared somewhat like a mirage to her eyes. She couldn't make sense of what she was seeing, and there was no time to squint the image into focus. She reached down to grab the anchor chain for the Suzuki's front axle while keeping an eye on the horizon with the occasional random double take. *One axle secured*, she thought. Just then, as she looked up to see if there was enough time to attach the rear axle, it came into focus. The horizon was now an enormous churning froth of dirty-looking water coming onshore toward them. The oozing blob of salt water had just begun devouring the first layer of trees back from the beach, which was about a minute away from their location for a world class sprinter. With a gradually loudening voice that intensified into outright panic, one of the two sentries looked up as he was opening the hatch and yelled the words everyone was thinking: "GET IN! GET IN! COME ON! "

Kahmay quickly dropped the second axle chain and dove down onto the pavement to run it through the rear axle and hook it to the anchor hoop while the first sentry was descending down the ladder into the bunker.

"WHAT IN GOD'S NAME ARE YOU DOING SERGEANT?! COME ON!" yelled the second sentry.

With one final strained reach, Kahmay finished cinching the rear-axle chain and scooted out from underneath the rear bumper. Running toward the hatch, she knew this was likely going to be one of the longest days of her life, and it would soon be dark outside.

The three made it safely into the hatch and hastily slid down the long ladder into the adjoining corridor of the sealed underground fortress of Detachment IV. They hurriedly scrambled toward the control room where the rest of the duty staff was sitting. All personnel were transfixed to the closed circuit cameras that kept watch over the installation perimeter to the east. Kahmay watched the monitors as the external cameras were slammed by sea water and became submerged under the awesome power of the wave. The mounting stand for the southeast perimeter camera buckled under the pressure of the wave and began leaning backward, changing the camera angle to a nearly straight up view toward the sky. The control room had now fallen almost silent as the flashing red alarm lanterns spun around and around in the darkness of the bunker without an accompanying audible alarm tone. Only the low rumble of the stampeding sea water above and the faint sound of the instrumentation cluster power supplies humming broke the silence. An eerie feeling filled the room as everyone began to simultaneously realize that people and animals were on the surface dying and suffering. Everyone seemed to draw a deep breath at once in preparation to explode into action. The swing shift NCOIC, Technical Sergeant Derrick Sanders broke the high-pressure silence.

"SNAP OUT OF IT PEOPLE! PREPARE THE RADERS! THIS IS WHAT WE TRAINED FOR... COME ON!" Sanders shouted, clapping his hands together to help snap everyone out of their naturally shocked state. Even the best training simulations could not come close to the real thing. He grabbed the public address microphone and allowed his process to fully kick in. "Launch bay alpha, report status over. Repeat; launch bay alpha, report status! How copy over?"

The robotic voice of one of the swing shift launch specialists broke the silence just as Sanders was preparing to really lose his cool at the sound of dead air.

"Copy control, tubes one through ten prepped and standing by over."

There was a total of 18 launch tubes available for the oversized RADER drones to exit the bunker complex. But the standard contingency for tsunamis specified that ten drones were to be immediately launched to an altitude of 300 meters before any threat to the integrity of the bunker itself could manifest all the way inside. In the event of an actual breach, the first ten drones would loiter around the sector at an altitude of 300 meters in a pre-programmed flight pattern, and would send live video streams to seaborne command if not manually redirected by the human RADERS in the first 15 minutes. After that initial 15 minutes, up to an additional 20 drones could be launched at the discretion of the NCOIC as long as there were enough personnel on duty to meet the minimum requirements for practical safe operation. The final 20 drones were swap-outs, and were launched one at a time after units from the first wave came back to recharge or be repaired. Today the swing shift RADER crew for Detachment IV consisted of 11 flight specialists, 2 ground controllers, and the NCOIC. Sergeant Kahmay and the two sentries brought the total head count to 17. But the two surface troops were not trained for flight operations. For this mission, the Det. IV RADERS would have to make do with 15 troops to perform reconnaissance and rescue for the entire sector, and two sharp troops to step in and help wherever needed.

    TSgt Sanders held his finger to his mouth to give the rest of the crew the signal to stay quiet. He was listening to the surface water and tried to envision what the water was doing on the surface. The video cameras were good, but only offered a limited view of the bigger picture. He tried to wait for the exact moment when the primary kinetic energy wave had passed over the surface so the launch tubes would have their best chance of surviving the pressure of the water that followed the initial impact. He could see the leading edge of the wave moving toward the village in his mind's eye, and envisioned the comparatively calmer water that was left behind in the wake. *Now, now, now...*, he thought.

"Launch Bay Alpha, you are clear to extend. Acknowledge over...," said TSgt Sanders.

"Copy control, extending in 2....1...extending" stated the voice without wasting a moment.

The gigantic initial ten hydraulically telescoping steel tubes began extending toward the surface along the east perimeter where Kahmay and the sentries had been moments earlier. The devastating energy of the water began impacting the outer knife edge design of the tubes, but was thus far being easily redirected around the main cylindrical structure of the tubes. The colors of the panel light indicators down in the control room now had flickers of yellow and green, which lit up the poised faces of the two young controllers who monitored the extension progress. Kahmay well knew that green meant nominal tube deployment, and yellow meant dangerous stresses to the pressure sensors on the knife edges were present. One of the status lights was now intermittently flickering from yellow to red. The energy of the wave was strong enough to push one of the tubes to the breaking point or at least, it was pushing the tube's ability to withstand the force much longer. Much of the outcome of the mission depended on the NCOIC's sense of timing and the surface instrumentation. Kahmay was there in the role of decision-matching with TSgt Sanders in the event he became incapacitated and she had to take over for him. The room remained tensely quiet as the tube indicators began changing one by one from flashing greens and yellows to all steady greens. Once all ten indicators were steady green, Sanders knew he was clear to blow hatches and launch the RADERS.

"RADERS sound off...," spoke Sanders with a calm urgency.

The specialists who would take over control of the individual drones began sounding off by the numbers in rapid sequence over the radio from the confinement of their water-tight pods. The Det. III/DET. IV med-bay NCOIC reported eight human medics and four robotic med-assist units as "available and standing by" in the 2 kilometers-long sealed corridor connecting the two bunkers. Once watertight integrity was verified, the bulkhead door latches would be disabled and the medics would be free to traverse the corridor between bunkers using the Mag-sled.

"ONE GO...TWO GO...THREE GO...,"and on it went until all ten pilots and the standby pilot had reported "GO" status.

"Alright people...here we go! Control, standby to blow hatches on my mark...in 2...1...EXECUTE, EXECUTE, EXECUTE," exclaimed Sanders.

The large 3.5 meters-in-diameter iron hatches blew open with a series of small synchronized explosive charges. The hatches were slowed to a stop by hydraulically resistive drag pistons. The ten frontline RADER drones were standing by at 85% of maximum rpms and were ready to be released. The release latches for the small swarm clicked open and the drones exploded vertically out of the tops of the tubes near their maximum launch speed of about 143 kilometers an hour. The RADERS screamed toward their initial altitude like they had all been loosed from their own giant slingshots. Kahmay remembered what it was like to be standing on the surface of Detachment IV for the first time as she witnessed this very same event during operational readiness exercises after her initial assignment to the RADERS. It was like standing on the shoulder of a stateside interstate freeway and getting nearly blown into the ditch by a pack of small passenger cars travelling at just under 89 statute miles per hour.

Each of the pilot specialists were now looking at the world through the electro-optical-mechanical eyes of the semi-autonomous rescue drones. Three hundred vertical meters offered enough panoramic vantage for the pilots to be able to see the leading edge of the wave as it rapidly devoured nearby spruce trees and small structures. The wave had already destroyed countless rice paddies and private vehicles during its approach of the inland villages. There was nothing behind the drones to the east but the ocean, some floating trees, and a few small positively buoyant fresh water tanks that had been ripped from their rusty bolted anchors in the paddy fields. The tanks were always left sealed and empty during the winter months and had not yet been filled with fresh water for the workers.

It was the job of RADER 1 to check the immediate area around the bunker complex while the other nine RADERS flew in the direction the wave was moving. The first few minutes would be the difference between life and death for many of the people living in the coastal area. RADER 4 was the first drone to make visual and thermal identification of a survivor.

"This is RADER 4. I have contact...descending to evaluate over..."

The pilot descended the drone down to an altitude of 10 meters through the group of private vertical escape airships being operated by civilians to get a better look at what was happening. The heads-up display in the pilot's pod began to clearly reveal a young child sitting atop a fast moving minivan as it bobbed up and down and floated in the direction of the wave's motion. The boy was in his pajamas shifting his position and slipping around trying to get enough traction with his sock covered feet to stay on the unsubmerged part of the van as the wave was causing the vehicle to roll and list unpredictably. The pilot skillfully maneuvered the drone into position to pluck the child from danger and wasted no time grasping the child with the padded grappling arms on the drone's underbelly. Once the first two arms of the RADER successfully wrapped themselves around the child, the other four arms completed the protective web and fully encaged the child as the propellers sped up to lift him.

"RADER 4 en route to return...standby to receive over..."

"Copy 4, standing by and ready..." said Sanders as the drone quickly returned to tube four for drop-off, and the medics down in the bunker scrambled into position to receive the first victim.

The boy was carefully descended through the open tube down to the landing pad where medical personnel were there to grab him. One of the medics slapped the plunger on the side of the drone, which sent a message to the pilot's pod that the drop-off had been successfully completed. RADER 4 was quickly back out of the tube and once again speeding toward the impact zone to rejoin the others.

The radio came alive over and over again to report multiple contacts and prepare the bunker personnel to receive victims in need of attention. Within the first two hours after impact, the RADERS had collected 37 humans, one dog, and two cats. It was not the operational practice of the RADERS to seek out domestic pets during natural disasters. But collecting the animals concurrently with human victims was encouraged if the human could hang on to the pet long enough to become safely encaged.

Most of the victims who had been safely delivered to the bunker were awake and coherent. But three people were in serious condition, and one elderly gentleman was in critical condition after his leg was severed at the knee. He had lost a lot of blood, but the human medics managed to stabilize him inside the containment room. The two surface sentries were busy helping the medics transfer patients onto gurneys and helping the standby pilot transfer depleted drones into the recharge area with portable lift dollies. Both young men were sweating profusely within the first half an hour. They were used to being above ground with a breeze and a water cooler. The bunker complex must have felt like a sauna to them, as full ventilation to the outside would not come for many hours, if not days. The best O_2 was closest to the launch tubes. The uninitiated almost always had a nose to seek it out, even to the exclusion of other priorities. It was sort of like looking for shade on a muggy afternoon in Guam.

Hours went by as the traffic to and from the tube array was non-stop and unrelenting. Personnel were beginning to feel the full toll being exacted on their bodies and minds. The grind continued without regard for tiredness or the degradation of sharp cognition. Vital equipment in the bunker was being gradually battered into disrepair, and the RADER drones were being torn apart by the devastation of the surface. RADER 22 was trapped inside tube one with no way out. It was painful to have a malfunctioning tube entrapment with a functional drone inside. The tube one pilot was so disgusted by the 6% mission capability degradation that she got out of her pod and started beating on the tube with a sledge hammer. She was trying to get the entrapment door relay to unstick and release the drone back down into the bunker. It was fortunate there were no victims trapped in the tube with the drone. But the tube was hopelessly jammed and her excess physical energy ended up being redirected to helping the two untrained sentries and the standby pilot. The surface sentries, medics, and standby pilot were in that group of double-timing troops who needed a drink of water and a breather before going back into action.

The sounds of the voices of the rescued victims in the containment chamber offered reassurance for the weary RADERS as they worked through the endless string of challenges on into the night. Beyond that one giant consoling factor, there was nothing but shortening tempers and degraded cognition. The crew was getting tired, and there would be nobody coming to relieve them anytime soon.

Reassigned

EARTH
Sector JP-0019
May 16, 2021 C.E.
Sunday
1732 HRS

The ill-fated events of Saturday afternoon had been the start of a seemingly unending nightmare. The Detachment IV bunker complex was a disaster area, and those who survived were indeed exhausted. Beholding the devastation on the surface with tired minds and bodies had initiated the subtle process of decaying the cognitive sharpness of the RADERS. The drone units had not detected any signs of life on the surface for many hours. By the time nightfall approached on Sunday, the hope of rescuing more victims was guarded, but remained strong. The first full 24-hour day of operations was finished, and the entire crew had been sheltering and working in place since the initial impact of the wave. Some of the crewmembers were now strewn about the complex fighting involuntary physiological shut-down.

One of the control room troops was snapping a rubber band onto the skin of his wrist to "sting" himself awake and stay focused. Sergeants Kahmay and Sanders had just sent part of the crew into the darkness of the back rooms to lay still on the couches and coffee tables. Their orders were to rest and report back to the control room at 2300 hours to take over for the others who had still not rested. They did not need to be told twice.

Word arrived midday Sunday that Detachments II and III had so far come through the ordeal with no fatalities, but had a few people in serious condition laid-up on the offshore medical frigate. One individual was being treated for severe shock after being trapped in his control pod. Flooding forced him to sit and watch the rising water level while he remained helplessly strapped in with the breathing apparatus. When they found him he was unconscious. His pod was filled with sea water and the mask was still sealed around his face with nine percent oxygen remaining. Apparently he had some kind of anxiety response that knocked him out and oddly saved his life, or maybe he had a seizure. Nobody really knew. The pilots' pods were not supposed to leak, but all of the pilots knew it was a real possibility. Claustrophobia was a disqualifier in training, but he probably just lost it when the water started coming in. Acute panic does strange things to situational human reactions.

Partial underground collapse of the main corridor wall in the Det. III complex severed the constant direct current power supply for the backup power system and electrified the six inches of standing water in the control room, which was completely counterintuitive given that the system was well fused and should have immediately allowed the fusing to pop open the circuits and power everything down. It sounded overly presumptive and irrelevant to the immediate crisis to already be hearing speculation from the non-forensically inclined. Those initiating the speculation were probably losing focus from fatigue and sustained high-energy vigilance. All three individuals in the Det. III control room were found barely alive with standard conductive boots on, which was very bad and should have never happened without the boots being connected through a regulated grounding matrix. The conductive boots are more comfortable, and some wore them on occasion to give their blisters a break. Senior personnel liked to use the pressure functions of the boots to stimulate capillary function in the lower extremities during periods of prolonged sedentary activity. It sounded like it was basic complacency; "...one of the most insidious mass killers of all time" as Kahmay so often tried to explain to the Det. IV team.

Detachment I over on the west side was a total loss. All 19 troops on duty were lost. Most of them were killed on the surface just a stone's throw away from the hatch. They were trying to rescue their family members who were there at the Detachment having a family appreciation picnic to celebrate the arrival of the warm weather and show their kids a little about their work environment. The drone footage of several families who were found deceased still clinging on to one another was thoroughly haunting. Sudden death could have come calling for any of the RADERS on any random day. One of the three individuals down in their control room died trying to outlast the wave so that the others on the surface could get in before the water swept them away. He couldn't bring himself to choose their death at that moment, and they just couldn't get to the hatch in time. They were carrying their small children while sprinting with bare feet across sharp gravel terrain. The guy's two teammates below were pinned and drowned by the crushing combination of heavy debris and seawater respectively. Nobody knew how he overrode the failsafe sequence, but that would have been the only way to keep the hatch open as long as he did.

    Kahmay propped herself in the standing position against the waist-level control panel, and argued with herself about why she should have to submit to the demanding screams of her body that she go to sleep. She took another gulp of her double black tea and stared down at the squadron personnel roster that was hanging from a small hook against the control array. She read the Detachment I names one by one, knowing that they had all died and would eventually be flown down to sector JP-0001 to be returned to their families in the states. *Nineteen brave souls*, she thought. *Why would they have built the detachment on a known fault line? Because they thought the odds were with them? Because they made a conscious choice to accept the risk? Yes, it had to have been the risk assessment versus the number of lives saved...damn the Tohoku demons of this land...damn the insatiable thirst of death,* thought Kahmay. She heard footsteps slowly trudging toward her through the small nearby puddle of standing water and looked up to find Specialist A.J. Conway standing there with a small scrap of bloody paper in her left hand. She was the last of the pilots to come out of the pod room.

"Fourteen home and charging...twenty-six afield for 'auto sys-grid'...three 'last-known-lokes'...five 'did-not-returns'...and two non-repairable with about half their parts stripped out to repair six others," uttered Conway, unable to summon much more than the two calories it took for her to read the words and numbers from the paper. "I just set R-49 down in tube 9. Is Sanders in the back?"

"Yeah, he's on the couch for a couple more hours. He was last seen drooling on his lapel. His eyes were involuntarily crossing. Rest and food are the only way we're gonna keep doing anyone any good. We're definitely gonna need...at least five by five for later. How long since last surface contact?" asked Kahmay.

"Six hours, twenty-eight minutes. Anyone out there still alive right now is in the 'less than three percent' survival bracket. We need fresh eyes pretty bad," said Conway, shaking her head side to side in frustration. The experienced specialist struggled to think of anyone who might still be available and was not already completely spent. Kahmay relied on A.J. to deliver timely information and experience-based damage assessments. In her position as senior specialist, A.J. was most adept at identifying the potential efficacy of repair scenarios and corrective action steps. Usually when Conway delivered her report, it was at shift change after she had already worked a full swing shift with the swings team. There was nothing more helpful to Kahmay at the start of the graveyard shift than to hear A.J.'s swing shift summary of the past, present, and recommended future.

"Alright then Conway...I need you to go into the back and wake up Zeke. Send him out here and then go get some sleep. I need him for a drop-and-seek before sundown, and then I'm going to need you later after midnight, so...do what you gotta do to get some sleep. We're going to ops-check tube 1 again tonight after we mop and dry all the excess moisture in here. This floor is a damn safety hazard."

"Rai-do then..." said A.J., doing her most complimentary impersonation of a nice Australian woman she had met at a space junk conference in Brisbane several years back. "If I'm not up in a couple hours throw some water on me."

A.J. turned away and walked slowly toward the back room where the others were sleeping. Kahmay looked up at the monitor array as she had done at least 500 times since yesterday. The scene had remained unchanged for many hours, but this time she caught something in her peripheral vision on monitor three. It was a child's plastic baseball bat gently bobbing on the surface of the gradually receding water. The orange colored child's toy mocked her for believing that she and the others could be so arrogant to think they could save everyone. It was daring her to be better, and simultaneously punishing her for being lesser. Her look of astonishment at the sight of the toy slowly transformed from shocked surprise to boiling anger. But there was nobody to blame...nobody to be held to account. There was only silence, the orange bat, and fermenting rage.

By the fourth night the flood waters had receded enough to allow shift changes to occur in the usual way for those who still had a barracks to return to. Everyone else had to sleep in the bunkers or stay in a friend's room. Instead of everyone using their personal vehicles to go into the village and pick up food and supplies as per usual, entire shifts drove to and from the village in large canvas-covered trucks. Big deuce and a half looking trucks with collapsible sides and pneumatically adjustable vertical flatbed controls were being used for moving large quantities of cargo over rough terrain. There was an airstrip about 15 kilometers inland that was used to medevac survivors out of the disaster area when advanced treatment was needed in one of the better-equipped southern sectors. The crisis management and rescue response cycle of the past several days had subtly morphed into poised search-and-recovery posture and expedient survivor transport. Hope of rescuing the missing was diminished, but not entirely gone yet. Some troops continued to treat the situation with the same urgency they had during hour one. Those were the ones dedicated at the ideological level; the ones who would keep on going even if they stopped getting paid for it. They were the best of the best.

The local people were joining together in the village to immediately address urgent resource requirements and temporary building strategies for those who needed shelter. They were eager to put their hearts into restoring the health of the community, and they welcomed the opportunity to show their people that they would fight to keep bouncing back. There was power in the postponement of mourning.

By the time the 35th RADERS declared an end to rescue and recovery operations a little over a month later, the environment around Det. IV was one of quiet, lingering shock. Despite the efforts of thousands of people and machines working around the clock over the course of nearly 750 hours, the death toll from the massive 9.6 magnitude earthquake and subsequent tsunami was still expected to be in the tens of thousands. The grisly remains of the many missing victims were still being found in unlikely locations throughout the sector. There were just too many unprotected people near the coast, and the epicenter was only a few kilometers offshore. While many lives were saved, few inside the squadron viewed the rescue operation as a satisfactory success. For the second time in a little over 10 years, the Northeast coastal region of Tohoku had been devastated by a compound natural disaster. Only this time, they thought the effects would be much less than the quake of 2011. Tens of billions of yen and hundreds of millions of dollars had been spent fortifying infrastructure, training personnel, and upgrading response and preparedness strategies. None of it was enough to change the stubborn fact that the Japan territory still only had an area one-quarter the size of the state of the California territory to grow food for 94 million humans. Infrastructure like the RADER complex, which offered little or no apparent value-added benefit, had to be immediately dismantled and replaced with agro buildings and vertical farming facilities.

Popular support for distributed emergency response along the eastern shores of Honshu had all but evaporated by early July of 21'. Those who believed the RADER system was a great idea that simply needed more procedural improvement were in the minority. The mission of the RADERS on Earth was discontinued without much of the world ever having known it existed in the first place. The 35th was a deep space unit that had never been deployed to space, and was likely never going to be. Earth was a proving ground for them. They proved that a small crew could have a remotely operated rescue unit in space, as long as the expected number of people in need of rescue was not beyond the capability of the unit's resources. Larger rescue operations needed larger rescue units. The only fact of history that made the RADER system seem appropriate at the time of its initial installation was that expensive concepts cannot be fully funded without first proving themselves on the micro-scale. The world only had so much wealth.

Most of the personnel in the 35th squad were to be reassigned to other experimental units. Sector HI-0002 needed most of the personnel from the 35th for volcano duty with the 8th RADERS. The bulk of the remainder of the personnel was sent to sector AK-0066 for Type III Arctic Prototypical Advancement and Research Trials (APART) duty. Sergeant Kahmay was reassigned to sector JP-0001 along with Specialists Conway, Hutchinson, Lenihan, Quire, and Monty. They were going to Edo; home of Headquarters/Deep Space Expeditionary Forces (HQ/DSEF).

The Future Has Changed Again

EARTH
Sector JP-0001, Edo
December 05, 2021 C.E.
4 Months since the Kibo attacks
Sunday
0147 HRS

There was something strange about being awake during the quiet, wee hours of the night in sector JP-0001. The largest, most densely populated megalopolis on planet Earth was always busy. But at night, the many noises of the daytime hours gave way to a uniquely peculiar silence. It was surreal to Kahmay when she thought about how millions of people could be so collectively quiet. When compared to the many other urban areas she had been to, sector JP-0001 was *conspicuously* quiet. Kahmay wondered from time to time if perhaps it was because the residents had an uncommonly profound appreciation for the healing properties of silence. She imagined every resident was out there savoring every single minute of the downtime to recoup the energy needed to perform their individual daily-life marathons again the following day.

By winter, the time Kahmay spent in the Blue Forest was already starting to fade into the background of her memory. It had been four months since the brutal attacks of last summer. But to those still on active duty, it felt like it had just happened yesterday in many ways. All DSEF installations worldwide had been at their highest alert level for months with no reprieve. Every day was like a repeat of the days from immediately after the attacks. Mission fatigue was really starting to kick in for the vast majority of field units, and the people in the dark bunkers of compartmentalized project missions were gradually transitioning from plain old stressed out to outright psychotic. By now everyone's patience with the Unified Global Council's (UGC) inability to think more creatively was starting to wear extremely thin. Failure to bring the responsible parties to justice was everyone's responsibility. But it seemed impossible to get the key decision makers to think in a more unorthodox way. Too many of the tactics being implemented in warfare were failing the efficacy tests of modern asymmetrical engagements. The enemy had adapted to advanced technology and had begun using reverse-engineered weaponry against the global establishment. The cutting-edge razor of global innovation had lost too much ground to the unexpectedly well-informed, well-trained vengeance movements.

There was no shortage of tough talk while the UGC general assembly was perpetually in session over the last weeks of summer and into the autumn. It took about a week after the *Kibo* disaster for world leaders to fully realize the implications of all that had happened. Heading into the autumn, the surface response team operatives had been overwhelmingly efficient at dramatically degrading some of the enemy's more advanced capabilities, and many of the allied special purpose neo-tactical groups had taken modern warfare to higher standards. Some of the stuff the neo-tac commando troops pulled off was completely radical.

The UGC was good at making sure the people knew that the advantage was in the "hands of the righteous". Showing certain things that were meant for public consumption in the allied media was one of the favored tools in the propaganda arsenal. Private citizens needed to know that there was more to it than anonymous bombs and bullets, and watching a new bit of technology play out in the media helped the people feel confident. But revealing too much conceptually-sensitive content in the main-stream media was a risky affair.

Civilian casualty rates were falling, and the people of Earth were so well connected that they began to see a more transparent view of everything around them. Many heroes had been born in the distant deserts and unexpectedly obscure pockets of battle. To date, there had been significant arrests in New York, Jeddah, Morocco, Paris, Brussels, Frankfurt, London, Mumbai, and at least two dozen other urban sectors around the globe.

The master planners of the *Kibo* attacks were still out in the bush somewhere, relatively safe from electronic trails, satellite surveillance, and armed hunter-killer drone patrols. Despite superior reconnaissance technology, the allies still had not searched the many deep caves and underground hideouts the enemy favored. There were just too many of those kinds of places to make quick work of it. The elite allied field operators were running low on fresh leads, and the trail was cooling off. Reconnaissance tech-heads around the globe were hypnotized with bloodshot eyes, and seated at their monitor arrays with cups of cold "BVIT-spresso" in their hands as they worked feverishly to locate what they believed to be the last of the enemy operatives connected to *Kibo*. Nobody believed for a second that the enemy had been eliminated. But the rats had obviously scurried off to an obscure new sanctuary.

Matters were made significantly more complicated by the outdoor winter temperatures, which were dropping like a lead balloon filled with heavy water. The average daily cost of the hunt was going up, and the actionable results were going down. The enemy had gone into hiding to celebrate with muted revelry.

Tough talk and the sacrifices of thousands of men and women would not be enough to ferret out the more cowardly remnants of the extremists' organizational hierarchy. The dirtiest of the dirty were still too successful at making clean getaways for the people to feel good about the completeness of the global reprisal. It had to be complete or it wasn't good enough. The war of good versus evil was going to rage on indefinitely as it had no doubt done for billions of years.

The old way of thinking about war was not going to work. Even most of the misinformed and under-informed civilians knew that this was not a 20th century style conflict. It was obvious that the kind of organization and sustained patience required to so thoroughly infiltrate DSEF was unprecedented in the history of guerrilla warfare. The unexpectedly amorphous nature of the terrorist tactics signaled a heightened resolve of extremists to carry out attacks that had been fermenting for generations. In fact, there were many allied active-duty military members, active DSEF, and assorted civilians who identified the likeliest *modi operandi* and wrote about the coming attacks years before they ever happened. But nobody wanted to hear the astute insights of "alarmist" academia back in those days. Nobody wanted to hear that the freedom-hating anti-establishment terrorist fighters, with scarcely enough food to feed their children, were armed with electromagnetic pulse charges, machetes, and unrelenting resolve. Media sources that leaned toward the "diplomatic solution" in the wake of the attacks were unceremoniously silenced by unseen power-entities. Both sides of the global oligarchy had their ways of silencing the people while they played power-chess with peoples' lives. Speaking out against the prominent hawks, who ignored the warnings of the experts in the pre-war days, was social and professional suicide in allied territory. People were unceremoniously forced to choose between being a terrorist, a pariah, a traitor, or an ultranationalist right-wing zealot. Moderates became "uncommitted scum" in the post-attack days. Even casual social environments like holiday gatherings and employee luncheons were filled with clucky ostracizing notions about the "...traitorous people down the road [who did not] have any patriotic flags up...and therefore must be terrorist sleeper cells." Fortunately, that kind of paranoia eventually subsided as unexpected patriots were revealed and reassessed by their actions over the long years. It was a real attention grabber when dovish high school English teachers and subdued computer programmers started turning up in the allied news-feeds as heroes for neutralizing terrorists with heirloom five-shooters and homemade booby-traps. One of the favorite stories in the land was the tale about the guy from Fiji who everybody thought was a terrorist. He ran a quiet little grocery delivery service with his young son just outside of Detroit and was a complete gentleman to all he encountered. He loved the Michigan territory, and he embraced the United States as his homeland. It bothered him that he was unfairly profiled by those who did not know him. He had been approached by black-flag recruiters who suspected he would be carrying bitterness in his heart about the way he was being treated. He accepted their invitation on a whim and proceeded to single-handedly dismantle the entire cell. He waited until he could no longer identify any new targets before he sent his video journal to the authorities. One careful target at a time, he hunted the extremists as a vigilante. The recruiters were planning murder, and he was planning their end. Once he identified a target, he would track them and determine their patterns. Then when they least expected it, he was there with a homemade zip-gun he had learned to make as a child. One shot to the head was his only method of killing. He carefully documented all of the smoking gun evidence and then sent the whole package to the International Criminal Court. The rumor was that he had disappeared to rural Montana after that. The fact that neither he nor his son was ever found again fueled the legend of the man who would eventually come to be known as "Zipshot: The Amazing Fijian-American Assassin". Zipshot was, and likely still is, an awesome American.

This "new war" was like launching a search for a gang of hive-minded rodents who didn't need technology to communicate with one another. Their goals were always the same; to take the blood of others and rebuild the world in their own image. It was a bitch of a broken record. The commitment-to-cause of the enemy was not a temporary phenomenon. It was a genuine case of perma-grudge, and these extremists were not going away. Their hatred and disdain for all things progressive was steeped and rooted in centuries of both real and imagined oppression. It didn't matter to them whether you were a "Repugnican", a "Libtard", or just one of the hundreds of millions of normal, ordinary "folk[s] who believe in a higher power"; their specific God apparently wanted you dead.

General isolation from the rest of the world had allowed these aggressors to spin traditional story-telling into whatever fantastic tale they saw fit to use in order to indoctrinate the next generation of fighters with the appropriate measure of blind rage. Stories of historical slight had been cultivated into horrendously disproportionate lies. Generation after generation had been carefully trained to hate with small doses of exaggeration and over-generalizations of the kind that go over well at picnics and wedding showers. The teachers of the new generations of hateful extremists were brimming with repressed rage, and their own children were to be the unwitting tool of their long-plotted vengeance. Dissenters had their children taken away from them by members of their own family through the use of social ostricization. Legal privileges were stripped from people when the church-state/mosque-state institutions felt one needed a tighter leash for their divergent beliefs. Their ranks were filled with people from every race because they used the universally human elements of anger and family to gain their following. But their days would be numbered, because their way was not the *right* way.

    The demands of her present duties now so thoroughly dominated Kahmay's changed reality that she could scarcely think of anything beyond deadlines and proficiency exams. She knew it was probably a good thing to occupy her mind with something proactive after all that had transpired over the recent months. She wasn't ready to be reassigned yet when she was told her time with the RADERS was going to be cut short. She kept telling herself that it was going to be for a good cause, and that transferring to sector JP-0001 for Operation *Kibo* was going to be a rare chance to make a bigger positive impact on the world than she ever had before. But on this night, she couldn't sleep knowing that her sister Rebecca would soon be going on her first break at the hospital back home in the states. It was the only time of day on Earth that Kahmay could get ahold of her sister without it being inconvenient for both of them.

The new assignment felt like a promotion in many ways. The mission objectives were different and for the time being at least, the training was a bit less action-oriented than back in the days of working with the RADERS. The chain of command wanted everyone in the ranks to train "in preparation for the next mission". Those in sector JP-0001 were being groomed for command functions and were still expected to keep up their vocational proficiency training and physical conditioning. This time there would be more lives at stake than was the case with *Kibo*. The next mission Kahmay and her troops would undertake would be carried out first on Earth, and then from orbit, and then from many millions, billions, or even trillions of miles away. Kahmay could hardly wait for another chance to come face to face with the opportunity to make a real difference. Training was necessary, and was a potent long-term investment that had always been proven to repay its initial cost in the form of "unending dividends of timely knowledge and experience". The operational execution of a mission really made the dead parts of

Kahmay's inner being feel more alive, and brought her sense of purpose back to life in ways that only a *hard thing* could do. She always tried to instill this point in the younger troops when they became demoralized by the eventual numbing effects of "all talk and no action".

Kahmay listened intently to the ring tone of the old ring-tip phone connection to see if she could hear the distinct crackling that so often obstructed or prematurely ended overseas voice calls. When there were cracks and static, she knew the most expedient thing to do was to simply hang up and try again for a crisper ring tone during the ring sequence. *Finally, a good connection at the right time, on the right day of the week, with the right planet alignment...I should buy a lottery ticket later...*, she thought to herself.

"Beck? You there?" asked Kahmay.

Kahmay's older sister was well rehearsed in the art of having a conversation with a systemic 917 millisecond delay, and knew how to stay quiet after coming to the end of a naturally finishing statement. One ill-timed sentence would result in the beginning of a tedious process of multiple consecutive interruptions when Kahmay called.

"Yeah, just started break time. What are you doing up at this hour? Isn't it the middle of the night there?"

"Yeah, it's just about two o'clock. Couldn't sleep...was thinking of you and the girls in your routines and thought I'd give it a shot. It's easier to get a good connection this time of night. I was just finishing up cleaning the sector-19 funk and salt corrosion off of the Suzuki's throttle-body. Last night it was the fuse and relay terminal blocks...that was loads of fun and lots of ethyl alcohol. I've almost got 'er back together over at the POV storage bay. I bring parts home and clean them up here on the weekends...out on the veranda. Everything alright over there sis?" asked Kahmay.

"Yeah...pretty much. It's a little quiet around the house since daughter number one moved out, and daughter number two is only a few months away from leaving too. Pretty soon it's just gonna be me and the quiet one. Oh yeah, and furry thing one and fuzzy thing two are here too, lest I forget. They are presently roaming the kitchen floor looking for fallen toast crumbs. They act so starved...you'd think I never feed them."

Kahmay replied as soon as the unmistakable cue of silence lasted longer than just the amount of time necessary for a human to take a breath before beginning to speak again.

"Oh really? You mean, it's just gonna be you and Bopp there with the dogs pretty soon?"

"Yuuuuup...and we're not sure if we're ready for all that potential peace and quiet around here.

Something about spending years surrounded by the chaos of youthful pursuits that makes all silence feel uncomfortable...errr, ya know, awkward I guess...is the word I'm looking for," said Rebecca with a slight laugh. "Are you still in sector one?" asked Rebecca in a hurried attempt to take the conversation in a new direction.

"Yeah, looking like I'm going to be here for at least another year and a half, maybe longer. Really miss you guys Beck. I wish I could just fly you guys over here with that spare twenty grand I have laying around " said Kahmay with a sarcastic laugh that implied an "as if" at the end.

"But do you think you'll be able to get away for a week or two at any point?" asked Rebecca.

"That, I do not know. They never really tell me anything. The new commander seems like a real know-it-all jackass type of guy on the personal level, so I'm keeping my guard up about any time off. They're all really serious about the leave cancellations since the *Kibo* thing. In all likelihood, they're probably listening to every word of every conversation worldwide right now. The word 'Zettaflop' immediately comes to mind. We're lucky to be allowed off the base *at all* right now with everything being the way it is. But I'm not sweatin' it. I'll find my way back to you guys somehow. I always do right?"

"I know you will" replied Rebecca, now slightly choked up with the sorrow of knowing that the conversation would soon be over. Telephone conversations with long-estranged loved ones rarely ever yielded much free-flowing communication, nor did they offer the more intangible benefits of close interpersonal bonds. Depending on mood and ambient stress levels, Kahmay found that the occasional call overseas actually made her feel *worse* than she did before picking up the phone. Fourteen minutes of awkward small talk could sometimes translate into days of unchecked worrying. This condition was spawn from the ignorance of not knowing *who* they all were as human beings anymore. Her own family was foreign to her. Ensuing post-conversation symptoms included decreased appetite, erratic sleeping patterns, and random tension headaches from prolonged sustained frowning, teeth-grinding, and jaw-clinching.

With her best effort to sound emotionally unaffected, Rebecca continued speaking before the delay could kick in and ruin the communicative uniqueness of the moment.

"We love you Sarge...and we can't wait to see you again. The time is going by waaaay too quick...it makes me sick to my stomach when I think about all the years that have gone by with everyone so far away from one another. It feels like you've been gone forever."

"I know...it's a rotten problem in need of a primary decomposer. But I *can* tell you that I'm working on a solution. I don't believe in the concept of impossible, you know that," said Kahmay with a hint of uneasiness. "I can't afford the pessimism, so I spend my free time investigating ways to win the long shot while I'm working the problems and duties of the present."

Kahmay stopped talking for a moment to allow the welling of emotion to pass. She could not allow the tree of sadness to blossom into full despair...not now. That would only make things harder on everybody. Once she felt like she could continue talking again without emotion getting in the way, she began to speak to her beloved sister once again.

"Gotta get going sis. I wanted to seize the rare opportunity to see how you guys were doing. There's supposed to be something important going on at the meeting later this morning, and I suspect it's going to be more important than the last 53 important meetings so...gotta try for a couple more hours of rack time if I can get it...please keep me in your loop?"

"Yeah...absolutely! Of course I will girl! You are always in our thoughts, and we love you and miss you terribly" said Beck, choking back the flood of contorted breathing and unintended tears.

"You're always in mine too. Give Bingo and Bullseye my toast crumbs and hug the nieces for me k?

Tell those girls to stuff themselves into a pressurized box with some protein rations and some water and then send themselves to me via overnight express. I'll reimburse with cold hard cash upon delivery. They still allow C.O.D.s in this sector! Can you believe that?"

Rebecca laughed as one of her sister's characteristic jokes came over the phone's speaker. She knew the only reason Kahmay cracked jokes was to break up the inherent sadness of yet another goodbye in a long series of too many inevitable goodbyes. But they learned to stop using the word "goodbye" when they had to go their separate ways or hang up the phone. Like so many other people who shared their circumstances of prolonged separation, they eventually began using phrases like "see you later" and "see you soon". The implied certainty of such phrases was almost as good as a *guarantee* that a reunion would happen...eventually.

"Okay..." said Beck with a courtesy laugh. "Give my regards to the nerd squad over there Poindexter."

"Will do sis. One of 'em wants to meet you by the way. The individual saw your picture and has been starry-eyed ever since. We're talkin' full-on crush. But I'll wait to tell you the story until we can talk without time-deficit anxiety. Love you..."

"K...I love you too."

Both sisters hung up and immediately felt better for having successfully pulled off another six-thousand-mile-long electric conversation. For now, it was their only option so long as video and holo-conferencing were restricted by OPSEC precautions. It was the best they were going to be able to manage without encrypted sat-phone capability. Kahmay walked out onto the covered balcony of her third floor, nine square meter apartment and stared out into the quiet, dimly lit neighborhood. She sipped some hot green tea from her mug as rain drops began to fall one by one through the conical light beams of the nearby street lights. Soon it was pouring, and Kahmay suddenly felt tranquility in her heart from how it reminded her of the rainforests of home. She wondered whether she should dare attempt a little more sleep before sunrise. She really despised waking up twice in the same day, but understood the need for it more and more as she aged into the mid-point of her expected lifespan as a human. *Yes, I'm going to need it*, she thought to herself grudgingly.

Adapt and Over and Out

EARTH, Edo
Sector JP-0001
December 05, 2021 C.E.
Sunday
1048 HRS

Whenever the entire training unit at Headquarters DSEF was called into session on short notice, the duty personnel typically assumed that something in the recent past was the impetus for the session. Most often, they were wrong and the session had been planned weeks in advance. There was a lot that went into scheduling the sessions. In order to account for all of the particular preferences associated with a handful of important people, the organizers needed all the time they could get to meet the micro-needs of the VIPs. Nobody wanted to upset the brass by putting too much sugar in their coffee. Speaking to a giant pack of cadet trainees made the brass cranky and generally inconsolable in the little ways. But for this session, it was in fact a recent event that led to this moderately impromptu recall. There had been protestors assembling throughout Friday afternoon across the various districts of Edo. They were assembling peacefully to advocate an end to tax spending on deep space exploration. By Saturday morning there were thousands of them blocking the entire crossroads in all directions. Anytime there were protests in Edo it was cause for alarm, because the people would not just waste their time on a pursuit that was not of the utmost importance to them in their daily lives.

The Headquarters/DSEF offices were located inside a high-rise office building in the Hamamatsu-Cho region of Greater Edo just outside the southern edge of the Tokugawa Yamanote line. Floors 48 through 52 were packed with the mundane functions of administrative processing and formal classroom training. Hand-to-hand combat conditioning was in an almost sound-proof room on the 49th floor and was the only thing occasionally breaking the silent torture of paperwork and ticking clocks. The half-penthouse roof area straddled the northern half of the building atop the 52nd floor and was used for operations, basic physical training, and ceremonial functions. Occasionally when newer, more advanced equipment orientations were required involving larger apparatuses, the equipment would be brought in by helicopter or drone so that the proper theory of operation instruction could be conducted atop the building away from the other mission functions. However, today was not about new equipment or bloviating brass. Today was going to be about a major strategic course correction for DSEF.

Sergeant Kahmay could see the demonstration group assembled at the main entrance to the high-rise as she walked from the train station toward the peaceful assembly. There they all were on their knees in complete silence facing away from the building. Their backs were bent forward at a 45-degree angle to articulate their loyalty to the authority of the state, and more importantly, to honor the modern cultural doctrine of "restraint before violence". But the obviously premeditated blockade to the entrance of the building screamed disagreement with both the state *and* its present-day cultural traditions. The ominous black kimonos being worn by the demonstrators spoke loudly to the objectives of the assembly. The red headbands were being worn by the members of the group to liken negative balance sheets to the spilled blood of benevolent 21st century Japanese national heroes.

Kahmay wasn't sure whether to keep walking toward the protesters, or to call in to the protocol office and request instructions for alternate action. She couldn't hear herself think clearly over the deafening silence of the protest group. Confusion seeped into her mind as she attempted to reconcile the competing variables of simultaneous mass protest and mass restraint. *Now we are the pariahs again? Was our bond with these people an illusion?* Kahmay tried desperately to find meaning amid the shock of the unanticipated demonstration. She did not want to believe that this contingent represented the collective consensus of the people.

Just as Kahmay began slowing the pace of her walking, she heard sounds of "*Pssst. Over here sarge.*" It was coming from her right. It was Monty, Quire, Hutchinson and Lenihan standing outside the Hai-Mart convenience store eating chocolate-bread and drinking canned hot coffee.

"Hey" said Kahmay with an instinctive whisper. "What are you guys doing here? They're supposed to get going in there pretty soon. We gotta get in there."

"Ain't gonna happen through the front door" said Monty without looking up from his newspaper.

"He's right ma'am," said Hutch. "Those peace officers over there just came over and told us to wait here. There's some kind of threat to the building. I think they're bringing dogs in. Might be a bomb or something. I just spoke with Conway. She called me from the roof and told me that Lieutenant Colonel Norris says we were all supposed to make our way to Meguro, and under no circumstances were we to attempt entry into Headquarters today. They've rescheduled the meeting for 90 minutes from now over inside of some schoolhouses."

"What about A.J.?" asked Kahmay. She looked up at the roof wondering how her most experienced specialist was going to get safely down and out.

"She's comin' over on the training drone...I'm gonna fly 'er there from Meguro once we get there" said Quire from his leaning position. He pushed himself off of the brick wall of the Hai-Mart with his upper back into the full standing position and made eye contact with Kahmay for the first time. "Lieutenant Colonel Norris flew himself over to Meguro with a mobile control unit a little while ago. He's sending the trainer over for Conway after it's fully recharged. I recommend we all get going that direction so we can get this show on the road sarge. He's expecting me to take over and bring her back, so we don't have a lot of time left."

"Right then, I'm going into the rear storage unit for the trike. You four head back to the rail station. I'm going to stay here with the comm-unit until A.J. is safely away. You're in charge Hutch. I'm counting on you to get 'em there safely and get the essential information from Colonel Kleen whether we make it there on time to hear it or not."

The four specialist-cadets quickly began walking back toward the mag-rail while Kahmay began walking around the block to gain access to the back of the high-rise where she hoped the storage locker would be accessible. Kahmay pulled her comm unit from her inside uniform pocket and tried to get A.J. on the line as she walked.

"Conway here," said A.J., answering her comm unit.

"Hey...you see your ride on the horizon yet?" asked Kahmay, beating feet toward the unattended double doors of the storage locker on the northeast end of the high-rise's ground floor.

"Negative Sergeant. Can't raise Norris. There's nothin' on the horizon. I think someone's jamming us from close by. I see uniformly spaced overlapping blankets on the spec-an...coming out at 13.4 dbm across all the operational bands. They knew exactly where to set the amplitude to stomp us out. Definitely a bunch of humans with access to high-dollar directional amplification equipment...no way they could achieve that kind of ambient signal amplitude up here without making a scene...probably cargo vans or...maybe they're up in one of the adjacent structures with something kinda big and hidden. They've *gotta* be close!" said Conway.

"But they left the comm-freq open? Have you swept for a microwave source up there yet?" asked Kahmay, now puzzled at all of the seemingly conflicting information.

"Yeah...and I'm gettin' a slight increase on the half-power probe level coming from the west side. They're not up here Sergeant. Whoever's doing this is using a ridiculously focused kind of power...and they're close...one or two blocks away at the most!" Conway said.

"Do you think you can get down here?" asked Kahmay, her voice filled with all of the intangible sounds of someone walking at an urgent pace.

"It's not happenin'...elevators have been remotely disabled," said Conway, frustrated that she could not think her way out of the predicament. She searched the surrounding neighborhood from her perch using her monocular hoping to see something that would trigger an idea. "Alright, alright, uh... damn it, how the hell did they get knowledge of the alternate location? That's the only way I can think of that would allow my comm-unit to work with you but not him all the way across town...unless he lost it or it was damaged maybe? Why isn't Norris answering?"

Kahmay's concentration was divided by what she saw after she unlocked the storage locker and swung open the heavy double doors. It was not the old trike-bike she was expecting to see. It was a brand new, urban over-under sidecar taxi with the HQ/DSEF logo stenciled onto the back end of the driver's seat. *What the hell is a brand new over-under bike doing in here?* she thought.

The over-under was twice as expensive as the various standard trikes, because they allowed local businesses to send two-person teams for onsite services. The teams brought whatever goods they might need to deliver to a customer, and also had the capability to provide tutelage, minor medical attention, and errand service. The over-under maintained two-wheel advantage in congested street traffic because the sidecar was designed to slide over toward the driver and nest itself into the space below the driver's femoral axis. Squeezing through the narrows between the lines of cars and buses saved thousands of hours per year for small business owners and was a priceless competitive advantage in the crowded streets of Edo for any organization seeking more efficient operational margins. Once through the dense traffic, the trike could return to sidecar configuration so the driver could once again engage high speed travel with a lower center of gravity.

Without thinking, Kahmay quickly grabbed a flare kit from the shelving unit inside the shed and threw them into the bike's rear storage box. She spotted a few other items on the shelving unit, but could not see any possible utility in them for the present. Grabbing one of several helmets setting on a small table next to the trike, she put one on and hopped on the bike. She attempted to raise A.J. again on the comm-unit as she carefully backed the unfamiliar bike out of the shed.

"Still there?"

"Yeah I'm here..." said Conway.

"Okay...listen...you're stuck up there for now. No practical way around that unless I can find out where the jammer is. Are you armed up there?"

"Negative...but I think I can bust open the weapons locker with the fire axe" said Conway.

"Alright, why don't you do that...I'm gonna find these untimely mosquitos so we can smoosh them and get the hell out of here. Check in if you see my flare. Look to the west" said Kahmay with confidence, this time speaking without quite as much urgency.

"Roger wilco...be careful sarge. We don't know who these people are, or whether they have anything to do with what's happening."

Specialist Conway immediately went about busting open the weapons locker and scanning around the roof to see if she could see anything that might help her make a quick unorthodox escape from her trapped position on the roof. She loaded up three M-4Zs and stuffed her cargo pockets with several high capacity magazines. She took up a defensive position and tried to calm her mind down enough to be able to think outside the box. But not knowing the nature of the threat was interfering with her ability to do anything but remain quiet and keep her situational awareness.

    Meanwhile, Sergeant Kahmay was speeding through the tight city blocks in the immediate area surrounding the high-rise looking for anything revealing about where these unknown blanket jams were coming from. Nothing on the streets of Hamamatsu appeared out of order, save the demonstrators and the ominous irregular daytime quiet. She tried to think of where she would hide if she were the one trying to jam an entire building from one or two blocks away. She came to a stop at the main traffic signal to the west of the DSEF building. She had a couple minutes to visually scan the area for anything that looked out of place. Bicycles, pedestrians, taxies, white cars, black cars, buses, *NOTHING*! Kahmay looked everywhere as the light turned green, and then she noticed something that fell squarely into the "suspicious" category. Two individuals above the Pachinko parlor were standing in the third floor window staring directly down at the intersection. There was nothing unusual about a couple of people standing at the window in a crowded city, but this was different. The building had all kinds of antennas on its roof, which again was not unusual. The unusual part the Sergeant noticed was that there were at least two well-hidden snipers on top of the building who were not maintaining their static discipline. Seeing a fidgety sniper in Edo was like spotting one of the last hundred Iriomote Mountain Cats at a dog show whistling Kimigayo; it just *shouldn't* happen in this dimension statistically. Furthermore, to seal the deal, some of the inherently directional-looking antennas were arranged in a pattern familiar to the Sergeant's memory. The bidirectional, like-banded array pattern was used specifically to either *facilitate* two-way ground communication, or to *obstruct* a predicted two-way ground communication.

Pulling the trike over about half a block down, Kahmay found a nice little cranny to squeeze into between the bumpers of two parked cars. She left her helmet on and hopped off the bike to grab the flare kit and head toward the Pachinko building's electrical panels on foot. The most expedient way for her to get the drone channels cleared up was to simply deprive the whole building of power and let A. J. know that she could try and raise Norris again. But it was a risky plan to assume that there would be enough time before the business owners came out to investigate the encroachment on their bottom line. Walking swiftly along the street-facing side of the building, Kahmay was nearly to the electrical panel when suddenly she felt a stinging sensation coming from the right side of her neck. She immediately began to feel dizzy. She had barely enough time to reach up to the source of the pain as she looked over her right shoulder to see a gun barrel being pulled back into the 2nd floor window of the building across the street. The black curtain of unconsciousness began falling across her field of view as she looked back down into her hand just in time to see a shiny dart with black fletching. The limp fall toward the concrete sidewalk was her last memory.

Specialist Conway was still crouched and trapped atop the DSEF high-rise. She could feel herself preparing to do something drastic to get free of the unknown doom that she anticipated in the coming moments. Over and over again she went through the scenarios in her mind that were most likely to occur, and how she would respond. She was relying heavily on her ability to reload the rifle quicker than the enemy could move in on her sustained fire. She resisted the temptation to stay solely focused on the elevator door and tried desperately to come up with something novel and opportunistic. But she could not pry her thoughts away from what she knew she would be forced to do if the door opened to reveal her unknown fate. She controlled her breathing and allowed her thoughts to carry her back to the facts. She had not tried to raise Lieutenant Colonel Norris for several moments and was just about to try again when she was startled by the sudden start-up of the building's air-handling system. The landing pad lights and perimeter lights flashed on and off simultaneously as they ran through their familiar power-up self-tests. Specialist Conway felt a sudden wave of relief come over her as she realized the power was coming back on.

Across the roof A.J. saw the elevator door open up and was glad to see the inside totally empty. Without hesitation she grabbed the two spare rifles and made a dash toward the elevator. She ran along the perimeter of the roof and peered over the edge as she kept her profile low. She rapidly continued moving her person in the direction of the elevator while observing the distant ground below. The demonstrators were walking in all different directions and clearing out of the demonstration area. She noticed they all looked like they were walking too fast, or that they were in a bit of a hurry for a bunch that had just been on their knees since well before the break of dawn. Approaching the elevator, A.J. could now see a small object on the floor of the spacious elevator service car. It was a tiny digital timer with four minutes and forty-six seconds left on it. It was counting down to zero! She slammed her hand onto the floor selection panel and repeatedly hit the "G" button. Her stomach became numb upon realizing that she may have made a mistake not taking the stairs. Her uncertainty was erased by the normal closing of the car door and subsequent rapid decent through the floors to the ground level. She knew she had no choice but to try and bust the ceiling of the elevator open to prepare a cautionary egress should the car suddenly stop before reaching the ground.

Kahmay opened her eyes and tried to focus on the light she could see through the blur of her helmet visor and her chemically mal-focused irises. She was face down on the concrete and her body was moving by itself. It was an odd feeling for her to know something was wrong and not be able to pinpoint the reason why. It was simultaneously comforting for her to know that if someone came to finish her off, she would be watching it through the blurry eyes of a limp body. She felt lucky, even *happy* to realize that she might not feel the pain of a bullet entering her brain, or a blunt object flipping her switch off with the first blow. She felt a tug coming from her right shoulder and could not even bring herself to be startled by the realization that it was someone *else* moving her. She had a vague notion that the person who had incapacitated her was trying to pick her up and carry her off to an unknown location. But then she heard A.J.'s voice through the fog of her aural incapacity.

"Come on, get up Sergeant! We gotta go! Come on...you gotta help me out here!" said Conway, maneuvering Kahmay's body into position for the fireman's carry.

"Wha...how did you..."

Kahmay struggled to maintain consciousness as she felt her body bouncing on A.J.'s upper back at a frantic pace. She tried to focus on the bouncing blurry images and managed to bring the high-rise into focus just in time to see that they were traveling away from it.

"I think something really bad is about to happen. We gotta get away from here *NOW*!" said Conway. "I think it's a bomb...!"

"Use the Trike" said Kahmay in the clearest voice she could manage.

A.J. spotted the trike still parked where Kahmay had left it moments earlier. She hurriedly lowered Kahmay into the trike pod and latched the door shut. She knew they had only seconds remaining before the clock hit zero, and was relieved when the bike started right up. She twisted the accelerator handle a couple times with the transmission in neutral to make sure she was oriented and had good throttle response. She hunched down and twisted the handle wide open until she was confident her center of gravity was low enough to really put some extreme demands on the vehicle. The bike quickly had enough forward momentum for her to place her feet on the foot pegs. *Two blocks, three blocks, five blocks, seven, eleven, almost clear...*, she thought. Just as her subconscious mind began to make the realization that they were more than likely safe from whatever was about to happen, she heard the sickening sound of an enormous explosion. The blast had come from behind her, but A.J. dared not look back until she could put more distance between them and the blast zone. She struggled to fight her urge to at least ascertain whether they were going to be overwhelmed by a speed-mismatched concussion wave so she could find quick shelter in a ditch or dugout. She opened the throttle as wide as she could and leaned down into the envelope of the natural aerodynamic profile created by the bike's piercing arrow-like design. She knew she had to keep her eyes forward. But the overwhelming curiosity that had built up in her mind about what had just happened caused her to finally glance into her side mirror. She carefully twitched her head over for an instant; just long enough to take a quick visual snapshot of the view behind her and refocus her eyes back onto the road in front of her. The entire building and everything in it was being consumed from the center by an M-Class implosion charge. But the initial outward blast of the implosion bomb had accelerated certain solid fragments beyond the escape velocity threshold requirements of the super-dense mass created at the center of the blast. The bomb's supercenter gathered and compressed the amount of material required to make the bomb's detonation point gravitationally attractive enough to pull the remainder of the material within the blast zone in toward the core. Specialist

Conway could feel her eyes widening into saucers as she observed various pieces of shrapnel speeding in their direction. She was going too fast to make any abrupt turns, and had no other practical choice but to continue speeding. The hair on top of her head strained to stand up against the wind as pieces of debris began impacting buildings to the left and right of them, making sharp cracking noises upon impact with other objects. Some of the pieces were landing on the road in front of them, and tumbling down the road with such tremendous energy they were obliterating themselves. The shrapnel cut through the surrounding area with energy and speed that was only rarely matched on Earth. A.J. could not believe that she had not been abruptly killed from behind yet. Finally, she managed to let go of her distracting concern for things that had not yet come to pass, and focused solely on speeding forward; unflinching, and determined to get them clear of the danger.

Do What You Will

EARTH
Sector JP-0001, Edo
December 05, 2021 C.E.
Sunday
1217 HRS

Specialist A.J. Conway was now far enough away from the scene of the high-rise implosion to begin thinking more seriously about the quickest route to Meguro. She felt herself becoming cold as the wind rushed into the spaces of her lightweight jacket, drying her sweat and carrying off her heat. In the chaos of their hasty departure from the Hamamatsu area, she had forgotten how she lost her left shoe. The sock-covered toes of her left foot were transforming into little frozen toe-berries from the hyper-cooling effect of high wind on moistened skin. It was strange to her that she had escaped with only one shoe. But the stranger part for A.J. was that she could not remember *when* she had lost the shoe. She occasionally glanced down over her right shoulder into the over-under passenger pod to see if

Sergeant Kahmay was showing any signs of consciousness yet. The Sergeant was still fading in and out of consciousness from the potent tranquilizer dart. A.J. could not get over the thought of how close they had come to death, and found herself wondering whether or not they were just plain lucky, or whether the perpetrators had intentionally meant for them to live. There was one thing she had learned about the people of 21st century Edo that shined above everything else, and seemed to be the most incontrovertible piece of evidence in support of their non-violent intentions: they were not known to kill people just to make a point when the bloodless, tidy destruction of inanimate "things" and "symbols" had proven to be more than enough to get a strong message across to the world.

    A.J. cruised along the lower urban highways of southern Edo and made her way through the nooks and crannies of the neighborhoods looking for an inconspicuous route to their destination. Once she had made her way out into a relatively low population density area, she thought it wise to pull over at a Ramen shop she spotted a hundred meters down the road or so. She pulled the trike into the tiny parking area beside the noodle house feeling lucky that there were two and a half square meters of parking space available when she most needed them. She turned the ignition off and reached inside her cargo pocket for her comm-unit.

There was a message indicator showing that Lieutenant Colonel Norris had attempted to contact her. She opened the message and hurriedly read the text in anticipation of its expected important contents.

"Hey Conway, this is Quire on Norris' comm-unit. When you get this, come to the dentist office that has the big green and white sign above it at the southeastern corner of Meguro township district 2. I can bring you guys over to the spot here. No hurry" the message read.

A.J. got off the bike and walked around to look in on Kahmay. She was a tad surprised by the sight of the Sergeant in a position that had intentionally been chosen for greater comfort. Kahmay slowly opened her eyes and looked up at Conway in a way that suggested she was about to speak.

"One miso chashu and a side of gyoza to go...for me...pretty please."

Kahmay managed a slight smile as she reclosed her eyes and trusted that A.J. would forgive her presumptuous request.

After a quick side trip, Specialist Conway came out of the noodle house bobbing up and down with her shoeless left foot and deposited the hot food into the trike's cargo compartment. The two were soon once again on their way toward Meguro. Conway managed to pull up a map of the Meguro area on her comm-display and was now following the prescribed course with ease.

She spotted Quire up ahead sitting on a small concrete retaining wall outside the dentist's office and was at last relieved to be regrouping with the others.

"You can pull the bike over into the parking garage there" said Quire, looking down into the passenger pod. "What happened to her?" he asked.

"She had a run-in with a bad guy who was packin' tranq-darts. She's alright. She's just resting right now" said Conway.

Sergeant Kahmay looked up at Quire with creased eye-slits and showed him her middle finger, as was their interpersonal custom for demonstrating the proper esprit de corps. Quire smiled and reciprocated the gesture after feeling the relief of knowing that there was nothing permanently wrong with her.

"Didn't find out what happened to you two until after the big 'ole void that used to be our headquarters starting popping up on the news a little while ago" said Quire. "We tried changing up the SCI band multiple times...messed around with some modulation that we thought had a chance of squeaking through...but it was like trying to shove a circle into a parallelogram party...ya know, it could happen... but it's not recommended...know what I'm sayin'? Feedback on the second harmonic fried the receiver sarge. We failed you. The training drone was out there loitering over some kind of company softball tournament and couldn't fetch the auto-return coordinates after bing-bat...we really had a case of the head-scratch on that one too because the auto-return should have been..."

"Hey Quire," interrupted Kahmay in her best-feigned voice of slightly mocking frailty, "I promise not to tell anyone in Idaho that you're making excuses if you promise to *validate my parking and help me out of this CASKET*!" The Sergeant finished the latter half of her sentence with a subtle crescendo and an abrupt dose of seriousness.

Specialist Quire offered up his hand to invite his senior-ranking teammate to grab hold while the two shared a laugh of grateful relief that the day had not been far worse. Kahmay viewed Quire like the little brother she never had. But there was plenty of mutual respect between them on the peer level as well. She was glad to have a finesse artist on the field operations team, and was always conscientious about how rare it was for someone to be able to perform as well under pressure as Quire. He was the one and only Field Support Operations Specialist Leonard Quire; tactical call sign "Trigger".

"It's this way" said Quire. "They all went into the bar after we heard you guys were alright. You were the last two unaccounted for."

Colonel Kleen and Lt. Colonel Norris looked up from their vodka-spiked melon sodas as Conway, Quire, and Kahmay entered the bar. Kahmay looked up at the sign above the door and smiled when she read the ominous-sounding "Bu-rak-ku Bi-zhi-on" kana script. The "Black Vision" bar actually looked more like a burger joint on the inside than a cocktail bar, but with slightly darker ambience than a typical family style burger restaurant. This tiny local watering hole, despite its dark name, was the kind of place people went to feel light-hearted. There were tasty snacks listed on small touch-activated menus, milkshakes a la mode, a full bar, and a generous twofold choice of tatami or booth-style seating.

One would never know from the appearance of the area outside the Black Vision that there was a bar inside the larger structure. To the unknowing eye, it looked like an apartment building that had various unseen little business enterprises embedded within it. Often times, undersized home offices in residential neighborhoods had their own little blinking phosphor-gel signs powered on at night. Working adults frequently commuted to salaried positions during the daytime hours, and then came home in the evening and turned on their multi-colored "[INSURANCE]...0120-YASUUUI" sign at night. One could make a killing conducting micro-business at all hours in Greater Edo.

"Have a seat. Make yourselves comfortable" said Lt. Colonel Norris, pulling out a few chairs for the latecomers. "Geez Sergeant...you look like I feel" he joked. Kahmay was not really in the mood for jokes, but she somehow found the fire within her to snap back at Lt. Colonel Norris to let him know that her toughness was still intact.

"Good thing I don't *feel* how you *look* Colonel" said Kahmay, opening up her to-go container full of miso-chashu ramen and pan-fried gyoza. "So, what the hell is going on? Where is everybody?" she asked, almost indifferent about what the possible answers to her question might be.

"This *is* everybody Sergeant" said Colonel Kleen. "We're done."

There was an awkward silence at the booth-table as Lenihan, Hutch, and Monty all looked at one another to see if any of the three were willing to take the others through the summary explanation of what Kleen meant by her statement. Specialist Mayfield was off in the corner heavily engaged with a gaming table and did not yet even seem to be aware that Kahmay and A.J. had made it safely out of danger. The Colonel saved all of them the trouble of guessing and cleared her throat in preparation to speak after one last sip of her drink.

"They're shuttin' us down Kahmay. As of 2400 tonight, the funding stops, the headquarters is shut down, and the agency formerly known to the public as DSEF will be no more. Those with fewer than six months of retainability left on their contract will have the option to stay here in the building across the hall and go home once their time is up. Those with more than six months left are being farmed out into the wind. Your choice is to either re-enlist and cross-train, or stay here for a few months pushing a pencil and picking up trash every day as a gesture of goodwill toward the community. What's your pleasure Sergeant?"

Kahmay did not immediately have a reply for the Colonel. She grabbed the attention of the bartender and requested a large Sojuzake-a-la-Seoul before turning around to once again face the team. She was hoping the Soju would kick in before the Sake. The bartender set the Soju beverage down in front of her and gratefully took the cash Kahmay had extracted from her sleeve pocket and flung onto the table in disgust at what she was hearing. Seeing the chance to add one more comment before Kahmay finished gulping her drink down, the Colonel started to speak one more time. She leaned in toward the middle of the table like a parent attempting to gently scold one of their children in public.

"It doesn't have to end this way...you know how these things have a way of fizzling out. By this time next year the heads at UGC will have..."

The Colonel was cautiously interrupted by Sergeant Kahmay, who had just finished swallowing her last gulp of soju.

"Ma'am, what can I do to keep the team closest to the stated objectives of those who understand the true meaning of the word 'COMMITMENT'? That's all I need to know" said Kahmay with a noticeably reckless tone of anger.

"Sergeant, my recommendation to you right now at this moment, is to avoid saying something you might regret. You're obviously pissed off, and you're definitely..."

"YA THINK? WHAT THE HELL GAVE YOU THAT IDEA COLONEL?" barked Kahmay.

This time the Colonel was abruptly cut off, and was moving to get out of her chair before Kahmay could even finish her sentence. Although the Colonel could have stayed and verbally wrestled with the Sergeant, she chose to close herself off and let the chips fall. She knew it would be hard to get through to Kahmay under the circumstances. She had to let go and trust that the veteran NCO would have enough restraint not to alienate her whole team during what remained of the evening.

"Before I leave Sergeant, you should know that we already spoke about this while we were waiting to find out whether you and the Specialist there had been smashed into the 'double-singularity with cheese' burger. We have no doubts that there is still a way to complete the mission...if not three ways. But that will be all on the subject until this group has had a chance to blow off some steam and assimilate the changes. I swear I just heard you start to forget what FUCKIN' PLANET you were on…barking at me like a *damned private? How dare you*" said Kleen in her angry whisper. "Do what you will Staff Sergeant, but lose your bearing toward me again and we're going to have a problem. Never sacrifice your self-control" said the Colonel, motioning nonverbally with her eyes and head to Lt. Colonel Norris that she was ready to retire to quarters for the night.

      Several uneventful moments passed following the departure of the brass. The junior enlisted personnel made themselves busy with several low-stakes games of 9-ball while Specialist Conway and Sergeant Kahmay remained at the booth-table without a word. They were too disgusted with all of the wasted effort and anxiety to feel anything but regret and disappointment. The monumentally screwed up day had turned into a quiet, mildly liquored-up reflection of the future. A.J. knew better than to start offering dime-a-dozen solutions to her partner in crime. They were both beyond needing to be told to "embrace the positive in life". They knew they were going to continue pursuing the mission objectives without regard to the demands of the opposition. But neither troop could yet fully fathom how this would be accomplished.

"You want those last two gyozas Tootsie?" asked Kahmay in her business tone.

"No, thanks..." said Conway. "You haven't had enough to eat yet anyway...get it done...or you know what will happen to you. That's all I'm going to say on the matter."

"I'd sure like to know why..." said Kahmay.

"Why? Why what?" asked Conway.

"Why is it still such an incredible mystery to everyone that Earth cannot survive within the current status quo? I mean, would *you* want your children to live in a garbage can that smells like an unintended mix of bleach and methane? I know that sounds pessimistic, but...I think we messed up...really. If we're all supposed to...exercise our free will...then...we're still free to pursue our free will...right?" asked Kahmay, fixing her tipsy stare onto the salt and pepper shakers at the center of the table. She was transforming into monologue mode, and was about to begin the familiar process of systematically purging herself of the frustration she felt. Conway was her most trusted ally and was often the only one who ever heard the Sergeant's innermost feelings at times like these. From the moment Kahmay's left eyebrow started to raise, A.J. knew the conversation was about to take a different turn.

"The thing few people ever understand about quantum physics is that adding figurative energy to your thick skin requires stealing energy from your inner atomic core. Thick skin cannot absorb and replace photonic energy efficiently enough to counteract the years of longevity you steal from your soul during high-quanta activity. In the flesh, I think the effect is felt in the form of an almost imperceptibly resolved 'pain-amplitude' knob that is constantly being turned slightly clockwise, or slightly counterclockwise...or sometimes up toward almost the maximum...and rarely...it *feels* like the dial is being completely still...maybe...in the zero-voltage ground-plane of electrical neutrality."

"Oh hell yeah" said Conway. "It might take longer than we thought, and it might feel like something is draining the soul in the process. But we can still pursue this. In the meantime, we have to do what we can to minimize the damage to this planet...ya know...heal it over while we're still here" said Conway.

"Yeah, I was thinking about the Carpenter homestead back behind my place. Ever been to the west side of sector AK-0006?" asked Kahmay.

"What? What are you thinking?" asked Conway.

"I was thinking about firing up the tractor and digging some holes. Mr. Carpenter has a bunch of old grain silos he brought up there from sector OR-0001 back in the 1970s. He was always talking about wanting to fabricate a giant telescope with them. But he's gone now, and his widow couldn't handle the upkeep on the place. Not many people in their eighties are tough enough to go to the store on a snow machine in minus 40. I used to bring her groceries and firewood back in the day. But then one day she was just gone. There were no tire tracks in the snow, not even old ones. It took me almost a month to find out that she had been taken into the city by helicopter to stay at her son's house. I went in through the side window of the cabin and found the entire place empty. The borough tax assessor's office said the property taxes had been paid *decades* in advance, and that they were not able to auction the place under the abandonment statute because the Carpenters built squatters cabins on the property, and at least one of them is occupied at all times by folks who just live out in the bush because they are free to do so. But the grain silos have been protected under the drunken spruce and paper birch trees for...I'm wantin' to say 15 years or so? I say we drag 'em out and build a training complex. You know how to weld?" asked Kahmay.

"Yes and no. But yes, I can do it. I can refresh my proficiency by reading and practicing on some scrap. I struggled with certain metals...Aluminum is a challenge if memory serves. No, I've never been to the west side of sector AK-0006. Always heard bad things" said Conway.

"It's gonna take more than just me and you" said Kahmay. "Do you think anyone in the unit would..."

Kahmay was surprised to be suddenly interrupted by Specialist Rufus Mayfield.

"Yeah, we would" he said.

Mayfield had been passively listening to the conversation whilst playing digital pachinko at one of the back tables.

"We all would...at least, everybody that's present in here right now would. I'm already writing up a form 1000 in my head right now. Maybe DSEF won't be the organization I end up giving the completed form to, but somebody in the government wants to save money, right? Anyway, that's just what I've been working on for the past few hours...and they haven't even officially dissolved the unit yet...right? So, the way I see it...we're already way ahead of their evil plan to close the book on distant space. All we have to do is show them how we swim upstream in the face of their crappy news flash, and they'll look to us again...once they realize that the middle fork of the crap river they sailed in on...is just too crappy to pursue. They'll admit their big mistake to each other, deny it to the public, and we'll all be back in business" said Rufus.

"Rufus, you are the man. What are you drinkin' dude?" Kahmay asked. "Have I ever told you about the river I live by back home?"

"Oh, alright," he said, moving out of his game-table and over to the larger table with Kahmay and

Conway, "um...I'm drinking green tea with a macchiato on the side. That is...only if you're buyin' Sergeant Kahmay."

"Yes, I'm buyin'" Kahmay said.

Kahmay pulled a chair out for Mayfield and patted it a couple times to encourage him to sit and elaborate.

"Tell me what you're thinking Rufus" said Kahmay.

"I'm thinking...you never told me anything about any river...and that we're going to have to go into space whether they would have us go or not...straight up. It really doesn't matter what they think the public can stomach, or who has a violent protest over it. Can't you feel people starting to dissociate themselves from all the old norms? Look at the last three to five thousand years...people just start malfunctioning when they get too bottled up...wars, overdoing things, under-doing things, trying to fix problems by creating new problems...endlessly. We aren't the kind of species that uses the bio-clock very well...it's like, we became these technological people, and now there's no going back. This so-called 'technology' truly was the work of Pandora. It's too late, we already opened the damned box...as long as just one tiny enclave of humans with a memory and the capacity to reproduce exists, technology will now forever be the go-to solution for all the problems we perceive need a..."

Conway interrupted Rufus to prevent him from getting carried away. He had a reputation for digressing too far away from the main conversation topic.

"Hey, whoa, whoa...Rufus, man...I hear you...and I kinda disagree with you about the Pandora thing...but you're preaching to the choir mostly dude...humans just naturally want to make tools and establish more efficient processes...and we measure those results in terms of the extra longevity that we receive statistically. We conclude that it's a direct result of not damaging our physiology as much as say, back in Neolithic times. But how can we do this...right now, in the present? How are we going to get our team into space? Because it's not a question of 'if' anymore...not for any of us".

"Well...how would you survive in the middle of the desert with no water?" asked Rufus as a way of challenging the real question into a natural, unforced solution.

"You would need knowledge, a strong will to survive, and at least some accurate instinct of what would happen to you if you didn't complete 'X' in time to preclude 'Y' from happening" Kahmay said.

"That's exactly right" replied Mayfield enthusiastically. "And you would do the exact same thing in space. It's not a question of 'if', it's a question of 'how'. That's all there is...'how'...and every 'how' has an answer in a multiverse with endless possibilities. But it's a race against time. More than likely, before you get close to the answer for the question of 'how', you are going to be on a collision course with questions like 'poverty, hunger, and disease'. We have to move quickly...and that means we're going to need to *avoid* reinventing the wheel as much as possible. We have to remain practical" said Specialist Mayfield.

"Alright, so now we have to figure out a little bit about the interim. We could get a lot done here picking up trash, or we could get a lot done here picking up trash and then taking this show into sector AK-0006...so we can practice sustaining life where none yet exists" said Kahmay.

"Yes, but with what resources?" asked Conway.

"It's going to be whatever resources we can generate, by whatever achievable means necessary. We have to utilize established networks of contact over here while we have local access to one another. How much service retainability do you have Rufus?" asked Kahmay.

"Eighteen months and seven days precisely" said Rufus. "I think I should extend my enlistment for three years, and then put in a request for follow-on orders to AK-0006. There are two Senior Specialist positions there for comprehensive celestial mechanics and deep-space perturbation fundamentals. If everything goes well I can extend again for another year to get in deeper with that approach. Those slots aren't on the termination listing for all the programs that fall away after tonight, because most of what is taught in those programs is funded as supplemental support programs for satellite communications and unmanned semi-autonomous drone programs" said Mayfield.

"That might get two of us there if we get on it immediately. What about the odd person out?" asked Conway.

"Don't you mean 'what about the others' A.J.?" asked Hutch.

A.J. looked up to see Monty, Quire, Hutchinson, and Lenihan all standing there leaning on their pool cues.

"How the hell are we going to fit seven people into two slots?" asked Lenihan.

"Lenihan, you above everyone else should know that little-big things can fit in anywhere they damn well want to...right?"

Rufus only answered the question in a deliberate attempt to capitalize on the opportunity to lighten things up.

"You know; you have a point there Rufe" said Lenihan. "I'll let my contract expire in a few months once both of the open slots have been filled by two of us. Then I'll go stay in the complex after we get 'er built and bring home the bacon in the form of knowledge. I wish to be the team's full time troubleshooter. I'll research, scrounge food, fish for food, grow food, attend classes, you know; bring something more than just my magnetic personality to the table."

"I think Lieutenant Colonel Norris is already working on the personnel problem" said Monty. "He was drafting up plans for a schooling program up there where you all are talking about, but not in sector AK-0006. He was trying to set it up in sector 99."

"That's Devil Dog country" said Quire. "It'd be a hard sell. There's no real legitimate mission correlation. I think we're better off trying to get the school going over in sector 6, but still include the Devil Dogs on the form 1000. Expanded combat capability and close air support will be needed on other planets. But yeah, we ought to ask Norris to change his solicitation for there in AK-0006, and sell it as a way to get the training done without using any big money...save the ration stipend of course. That way we can get the slots and stay together as a team. Any training that needs to be done between us and the Devils can be done once the Earth phase of the original mission is complete."

"Alright then, pitch it to him...in the morning. Like Rufus said, we've got a really good head start here. We have to use the remaining time as wisely as possible. Let's gather here again tomorrow and hash it out some more. I like the way this is headed. Feel free to relax tonight. It might be the last time you all get to let loose for a while" said Kahmay.

Embracing the Impossible

FOUR YEARS LATER

EARTH
Sector AK-0006
November 8, 2025 C.E.
Saturday
0256 HRS

Approximately 21.32 simulated meters down inside the underground command post of Deep Space Expeditionary Technical Squadron (DSETS), Detachment IV, Technical Sergeant Kahmay awoke to the sound of the surface alarm. She rolled her eyes in mild disgust and allowed her head to drop back onto the pillow with a soft thud. Now caught in the middle region of sleep, she heard the voices of her graveyard crew shouting back and forth at one another about whose fault it was that the ventilation shafts were not sealed in time to save them all from certain simulated death. She wondered what on Earth it was going to take for them to treat the exercises as reality. She knew that the bitter-cold vacuum of space would never forgive such petty mistakes, and that her crew would never be prepared on time for Operation *Kaminari* at this rate. There was no tangible consolation afforded by the subtle realization that if her crew members were apathetic about the mission, they would surely not bother to expend so much energy on a *meaningless* heated argument. But all of the wasted emotion in the solar system would still be inadequate to save an individual from basic lack of preparation.

Kahmay sat up onto the edge of her bunk and exhaled a burst of pressurized disgust at the realization that her conscious mind had now fully commandeered her dream-state. Going back to sleep until 0500 to get those extra two hours was no longer a realistic option for the Sergeant. She hopped out of bed in preparation to begin her day. She grabbed the public address microphone and simultaneously twisted the volume knob clockwise to the specific threshold that just approached the level of "startle". She cleared her throat and took a sip of water through the straw of the sealed cup she always kept by her bedside.

"Attention, attention...This is the NCOIC. This is the NCOIC. All personnel will report to the conference chamber at 0430. All personnel will report to the conference chamber for a mandatory meeting at 0430 hours. Kahmay out."

The abrupt absence of sound, followed by the faint sound of 44 boot-covered feet shuffling all around the hard clay floor, reassured her that the entire crew was at the very least, serious about compliance for this meeting. The louder sounds were coming from the day shift crew piling out of bed like 22 Alder logs being dropped onto a concrete floor. The softer, more focused sounding 22 boots were the tired ones from graveyard shift. She perceived this latter bunch were primarily moving with increased urgency due to the anticipation they felt about spending the last 30 minutes of their shift at ease in a sitting position with a cup of something hot. The loudest discernable sound from their area was undoubtedly the sound of the Mobile Tooling Station (MTS) drawers being closed with a bit too much force. She knew precisely what both shifts needed to be told in order to fully understand the seriousness of the training. Her thoughts were exclusively focused on the words and expressions she would choose to accomplish the accurate conveyance of her extremely important message. She filled the tea kettle with water and began heating it for her morning Kilimanjaro French press coffee. Only the penetrating aroma of the finely ground coffee bean could properly sharpen her verbal scalpel these days.

She casually walked into the conference chamber at 0429 and made a straight line for the offset podium and microphone combination. Just stage right from center where the presentation screen hung, Kahmay picked up the slide advance control and brought up the first slide. She then fixed her eyes upon her 22 crewmembers and began methodically making eye contact with each and every one of them individually. The screen was tilted a few degrees downward toward the semicircular amphitheater style seating pattern, so that all attendees would have the most perpendicular view of the screen. All were quiet within seconds, and as the last person finally stopped talking, the clock struck 0430 and without hesitation the Technical Sergeant began to speak with controlled speed and emotionless military precision.

"Good morning. All those on graves who cannot stay awake through this meeting will get with their crewmates after this is over and go through what I have told you so that nothing is missed. I know you night owls have been at it all night and that you couldn't get your act together for the drill earlier this morning. For you people on days, you guys are going to go through the same routine today as graves did last night. I want all MTS units and systems rips signed by both shift leaders before you go home. Now to business. You are all here because you want to be. You all know that it's a long shot that you'll receive anything in the way of compensation by the time our mission has moved into the contract phase. In fact, if we get a letter from DSECC that says nothing more than "piss off", we should all consider ourselves lucky. I appreciate the fact that you believe in something greater than yourselves, and I fully intend to do everything in my power to ensure that you are rewarded with untold intangibles for all of your commitment to this endeavor. But people, we have a long way to go to get back to zero...and rewards are the least of our worries. We have just under five weeks remaining until we are required to submit our ops-plan to DSECC, and *THIS* is how far we have come!" With a pointed snap of her arm, she advanced the slide forward to the primary metrics page and then quickly moved her head back to the crew to see their expressions as they saw the primary metrics in all of their abysmal underperformance. She noticed them all squinting out their own renditions of pained frowns, and that they were randomly lowering their heads in frustration. Immediately the low roar of disappointment was interrupted by the NCOIC. "Now, obviously the operational numbers are unacceptable. We screwed up six out of seven categories, and have failed to respond appropriately in dynamic life threatening situations over 82% of the time. That is horrendous... and frankly, it's embarrassing. Yes, the trials and procedures have been designed in a way that maximizes unforeseen variable interruption. Yes, there have been several impressive successes along the way. But we are not ready. Not by a long shot."

Kahmay allowed her initial talking points a few moments to ferment, and then asked a question of the entire crew.

"Can anyone tell me in one minute or less why we are *STILL* having so much trouble with surface response?" she asked.

Instantaneously three hands popped up and Kahmay quickly pointed at the always razor sharp Specialist A.J. Conway.

"Go for A.J...." she said.

Specialist Conway sat at attention and began explaining, "Ma'am, we've been runnin' twelves or longer every day for weeks, and the primary metrics don't even come *close* to..."

Kahmay calmly interrupted in a slightly louder voice before A.J. could finish her specially prepared thought.

"You're exactly right, and no further discussion will be allowed on this topic or any other operational topic for the rest of the day. You all need rest, and I need time to think without all of the racket around here. And what the hell are we doing HERE... ON SATURDAY...AGAIN? Go see your families! Go have fun doing your favorite things around your favorite people for a while and clear your heads. I need you all back here at 0500 on the 20th, and I'm going to need *all* of you at full strength. Dayshift, if you will please finish up comprehensives on bays two and three before you go."

The 11 well rested troops enthusiastically spoke their "yes ma'am[s]" and "copy that[s]" in low excited voices.

TSgt Kahmay trained her look upon the tired faces in the crowd that she knew to be the night shifters of the bunch, and then spoke their instructions.

"Graves...you all hit the showers, grab breakfast, and go immediately to bed without passing go...you guys are dangerous when you're this tired. DETACHMENT DISMISSED! Don't call me unless you have a death wish, a brilliant idea, or a genuinely boring adult problem."

Again the 44 boots began shuffling and rumbling across the floor, hurriedly moving into the last phase of their respective pre-work and pre-relaxation routines. Kahmay returned to her quarters in Bay 1. She took a deep breath and smiled as she exhaled and laid her thumb across the coffee bean grinder's power button and started it whirring away at the morning silence. She knew the crew had earned it, and she knew the metrics were not an absolute quantification of their ability to do what would be expected of them. The technical response capabilities were scoring high every time, and the ship's comprehensive systems checks were coming back at 99.2% capable on average. All discrepancies identified during comprehensives were 100% repairable, and follow-ups on repairs had been reliable in random selection processes so far. But the toughest part was still ahead. The 23-member Det. IV crew had no *real* ship, and running operational and technical drills in a homemade deep underground bunker was a crude simulation of the reality aboard a multibillion-dollar cruiser. But that was not a problem in the risk-taking business. The entire crew was betting the farm on the idea that even if they didn't somehow procure a ship, their ops-plan would be so undeniably strong that they would get their approval from DSECC and make it out of Earth orbit with or without public funding. They were hoping that philanthropy would find them to be at least utilitarian enough to be deployed out there somewhere in the solar neighborhood. They believed in themselves *that much.* They knew what they were doing, and had been trained to do the *exact same things* that the brave souls of the original Operation *Kibo* were trained to do. But the annihilation of the *E.S.S. Earth 1* had taught everyone the hard way that the *exact same things* would not suffice a second time. Somehow, they would make this mission happen. Failure was not an option for any of them, and they were all ready to do whatever it took to get the distant outpost built and settled.

Kahmay gave her brew a final stir and took her first frothy caffeine-laced sip as her thoughts turned toward her objective for the next two weeks. She had business with family, and it was her turn to go home too. She loved going home, because it was like traveling to another world within her own world. Home was a magical place, deep in the temperate rainforest of sector OR-0042, not far from the beautiful Pacific Coast. Mom's home cooking, Dad's latest project, and lots and lots of green plants and evergreen trees surrounded every inch of the heavily fortified perimeter of the homestead. She thought about how she was going to survive in space with no forest. How was she going to convince the family that they had to leave with her? *They would never leave the planet...not until after that glory-seeking black flag army of AK-47-toting losers comes into the river valley to take delivery of their well-deserved annihilation.*

The whole family had spent most of their entire lives preparing to defend this enchanted forest from such threats, and they weren't afraid to die protecting the land and their way of life from parasitic thugs. In fact, they were all way more interested in the potential gratification of revenge killings than they were in some far out space journey. For Tech Sergeant Kahmay, her revenge was going to be watching all of the self-righteous idiots kill themselves from the remote surveillance network as the team plotted an intercept course for Edo-00010011. But there was no plan for the innocent masses, and this was unacceptable. She knew she had to do more. She had to be better than her former self. She needed transcendence for herself and as many others as possible. The Command Council would likely be glad to choose a variation of the original ops-plan that included provisions for the mass evacuation of the innocent if they believed it was feasible and achievable without sacrificing the survivability of the larger human race.

The idea of leaving Earth would just seem wrong to the McGrady clan. Kahmay had no idea how to convince them that the threat was likely not going to be what her tribe had anticipated throughout the years. All she knew was that the *capability* to bring the tribe to distant safety needed to exist long before the capability to repel an army of human oppressors. All of the McGradys including Kahmay were itching for a fight. Much unprovoked hatred had been brought to bear against them. But the next fight would *not* be the enemy they could see with their own eyes. The next threat was going to be carefully chosen by the oppressors to be stealthy, 100% lethal and utterly inescapable for those that had not taken the necessary precautions. It would come *"like a thief in the night"* as papa Church would say to bring attention to the biblical reference of a thing. God knows evil had come calling like such a thief in the past. The tribe knew that the thief now drew near, and probably lurked right around the corner more often than anyone suspected. The armies of people who publicly hated entire civilizations would keep coming and coming without end. It was in their nature to kill, and to be killed, and to have a glorious romantic time of it. To do so in the name of their God was simultaneously the source of their ridiculousness, and their uncommon will to commit themselves to martyrdom. Who would restore life to all of the families that would surely perish in a clash of civilizations? Would it be the same foul malevolence that brought death to their loved ones when they were so terminally offended in times past? Yes, the black flag armies had now earned their right to be slaughtered. The atrocities had cut into the fabric of the people too deeply to be forgiven, and the fever of revenge was upon the land. Even the pacifists knew enough to know that reasoning with those people would be out of the question. Kahmay had the thirst for their blood now too like the others, and with that thirst was loosed her most potent weapon. She had so much pent up anger toward the evils of the world, and had repressed her anger for decades. She always felt like it was her duty to turn the other cheek, and she regularly did so, often to an unhealthy degree. But now the full fermented rage of it all was ready to be unleashed upon her enemies. She would be more than happy to announce the failure of her will to be patient any longer than she already had.

Kahmay was not finished stealing happy times with her family, even as the evil struggled to gain ground all around them and from within them. But happy times would have to wait now. The indefinite postponement of joy and peace was never more necessary than it was in these days. Kahmay took another deep breath and sipped her lightly sweetened brew as she envisioned the arrogant demons multiplying across the land. She had seen them rally in numbers before, and took solace in knowing that the final chapter for evil always ended the same. *One day at a time...one day at a time,* she thought.

Winds of Change

EARTH
Sector OR-0042
November 10, 2025 A.D.
Monday
0923 HRS

It was almost 9:30 AM break time at the Coastal Forest Sawmill. There were only seven more minutes until Church McGrady would be allowed to eat his morning cottage cheese and fruit for the 3,107th time. He had learned to savor the finer aspects of the fruit flavors as a way of defending himself against the creeping boredom that befell him after so many years of dancing with his deadly sawblades. He wondered if his beloved Marie had remembered to include one frozen green grape so he could keep it in his cheek during equipment power-up. He liked to poke a tiny hole in it with his teeth so the grape juice would slowly leak onto his taste buds. Marie discovered his appreciation for small gestures of affection back in the late 1980s when they first met, well before they were married. That solitary frozen green grape was one of the many ways he deliberately distracted himself on his work days. By forgetting the minutes, he would be pleasantly surprised by the passing of unanticipated hours. As long as he didn't completely bite into it, his break time could last as long as he wanted it to without even needing to leave his work station. *Four more minutes*...he thought.

Those few others at the mill who predictably began casually meandering toward the break area four to six minutes early were beginning their careful daily ritual of wandering away from their work areas. Church knew he would never be one of those people. He knew his life was something else entirely. He had known from a young age how futile it was to spend one's limited energy pretending to be valuable. *How could they feel good about rehearsed deception? Where could they find the mental energy to even pay attention to the time that closely, whilst being simultaneously careful not to give away the true shirking nature of their premature migration to the microwave? Two minutes left.* It was time to safely begin the shutdown sequence and secure the control panel in accordance with occupational safety protocols. *Yawn.* The decrescendo of the giant log-cutting blade was profoundly calming to his senses. Now he could safely think about the future for 13 minutes. These were 13 of his most favorite minutes of the entire day. The wood chip processing foreman Delmar Post walked toward him in a purposefully relaxed straight line, doffing his face shield with his right hand as he walked. Del's characteristic smile and enthusiasm for each new day rarely failed to impress, especially if it was a Monday.

"Hey Church-man! How was your weekend my pale-faced Viking friend?"

Laughing in his unique way, Church replied, "Hey Del! Seems like it was too short as usual. I think something about the time speeds up on the weekend days as soon as I get home every Friday. I love being at home, and that's my torture when I come here. I'm not ashamed to admit it."

"I feel ya man. I think about that every day. Time is gonna catch up with all of us eventually, and I was really hoping to get a different view than all of this before that Reaper comes calling. But right now, this is the only view that consistently pays the kids' tuition isn't it?"

"Yeah, or it just pays for the food and heat," said Church with a subtle laugh, as he opened up his Therma-keeper. "My kids are all too hard-headed to accept money from me, so no tuition problems to speak of. It's just me and Marie versus the mortgage and the high cost of living, and even *that's* projected to sink me by next year if I don't get a raise soon. Lord forbid one of us becomes disabled. That would be the END of a 65-year-long nitrous burn."

Del assumed the floor again and let his thoughts flow out freely, as was his way when he was filled with the temporary happiness that break-time brought.

"Church, I think between the two of us, we have enough sawdust in our lungs to power a small pellet stove. I'm thinking about having one of my lungs removed so I can sell it back to the old man for the multi-fuel pile. I bet one lung would be enough thermal energy to keep the house warm for at least a couple hours. I think we could do it Church. Seriously, we could go off the grid and just pool our resources together until they find the cure for time and all of its ugly side effects. That's gonna happen soon right? I *know* they're about to figure *that* one out right? And besides, my kid is about to discover all that in his bedroom by accident while he's doing his homework. Did you know my little Thello is mixing up his own aspirin for the science fair this year? Man I swear, that kid is going to be set. I know if anything happens to me, he is going to take care of his mama and his big sis. I hope he'll be able to hook me up to the hi-test meds before my Uncle Sam-in-law realizes that boy's aptitudes and snatches him up into 'The Machine'. Hell, I wish that kid would just hurry up and figure out how to download my brain into a new body and be done with it ha ha ha! I can feel it...it won't be long now. We're all gonna be hanging out in the master nonvolatile computer storage locker, and we'll be sweatin' about how many back-up copies of ourselves to make."

"Upload Del... upload" said Church with a half-grin. He was proud of himself for having remembered some of the details of all the boring conversations he had been force-fed by his daughter Kahmay over the years. "You have to know your up from your down man". Church always finished with a psychotic-sounding, bouncing three-part chuckle-laugh when he surprised himself by recollecting obscure facts.

"Upload, download, side-load...all the same to me man," said Del, shaking his head slightly from side to side.

"Del, man, stop pretending to be less. I know your secret. You have three degrees in Advanced Mathematics or some shit...and a PhD in Theoretical Propulsion or some damn thing. Who exactly are you trying to fool?"

"Church, man...I keep tellin' you...it's PHYSICS! It's Theoretical PHYSICS! Advanced propulsion prototyping was that last gig I had up there in Washington...and none of that matters anymore anyway", said Del with a concurrent deep inhaling breath. "Most of the theoretical stuff I was working on has been either disproven, or has become accepted fact. Application of the knowledge is a lot riskier than just understanding the principles. You don't have to comply with physics if you can do a good enough job convincing the idiot rookie manager that your hair-brained idea is worth writing a check over. I always stayed true to the physics though, but I never tried to sell a bullshit idea to a naïve kid with lots of money. I guess that wasn't good enough for them, so don't be surprised if every so-called advanced technology for the next 20 years just falls out of the sky from pure greedy ignorance...or, maybe indifference is the word I'm thinking of. Naw, the only things that matter to me right now are here...in this rainforest. No amount of special obsolete knowledge is going to help me pay for Nadia's treatments. Only 40 hours a week at this place is going to keep that going now. The downside of receiving so-called futuristic medical treatment is the limited impact of the 19th century wages one often has to keep it all going in a positive direction. You ever try to stop a bullet train with a slingshot? Ain't gonna happen man."

"Futuristic? I thought they were just pinpointing the tumorous masses and the oncogenes in her system with a Uni-scan, and then shootin' her up locally with crazy gene therapy cocktails." said Church.

"Yeah...and that's enough red tape and special line-items to keep me coming to this mill until I draw my last breath...even if I live to be a hundred and fifty. They're required to deliver the drugs in a certain order according to efficacy ratings, but a talented doctor knows things that the GMA doesn't. Did you know...that one pillow costs the hospital almost 900 dollars. I had to cash in a couple bitcoins already."

"So, the hospital is using 20th century quick-fix tactics with a 21st century cost structure to make it seem like a more advanced treatment...sheesh...there's gotta be a better way man. Those med-beds at the primary treatment center up there by the Columbia River do those complete immersion therapies for 20 grand. But over 90% of those people are living past 105 now...so it might be worth it to a lot of people with guaranteed pensions and fat life insurance policies."

Del quickly replied with a huge grin that only came onto his face when he knew he would have an opportunity to reply in song.

"Of course there's a better way my naive friend! It's called, 'NOT TELLIN' YOUUUUU Oh whoa whooooa, 'TIL AF' TERRR, I HAVE SECUUUUURED...THE PATENT RIGHTS'!"

"Ha, whatever you say man." Church was not entirely sold on the idea that Del had been experimenting at home with bioengineered cures for his beloved wife, but he knew anything was possible where loved ones were concerned. "Just remember though; obsolete knowledge is nowhere near as dangerous as obsolete aptitude Doctor space-man."

After sharing one last laugh at Del's light-hearted musical remark, the two sixty-somethings sat quietly and finished their food, staring out into the dairy pastures. Church looked out at the endless green grass that stretched from the mill property to the distant edge of the coastal mountain range on the Western horizon. He thought to himself about how all of those cows could possibly be satisfied with the same routine over and over, day in and day out. But he quickly denied himself access to the rest of the thought, because he didn't like how it ended. He'd be damned if he was going to sit there and spend his last three minutes of coffee-sipping involuntarily convincing himself that he was just a cow to be milked daily until he could no longer produce anything nourishing. He knew he was more than that, and he knew he had to make a change to his situation...somehow, someway, he *had* to come up with a different formula for life. Only during these tiring, punishing days could he begin to feel those familiar winds of change stirring in his heart. Things were lining up, and he knew he would live to fight a different kind of fight. The future would be different for sure. But the basic structure of how it would all play out eluded his experienced mind. Intangible, *real* things were changing all around him. He only wished the physical pain of 66 years' worth of cumulative chronic injury would go away long enough for him to be able to think *clearly* about something besides how to continue going on like this. After decades of wrestling every cedar, maple, and fir tree within a 200 statute-mile radius, his muscles and joints could not take it anymore. Church looked down at his old digital watch he purchased back in the 1980s at a gas station for five dollars. He always kept it in the bottom of his Therma-keeper so he wouldn't be tempted to look at it before his food was consumed. It was 0942- time to stand and begin walking toward the saw for power-up. He popped the lone frozen grape into his mouth and forced himself to stand. He began walking toward his work area and did his best to ignore the pain, just like he had always done for so many years. He managed a tiny genuine smile that appeared to form on his face without regard for the grape in his cheek. He was happy knowing he was going to get to spend a week with his middle daughter Kahmay, and he could feel how it inexplicably lightened his step. His experience of time sped up again as his mind began trying to focus on not harming the grape. Turning on his machines, he stared at the enormous uncut timbers lined up behind his saw and noticed they reminded him of a line of cars waiting at a quick-charge station for their daily electricity rations. *I think I'm gonna make it to quittin' time just on time, but damn this pain...damn this relentless pain. Is it really supposed to hurt this much? Man... I'm screwed...something has gotta give or I ain't gonna make it much longer.*

Mother Earth

Earth
Sector OR-0042
November 14th, 2025 A.D.
Friday
1605 HRS

    It was already five minutes past quitting time for Marie McGrady at the Shooting Star Center for developmentally disabled adults. Mrs. McGrady rarely ever left work for the day on-schedule. With routine timing, individual members of the organizational staff leaned into the threshold of her office door as they filed past. Most of the staff was simply seeking a quick conversational mood boost before going home to get rested up. Marie certainly had a reputation for pointing out the positive, and had been transformed into a kind of transcendental guru by her colleagues over the years.

    The anticipation of the coming weekend had everyone in the building buzzing around excitedly, like somebody had doled out an eight-ball of perma-happy in the back parking lot at lunchtime. Marie rarely interrupted them over the years as they shared intimate details of their personal troubles, and news from their home lives with her before leaving the building. She refused to interrupt them, because she wanted and *needed* them to know their lives truly did matter to her. She chatted with them, and appreciated what a rare thing human trust bonds can be. She had learned the hard way too many times just how fragile and delicate the traffic lanes of bidirectional verbal communication often were in her life. No interruption of a happy person on Friday afternoon was ever worth it. She knew the value of fleeting opportunity, and the concept of *Carpe Diem*. One of the many reasons she awoke each day at 0500 was because of the mission of the organization and all it stood for. She looked up from her slightly cluttered desk just in time to see the boss approaching from out of his office.

"Hey Kurt," she said. "You headin' out for the day?"

"Naw...just wanderin' around trying to find my Z-bot again. Dang thing never comes when I call to it."

Dr. Kurt Pittman came to the Shooting Star Center back in 2001 from sector Cal-33 down in Frisco. In his youth, as he did his best to navigate the challenges of life as a 20th century unsupervised emancipated citizen-youth in the United States, he was also a natural intellectual warrior without even knowing it. He ate problems and bureaucratic barriers for breakfast. Losing both of his parents by the age of 14 had toughened his soul. He wanted to live, and being an emancipated citizen-youth forced him to choose between dying the predictable death of poverty, or living with utter abandonment of fear. Fear, doubt, loneliness, and imagined regrets were something he could not afford. He chose the hard course in life with immediate zeal and determined efficiency from a young age, and then never looked back. The hard course was the *right* course. Now independently wealthy, and unhindered by the destructive trappings of a paycheck-to-paycheck lifestyle, he was free to light his own fires and kick his own tires. Helping the developmentally disabled was part of the circle of life to him, and only those who were willing to go down the path of selfless and dutiful dedication to the cause of compassionate care would be afforded such care themselves in the end. All humans who enter into the uncertain grey areas of erratic or attenuated cognition in later life needed a custodian unmotivated by profit. His only secret was that he never allowed his personal flame of hope to extinguish. He refused to allow himself to be discouraged or demoralized by anyone or anything.

    Marie managed a tired smile at the Doctor's strangely humorous comment and then raised her right cheek up in a half-grin as she asked him, "Are you getting your vacu-bots and clerk-bots mixed up with your Senior VP again silly?"

"No, no, the Z-bot is totally different looking. I'm helping these whacky college kids with their start-up business. I told 'em I was interested in helpin' with the Z-bot's proving phase. It has the new Gen-33 holo-cell in it, and my webinar is about to start. I gotta find that sucker or I'll be forced to lower the shades and turn off all the lights at 1630 to start looking for the hologram light in the dark. I hope it's not stuck somewhere with no spare tire or roadside assistance coverage. I think I'm going to put it into the critique form that this robot is too independent and generally disobedient."

The good Doctor did occasionally try his hand at humor. But he always felt like his jokes and innuendos were lacking some essential ingredient that had always escaped his understanding. Still, at some point in his life, someone had appreciated his dry brand of humor and he never forgot that part. However, he struggled to remember who they were. He wanted to find them and tell them a long story over a round or two of fine spirits. He looked over at Marie and was a bit surprised to notice that she was gathering her keys and her Therma-keeper in preparation to leave for the day already. He was disappointed that he wouldn't get to chat her up a little, but he also knew she had to get home to Mr. McGrady.

"Okay then Marie, careful out there on your way home. Give my regards to Mr. McGrady. Do me a favor before you roll out of here and just check around your vehicle for a little twitching utilibot lookin' thingie with a purple 33 stencil-painted onto the side of it...pretty pleeeeaze? I think it might have escaped the building...I can't seem to find it anywhere around here." said Dr. Pittman.

"Sure will...see ya in the mornin' Kurt. Good luck with your webinar."

Marie hurriedly made her way through town and onto the highway entrance. She usually felt a greater degree of stoicism on the 28-minute drive home, but today she was filled with emotion. She even smiled as she blew by the speed limit sign doing 3 miles over on her way out of town. She thought about her middle daughter Kahmay at home building a fire in the wood stove waiting for her and Church to get home so that they could all talk about the day together. *This is Kahmay's only Friday before she goes back. Maybe it would be okay for me to go as much as 5 over just this once. We're going to have pizza, because I know it's her favorite. I wonder if the others will show up for dinner. It should be a proper party, so maybe I'll go to Daikon's and see if they have any of those triple chocolate cupcakes. Calm down Marie, calm down. This isn't the last time you're gonna see her. God I hope it's not the last time...*

Transcendental Logistics

Earth
Sector HI-0007
Autumn, 2025

Many years had passed since construction of HEIWA-1 began in earnest in the summer of 2016. By the autumn of 25', nearly everyone on the planet was still under the impression that the completion of the space elevator project was being stalled by two problems; inadequate installed solar collection panels for the ascension pods, and not enough mass on the geosynchronous counterweight. It was well known to the throngs of craft-workers, design teams, and government agencies that were privy before construction ever began that the project would be slow going until the two main problems were addressed. Very few people knew the real truth about what was *actually* happening with the project since the news reports began fading into the background of global chatter. For the fifth time in many decades of humanity doing everything it knew to get the damn thing built, construction was once again progressing forward. There was just no way around the inevitability of it all. Boron nitride nanotubes provided the missing link the designers required to achieve the strength necessary to make the physics of HEIWA finally come together. Micro-polymers extracted from the Pacific Ocean garbage patch were used to help produce large onsite "starter" batches of boron nitride nanotubes. Other global gyres were targeted by enormous collection vessels and brought their partially disintegrated cargo into the HEIWA project. The initial batches of nanotubes were immediately retrofitted to the existing superstructure at the base so that new strength tests could be performed on the macro level. The energy-collecting properties of the new polymer-bonded nanotubes allowed polarity-manipulated piezoelectric shunting to facilitate the flow of the unfathomable number of collected electrons to the harvesting array, which helped to feed the project's notoriously hungry local remote power grid.

Because enough people with authority believed HEIWA was a necessary thing, fiction was forced into reality with unprecedented urgency behind the scenes. HEIWA was truly the most efficient, expedient way we could collectively conceive of as humans to get large quantities of materials both to and from space in a practical, affordable manner. The problem with humans though, is that we all have our own unique cardinal references we use to bring perspective and validation to the concept of "affordable".

The HEIWA system involved anchoring the tether and counterweight satellite to Earth at the equator along the meridian that intersected both the equator and the southernmost access to the clockwise-churning Great Pacific Ocean garbage patch. The system included onsite power-generation for the ground station. At the other end of the tether, periodic maneuvering of the counterweight was required to maintain a finely aligned altitude of 100,000 kilometers above sea level. Power for the counterweight's primary orientation thrusters and secondary alignment booster matrix had to be collected initially in space using solar arrays. Human astronauts were needed in geostationary orbit to physically inspect the counterweight thruster plenum exteriors, power storage modules, propellant pressures, and flow rates. Solar panels were periodically maintained using a turn-in process, which involved the use of two fully space-borne drones and a two-human assist team aboard the old International Space Station (ISS). Those two human maintainers were the busiest known extraterrestrial workers in the solar system for many years.

The HEIWA project underwent a high degree of global criticism in the construction phase for being so geographically inaccessible to most of the world. The global financial system was on the verge of collapse in the summer of 2016 and the investors needed to find as many leverage points and competitive advantages as possible to stay above water on any commitments. Companies wanted to conduct business using HEIWA. But they did not want to ship so much expensive hardware out into the middle of the Pacific Ocean.

Critics of HEIWA eventually ran out of legitimate arguments against the idea of building it in a remote location. Once the assertion that the tether would be vulnerable to extremist attacks was proven correct, the primary opponents of the location abruptly settled into relative silence. The failed attempt of highly organized terrorists to detonate a tactical nuclear bomb at the base of the superstructure guaranteed that the world would come to see the remote location of HEIWA as the only logical choice. Surface logistics for contracted suppliers and freight movers were complicated by the need to ship everything out into the middle of the ocean under a veil of secrecy. Business managers considered the inconvenience of distant access to be a small price to pay for the security assurances. This so-called "Tower of Babel" would indeed be safe for as long as it took to complete construction and demonstrate proof of the macro-concept. Proof of sustainable reliability would take some time. In the meantime, shipping companies had no problem finding crews that would be willing to work ridiculous hours around the clock getting paid for load after load of pristine raw material. Companies providing shipping out of Asia armed their surface ships with large guns and depth charges. Pirates could usually be taken care of long before coming into clear view with the naked eye. But occasionally a homemade pirate submarine could position itself in such a way so as to be undetectable as long as it remained motionless. The increasingly novel evolutions of the pirates' tactics had the DSEF HEIWA crews walking around on eggshells pacing the base complex perimeter with small arms and enhanced nocturnal targeting masks. Somehow "resource protection" seemed like a grossly inadequate official description of the job they were *really* doing. The sentries quacked at one another in the mornings to let one another know that the word on the street was that they were all sitting ducks waiting to be obliterated in the name of terrorism. Freight crews, traveling to and from the complex to deliver bulk materials, carried military weaponry onboard their ships. It was mostly stuff that had accumulated over the years as the freight crews repeatedly outfoxed the marauders over the course of time and absorbed the pirate resources for their own defense purposes. It was strange to see an old civilian sea captain walking around smoking a pipe with a modern M-27 pulse rifle dangling in front of her, and a 50-year-old rocket propelled grenade launcher strapped to her backside. While moving about the ship completing their daily duties, all the freight crews were packing some kind of anti-pirate heat.

In the late teen years of the new century, most of the world did not know that the "old-news" problem of inadequate energy collection for the system's many moving parts was being rapidly remedied with Chinese, Indian, and Southeast Asian production capacity. Transoceanic collaboration joined the Asian production entities with those of the United States, Japan, Canada, Mexico, Peru, Bolivia, Brazil, and most of the rest of South America and Australia. Technological solutions had been hashed out on artificially constructed islands years ago, and the place most people thought of as the ocean's landfill had turned into an enormous 846.7 Gigawatt power generation array. That amount of power output capacity was roughly equivalent to the combined output of all the hydroelectric power plants of the world combined at the time. The project was only just beginning to pick up momentum when the 850 Gigawatt mark was swiftly surpassed in late 2016. The ocean was indeed more powerful than the combined forces of the Earth's rivers.

Hundreds of thousands of ultra-high-efficiency wind turbines were leaving Chinese coastal ports disguised in plain sight as "more mass-produced stuff headed for the rest of the world". To all of the millions of Chinese citizens who saw the massive turbines leaving their ports around the clock for so many years, there was absolutely nothing suspicious about it at all. While it was true that a good portion of the materials leaving the ports were headed for foreign consumers, it was also true that the bulk of it was headed for the HEIWA site out in international waters.

The subsurface part of the system utilized composite parallel power-generation equipment under the surface of the ocean to capture immeasurable amounts of energy from naturally occurring tidal currents. Capturing all of that energy was kind of like trying to lasso a freight barge with dental floss in the beginning. But with persistence and the willingness to try new solutions, the painful trial and error stages of development were conquered.

The problem of the geostationary orbital counterweight was a more difficult problem to solve. It was kind of like walking into the desert for days in the scorching heat to place emergency water rations there so that you would not die of thirst on your second trip. The problem of 'how [to] get an egg without a chicken' left the early designers bewildered and frustrated.

Many ideas had been tossed around over the years for how to solve the problem of keeping the line *just* taut enough to handle the anticipated loads. Without taxing the carbyne-graphene cable braids beyond their design limitations, project engineers had to find that "sweet spot" where aggregate centrifugal forces were in equilibrium with aggregate gravitational forces. Yin and Yang had to offset one another with near perfection, or years of work would have to start over. Some implementation problems were so bad that entirely new technologies had to be developed before even starting the tether attachment procedure. Space junk orbitals had become so complex and numerous that 11 years of autonomous collection and disposal operations had to be completed in relative secrecy before the final tether attachment.

Once the system was operational, the expected reward was for the ascension pods to crawl their way up and down the tether and deliver bulk quantities of everything imaginable into various Earth orbits. In the beginning, the vision of efficient delivery of parts, fuel, food, and personnel up and down the tether had the whole world buzzing with excitement. The unsustainable expenditure of finite resources for rocket technology deployment had created the need for something better, and HEIWA was considered a complementary solution that would offer benefits far in excess of the cost.

In practice, exhaustive testing and simulation of the macro-concept showed a pattern of increased confidence as new and improved variables were plugged into the modeling concept. Greater and greater amounts of simulated cargo were being successfully delivered without ever coming close to the deliberately prohibitive margins of error. The ascension load variables were calculated and recalculated in real time to be directly proportional to the corresponding degree of correction that would be required for each and every vertical millimeter. But proving the concept to be scalable all the way to the target altitude would remain stubbornly elusive and intangible without a significantly more risky upfront investment.

In the bathrooms and boardrooms of nation-states and aerospace companies, people interested in the idea of developing the "space elevator" were often quick to abandon the idea of an elevator in favor of reverting back to the apparently insolvable riddles of rockets and finite resources. The challenge of making sure the tether was stable enough to be used and abused by countless trips into space and back was just too much for most to live with. But for a small faction of visionaries, primitive ideas about raw steel and untold human resources gave way to carbon nanotubes and semi-autonomous robotic construction crews respectively. Enter the Koreans.

The task of putting a giant army of mechanized employees to work was delegated to the Koreans because of their proven aptitude and breadth of experience in the field of robotics. They were well known to have the most advanced knowledge of the networking arm of robotics on Earth, and would help the collaborative transoceanic effort tremendously. Humans known as 'catalyst' workers were hired and relocated throughout Eastern China to build robotic infrastructure. Each 'catalyst' worker spent three months working 18-hour Earth shifts in rotating rosters, and then spent 30 days paid leave at home for reconnecting with family and resting. They did this over and over again for many years. The contractors who employed the catalyst workers were forced to draw workers from far off locations so that the true purpose for all of the activity could not be discovered.

The anti-establishment terrorists hunted the technological enclaves relentlessly, but could not stop the inertia of mankind's innovative predilection. Robots that were built for the sole purpose of manufacturing other robots were considered one of the greatest sins of man by the terrorists, and China was acutely aware that the secrets of Eastern China had to be guarded with the utmost vigilance and alertness.

The road to completion for HEIWA was full of figurative potholes. By the winter of 16'-17', the entire world had nearly come to war as the result of grand scale omissions of truth. The governments of nation-states did not want the world knowing that so much money was being spent on technology while people were suffering through the ravages of poverty, pestilence, and famine. Rapid Chinese naval expansion in the East China Sea throughout the latter half of 2016 had the billions of working class civilians wondering why a global war had not already started. Everyone expected anarchy to come at any moment in 16'.

By the end of 16' there were several thousand electronic eyes on the South and East China Sea regions. People began to see things that could not be explained. The elaborate broken-record cover story of "hegemon-like nation-state becomes power-hungry and transforms into a blood-lusting imperialistic global threat" was falling apart. People of Earth had an informed suspicion that larger forces were at work. Ultimately, the people demanded that world governments come clean with the truth. When truth did not come, the world lost its sense of direction and purpose. Subsequently, the disintegration of human empathy began its snowball toward an emotionally indifferent era of human existence. Interpersonal human bonds had been irreversibly devalued by a cultural shift toward survival. It happened gradually enough to trick the people of Earth into assuming that everything was going to be okay. Every bad thing was dismissed as another one of the quadrillion renditions of a classic "bad day". Resilient pockets of the Old World still lived and thrived in their own ways. Ultimately, the enclaves of the Old World were to become the uniquely variable seeds of a new human garden. They would now be sown across the Universe in search of fertile ground to replant the species.

To Stay or Not to Stay

Earth
Sector OR-0042
November 15, 2025 A.D.
Saturday
0413 HRS

    Everything was quiet at the McGrady household as Kahmay sat out on the front porch in the dimly moonlit pre-dawn hours. The quiet morning hours were her greatest moments of clarity, which was a decreasingly good thing. She sat staring out at the evergreens trying to navigate her way through the tortuous thoughts running through her head. Last night had been such fun, and she did not want the feelings of joy in her heart from her week-long visit to fade away. There was outstanding company, Hawaiian-style pizza, karaoke, and top notch extra stout homebrewed beer. *We are all so fortunate and blessed. I must go forward and do the hard thing*, Kahmay thought to herself. *I must do what I was meant to do.*

    The first birds of dawn had not yet begun chirping when Marie carefully pushed open the screen door that led out to the porch with her hips. She was in her slippers, and had a sleepy smile on her face. She was fully equipped for a nice peaceful morning on the porch with Kahmay. She had two fresh cups of coffee in her hands and looked highly skilled as she went through the door in reverse without spilling a drop of coffee along the way. It took years of experience and black belts in child rearing for her to do so many things at once.

"Hey you," said Marie in her quiet morning whisper. "What are you doing out here at this hour? Got some fresh here for ya if you want it."

"Sure, sure! Thank you!" said Kahmay. "You know; I could ask you the same thing mama. Did I wake you?"

"No, no honey. You were quiet as a mouse, just like always. I have been waking up all night off and on. I knew you were out here because the porch light was on, and we never leave it on at night anymore. I can see it on the ceiling reflecting through the stained glass at night, and for some reason I just keep looking at it waiting for it to flicker or something. Plus, Church keeps his night vision by the bed because he recently learned that survivability during a nighttime home invasion is dramatically improved if you leave the outside lights off and give yourself the ability to work in the dark while the vermin are busy struggling to figure out where you are. I guess the average dimwit petty thief doesn't go around the neighborhood with night vision equipment so..."

"Ah, that's good thinking" said Kahmay. "Ya never know when someone is going to come up the hill at night, or for what reason. They could be cracked out, whacked out, or just plain tapped out and desperate."

"Yup" Marie replied, sipping her coffee and settling back into her canvas chair. "So, why are you awake at this hour? I guess you're probably just used to it with all the graveyard shifts and jetlag-filled traveling years. What's on your mind honey?"

Kahmay didn't know whether to ruin the tranquility of the morning with the truth, or whether to let it ride a little longer so she could savor this precious time with her one and only biological mother.

"It's nothing we need to get into so early in the morning mama. But I see you haven't lost your ability to sense when I have something on my mind. It's just work stuff."

"Okay, I'm listening. Let me have it now while it's quiet and there's nobody around."

Marie knew better than to wait for people to ambush her with unexpected truth. The years had taught her the hard way to proactively seek answers when she was most prepared psychologically to deal with the findings of her questions. Kahmay decided to walk through the door of opportunity and go ahead and break the news to her mother, accepting that she would likely need to explain it over and over again to the others as the day went on.

"There is a good chance the council is going to approve our plan. My team doesn't know it yet, but they are one of the most prepared crews I've ever worked with. The problem is that nobody has any appetite to go into space anymore. Everybody was watching with hope and optimism before *Kibo*, and then it all turned to hate and division. It's like...this crew could be *half* as good as they are, and still be almost a shew-in for one of the supercruisers. But I don't want them to stop trying their best. When we go out there, they are going to need every last bit of their training and their strength to get through it."

Marie set her coffee down on the little table in between the two of them and reached into her nightgown pocket to pull out a pack of cigarettes and a lighter. The most recent situation report Kahmay had concerning her mother's smoking was that mom had altogether given up the consumption of nicotine. Kahmay looked at her mother with shocked surprise, as her mother convincingly pretended to light up before grabbing her coffee again to begin talking.

"I want you to know I'm with you no matter what child...and the only reason I started smoking again is because I know they have those fancy med-beds on the supercruisers right?"

Kahmay was caught off guard, but managed to begin forming words. "Uh...yeah, but...they're actually limited intelligence machines that can..."

"But *nothing* kiddo..., I'm sure they're the greatest thing since sliced flax-bread. But I don't think I'm ready to listen to the specifics about all of that jargon this morning" Marie interrupted. "If you want me to live long enough to be the ship's onboard yoga instructor slash gerontological therapist, you had better get it done. Cut to the chase already... Sergeant Storyteller!"

"Okay, okay...sorry, I'm still not convinced I'm on leave yet. It takes a while to decelerate... hypervigilance can be a vicious consumer of human life force" said Kahmay, vaguely chapped by her mother's abrupt intolerance of the technical details.

Marie was smiling at her own abandon, and couldn't resist the temptation to think herself pretty clever to have fooled her so-called brilliant child into thinking her realistic looking virtu-cig was the real deal. She noticed Kahmay's eyes squinting toward the device to try and validate its authenticity. Alas, the tiny metal collar at the border of the filter and the tobacco betrayed the true nature of the object Marie held. It didn't take long for the tension of the moment to give way to laughter and relief as the two slowly began coming to life and waking up together for the day. Marie's relaxed demeanor became a little more serious now, as she pressed Kahmay for details about the ops plan, and the stuff that Operational Security demanded must be guarded with the utmost trust and vetting.

"Okay, give me the scoop. What's going to happen hon?" asked Marie with deliberate seriousness this time.

Kahmay chose her words carefully and calmly and replied, "Well, the council's main requirements for being in compliance are that your personal effects and preselect lists are logistically ready and up to date respectively. Nondisclosure agreements, in-processing paperwork, container plans, you know...all the usual stuff governments want to know about you in order to quantify the quality of the various qualitative quantities, and to evaluate the evaluations in life's variegated figurative evolutions and empirical creations. In other words, they just want to make sure that everyone leaves at the same time so the security risks are minimized."

"Well...," said Marie with a follow-on pause that allowed a few long seconds to tick by. "When do we need all of this to be done and ready honey? Because Mr. Church in there is falling apart and losing hope. He's so tired all the time anymore...I mean...he gets wore out from too much Scrabble and Sudoku with the nieces...and ain't none of us getting any younger around here...catch my drift there sarge?"

"Yes ma'am, I do. More than likely, we have until spring. No matter what happens, your container will be ready for pick-up and I will try and give you guys as much heads up as possible once I know more...but there's the other thing too mom...about the war. Have you guys talked at all about how you think you wanted to..."

"If the sector is being overrun as we are all getting ready to blast off, you will go with your team...they are your family too, and they need you honey" Marie interrupted.

"No they don't actually. They would get along just fine without me, and I would get along just fine without them. Every last one of them ended up on the mission as the result of their lifelong pursuit of knowledge and scientific discovery. Take any one of them, put them on a spaceship, and kick them out there into space...and they will begin forming social bonds with the onboard Artificial Intelligence. They know how to eat the fruit of the tree of life. They're good people. They definitely don't *need* me...they're pretty resilient to changes in group dynamics. They just want to do something *good* for people. They spent the years studying space...and a growing minority of people on the planet seems to be in favor of finally building the interplanetary highway system.

"Why would you want to stay here?" asked Marie.

"Well, I don't really...but stranger things have happened. You guys haven't gone anywhere in almost 30 years, and something inside me tells me that your enthusiasm for leaving might be temporary. Has the other half mentioned anything to you?" asked Kahmay.

"Yeah, he mentioned that Delmar Post has an idea to cure Nadia...and he also mentioned that he thinks it might have something to do with what you are doing...with the ships...err...superships, or whatever the heck you call 'em...the big space ships in the sky" Marie replied, wiggling her toes and methodically sipping her coffee.

"Supercruisers...so...does that mean if he finds out that Del and Nadia are leaving too that he might be more open to the idea than he was on my last visit?" asked Kahmay, this time unsure of whether or not she wanted to hear the answer.

"I don't know honey...and honestly, I don't think *he* even knows for that matter. Delmar is being necessarily coy, almost like, the consequences of letting out his secret could endanger Nadia's chances for survival in some way. Mr. McGrady's decisions will be his own, but I'm sure he would be excited by a possible future that included old friendships. When he is feeling good, he seems optimistic about all of us leaving. But when he's tired, he goes into himself and gets quiet and seems filled with hopelessness or...something like deep concern maybe," explained Marie. "Maybe if you laid it all out with everyone this morning after they all wake up; you'll get more information out of him."

"Alright then mama," said Kahmay, "but hopelessness though?"

"No, no... not hopelessness exclusively" Marie said. "I misspoke. It's not quite that serious, no... I just think he has been physically exhausted for so long that I fear he is starting to feel like...like, we're all going to die working for a better tomorrow...and taking care of *today* is really all we should dare to do...right?"

"Yes, I agree...that we should do everything we can today to make sure the plan for tomorrow is in better shape by the time we go to sleep tonight." Kahmay said, giving her mother a glance that cautiously dared to tactfully disagree. "I know; I know...it's pretty easy for me to say these things as a younger person. But I *do* believe it...for now...incidentally. And I'm not that young anymore...physically."

"Right about now, papa Church is probably struggling with the question of whether or not to occupy the rest of his days engaged in guerilla warfare, or to spend it bringing everyone he loves into 'space' as it were." said Marie, using her fingers to paint invisible quotations around the word "space".

"Well, that brings me back to the point I was about to make about the war. Our ops-plan includes combat provisions. If you do come, you are going to be onboard while we are attacking from orbit. All the civilians are doing it these days ha ha. The Joint Chiefs and pretty much everyone in the entire Defense department from the top down wanted to send hypersonic..."

The morning silence was unexpectedly broken by the faint sound of the front door quietly opening, followed by an abrupt swing of the front porch screen door as Church burst through in an attempt to surprise the two and catch them unaware.

"WHAT!?...the hell is going on out here?" asked Church with a look of mischief on his face. "You two gonna sit here and drink up all the coffee, or are we going to get busy doing something?"

Kahmay and Marie felt almost guilty for not reacting as Church had intended. He had chosen a moment of conversational climax for his playful surprise attack, and the effect was a complete anticlimax. Even the birds were strangely quiet, as if listening for the other Church-shoe to drop. Marie was just waiting to hear about something hypersonic 'er other.

"Top o'the marnin' sir! Did you sleep well?" asked Kahmay.

"Yeah, slept alright...all things considered. Thought I heard two hens out here cluckin' away...figured we could use the eggs. Why are you two up so early?"

"We're having a top secret discussion about the price of two by fours...*nosey*!" said Marie with her intentionally playful harassment.

"So, what would your people think about us driving our own stuff in the GEMINI?" asked Church, directing his abruptly serious face toward his middle daughter.

"Oh, you heard that? I actually don't know what they would think. The destination is sensitive compartmental information presently. So they aren't going to tell me where it's at until right before departure. There should be enough time for me to get you the information you need. That GEMINI gets way better gas mileage than the hog they would send to get it themselves, and you've probably got way more experience on the rough northern roads than anyone I ever saw come through DSEF's transportation doors. These days they're all about saving money. So when I ask them, I'll be sure and mention that your truck gets better mileage and is equipped with the latest mil-spec safety upgrades. They'll eat it up hook, line, and sinker. They might just go for it based on cost-comparison analysis alone. In fact, one would hope they do it that way every time...as long as they don't sacrifice quality or national defense it's all good right?"

"You think we'll need the sleeper? Rough Northern Roads?" asked Church with his head tilted to the side. "I thought you said you didn't know where they were sending everyone's stuff."

"Officially, I don't know. Unofficially...I'll just say that Det. IV has made this question one of their pet projects. Best we can figure, the one nearest place to get a big load of household goods into orbit is at least a few thousand miles from here." said Kahmay. "But we can neither confirm nor deny any of that yet because the fact is, we haven't become privy to anything official.

"Understood sarge. Please make sure they understand that I'm not leaving the planet without the gun safe." Again, Church delivered his crazy-sounding three-part chuckle. He was in a sense, nervously giddy about the thought of just "moving into space".

"No worries dad. The onboard small arms vault has plenty of room for the safe. We just have to enter your retinal scan and left palm print into the central computer. The vault will be climate controlled to 73 degrees Fahrenheit and 35% Relative Humidity."

"Just let me know what the temperature and humidity are going to be in my bedroom, cuz that's where I'm keepin' everything. Is that gonna be a problem?" Church asked.

"73 Degrees...35 percent humidity...the environmental targets are the same everywhere on board...with a few minor exceptions related to research and development...and food storage, and production areas." Kahmay's brow was now slightly furled in low-grade concern at the notion that her dad might possibly consider disqualifying himself over something that the crew had not thought about in the planning stages, like emergency road flares, or extra jumper cables. "The cruiser also has a quarantine chamber that can be adjusted down to..."

Kahmay was suddenly interrupted by her mother. Marie had become exceptionally skilled at gently interjecting a train-halting "but ya see...", or a "HOWever..." in conversation with her middle daughter. Misses McGrady knew she had to redirect the evolution of the conversation early, before Kahmay could get going too much on a detailed scientific explanation about things that were not pertinent to the big picture.

"Your sister over there in the valley is bursting at the seams in anticipation of all this. Can't say the same about Beck though," Marie said.

Over the years, Kahmay became more adept at knowing where to draw the line in conversations that lent themselves well to excessive detail, while Marie learned to try and care a little bit more about "...carbon dioxide fixation of mycelial *Ganoderma Oregonensis* at surface concentrations of greater than or equal to 5000 parts per million...especially above 24 degrees Celsius."

Mother and daughter both knew just enough about life to consider the very likely possibility that a little more patience might spur an unexpectedly beneficial result.

In Marie's mind, she was saving Kahmay the embarrassment of becoming that person that nobody wants to become trapped in conversation with. But in Kahmay's mind, she really thought everyone needed to know what the achievable minimum temperature capabilities of the quarantine chamber were. It was always challenging for humans to bridge these nuanced gaps in understanding between professional and social groups. To a scientist, discussing the minutiae was just as natural and socially condoned as a conversation about why her older sister Rebecca was having second thoughts about leaving the planet.

Kahmay was moderately surprised to hear that her older sister was less than enthusiastic about leaving Earth. But Beck was a skeptic at heart, and was well guarded against believing in something that sounded too fantastic to ever materialize into reality.

"But Lace is on-board though?" asked Kahmay, inquiring about her younger sister Lacey in sector OR-0005.

"Yup...she has been studying sustainable closed-loop farming processes since you left Edo. When we first confided in her about all of this, it only emboldened her to turn that cactus farming hobby of hers into a full-on agricultural pursuit. She wants to be on the farm squad," said Marie, smiling from her mental image of Lacey hunched over a hydroponic cabbage with a magnifying glass searching for irregularities and parasites.

"That is truly inspiring to hear" said Kahmay. "There will be plenty of that kind of work going on aboard the ship. I haven't spoken with her in so long... she's probably interested in a great number of things that I simply have no clue about."

"Yeah" said Church. Actually, I told her about the work you guys were doing with the nutrition budgeting and gave her the Kahmay version of the 'low overhead input, high-protein content, freeze-dried longevity, dynamite medicinal efficacy' speech a few weeks ago and she seemed really, *really* interested in that."

"I am really excited to hear that," Kahmay said. "You should tell her to try some of the mycological practice exams on the Z-drive. We're going to need someone who can pay close attention to detail in the incubation and fructification rooms. Humans need protein...*period*!"

"Roger wilco...we're havin' a virtu-visit with her tonight. I'll let her know the position is open for now" Church said.

The tone of the conversation on the McGradys' front porch had gradually turned more serious over the period of time that had passed since Church made his surprise entry moments earlier. Kahmay attributed that to the fact that her dad was the kind of guy that would start immediately to work on something he truly believed in. One of the things she admired most about his general character was that he was greased lightning once he was decided about an objective. The Sergeant knew well that all too often, the only thing preventing a task or process from being fully completed was the swift, decisive move to act. Of course, knowing a thing alone was not enough to ensure the avoidance of failure. Kahmay also believed one had to learn to *identify* decisive actors, and subsequently also be able to call on that person *when* their special skill was needed. Only togetherness and familiarity with personality nuances could deploy a team-specific weapon of such efficiency.

Operation Oblivion

Earth
Sector AK-0006
November 20, 2025 C.E.
Thursday
0459 HRS

    The Non-Commissioned Officer in charge of Detachment IV made her way toward the stage-right podium so swiftly and quietly this day that scarcely three or four of the sharpest troops noticed her glide in like a super-featherweight boulder. Just as the clock struck five, she began writing on the old whiteboard the crew had dug up from a burned out abandoned school, not far from the Detachment-IV bunker complex. The 22 crewmembers abruptly toned down the chatter and tuned in. They noticed that the Tech Sergeant had written the words "Environment, Longevity, and Response" on the board. She turned around to meet their eyes and began to speak.

    "I am pleased to see that you all made it back in one piece. Hopefully you were allowed to spend some quality time with loved ones and take care of some of the things that could have been distracting for you here. We should all be well rested and ready to move directly to business. Given the nature of our mission here, which we have crafted for ourselves, I am compelled to ask if any of you have any updated information for me regarding your families and how things are coming along on that? If it's too personal and you would prefer to let me know in private, then you can get with me after I finish laying out the mundane stuff here this morning. Anyone? Okay then, I'll go ahead and let you know what happened while I was at home. I was honest with my family about our progress. After gathering them all to the homestead this past Saturday, I told them that I believed our ops-plan would pass DSECC scrutiny, but that anything that happens after that is too hard to predict. I carefully explained that it could be either extremely hard, extremely easy, or a frequent homogenous mixture of the two. I asked them what their decision would be in the event that we are required to stay in space for many years after the primary *Kaminari* objectives are completed. By the time I finished explaining the worst case scenario to them, not all of them remained willing to go with us. By show of hands, did any of you experience difficulty with any of your family?"

    Kahmay was slightly surprised to see a few hands go up, but then quickly regained her composure as she realized that she had prepared herself for this in her mind many hundreds of times. It was Schuler, Manuel, and Ragland; the three flakiest, most unreliable characters of the present bunch. If they decided to back out, the crew would be without the petty-thief con-artist, the sociopath, and the cut-throat self-glorifying narcissist respectively. Kahmay figured that perhaps she would be able to get replacements for them quickly if she pushed the issue now instead of later. She began to focus a little more on these three, specifically about the implications of their raised hands.

"Out of you three who care to share at this time, did the difficulty you experienced affect your resolve to see this through? Please lower your hands if you are still on board."

All but one hand went down. *And then there were 22 of us*, thought Kahmay.

"Okay then Schuler, you are permanently dismissed. I'm sure you have no desire to sit through any more of this."

The young specialist asked in her best sniveling manner, "But don't you at least care about...,"

Kahmay interrupted the junior Specialist with an immediate "No, I don't care Schuler. All I care about is getting back to the mission. That will be all. You are relieved. For the rest of you, we are now seven minutes behind schedule so let's get busy. Starting with the topic 'Environment', let's talk about the side effects of being around the same people for long periods of time in confined spaces. Who can tell me what the worst hazard related to this is? Nobody? Okay, I'll just go ahead and tell you. Death. Death, as a predicted outcome, and the preceding depression of being in deep space is the worst consequence of a bad environment. Confinement anxiety has been known to seriously degrade human health, particularly those who are prone to the classical physiological responses observed in claustrophobic individuals. The objective is to live and complete the mission. Logically, death is the biggest threat to that objective."

Just then a hand came up.

"Yes, go for Hutch" said Kahmay.

The tall slim specialist from Texas, Jimmy "Hutch" Hutchinson, always popped up like his posterior was on a spring, and like his feet were bolted down to the floor. He frequently made a habit of standing when speaking to anyone. Once rooted, some aspects of basic military training were known to remain in an individual's personality forever. In this case, every single bit of training left over from the DSEF days would serve the team well. He snapped up and pasted the unruly black hairs on top of his head down with his hand all in one fluid motion. With intense enthusiasm Hutch asked his question with the sharpest grammar he could manage. "Ma'am, do we really need to rework the contingencies for that?"

Hutch retracted his invisible spring and sat down with such edgy quickness that he drew winces from his colleagues. They expected him to hurt himself from sitting down into his seat too quickly.

"No, the present contingencies for the problem of 'lurking death as the result of avoidable hazards' will be satisfactory. You all know the dangers of space, and you have spent a lot of time thinking about all the many different ways to die out there. Contingencies are not meant to shepherd you through every possible outcome. However, as per usual, I expect continuous process improvement to be a part of your daily life. When you go back over the contingencies, you should be making proactive efforts to understand the implications of every word. If the language of the written plans is too boring for you, then I expect you to rewrite the plan with a more interesting tone applied to it. Please submit it to me for approval and intrigue evaluation. When people get bored, they become complacent. I am sure you have all heard me say it a thousand times that if we are allowed to become complacent, then death will seek us out far quicker than if we are prepared. I'm sure many of you have heard the phrase 'move to live'. I know by the time we leave the planet the remaining crew will be made up of the individuals who want it the most. By default, you will also be the crew that has the most intense will to live. When I say 'environment', I am thinking about how you will adjust your actions and your expectations of one another as months turn into years. I am thinking about how your environment up there is going to be absolutely what you make of it. Sometimes it will be more than what you were prepared to handle. Sometimes, despite your best efforts, it will be far below your expectations. You will need to learn how to adjust your own thinking, and set personal goals for yourself to improve your quality of life. Have you all completed the exercise I assigned before the break? I want to hear from someone who actually remembers vivid details of what it was like experiencing the exercise."

Just then a hand popped up.

"Go for Ragland" said Kahmay.

The so-called cut throat began to speak.

"Well, I tried to do it just like you outlined. I imagined I was the last remaining survivor of the team and had chosen my off-Earth place I would call home, and then...the first thoughts I had about the final step, with regard to finding a life purpose...I had trouble with that. It was hard not to conclude that the reason why that last step was so hard was because right now our purpose is so absolute and all-consuming. I mean, we are about to go into space, and uh...it's enough to think about how to do *that* without dying. If I had to give an answer, I'd say that I would immediately begin training my thoughts on how to get more of the people I love out there with me. Put it this way, I'd rather they came out to space with me than stay here on Earth. But I know space would be too hard for most of them, so I am fighting with myself about how strange it would be to lead my loved ones into danger in the name of getting them out of danger. It's like, there's no safe place *anywhere* really."

      Kahmay was shocked to hear such profound sentiment and depth of reasoning from someone who had a reputation for being a shallow, indifferent narcissist. Maybe the narcissism was a defense mechanism. Maybe Ragland's cut throat nature had to do with the things he had done to survive in his younger developmental time. But now, one thing seemed more obvious to Kahmay than ever before: Ragland was committed, and had likely been faced with the harsh reality over the break that someone he was counting on to come with him was probably deciding to back out. He seemed determined to confront the difficulty with strength and courage. But Ragland's attachment to the euphoria of being in control of social situations could end up being his undoing. If he gets out there and abruptly finds out just how small and vulnerable *all* humans are in the big picture, he may choose to go out in a blaze of pride-fueled glory. Kahmay knew that she was going to have to keep a close eye on him and Manuel. Others would need to be more thoroughly cross-trained on their mission specialties if Manuel and Ragland ended up quitting. Personnel rosters and individual assignments would change over and over until the NCOIC knew she had the rare, sweet team chemistry elements pinned down. Once more she addressed the remaining twenty-one crew members before releasing them to their new projects.

     "Okay, I really do want to hear more from the rest of you about the exercise, but I need to know you are all going forward on the new projects. All matters pertaining to the ops-plan are now considered priority nine. We have a new top priority on this fine terrestrial Monday. It's called 'Class B integration and the hellish nightmare we will all be in if we don't secure one of the supercruisers from DSEF'. Daytime folks; I am going to be with you today for the start of the Class-B integration and hull design modifications. Graveyard shift; we are going to leave you a detailed log of everything we tested and/or concluded today, and I do expect you to look it over when you first come on shift tonight. Your work this evening will be directly related to what we come up with today on dayshift. You are going to spend your entire shift tonight making changes and refinements, and don't forget to include your written empirical counterpoint in bullet statement format. That will be your opportunity to bring up anything novel that has not been previously dismissed under the 'guidelines of dismissal' criteria found in the master continuity guide. The half-life of the reactor is long enough to allow wiggle room on tactical design. Just don't skimp on the power availability for the latrines and the mess hall. If we lose our ability to maintain nutrition and sanitary conditions, everything will come to an abruptly grinding halt. I'm sure I don't need to remind you that we DO NOT have time to discuss things merely for the sake of discussion. We only have time to discuss things that will result in improvements, breakthroughs, catastrophic mission failure, or previously unconsidered mission threats. I'll be gone today for a while before noon. Graveyard shift, I'll see you tonight. You're all out of here for the day. Days; you know what to do. If ANY of you come up with something that passes the litmus test for catastrophic mission failure, you should call me without hesitation. Even if I chew you a new one, you would rather me do that than keep it to yourself and wait too long to tell me. I can only help you solve the problems I know about. But none of us can solve a problem that we waited too long to begin solving, because we ARE on a time limit people. Be back in a bit. Get it done! DETACHMENT DISMISSED!"

    Kahmay tossed the folder full of papers onto the table and pointed to it as she made eye contact with A.J. on her way out the door. She knew that A.J. and the other nine of them would have no problem getting right into the meat of things. With A.J. Conway at the helm, things got done every time. Specialist Conway was the team's fourth in command.

Kahmay's thoughts turned to her meeting later on in the morning. She let her thumb rest on the coffee bean grinder button and took in the aroma as she calmly closed her eyes and began thinking of how to make her plan B work. She told herself that two hours was plenty of time to think up 10 poignant questions for Colonel Kleen. The price of not being prepared for a meeting with the Colonel was measured in self-loathing and regret. Experience had proven that the only way one could ever feel like an above par human being after a meeting with Kleen was to basically read her mind and anticipate her moves. There was only one way to have a say in the outcome of the meeting: you had to anticipate when she was going to bring up a certain point, then make sure to hit that point before she could really get going on the topic. If you struck too late, she would transition her way into a lecture that assumed a much lower level of intelligence than the reality. If you struck too soon, the lecture would still come. But it would come toward the end of the meeting, as a sort of drawn out inspirational reiteration of the points discussed. Yes, there was a magical spot you had to hit with her. You had to strike at the precise moment that she would begin to think about saying a certain thing. She would be so perplexed by the fact that you knew precisely what she was going to say, that she would hold her breath for almost a full 30 seconds waiting for a chance to finish your sentences. After letting out a pressurized exhale, she would then immediately conclude that wasting her breath would be entirely wasted on you. The end result was the illusion of significant progress and traces of the Colonel's approval. Kahmay often passively feared what would happen to her interpersonal relationship with the Colonel if push ever came to shove. But the truth had shown that push often *did* come to shove, and the only option was to get tougher. *Don't ever be the one to allow animosity to morph into hate or physical harm,* she often thought to herself.

Just as the opening minutes of her trip trance music-mix recording really started to ramp up, Kahmay let her head fall slowly backward until all of the muscles in her neck were relaxed. She loved the part when the music accelerated and transitioned at just the right speed to match her mindset. She felt control, and then she felt intense peace from that control. She knew she only *needed* to control herself, but stubbornly clung to the illusion that she could influence her reality through patience, hard work, and a meditative approach to all of the day's problems. The music brought her to the place where she liked to be at all times. She preferred to be traveling at high speed in her mind, feeling good health, and doing improbable things with raw go-getter energy.

She sought a rich sense of purpose in her life, and she was exceedingly focused when pursuing that purpose. When the time for execution came to pass, she would be ready. She reminded herself that her goal was to be a selfless protector of her people, with or without their approval or admiration for it. Question number 1 for the Colonel's impending visit began forming in her enhanced state of consciousness. *"Ma'am, what is your assessment of the supercruiser X-Tensai and her present state of reconfigur..."* Kahmay was unable to finish her thought, because she was interrupted by the vibration of her comm unit and a grossly premature knock on the door. It was A.J. on Comm 1, and Colonel Kleen was simultaneously arriving auspiciously at the door. She enabled her comm-unit and told A.J. to standby for open audio.

"Colonel Kleen, come in, come in." The look on the Colonel's face was one of uncharacteristically pained features. It was a look that had only been seen by the others during times of desperation. Kleen hastily came across the threshold of the Tech Sergeant's door and made a direct course for the freshly brewed coffee carafe and sugar bowl. The Colonel poured herself a fresh cup and allowed the silence to remain a prelude to a lingering question until after she had her first sip. Only then could she begin communicating with Kahmay.

Everything in Kahmay's instinct told her that the Colonel was there to deliver some horrible news.

"How confident are you in the ops-plan Sergeant? Give it to me straight."

Direct and blunt was the only way the question could be answered thought Kahmay.

"Confident enough that even if they deny us, I would still bring this team into the execution phase aboard a commercial-sponsored rig without a second thought ma'am."

"Are you sure you're not being a little reckless with that notion Sergeant? This whole fiasco has been *NOTHING BUT* one giant second thought!"

"Ma'am, you agreed numerous times...we're going to damn well do this with or without DSECC...even if it kills us all. Besides, if we stay, then who will go in our stead? The Rabjohns crew? With his pack of racist, xenophobic haters representing all of humankind? Or...perhaps we would all feel better about being represented by those anarchists who burned down a hundred and seventeen churches so far this year? They even had a name for themselves... what was it? The Brotherhood of Power-Hungry Self-Serving Narcissistic Neanderthals I think it was? You know the trappings of all this Colonel and you know I'm not in this to simply flee into space with my family as an alternative to fighting an honorable apocalyptic war. I'm in this because it is *WHAT...I... DO...it's what I've always done*! It's what people are expecting me to do, and I love doing it...especially when it's needed like it is now ma'am."

Kahmay slammed her fist down on the coffee table to emphasize the second syllable of the word "especially", and stared the Colonel in the eyes to try and eliminate any doubts the Colonel may have been having about her resolve.

"Alright then, calm down! Calm down...and tell me where we're at on plan B Tech Sergeant! Have you thought about any other places to stick the ship besides the ones we talked about last week?"

"Plan B analysis has commenced as of 0521 this morning ma'am. The dayshift team is moving into fundamentals and catastrophics as we speak. They're itching to get to the good stuff, so I'm sure the compulsory aspect will go quick. Identifying new locations to hide the ship is only a small part of the bigger picture as I am sure you are well aware. A.J. is under instructions to organize a team for Kodiak. The seaborne approaches are being heavily mined, and the air approaches are still just as problematic as they were *before* D.O.D. authorized a portion of the remaining seed money to be used for upgraded EMP charges on the perimeter. They are obviously preparing for threats to come from anywhere and everywhere. I'm sure they have no idea that some of their trusted friends are prepared to commandeer a vehicle off this rock. Best I can think of on the air approach is to use a glider in tow from the Petersburg narrows, and then release it from just beyond the range of the early warning system under cover of darkness. But these kinds of operations are not part of my inherent aptitude ma'am. The weather is only getting worse out there this time of year and by next week a glider might end up being such a ridiculous idea that we'll have to choose a different approach. Nothing is completely off the table yet. I am pushing them hard today to get the worries of family off of their minds. They all looked like a bunch of deer in the headlights this morning. And by the way ma'am, what is your assessment of the soon-to-be-abandoned supercruiser *X-Tensai* and her present operational assessment?"

"The *X-Tensai* was built solid" said the Colonel. "She's the only one out of the seven built so far that uses the 50/50 style chassis concept. Her mission flexibility rating came off the drawing boards at 64%, and then they upgraded her to 75% after they realized that the Class B reactors were going to be retrofitted for the top 30 design concepts. She's so reconfigurable that my five-year-old grandson could think his way out of a crisis with 'er. And once we're too deep into the black to turn back, if a five-year-old is what we end up needing in order to bail ourselves out then...well, I just don't want to get started on anything overly negative. But I think you get my drift. The only other chassis that comes close to the *X-Tensai* in my opinion is the *Hell Cat,* with her 72% rating. But the *Hell Cat's* blunted trapezoid 70/30 design shows over and over in the simulators that she would be too hard to recover in zero gravity if control was ever lost in the High-G range. Plus, there's no obvious way to fit two reactors inside. I'm inclined to believe that space will be very unforgiving for anything that isn't inherently balanced and engineered to be multi-purpose from its inception. The other thing is that the *Hell Cat's* electromagnetic shield won't handle as much speed as the *X-Tensai*. She was built for close support. Anything above 0.17c in the *Hell Cat* would kill us all with many quadrillions of little dust particles that will all have enough mass at our preferred target velocity to cut us and the ship up into little pieces like a 50 cal."

"We'll take that into consideration ma'am. If we end up on the *Hell Cat*, then we'll make changes somewhere in Partial-G. There are several 'somewheres' that are suitable for the fabrication unit to get her modified. The crewmembers have all been warned *NOT* to pin their hopes on arriving at a certain place by a certain time. They know there is a strong possibility that we will be held up for months or years on a regular basis. Those unaffiliated with the fabrication crew will move into support roles and cross-training drills once onsite.

But our preferred ship is the *X-Tensai* if you are in agreement with that ma'am. She's the best bet out of the gate, and the intrasolar layover period will be less than half the time of the next best thing. If we get the ops-plan approved, then we'll get another reactor and we'll have an efficient way to execute the ice-retrieval mission when the time comes."

"Yes I am in agreement, and God speed to you and your crew on plan B Sergeant. If we don't end up needing it right away, it'll still come in handy one of these days. There are elements of the plan that can be used regardless of the problem. There are enough novel processes inside that file jacket to turn any situation into a good situation. Please have the crew cull and duplicate any useful closed-loop processes. Moving copies of those processes into separate file jackets with intuitive titles and nomenclatures will be a force multiplier Sergeant. Thank you for the coffee. If you have anything more for me in the next couple days, pass it on through Lieutenant Colonel Norris and I'll get back to you directly just as soon as I can. I have to go see a man about a dark horse tomorrow and I'll be out of contact until Wednesday."

"MA'AM YES MA'AM!" said Kahmay with subdued volume and maximum intensity, as she popped up her salute and awaited the Colonel's exit. With that, the Colonel was on her way out and returned Kahmay's salute while en route to the door. Kahmay immediately began thinking about what had just happened to make sure she didn't miss some important detail of the Colonel's visit.

"Did you catch all of that A.J.?"

"Yeah, solid copy" sounded the voice of Specialist Conway through Comm 1.

The look Colonel Kleen had on her face when she first arrived at Kahmay's duty post was one of tired determination. She wasn't there with bad news per se. She was only there to convince herself that everything was still going to happen in accordance with the plan. Some people down the chain of command remained disproportionately sensitive to the possibility that the mission would fail as the months wore on. Those few doubting personality types were actually subconsciously *looking* for a reason to finally declare it *absolutely impossible*. Kahmay knew this outcome could not be allowed to gain any momentum. Once the first naysayer was allowed to germinate the seeds of doubt, many of the others would rapidly catch the contagion of resignation. Together in their pessimism, they would all become mathematically tantamount to an immortal optimism-parasite during one of the most uncertain and dangerous periods of human history. Resignation to failure would mean resignation to extinction. Kahmay knew the first person to cast a groundless shadow on the hopes of others *must* be rebuffed. It had really come to that. Reckless pessimism was *everyone's* enemy, and it was cloaked in the disguise of gritty realism.

Colonel Kleen's insecurity about plan B was really starting to show, and her apparent panic threatened to develop into full blown paranoia about being caught or otherwise blocked. Something had to be done immediately to calm the veteran officer's nerves. *But what?* Things were very slow going at the moment. The ops-plan was on autopilot, plan B was still an organized fiasco, and no amount of wishing for their grand alternate plan to just suddenly materialize out of thin air was going to make it happen. It was time for Det. IV to get serious about acquiring the materials that would be needed in the event their primary plans for departure from geosynchronous orbit in the *X-Tensai* failed. Kahmay looked down at the folder on her desk that contained one of the only two hard copies of the mysterious alternate plan in existence. The Colonel had left it to be placed in the safe until her return. Kahmay opened the folder to sign the chain of custody form, and to check for any additions or recently documented subtractions before placing it into the safe. *Operation Oblivion*, the cover page read. *Yeah, you can say that again*, thought Kahmay. She flipped open the cover page expecting to see the same old page number one she had been looking at for months now. Instead, she was mildly surprised to see a photograph with a caption underneath it. *K Eki mae. It's a Japanese train station named "K"...what the...? What is this? What the heck does Kobe have to do with...? It's that supercomputer at RIKEN! But why...?*

After several long minutes of staring at the photo and looking through the rest of the folder for anything else she didn't recognize, she gradually convinced herself that the Colonel was interested in the K computer. It was a cutting edge supercomputer many years ago at the RIKEN Advanced Institute for Computational Science in Kobe. But she had no idea what on Earth the photo was doing inside the Ops jacket. *What in the world are we going to do with…*, and then it struck her in the head forcefully, like a basketball thrown toward the hoop for a full court clock-draining shot. They weren't going to do anything with it on *this* world. They were going to use it on the *X-Tensai*. Kahmay did not immediately know why K was so important, but she knew the Colonel knew somebody who knew somebody...and *that* somebody must have persuaded her to focus her attention on the mighty K. She placed the jacket into the safe wondering whether the K was intended as a mainframe supplement for the *X-Tensai*.

Reverse Engineering 101

Earth
Sector JP-0005
November 21, 2025 C.E.
Friday
0430 HRS

Yasunaga Atamagawa-san was enjoying his favorite recurring dream of transferring the sentient conscience of his human loved ones into an experimental solid state data-storage matrix. He was just about to make back-up copies of his Aunt Reiko when, for the 98th day in a row, his alarm signaled the start of his decidedly less exciting waking reality. The whole idea of taking a break away from work just seemed foreign to him, but the grind was really starting to get under his skin. Half a day off on Sundays was not enough to repair the psychological damage of an entire week tinkering with prototypes and rewriting firmware sequences. He loved work and many of the people he felt the strongest human connections to in adult life were the people at work. He walked a few paces from his bedroom into the kitchen to make sure his programmable espresso machine turned on automatically, and then went to the washroom as usual to clean up. He tried to push himself to get something useful done while he was waiting on the inevitable three-minute brew cycle. He loved how the 28.4 cubic meters of atmosphere in the apartment would be filled with the scent of fresh roast by the time he was done cleaning up. He had a long day ahead, and recently the train he relied on every day to deliver him to work in a punctual manner had experienced an unscheduled 52 second delay. It was hard for him to live with such uncertainty in his life, and he had recently been developing an algorithm to help him determine if getting up earlier and catching the train at the next stop after walking the first leg would be the more statistically reliable way of getting him to work at least 13 minutes early 99.95% of all the remaining days of his life. The only leg of the train line that had been more than 10 seconds late in the past three years was the leg between his neighborhood and the next neighborhood over. The train delay would not have been so concerning, except it happened on the way to work in the morning when tardiness was indeed one of the most unforgiveable offenses of all.

The RIKEN Advanced Institute for Computational Science (AICS) was 4.3 kilometers away, and would appear somewhat different to Yasunaga's eyes today compared with usual days. Today he had to go outside his normal routine. Colonel Tabitha Kleen from the American branch of DSEF had asked him over the summer if he could procure detailed theory of operation and technical data for the Taurus interconnect architecture concept. She specifically requested durable modular hardware mockups, complete with 3D printing specs and fabrication process papers for all of the component level multi-layered circuit patterns. Before *Kibo*, the thought of doing something so shady would have been an affront to Yasunaga-san's sensibilities and loyalty. But the Colonel had met him on the old Internet Relay Chat (IRC) infrastructure, and knew the truth about his core belief that humans would soon destroy the planet and everything on it that qualified as "life". The fact that he worked at the institute was an irrelevant coincidence before this past August. Tabitha was merely in the IRC chat room because it was one of the few places one could go where intelligent conversation about technology could still flow freely for longer than two sentences. It was a virtual think tank that was so boring to strangers that they couldn't wait to bugger off once they realized they were in the wrong cyber lounge. Even the most dedicated trolls were falling asleep at the mention of fully scalable six-dimensional adaptable interconnect framework. It was in that boring virtual construct of dry scientific repute that Yasunaga had met one of the most interesting people of his entire life-someone who was actually prepared to act on the unmistakable instinct that something dark was coming to Earth.

To the keepers of the prized intellectual property that lay within the institute, today would be just another day in a series of unrelenting work days that seemed to offer no hope of change in their near futures. The economics of supercomputing had changed dramatically in the late 20th and early 21st century. Government sponsored projects like the one at RIKEN were being mothballed everywhere. It seemed as though the only extra money that could be spent was cash spent to wage a more potent war. The world had stopped believing that supercomputers, advanced processing technologies, and artificial intelligence were worth the money that had been pumped into them so regularly for all those decades. Most people scarcely had the money to buy their daily rations and keep their electricity turned on. But they didn't much mind paying a portion of the cost for national defense, and doing what they could do to provide extra resources to ensure that their own country could annihilate an invading enemy long before their day-to-day security would be threatened. These were the choices people had to make as the bullet train of technology slowed to a coal fired steamer that was bent on death, violence, ethnic cleansing, and raw suffering.

Sociologically, one could never again hope to have a respected place in society by placing the needs of humanity above the needs of the kitchen pantry at home. Humanity had subtly gone into "survival mode".

The AICS was off by itself in a fairly remote area of the Kobe territory. Many times when Yasunaga stepped off the train to begin the 248 meter walk to the institute's front door, it was eerily deserted in the immediate area around the institute's structures. There were often only one or two other pedestrians in the area for many blocks. It had become so deserted for several kilometers in all directions that rare wildlife species would sometimes be spotted in the area around the main building, as if it were the last place they could go without completely vacating the local ecological uniqueness. Perhaps they were avoiding the need to place themselves in overlapping conflict with another species.

Today the institute was about to become the target of premeditated espionage. At least Yasunaga would not have to do it alone. Every day at the same time, Yasunaga met Mizuki Kurohaisha at the institute's cafeteria. The Computer Science working group that Yasunaga belonged to let out for mealtime at the same time as the coders' lair where Mizuki spent most of her time. The two, in their different niches, were great friends socially and professionally. They helped each other through the uncertain times of wondering whether they would live to see further advancements in the fields they were both so passionate about. Sometimes they commiserated about what would become of them if they had to change course and pursue a different path to reach their intended ends. But together, they never once spoke about "the end" of their human lives as if it were a foregone conclusion that they would inevitably die at all. Today, instead of talking about bio-mechanical interfacing, they were going to talk about nothing...at least not with their words. Each of them knew what they had to do to pull off the removal of the target items from the institute. The items were gradually going to be staged in a maintenance closet at the rear of the main building, close to the double doors. After their shift period, they were to go to the rear door and very methodically load the items into a waiting cargo truck. Once the smaller items were safely stowed, Mizuki would lead the falsely credentialed loading crew from the truck to the primary controller array. Two towers had been preloaded with the remainder of what they were going to steal. In recent weeks the two towers had been carefully filled with four of each primary hardware exemplar, and boxes of various accessories associated with operation, service, and maintenance. All of the technical reference information was safely digitized in triplicate. The keys to the tower access doors were safeguarded under a leg of the pallet jack that would be used to load and off-load the towers once they arrived on station up north.

"Ohayou" said Yasunaga, as Mizuki came and sat down at the cafeteria table with her orange juice and chocolate chip melon bread.

"Ohayou. Mou tsukareta yo" said Mizuki unenthusiastically as she let out a slight yawn to make herself comfortable in the role of "prematurely tired, overworked master-coder". Long hours at work and at home had a way of degrading the efficiency of human cognition, and the witnessing of brain-tired computer geeks was commonplace at the institute. The last three times the two of them took head-to-head intelligence tests on a Saturday, she outscored him by five, seven, and fifteen points in consecutive victories. Saturday evening was the end of the work week, and was the one time of week when a test of "intelligence" would most clearly reveal chronic cognitive degradation.

"Yoku nemashita ka Zu-Chan?" asked Yasunaga in an attempt to discover how well rested his partner in crime was before talking about any specific details.

"Zen zen chigau..." muttered Mizuki with a subtle rolling of her eyes. She had not slept well in many days. It was not in her nature to be sneaking around the facility stashing things like a squirrel tucking away its winter food supplies. "I feel like a thief tip-toeing around here, dorobou na kanji shinai no?" she asked Yasunaga, tearing off a piece of her bread and stuffing it into her mouth with a discontented frown. Yasunaga-san tried to console her while she washed her bread down with a generous gulp of orange juice.

"Don't worry about it...we are not thieves...just go into the back terminal area and spend the morning double-checking the data package. Remember, the hardware was going to be destroyed...and we are not spies preparing to sell secrets to an enemy government. What we are doing is an honorable thing, and it *MUST* be done Zu-Chan. The world cannot wait for bureaucracy. Besides, K is an older technology and has been officially obsolete for years. Nobody cares about her except us anymore...and the future humans hopefully."

Mizuki hung her head in resignation, and was nervously stirring her orange juice pulp back into solution with her tiny straw. Several moments of silence passed before she found her conversational direction again. "Let's just hurry up and get it over with, or I'm going to end up being a grossly overqualified parking-garage valet by the time this is all over" said Mizuki. Yasunaga was used to her moderate pessimism and was not deterred by his friend's troublesome vision of their shared fate. His primary goal was to remind her that their lives were about to become mostly unrecognizable to their former selves.

"Just think...you are going to be so happy tonight when you go to sleep. By the time your eyes start to get too heavy, you will have realized that K's obsolete parts were cast into oblivion a long time ago. Most people around here don't even remember why she was so special all those years ago" said Yasunaga.

Mizuki slowly lifted her head from her tray and looked Yasunaga in the eyes with a slightly improved look on her face. "You can stop trying to make me feel better now. I think I can be stoic for the rest of the day until this is done. When was the last time you heard from Tabitha-san?" Mizuki asked.

"She sent me an encrypted message two days ago to tell me where to meet her. We are to drive the truck on the expressway toward Northern Hokkaido this weekend" said Yasunaga as he disengaged his eye contact from her in anticipation of a slightly negative response.

"It's a good plan...hundreds and hundreds of kilometers heading north in the winter with highly sensitive equipment...nobody will ever suspect anything. Let's get to work" said Mizuki as she stood and slid her empty chair back under the table.

Yasunaga excitedly stood and followed suit with a widening smile on his face. Just as the two were going in different directions he leaned in to whisper one final thought to Mizuki.

"You should be excited. You are going to be a space-nerd computer-pirate Zu-Chan. What more could you want in life?"

The two shared a subdued laugh and exchanged a final "Jaa ne" before energetically striding off to go accomplish their separate tasks as if they were part of their normal daily routine.

Middle of Nowhere

Earth
Sector JP-0046E
November 22, 2025 C.E.
Saturday
0337 HRS

The relentless snow from the pre-dawn blizzard on Etorofu Island was coming in sideways, and the ground crew at the remote surveillance outpost was having trouble keeping the helipad clear in the minutes leading up to final approach. Colonel Kleen's helo was arriving from the recommissioned CV-64 *USS Constellation* after a quick 17-minute hop across the angry ocean. "Connie" as the *Constellation* was still affectionately called, had been quite busy in this part of the world since the signing of the Defense Reconstruction Act (DRA) in 2019.

Many of the 20th century's mightiest steel instruments of war had been retrofitted, redeployed, and repurposed in the years following the implementation of the DRA. Once the military industrial mechanisms were adapted to accommodate robotically assisted maintenance processes, old machines were being put back into regular use at a fraction of the original historical operating cost. Those who were worried about losing their jobs to a bunch of wage-thieving robots woke up one morning to discover that ten years' worth of work at the triple-time pay rate was waiting for them. Dry dock maintenance in the Virginia territory of the United States was expanded two-fold, and teams of human controlled robotic welders roamed the docks tirelessly. Governments of nation-states in the Pacific region that had spent enormous quantities of resources maintaining larger, more advanced military forces to deter the U.S.-Japan alliance were not happy that the DRA had put them behind the military power curve again. Political movements that had been historically adversarial in their dealings with the United States and Japan had once again undertaken the futile process of harassing and threatening allied movements of materials and personnel. The situation in the region was tense, and was often likened to the old 20th century Cold War.

The Colonel had not flown into the Kurile Islands strictly for intelligence sharing with the Japanese Maritime Self-Defense Forces (JMSDF), nor was she there to discuss the ongoing escalation of the situation in the Sea of Okhotsk. There were others who could have been sent in her stead for those tasks. Part of the reason she volunteered for this trip was to pursue a more personal agenda with her old friends Yasunaga and Mizuki. Of course, as far as Seaborne Command was concerned, she was only there to brief the JMSDF Intelligence Element for the Strategic Joint Task Force, and to deliver an important dry speech to the junior enlisted personnel about operational and informational security later in the day.

"Echo 1...this is Echo base...how copy over?", asked the traffic-controller-afloat.

"Solid copy Echo base...Echo 1 commencing final approach to LZ-46 over" the pilot replied, as he struggled to fight the fierce crosswinds of the intensifying storm. He took long, deep breaths as he began his controlled descent to the helipad. It was typical in this part of the Pacific Maritime Defense Zone (PMDZ) to have to deal with these conditions, especially in the late Autumn and throughout the Winter. Pilot anxiety while flying in blizzard conditions was heightened by the forehand knowledge that survival time on the surface while exposed to the elements was dramatically reduced. Ditching meant death.

There were a surprising number of people there on the apron to receive the Colonel considering how bad the weather conditions were becoming. New security protocols could be observed almost everywhere on Earth these days and were not unusual. But the security detail for this landing was not commensurate with the current threat levels. They were there to provide extra protection for Colonel Kleen, and only a select few individuals knew the specific reason why.

The Colonel refastened the upper three buttons of her winter parka and grabbed her briefcase so she would be ready to quickly make her way inside the command post and get down to business with her foreign liaison. She had a lot to do in the next 24 hours and could not afford to waste any time. In order for her plan to successfully execute, she needed Yasunaga and Mizuki to gain entry into the installation and get the parts they were transporting aboard the C-330 before its scheduled takeoff just before sunrise the following day. *Come on guys...please be there tonight...please...,* she thought.

She was met at the chambered entry control by Commander Michio Yomu; a long time jewel of the Japanese tree of the knowledge...of the difference between good and evil signals.

"Irasshai, Irasshai Tabisa-san..." the Commander said, hurrying Colonel Kleen into the entry with one arm.

"Thank you Commander. Thank you. Didn't think I'd see you out here on such a gorgeous day" said the Colonel sarcastically as she looked up at the raging dark sky full of swift moving snow and clouds.

"In two months this will be far worse Tabisa-san. You should be glad we are doing this in November and not January."

"I'm just glad you came up for air Commander. Staring at candidate signals all day can be detrimental to your mental," joked Colonel Kleen with a rare smile.

"Speaking of signals, I have something I would like you to have a look at once we are inside. There has been some unusual activity coming from the north-northeast for the past couple days. We have been in contact with your Army Air Corps a couple of hours ago. They are on their way to the area of interest right now to form a threat assessment. I am expecting their summary report to arrive within the next few hours."

"Yes Commander, I believe I know what you are referring to. Let's talk inside."

The two veteran officers made their way into the mudroom without delay and shed their heavy winter clothing. The Intelligence Element bunker complex was bustling with espresso urgency, as people swiftly walked around with papers and coffee mugs to accessorize their permanently pained faces. Video monitors crowded every corner and cubicle wall. But all of the technology was upstaged by the giant three-screen main event. Commander Yomu-san led the Colonel to the far left map screen where they both were soon left in privacy by their scattering entourage. The six non-commissioned officers and two lieutenants who accompanied them inside were all incrementally absorbed back into the black hole of unanswered questions within the complex. Every minute was precious when pursuing an elusive enemy with sophisticated encryption and unknown operational methods.

"Look...this is the intercept we started picking up from the Western Aleutians 36 hours ago" said Yomu-san. He directed the Colonel's focus to an embedded screen just below the Central Aleutians where a direct feed from the North Pacific sub-surface extremely low frequency antenna array was being translated into a compressed waveform intelligible by humans. It was obviously an intelligent signal that does not occur in nature, with pulses and equally spaced packets of comb-like signal peaks. "Now look at this," said the Commander, redirecting his pointer finger as he walked toward a small screen sitting atop a four wheeled cart beside the giant map screen. The smaller portable screen showed another waveform that appeared to be in sync with the sub-surface signal. But it was different. It was an aberrational high-frequency modulation product of the low-frequency signal. The sub-surface signal was informing the intelligence contained within the higher-frequency signal.

"The source of the second signal appears to be emanating from Kanaga Volcano. And that's not even the strange part. What is most unusual is that even if we had ever intercepted a signal with such a high frequency before now, we would never expect to see such high energy levels for such an exotic signal. On Earth we have not yet needed these kinds of energy levels for this frequency band. Sometimes we catch bits and pieces of signals like this from other parts of the galaxy, or from *other* galaxies entirely...but that is *after* the signal has traveled thousands or millions of light years across interstellar or intergalactic distances. There are so many things that can attenuate and distort the signal across those distances that we can hardly pluck them from omnidirectional space. But the magnitude of this second signal suggests something on the order of interplanetary communication. The way it has been amplified suggests a technology significantly beyond what we have been able to accomplish here on Earth to my knowledge. Whoever is transmitting these signals must be using geothermal energy to amplify them. We have absolutely no idea how they are doing it, but I am inclined to think they have been doing it for a very long time. Kanaga Volcano is many years overdue for an eruption. Perhaps the reason it has not erupted is because the thermal energy build-up under the crust is being consumed by this exotic unknown source before it can build up enough to cause an eruption."

Tabitha's eyes were glazed over as she came to grips with what the Commander was telling her. She pulled a small storage media drive from her cargo pocket and handed it to Yomu-san with her eyebrows raised.

"Take a look at this Michio-san. They're high-res shots from yesterday morning."

Yomu-san grabbed the drive from Tabitha and anxiously plugged it into the nearby access terminal. Several high-resolution photographic images immediately popped up on the access terminal screen and appeared to show an island with a large cargo barge floating nearby in one image. But the Commander could not make sense of what he was seeing. The other images showed a more magnified view of the shoreline on the southwestern corner of the island. Tabitha began explaining the significance of the photos to the best of her ability.

"These over here are just incremental real-time shots the StratoRaven took after the barge caught its attention. What does that look like to you?" asked the Colonel, pointing at one of the photos.

"Are those people?" asked Yomu-san.

"That was our analysis as well Commander. Notice over here after only five minutes, the inflatables they used to get ashore are gone. Something is going on inside that volcano, and we do not really understand enough to know exactly what that could be."

Commander Yomu-san began typing away on the holo-keyboard, sifting through the signal logs to compare the time stamps on the photos with what the signals were doing before and after this strange covert landing of humans took place on a seemingly insignificant volcanic island.

"Here... look at this" said Michio. "The EHF stops for almost twenty minutes, and then when it starts up again, the pattern is different. Do you think these people are manipulating the signal and communicating with someone?"

"I'd say there's no doubt they're communicating with someone. The question we really need an answer to is: Where is the receiver?" asked Tabitha. "What on Earth is going on here Michio?"

"I don't think it's on Earth my friend. I think they are talking to someone out there," said Michio, looking slowly upward toward space. "But if there are two sides to this conversation, then we must find out who they are talking to."

Neither the Commander nor the Colonel knew what to say next. This was a lot of new information to take in for both of them. But they both had the sense that whatever the mysterious signal activity was, it was going to lead to something strange and unprecedented.

The silence of their mutual contemplation was interrupted by the arrival of a junior enlisted messenger.

The young man cautiously knocked several times with a low volume tap to the edge of the threshold wall to get their attention. After waiting for the Commander and the Colonel to make eye contact, the messenger began to speak.

"Excuse me, I have a message for you ma'am."

He handed a folded piece of paper to the Colonel and hastily departed with a bow.

"Is everything alright?" asked Commander Yomu-san.

"Yes," said Tabitha, "everything is as it should be Michio-san. Are you sure I can't convince you and your family to come with us? We're really going to need people with your experience up there."

"I'm sure I have absolutely no idea what you are talking about my friend" said Michio. Without saying a word, he reached into the small inside pocket of his windbreaker and produced a small removable holographic data storage device.

Tabitha appreciated his discretion and quickly hid the device in the depths of her winter parka for later review aboard the Connie. She felt bad questioning his well-known resolve to remain on Earth as a vital scout for the resistance. But she had to know for sure that Michio-san had made peace with his decision to remain on Earth and hide his family. All she knew for sure was that if he and his family stayed on Earth, they were going to be joined by others to form an eventual counterattack. Such was the mission of the remaining allied terrestrial branches. They would be the ones given top secret friend-or-foe information and protocols. In the event they were to be the last ones in theatre, they would be evacuated by any means necessary. If all allied sovereignty on the planet were thoroughly lost to the enemy, then humanity would likely be split into two cardinal worlds for an exceedingly long time.

Commander Yomu gave the Colonel one last wink of the eye and saluted her with perfect military bearing one last time, knowing that there was a high probability that he would never see her in person again.

"Very well then my friend. We will meet again. I'm sure of it. Until then Commander" said Tabitha, extending her hand Yankee-style, and simultaneously bowing to express her commitment to their friendship beyond the challenges of the approaching calamity of what appeared like it was going to be a World War.

Los Diablos

Earth
Sector AK-0099
November 23, 2025 C.E.
Sunday
1612 HRS

The call to deploy came from Headquarters Joint Task Force (JTF). The operational request for an armed reconnaissance patrol out on the Aleutians came in from the Japanese side of the PMDZ in late afternoon local standard time. Senior leadership within the JTF was based down in sector HI-0007, and had become quite accustomed to calling upon the 7th Combat Devils of sector AK-0099. The 7th was called in for anything that involved offensive foreign contact or otherwise unidentified threats inside the defense zone. This time was no different.

The Devils were a combat reconnaissance unit trained in other such specific occupational specialties as counterterrorism, advanced counter-surveillance, and high value counter-insurgency target hunting. They really preferred to work in the dark these days if possible, which wasn't a hard thing to come by in sector AK-0099 this time of year. They got a lot done in the dark between November and March, because it was *always dark* between November and March, more or less. The members of the hardened combat recon-unit drank a lot of milk and vitamin-D3 shakes during the peri-solstice period because "A HAPPY DEVIL IS YOUR ONLY DEFENSE AGAINST AN ANGRY DEVIL" as the giant sign in the artificial sunlight-room read.

The 7th Devils were actually a company of three separate platoons under the old system, each with their own exclusive function within the larger mission of the 7th Devils. The "larger mission" was the same mission that was formerly the responsibility of the 1st Marine Expeditionary Unit (MEU) pre-17'. First and Second platoons were both made up of human commandos trained in advanced hand-to-hand combat techniques, in addition to all of the basic School of Infantry (SOI) principles taught to every Devil regardless of specialized aptitudes. Many of the initial recruits at the time of the unit's inception in the summer of 17' were United States Marines. Those first Marines from the old 1st MEU were given the honor of naming the new hybrid unit, and they decided it must be a Devil unit. The jurisdictional argument about which department of the DOD the unit would fall under was inconsequential to the unit operatives themselves. They just wanted to serve, and to make a difference in the world the way they always had, and always would. Once the unit was dubbed a Devil unit, it would always be a USMC creation. But currently, the unit's status was the subject of constant argument at the highest levels. Every branch wanted operational control over the Devils due to its prototypical nature. In 25', the unit was being controlled by the Army Air Corps. The operational members were an eclectic hodge-podge mixture of "any active-duty troop[s] who [could] stomach it".

Platoon assignment selection for individual candidates was accomplished in accordance with strengths and weaknesses. Those who aspired to train themselves to personally use almost any kind of human-wielded weapon were the kinds of operative-archetypal personalities that were selected for First platoon. Provided they were qualified, and met or exceeded standards, they were the point-personnel and were afforded the largest amount of field-autonomy for critical aspects of human combat operations. The majority of First platoon members tended to descend from the ranks of the Marine Corps, while Second platoon was Army-heavy, and Third platoon was almost always exclusively troops with a background in the Air Corps.

First platoon sometimes adapted and modified on-equipment weapons systems so the systems could be manually removed from malfunctioning Mech-dog units. In order to be used by humans, in the event of catastrophic failure of the Devil Dog system network, the systems had to be human-portable. But only a select few foes had ever managed to take the system offline in the past and it usually only lasted as long as it took the Zooms and Devils of Third and Second platoon to wrap their heads around the problem.

The operation and maintenance of the non-human Devil Dog system was primarily the purview of Second platoon. The Dog units themselves were a pack of armed, electromechanical, quadrupedal, canine-appearing robotic warriors. Whenever the humans of First platoon were within range of an active target area, the human controllers of Second platoon were usually close by and slightly to the rear of the action zone in mobile command and control bunkers. These Manual Human Operators (MHOs) of the mechanized Devil Dog element were combat trained, and were always onsite to provide whatever was needed by the human First platoon combat leader.

Typical deployments required two to four Mech-Dog units up front with First platoon, while a number of Mech-Dog units, usually from three to five, were held back in tactically advantageous flanking positions. The flank Dogs were often crouched down motionless and concealed with adaptive camouflage after they were in position. They mechanically assumed an alternate shape to most closely mimic some existing feature of the surrounding tactical theatre. If the flanking position was in the water, then they lay in wait under the surface of the water, often in the form of a big rock at the base of a reef, or the bottom of a lake or riverbed.

Second platoon members were often just as skilled at hand-to-hand combat techniques as their First platoon teammates. But rotating individuals back and forth between First and Second platoon was something decided by platoon commanders and company leadership well in advance of any deployment if possible. Of course, certain individuals were obviously more adept at performing one role over another. Attempts were made to cross-train everyone into higher states of proficiency and readiness across all of the other duty positions.

The day's call to action from HQ/JTF concerned something going on in sector AK-0099. The Third platoon "Zooms" were the air arm of the 7th. They were scrambled and given coordinates to bring the lead-team over to a point slightly east of Kanaga Island in quadrant 17E of Autonomous Zone 2. On this day, it took 4 minutes and 19 seconds for everyone in the unit to be prepped, geared-up, and boarded. Scramble time would have been much shorter if not for the gnarly hangover of one of the Third platoon troops.

The Devils spent most of their down time less than 200 feet away from the Serpent aircraft that flew them into danger for each call. There was no greater feeling of satisfaction for the Devils than the one they experienced while heading into danger at sunset; usually five hundred feet off the surface of a choppy black ocean in the dark.

All equipment was pre-loaded into the fuselages of three separate C-3 Serpent multi-role combat aircraft. First and Second platoons traveled together in mated configuration while en route to target in order to minimize their reflective profiles. They would then split off into separate directions as they approached the landing zone. The third C-3 contained two Mech-Dogs and a miscellaneous mixture of Second platoon operators and Zoom-crew. Zoom officers piloted and navigated, while Zoom NCOs and junior enlisted personnel worked in the middle fuselage area. The Zoom-crew specialized in unconventional weaponry and electronic countermeasures tactics, and worked with members of Second platoon to solve operational problems in real time. Lessons shared during debriefings were incorporated into the back-up Mech-units and often resulted in the comprehensive retrofitting and upgrades to all Mech-dog chassis frames.

Everything was business as usual inside Serpent 3 en route to target, as Senior Airman Raven Madrone observed her instrument panels for the electromagnetic presence of anything more threatening than a school of radioactive minnows. The whir of the high speed hover turbines filled the middle fuselage of the Serpent with a high amplitude audio noise floor, and meteorological turbulence outside was adding a vibration element to the noise sweep on both sides of 20 Kilohertz. Not that it affected much down in that band, but Sra Madrone preferred to think that every sub-system should be treated like it was the last of its kind on Earth. It was annoying to think that an entire set of expensive frequency-sensitive components were being used unnecessarily in a non-operational band. But the low band antennas had been known to pick up distress signals transmitted from the surface by the occasional marooned human, who had somehow managed to scrounge and/or fabricate the parts to transmit a signal of sufficient amplitude to be detected. Orders from JTF were to attempt rescue on any such signals *after* completing the primary mission.

Raven appreciated the fact that only the most important information was ever vocalized by the other humans in the Company while underway. She was reared in a quiet environment, and never taught herself to care much for civilized small talk. She knew that becoming exceptionally engaged with the inanimate world would likely not have been possible if her childhood had been filled with the drowning unchecked ambience of so many city noises. She was a rural-minded creature through and through. Despite her intense focus and rare keenness of intuitive observation and situational analysis, her doctors had recently been put in the position of having to clear her for duty with a 5-milligram maintenance dose of diazepam to combat the inevitable acute anxiety she felt once jabber-mouths began predictably jabbering. She did not hate or loathe the people themselves but rather, she hated sitting in silence while she involuntarily listened to them waste their lives spinning elaborate, pathologically inefficient tales about inconsequential matters. It was a nasty kind of narcissism that was supposed to point back to the human source as "an indicator of self-loathing" according to one common school of thought. But if you dared ask Madrone about the nature of her "problem", she would likely just look you in the eyes and become distracted by her own contemplation of all the possible reasons you would ever want to waste your precious time pursuing the boring truth of it all. Hypervigilance had transformed her life into a terminal search for absolute truth within all things at all times.

    Senior Airman Madrone's journey to the ranks of Third platoon had landed her right where she had so often dreamed of ending up throughout her youth: in a valued high-technology specialty that brought her into close contact with the enemies of her people. Growing up in sector AK-0099 meant that she had been watching the 7th Devil Dog take-offs and returns for many years going back to the era when the MV-22 Osprey and C-130 "spooky" gunships were the primary airframes used by the Air Wing of the 1st MEU in the pre-7th days.

When the 7th wasn't frequenting the local airways on a given day, Raven occupied her time watching the scheduled launches of the VANGUARD rockets that so thoroughly dominated the news of the day. The public was told the rockets were for seeding nearby planets and moons with supplies and equipment so the conditions would not be so hostile to the first off-planet human colonists. But the project was defunded, and half of the tooling and spares went missing within the first six months thereafter.

Raven was deeply cared for and guided by her father Mekmech Madrone, who had made laminated circular mealtime placemats of elaborate digital logic circuit schematics for their half-barrel tables when Raven was young. From an early age she absorbed information like an enchanted sponge. After the evening meal was finished, Mekmech would challenge her to trace out the different manifestations of the circuits by first applying theoretical stimulus to the circuit inputs. Raven was initially motivated to succeed by the thought of receiving the simple approval and praise of her father. But eventually, she was drawing her own circuit diagrams and challenging her father to accurately complete the circuit outcomes. She was falling in love with science all on her own, with or without the approval of any other. But Mekmech never scorned her for failure. He only reminded Raven of how blessed she was to have her gifts, and encouraged her to look at failure as a priceless way of toughening her soul and her abilities. They were best friends together in their sadness. Many were the constructive habits they formed to keep from thinking about the horrible passing of the others in their small village of Mekoryuk. Father and daughter were away from the village attending a weekend seminar about dark matter on Kodiak Island when a North Korean hydrogen bomb claimed the lives of their loved ones. It was profoundly ominous to both of them that they survived. It made them feel that they had to somehow earn the forgiveness of the divine ones that spared them that day, lest they wished to suffer the consequences of the unredeemed. They did not have ears to hear lectures about survivor's guilt. If pushing themselves to be better human beings meant more wear and tear on the vehicle of the soul, then so be it. They burned with thirst for revenge so intensely that it could not be quelled by any earthly means. The instinct to exact retribution was the hell-fire that fueled them every day. The fight to have the last word would be their honorable objective, or it would never be over for them.

Raven always paid extremely close attention during pre-op mission briefings. She wondered about what they might find once onsite, but tried not to let that distract her from her primary duty, which was to seek out, identify, counter, evade, and manipulate hostile or unknown signal sources. She was also relied upon to alter the mission's signal strategy if necessary so the mechanized element could operate freely with First platoon humans to isolate and contain threats without any electromagnetic hindrance. No matter how many times they deployed, she always felt the butterfly effect in her stomach as First and Second platoon made their split and the encrypted handshake of the day was exchanged to signal the execution phase of the mission.

"Viper 3, Viper 1 how copy over?" came the pilot's voice from the conjoined team's First platoon cockpit.

"Copy 1, go ahead" replied the pilot of Serpent 3.

"Be advised, we have...nasty conditions aloft and dung stew at the surface...as per usual over." said the Viper 1 captain.

"Solid copy Viper 1...you...were expecting a vacation? Or...are you...dissatisfied with your raw deal in life or...can you elaborate on the nature of the 'it' in the dung sham-wich over?"

"Roger 3...swells to one eight meters...lateral crosswinds bearing two seven three...sustained at six zero knots...gusts to eight zero knots...over..."

Raven did not mind listening to serious people talk in an adversarial manner to one another, as long as it was always obvious that it was being done in a joking manner. Deriving entertainment from the cryptic verbal daggers of her peers was a variety of discourse that interested her. It somehow reminded her of what it felt like to have siblings. She missed her teammates when they were all separate from one another. They were her extended family. But she could not fully enjoy the day's radio roasting exchange. She was overly concerned that she would not catch the important operational details of what they were up against in time to make up for what she *did not* know about signals above 53 Gigahertz. She rarely ever had to deal with carrier signals in that range. To indirectly spot a carrier above 53 billion cycles per second meant frantic combing of the subharmonic mixing channels for mixing products that gave away the EHF intelligence carrier. She checked everything from 85 down to the relatively unmixed native bands with five and one gigahertz spans, and had eventually started into the 500 megahertz chunks by the time her experience was telling her to try something else. She used higher resolution bandwidth settings and half-second sweep speeds so she could sample more cross-sections of the unidentified source carrier before they were right on top of it. Only if she found what she was *expecting* to find would she be able to zero in on it and begin demodulating anything useful out of the "noise grass".

The tiny hybrid force signaled the initiation of radio silence to one another as they sped fast and low through the 150-kilometer range-to-target checkpoint into the probable early surface detection zone. The encrypted sat-com transponders of all three craft entered digital hibernation and ceased transmission of all static-pattern beacon reports. They were electromagnetically isolated from one another for the time being.

The C-3 turbine rpms were set to track and phase-match ambient vibration with a 180 degree offset in order to minimize the risk of sub-surface detection of the Serpent. The ambient surface vibration pattern data was measured and transmitted by thousands of PMDZ buoys in the area that were all disguised as jelly fish. The Asymmetric Projects Branch(APB) of JMSDF in Edo had convinced the JTF that saline filled jellyfish swarms, fitted with radioisotope Geiger-detection equipment, could monitor the Pacific for residual manmade radiation and transmit ambient surface signals to allied aircraft on the SCI band when called upon. After the remote initiation command was received via satellite by a jelly fish, it would begin gradually biasing on the flow of power to the transmitter encased inside the artificial biodegradable blob. The transmissions were made throughout the tactical area with subtly increasing amplitude to emulate the same kinds of noise patterns that were naturally produced when large doses of solar radiation struck Earth from the sun, or when the jelly fish transmitters came into contact with aberrational human-produced radiation.

  Senior Airman Madrone tuned everything else out after seeing the illumination of the dim red separation lamp on the overhead indicator panel. This was the part when she would transform into someone else-someone possessed by so much bottled rage that a kind of extrasensory ability began manifesting within her. She could see precisely what everyone was doing in her predictive mind. Serpent 1 and Serpent 2 were now separated and headed in different clock directions. Serpent 2 went counterclockwise on the tactical clock-face to drop the flank Dogs and MHOs off on the northeast side of Kanaga to wait, while Serpent 1 continued clockwise to the target area. Raven began noticing an intermittent spike on the subharmonic band of interest and determined that it had to be the unknown signal starting to creep into range of one of the

Serpent's Q-band antennas. She tried switching several of the various EHF band-reject filters into the EHF antenna input circuit to see if she could isolate anything intelligible and cleanly demodulated. The Serpent 3 craft bounced and strained against the volatile mix of pressure extremes and subsequent turbulence outside. Raven took no notice of the meteorological beating they were taking as she projected herself into the airspace they were now entering with her visual mind.

The mixing remainder that kept spiking into range was centered at around 37.5 Gigahertz, give or take a hundred million cycles. But none of the experimental carrier filters around 75 Gig yielded any intelligent demodulation product. No digital, no cyclical-analog, and no repeatable trigger threshold. The local oscillator chart for the past five minutes was clean and flat, and was not the cause of the apparent spike. It was coming from somewhere outside the Serpent. But it was still too random to make anything out. Raven hurriedly gulped her honey-sweetened hot black tea and tried to rethink the problem while passively observing the known spectral trouble spots on the spectrum-analyzer in the tactical bands that had been recorded within the region in the recent past. Whatever this signal was, she knew it was likely not one of their usual foes. This was something else entirely and left no medium-range electromagnetic footprint. So far, there wasn't even enough data to match it up to the JMSDF exemplar signal.

It occurred to Raven that KA-Band signals were significantly more susceptible to precipitation and other atmospheric disturbances then KU-Band, and that they may need to loiter almost directly over Kanaga to get a fix on exactly what was happening. They were flying headlong through a lot of really nasty weather, and that could have been what caused the intermittent detection. She tapped her microphone on to inform the pilot.

"We're going to need sustained medium altitude loiter over the target Captain. Too much attenuation in these conditions sir" she said.

"We can do that Madrone. We're unrestricted from 500 feet on up. Radar is quiet as a church termite. Give me a number..." said the Captain.

"Copy that captain. Recommend Y equals two zero kilo foxtrot, X equals five zero kilo Mike, entry to tangent on Z bearing zero eight seven decimal five over" said Raven.

"Solid copy Madrone" said the Captain. "Moving in close..."

The Captain maneuvered the Serpent and began climbing to 20,000 feet in preparation for a circular loitering pattern around an imaginary path that would bring them to within a 50-kilometer radius around Kanaga.

Meanwhile, both First platoon and Second platoon were in position, and First platoon had begun making their way to a point about one-third of the way up the side of the volcano where they would send the Mech-units up into the suspected ingress of the unknown human operators from the StratoRaven photos. The humans were assumed to be inside conducting an unknown operation for unknown reasons. Senior Airman Madrone observed the live positional feed from First platoon. They were all safely on the ground, now moving by twos through the topographical cover, positioning themselves as close to the entry as possible without giving away the element of surprise.

Over on the northeastern shore, Second platoon was dug in and following First platoon with one Mech-dog per human pair. Serpent 3 was quickly running out of time to give the ground operators some inkling of what they were going to encounter as they entered the mountain. The First platoon point man, Staff Sergeant Rahiko "Supernova" Bakuhatsu waited patiently from a crouched position 100 yards south of the entrance to hear what the nature of the evil inside of the mountain was going to be. The entire First platoon was in position within ten minutes, and was awaiting any potentially helpful word from Serpent 3. Nobody on the ground wanted to just waltz into the unknown as long as the possibility of more information still existed. Sergeant

Bakuhatsu's patience was wearing thin when suddenly he heard his comm-unit come to life with Raven's voice on the other end. The sound of her voice automatically triggered additional adrenaline release for the Sergeant and the others on the tactical channel, because her voice at this stage usually signaled the start of high intensity, near-death experiences. She spoke calmly into the microphone to relay her information to the Sergeant.

"Viper 1, Viper 3 over…" she said.

"Go ahead 3, whadduyuh got?"

"Looks like basic global web stuff sarge" said Raven.

"Okay, this just got really strange. Mech reports no contact or visible countermeasures. Whiskey Tango Foxtrot over" said the Sergeant with an intense shallow breath.

"Standby Viper 1…got some more coming in…looks like…educational domain servers…lots of 'em. University databases…and The United Global Library repository? Looks like someone is in there dumping information into space like they stole it…D.T.R. effective is…wait for it…500 Gigabits spread out over multiple channels. Data pirates maybe? Proceed with caution Viper. We're moving in weapons hot. ECM and Counter-Counter(C^2) standing by over," said Raven as she flipped the ECCM master switch to engage the Serpent's advanced counter-countermeasures transceivers, and to bring the back-up Mechs aboard Serpent 3 out of standby mode and synchronize them with the Serpent's command and control computer.

"Copy 3, we're gonna go knock and see what happens. Standby..."

First platoon fell in almost single file as the group moved to close in on the passageway that led into the mountain.

"I've got multiple footprints up here...cigarette butts...I'm going in," said Rahiko.

"We got your back man" said Raven.

The Sergeant sent Mech-1 ahead into the passageway and signaled the others to file in and leave the door open, which meant the anchor pair was to wait in defensive positions just outside the passageway. Sergeant Bakuhatsu could see what the Mech-dog was seeing in real time, and so far, it appeared to be a natural tunnel system with two forks leading down. The Mech had been able to identify which fork the footprints led through and led the team to a point just inside the high-traffic fork. The Mech-dog then released its micro-scout from its right hind quarter compartment, and the Second platoon MHO guided it down the other fork to inspect for the possibility of an alternate approach. Everything appeared normal until the micro-scout abruptly fell out of contact. The last four frames of the video-feed showed something that looked like a metal rod crashing into it.

"Viper 1, Viper 2…heads-up, looks like someone or some-*thing* just obliterated the scout…possible hostiles, range four zero meters" said the Second platoon MHO.

"Copy 2, prepare to engage," said Sergeant Bakuhatsu, motioning to the other First platoon humans to follow him into the passageway. "Mech-2, deploy your scout" said Rahiko to the Second platoon MHO controlling Mech-2.

"Copy Viper, releasing scout" said the MHO.

This time the MHO flew the micro-scout into the passageway at high speed to try and get a full picture for First platoon before someone took a baseball bat to it. The scout raced high and fast through the passageway until the MHO could see a wide-open area filled with various humans and a large assortment of exotic-looking hardware. The MHO noticed a large transmission antenna in the center of all the supporting hardware. The antenna looked like it was pointed up through a fissure in the mountain that led to the open air. The MHO maneuvered the scout through a stand of three humans who were all swatting at the scout like they were trying to swat a fly, and reaching for their weapons. The MHO immediately keyed up Sergeant Bakuhatsu to let the team know what was coming.

"Whoa! WHOA! TAKE COVER, TAKE COVER, HERE THEY COME!" shouted the MHO.

First platoon took cover with their rifles aimed at the coming onslaught. Mech-1 and Mech-2 rushed in ahead at full gallop while the team rushed in behind them prepared to fire. The unknown humans immediately dropped their weapons and raised their hands up at the sight of the giant, fierce-looking robotic Devil Dogs. Both Dogs had disabled their adaptive camouflage and had their primary head-fired pulse weapons locked into position with the targeting lasers painting motionless red dots onto the foreheads of the three humans. First platoon quickly came in behind the Dogs and held their weapons pointed at the humans while one of them went around and patted the humans down to check them for back-up weapons. There was about 20 seconds of silence before one of the unknown humans began to cautiously form words.

"No wonder the government's broke. They sent you guys? For us?" said the man on the far right across from Mech-1's unflinching mechanical stare-down.

"Sir, you are operating on an unlicensed frequency band. Please identify yourself immediately, or really bad shit *IS GOING* to befall you and your colleagues here," said Rahiko.

Several moments went by without any acknowledgement from those who had their hands in the air.

"This is your last chance sir, or I might be inclined to think your intentions are threatening," said Sergeant Bakuhatsu.

"Alright, alright…and by the way, who's threatening who here? We weren't hurting anyone in here. My name is Prescott McGrady. My friends call me Presto, but you sir are not entitled to that honor…because you are obviously *not* my friend" said Presto.

"Tell me then Mr. McGrady…if you're not doing anything wrong then why do you need those rifles?" asked Rahiko, steadfastly holding his rifle on Presto.

"Bears…DUH!…Russians…DUH!…rabid foxes…DUH!…oh yeah, and we were also planning on taking out an armed, mechanized combat unit while we're in here just sipping nasty coffee and uploading the knowledge" said Presto with his tone transforming into fearless, condescending sarcasm on the brink of anger.

The Sergeant began to sense that these two guys and the young woman they were with weren't really a threat at all.

"Stand down Devils. Lower your weapons, take a breath. Looks like a damn nerd project in here" said Rahiko. "Viper 3, Viper 1…there's no immediate threat here. Bring her down on the south beach and save some fuel. Viper 2, bring it in. We're green" said Rahiko.

Second and Third platoons began making their way to the south beach rally point, while Sergeant Bakuhatsu and the rest of First platoon continued questioning the three strangers.

"Sir, we are the 7th Devil Dogs. They only send us out for the worst kind of high-risk threats. Now, you wanna tell me what the *HELL* you and yours are doing in here transmitting some kind of fancy information bundle into outer space for?" asked the Sergeant.

"Oh yeah, sure thing Sergeant Devil sir. We are filling up an ultra-high-capacity data storage unit that has been installed on board the *E.S.S. Hell Cat...um,* with all the knowledge" said Presto.

"What the hell do you mean, 'with all the knowledge'?" asked the sarge. "*WHAT* knowledge?"

"Um...uh, let's see how can I put this, um...ALL...OF...THE...KNOWLEDGE..., ya know, like, EVERY LAST PIECE OF STINKING KNOWLEDGE...IN ITS ENTIRETY...THAT...HAS...EVER BEEN ACKNOWLEDGED...AS...KNOWABLE, or catalogued, or forgotten on a hard drive, or dropped in the recycle bin without a paddle, or has been spoken and recorded and digitized...LIKE...EVERY FUCKIN' THING THERE IS TO KNOW...THAT WE'VE EVER KNOWN...EVER! I'm not sure if I made that clear or…did I just confuse you again?" joked Presto with his characteristic recurring sarcasm.

"What the heck is this contraption here?" asked the Sergeant, motioning toward the giant antenna in the middle of the room.

"Hey, now *THAT*, is a really good question Sergeant. It might even be the smartest, most philosophically *deep* question I've been asked all day long. *That*, is lightning in a bottle…*SUCKA*! Woo-ha! You guys all thought we couldn't do it, or that it couldn't be done…talkin' about 'I can't, it can't be done, it just isn't possible, wha-wha, goo-goo, poor me…oh, yeah right'" said Presto rapidly snapping his fingers numerous times as a matter of compulsion. "*That*, is an experimental Extreme-High-Frequency multi-channel data-transmitter. And if any of you even so much as breathe on it, I will dedicate the brief remainder of my unnatural life to making sure I breakuh your face."

Sergeant Rahiko took a few moments to think about everything he was seeing, and what he had been told by Presto. He was trying to make sense of it all situationally, but there were still a lot of pieces missing. It occurred to him that a bunch of civilians would not be in a volcano uploading the balance of all the knowledge humankind had ever accumulated unless they had been authorized or otherwise conscripted into service by those "deep-space people in D.C.".

"Mr. McGrady," the Sergeant began, "how did you come to be here? Why are you all here doing this? Who authorized this?"

Presto remained quiet in contemplation of whether or not revealing the truth would create more problems. Their motives were honorable, but their means were not necessarily legal. They were in league with some people who had managed to crack into the *Hell Cat's* master non-volatile data storage matrix.

"Why do you want to know sarge? You all thought we were a threat to...what...national security or something? HA! Well, you're right! We are a threat to *somebody's* national security...but not yours. From what I can tell, we're on the same side man. Your nation is my nation, and it's gonna be up to all of us to secure it. The last update we have is that we're putting information into a ship that doesn't quite have a full crew. So all of this might be for nothing" said Presto, sweeping his arm out across the room to draw Rahiko's attention to their little covert camp inside the volcano. With all of its exotic hardware, empty ration bags over-flowing the garbage receptacle, and awkwardly steaming geothermal transducers, the place generally looked like it had been lived in for at least a few weeks.

"Spit it out Mr. McGrady..." said Rahiko, clinging to the last remnants of his patience. "Who are you working with?"

"We were contracted by the Deep Space Expeditionary Command Council" said Presto. "They told us we could take our families into space once we were finished here...provided we're still allowed to do so of course". Presto looked over at his two children with a serious look on his face so they would follow his lead into diplomacy. Daven and Darby McGrady stood by their father, and were his exceptionally knowledgeable apprentices.

"Space? Really...they told you that huh?" Rahiko's train of thought was interrupted by a hailing-tone on his comm-unit, followed by the voice of Sra Madrone.

"Hey Sergeant B...they're for real sir. We gotta let 'em go. Their mission is federal priority 1-E. Whatever they're doing, D.C. considers it an emergency."

"Solid copy Madrone. You heard the lady everybody...release the nerds. We're outta here."

First platoon was trickling its way back out of the volcano when the command terminal of the experimental transmission system delivered its completion message. Presto could not help but clap his hands together in celebration of what the message actually meant. The last data update was complete, and they were clear to call in their final situation report to their DSECC point of contact. It was time to pack everything up and bug out to the *E.S.S. Hell Cat*. They were several days overdue to leave Kanaga and head for sector HI-0007.

"Hey sarge" said Presto to get Rahiko's attention before he got away. "You guys may as well stick around for a few minutes. We just finished here, and they intend to direct the nearest transportation resources to our location to get us up there as soon as humanly possible.

"Great," said Sergeant Bakuhatsu, "we get to deliver you out into the middle of the freakin' ocean now...lucky us! I'm sure nobody's going to be upset about that *at all*" said the sarge with his forehead crinkled down in frustration at the bad luck the high-maintenance nerds had brought them all.

Iwaizumi

Earth
Sector JP-0046E
November 24, 2025 C.E.
Monday
0637 HRS

    Everything was normal aboard the AH-64SX Super Apache, as the skillful Army Air Corps Captain brought them all safely back to within 15 clicks of the "Connie". The skies were clearing up and the equipment and data from RIKEN were safely aboard the C-330 and on the way to the HEIWA complex. The *Constellation* was prepping to leave the Kuriles before the ship's presence could attract the attention of unwelcome observers to the north and west of their position. Colonel Kleen was satisfied that everything had gone according to plan thus far. But over the years, Tabitha had learned that she had an innate sense for knowing when something was risky. She looked out her window to the port side of the aircraft around the part of the northwestern horizon that she could see from her seated position. She was scanning for something that she knew was out there lurking and waiting for them to accidentally stray just far enough into restricted airspace to legally justify an attack.

The brief trip to Etorofu Jima brought them perilously close to the periphery of sector RU-0105, which was an internationally agreed upon no-fly zone that was meant to address the problem of territorial conflict between Japan, Russia, and Autonomous Zone 3 of the Yup'ik Tribal Autonomous Region along the eastern shores of the Kamchatka Peninsula. Many years had passed since anyone from the Western world or the Far Eastern allied territories had been inside the RU-0105 no-fly zone. But occasionally, members of the Alutiiq and Ainu tribes brought out fresh human intelligence. This was the natural result of their being allowed to traverse Zone 3 in pursuit of subsistence game and for intertribal affairs in sector JP-0046. Additionally, the North Pacific tribes were suspicious about the behavior of Russian and Chinese vessels in the area.

The back and forth of seafaring tribes was a historical metronome that had not wavered, and would not be deterred by anything human. Despite the changing face of modern human affairs, the sea routes connecting the Ainu tribal groups of northern Japan with the North and South American tribes had changed very little over the millennia. The Alutiiq business of fishing, fellowship, and meetings with other tribal groups extended geographically all the way into the northern half of Japan's main island of Honshu. Despite the changing face of modern human affairs, numerous Russian and Imperial Japanese occupations in the 20th century, and NBC toxicity in the waters of their timeless hunting grounds, the sea routes connecting the Ainu groups of northern Japan with the indigenous tribes of the Americas were still their home, for better or for worse. They didn't need polymerase chain-reaction DNA analysis to tell them what they already knew about themselves. They could go anywhere they needed, whenever they needed to. Russian patrols were just another problem to be solved throughout the course of any given day of work.

Most of the known Russian patrols were originating in the Sea of Okhotsk. For all but the original humans of the region and the modern newcomers who sought to control the region, the Sea of Okhotsk was even more of a mystery now to scholars and researchers than it had ever been. Satellite reconnaissance photos revealed massive construction projects and unprecedented logistical activity in the region. But intelligence analysts could not figure out what a lot of the new construction projects actually were. The photos and high-altitude reconnaissance drone videos defied the usual laws of analysis. The informed speculation was that half of Russia was "chunneling" its way over to the east coast and living there underground between Vladivostok and the northeastern corner past Anadyr for some sinister reason.

The last known strategic military situation in the area had seen the Russians rebuilding old 20th Century World War II military outposts, and breaking new ground on advanced naval installations and state-of-the-art electronic and physical fortification projects. But all of that activity was above the surface and being done in plain sight. Like the Chinese in the South and East China Sea regions, the Russians sought to construct artificial islands at strategic points throughout the contested territorial confluences of the far northwestern Pacific region. The politically moderate talking-heads in Moscow had very little trouble convincing the UGC that their activities were related to an ongoing marine wildlife restoration project. But the hardliners in Moscow and the global environmental hawks knew better. On paper, the project was supposed to benefit the environment and help repair the damage of over 100 years of wanton destruction to the marine life and island ecology. Confirmation of the extinction of countless numbers of species in the years preceding the project compelled the minds of non-Russo optimists to be accepting of new ideas, even if the new ideas *were* founded on ill-intentions, and by ill creatures stuck in the realm of *old* ideas.

The damage brought on by the first industrial revolution, and the carbon ages that followed, left the door open for evil people to hatch evil plans. None of the countries in the general assembly who allowed the Okhotsk-Kurile restoration project to go forward were really naïve enough to think the hardliners were *really* worried about the presence of excessive heavy metals in the tuna population. Most of the veto-wielding nation-states voted yes just to see how much hardship the old guard in Moscow would be willing to endure to maintain the facade of benevolence.

The Colonel was scanning the horizon for something that was being reported recently by the Alutiiq as being an "invisible scout" craft of some kind along the southeastern perimeter of the no-fly zone. The boundaries of Autonomous Zone 3 were marked with standard Vector Oriented Transceiver Radar Reporting (VOTRR) beacons. All boundary violations worldwide were reported to a secure public domain server in Geneva so that anyone on Earth could corroborate a reported violation to a quote or news story involving the concerned parties. Colonel Kleen knew they could be harassed, but she didn't believe it would happen while they were so close to the *Constellation*.

The "invisible scout" aircraft sightings were initially being reported at the rate of one or two sightings per week. But in recent weeks, the number of reported sightings had gone up into the twenties and thirties. Whatever the phenomenon was, it was establishing regular traffic patterns in the area, which made the command staff at HQ/JTF extremely nervous. The AH-64SX pilot's voice came over the internal comm-channel to alert the Colonel and the other passengers that they were approaching the *Constellation*.

"Echo base, Echo 1...inbound on final approach, how copy over?" asked the pilot.

"Solid copy Echo 1, you are cleared to starboard, go ahead" said the traffic controller on the *Constellation*.

Before they could make their touchdown, the unexpected happened. The cockpit Radar Warning Receiver and Tracking began sounding off with the indication that they were being engaged by one or more unknown craft. The close range scope showed the physical threat coming in from the northwest just off the surface. Everybody immediately began looking around to see if they could make visual contact with the unknown threat outside the windows. The Colonel spotted something in the still dark blue western horizon. But it wasn't anything that could have been described as an "invisible scout". It was quite visible as a couple of black dots just off the surface in the distance. Right in plain sight racing in from the port side were two Mig-41C fighter-bombers, and their targeting lasers were locked on to both the AH-64SX *and* the *Constellation*. Just as the Captain was keying up to request permission to engage the Migs, the jets blew past them burning low and fast through the approach vector and the AH-64SX's Radar Warning Receiver went silent. It was typical taunting for this area, and would be reported to the JTF and the UGC up the chain. The Migs streaked off to the east-northeast and circled back toward the Sea of Okhotsk. The Colonel privately thanked God that the incident did not escalate into something more serious.

"Way to keep it cool Echo 1...we almost pulled the trigger on the Vampire last week over that horseshit...did you get a look at the tail numbers?" asked the *Connie* controller.

"Negative Echo base...they're all sync to the same elusive flag story...could have been Pyongyang, Beijing, or inner Siberia...no tellin' not knowin'. Clear a spot for us...we're ready to put 'er down and get off this ride," said the Captain.

It was true that there were three countries in the region using the same military hardware and the same tactics of harassment. It was all part of a larger game of chess that kept the friendly operators in the area guessing about who, what, and why. The Colonel's only concern was making sure she did her duty and completed her mission. The sooner the *X-Tensai* got underway and set up shop off-world, the sooner the

UGC could begin the evacuation of all who were still in the path of the reckoning.

"Fine job Captain," said the Colonel as she disembarked the Super Apache. "For a second there I thought they were going to be fishing pieces of us out of the North Pacific...or picking us up by the shovel full off the beaches of the Aleutians. Either way, I'm just glad to be back on solid iron again."

"No problem ma'am...if you need me later I'll be down below decks...hosin' the cheap vodka out of my eyes so I can see my Scotch" said the Captain.

For as much as the Colonel wanted to go and relax for a while, she had a lot of things to get done aboard the *Constellation* over the next couple days. It was time for her to issue the order to load everyone into the *X-Tensai* and get back across the pond to oversee the last phase of Earth operations from the HEIWA complex. The Colonel did not like dragging things out longer than necessary. If the objectives were already clearly defined, and there were no additional practical reasons why the crew and civilians should not already be aboard the ship, then going through the orientation and getting to know the ship as a team was top priority. Tabitha also wanted to be the first to tell the Detachment IV group that final approval of their ops-plan came through from DSECC, and that their plan was heading to the special budgetary appropriations committee for further resource assistance.

The special committee's decision to grant additional resources was becoming increasingly less pertinent to the more urgent part of the information she wanted to pass along. They were going to board the *X-Tensai* now, with or without additional resource assistance. The only question that remained was whether they were going to accomplish the next phase of *Kaminari* with ample resources, or with limited resources dangling over their heads as a constant reminder of what lies ahead. The importance of the sustainable elements of the plan would need to be stressed to the civilian staff and operational crew over and over again until every single member of the symbiotic ecological circle understood the consequences of losing sustainability in a vacuum.

The other important thing on the list of things that needed to be briefed to Kahmay regarding the DSECC approval was the subject of the government's specific request for the Det. IV mission. It was important the crew knew that they were being asked to go set up a place for refugees on Mars, and to produce a replica of the *X-Tensai* among other things. The plan called for indigenous iron deposits on Mars to be used in the parts fabrication printers. In fact, the original copy of the first draft plan included no less than five separate scenarios that could exploit the capabilities of the *X-Tensai* while she was still inside the solar system. Five separate scenarios, each of which assumed a more generous time frame for relocating the humans than the one specified in the conditions of the Council's decision to approve the team's request for the *X-Tensai*.

The Colonel was spending a few moments of relaxation time in her quarters with her feet elevated, and was attempting to train her mind on something else besides the dangers that lurked in the waters between Etorofu Island and the HEIWA complex. The East-Northeasterly course the *Connie* was on was not guaranteed to be entirely free of enemy presence. The entire northwestern quadrant of the Pacific was still turning up the occasional scout submarine, particularly west of the International Date Meridian. Tabitha sipped her eight-ounce cup of decaffeinated coffee while she reflected on the possible futures of all who would be temporarily left on Earth struggling in battle. While the search for permanent human refuge was being carried out in space with a practically indefinite time limit, hundreds of millions of civilians were being instructed by local authorities to fortify their homesteads and arm themselves to the teeth. She thought about Michio-san's family, and how they would fare as the enemy drew closer and closer to Japanese territory. Michio-san's skill set was needed on board the *X-Tensai*, and yet it was critical for someone with his knowledge of electronic communication to be on Earth. Intelligence from the ground would be vital in securing safe passage for the refugees.

In her quiet reflection, Tabitha reached into the deep inside pocket of her winter parka and pulled out the holographic data storage device the Commander had given her a while ago at Etorofu. Her sleepy, fatigued state from the long day was gradually transformed into eager curiosity as she plugged the device into her personal data management device. The file directory on the device revealed numerous folders segregated by text, graphic, and analytical file types. She opened the top folder and began scrolling through the photos it contained. The three-dimensional photos showed numerous different features of the inside of a cave network. Underground fresh water lakes and areas of cave that looked to have been carved out by humans were among the photos in the folder. The modifications made to the caves were done in a way that would accommodate thousands of humans for sleeping. The last photo in the bunch was biometrically protected, and was revealed after the Colonel allowed the retinal scanner to confirm that her retina was on the list of authorized viewers for the file. It was a high resolution photo of a map that showed a magnified section of the northeastern coast of Japan. It was obviously the location Michio-san and his family was going to be sheltered until they could be evacuated to Mars. The Colonel breathed an anxious sigh upon realizing what she was looking at. She knew that even if the fresh water supply was carefully rationed, it could be discovered by marauders, or contaminated by surface agents from a nuclear, biological, or chemical attack.

The hidden caves of Iwaizumi were not entirely known to the Earth public. The full extent of the depth and reach of the cave network at the Ryusendo branch of the network was a Japanese state secret because of its strategic value in the event large numbers of people would one day require hidden shelter. The central government in Edo had been working on it for decades as a contingency for the kind of events that were presently happening on Earth. Expanding the network was exceedingly easy once a secure, covert section was set aside.

Tabitha was relieved to see that multiple sites within the cave network had been set up over a broad radius to account for such necessities as communications transceivers and fall back rally points. She knew her friend would be alright. But she worried that the *X-Tensai* was going to take too much time getting the sanctuary set up on Mars to get them all out of there in time to avert a catastrophe.

One last glance at the accompanying encrypted text files reassured the Colonel that secure interplanetary communication with the Commander's outpost could be maintained indefinitely. There were areas throughout the entire region where ducting and conduit networks gave the future residents of the cave system access to the surface. Antennas, exhaust vents, elaborate fresh air intake systems, sewage outlets, and a good number of launch bays for light and moderate duty drones speckled the map of the cave network's infrastructure plan. The tiny hairs on the back of the Colonel's neck stood up as she made the realization that if the information on the drive were ever lost, it could never be recovered. She shuttered to think of what would happen if a secure copy of the information on the drive were not created immediately after boarding the *X-Tensai*.

The power needs of the cave network were to be met by a three-tiered system of capability that included eighth generation "second-skin" solar collection throughout the surrounding forests, over 150 micro-hydro collectors installed in the small-diameter freshwater capillaries, and a thrice-redundant charge-controlling system with over 50 megawatts of battery capacity. It was all being kept below the surface and up-to-spec to be ready for whatever doom may befall the humans that would soon be relying upon the cave network for their temporary survival.

Improvise

Earth
Sector AK-0006
November 25, 2025 C.E.
Tuesday
1530 HRS

Most of the Detachment IV night crew was busy unpacking their Thermakeepers and salivating over the contents therein when Specialist "Psycho" Manuel came into the break area and laid down a small piece of gear on the lunch table. To the rest of the crew it looked like something mysterious that might attach to a human hand. It was very similar in appearance to one of those orthopedic wrist support braces with the adjustable Velcro cinching straps from the 20th century. But this device was obviously a step up from something you wear on your wrist when you go bowling. It was a superconducting quantum entanglement accessory. The United States Marine Corps Counterterrorism Units and Navy Seals used them in their extreme cold weather training exercises as a way of training their minds to get used to "tactical zero". Tactical zero was the way they described the state of being in a microgravity situation during tactical military operations of all varieties. When Marines were operating in space, stealthy movements during reconnaissance and quiet positioning before operational execution were part of their standard operating procedures. Only a Marine trained to pick the specific spots that would offer the best angle of entanglement would reach his or her target. All of the old school Marines carried a set of these babies in their "ghost kits."

But what did Psycho have in mind with that blank stare of his? Was he suggesting something that had to do with a possible solution for the problem of how to get by the low-earth-orbit security drones? Could this be a possible solution for quietly loading the *X-Tensai* before commandeering her? Finally, the anticipation gave way to direct inquiry. Specialist Victor "Special Vic" Doyle could not wait any longer to find out what was going on and spoke up.

"Hey man, where'd you git that? What are you going to do with it?"

Manuel replied in his typically adversarial manner.

"Is that your business Doyle? Why do you need to know?"

Doyle let out a disgusted huff and went into gentle admonishment mode.

"Boring brother...just plain boring. We're here trying to bring ourselves up to speed and you're still so void of purpose that you have time for playin' games? Now, I believe you are intelligent and that you conspicuously placed that on the table because you have a good idea. I would like to *hear* your idea. Will you share it with the group, or are you just gonna waltz around here with that smirk on your face being all condescending and proud of yourself while we guess at your motives?"

Without saying a word, Specialist Manuel gave a short nondescript gesture laced with contempt as he turned his back on the group and went walking at a good clip into the supply closet. It was his typical half-word/half-tsk gesture that translated into something like "you annoy me so much I scarcely have the patience to form two words for you."

Many people in the group thought Manuel's attitude problem was related to some horrible traumatizing experiences he went through in his younger years. Sector CA-14 was known for its abnormally tough neighborhoods. There were many places in the United States like sector CA-14, but few areas on the map were harder on the soul than sector 14 of the California territory. They thought maybe he was bullied in school, or harassed by cops, or maybe even ridiculed in some way by someone he trusted or loved. The bottom line about this guy though, was that he had probably gone through most everything a person could go through and still survive. Everyone was pretty sure that he had been through some really bad experiences to become as jaded as he obviously had. But something had to give way with his negative attitude. If he didn't start learning how to trust, the crew was going to have a hard time going into space with him. He was so untrustworthy in the eyes of the crew that some of them thought he was a subversive working against them all. His innuendos and odd behavior made people uncomfortable. There was no room for passive-aggressive time-bomb personality types on this mission, even if it was done in the name of misplaced compensatory verbal self-defense. One of the few things the crew expected in exchange for a potential lifetime in the abyss of space was to know that when they went to sleep at night, a disgruntled peer was not going to come and poison their coffee or blow the airlock! He scarcely seemed to have the minimum social investment required to change his facial expressions.

     Just about the time the first derogatory comment about Psycho was due to be spoken by one of the group, Specialist Manuel emerged from the supply closet with a large cardboard box full of more of the same entanglement accessories. The box was overflowing with several different variations of the item placed on the table just a moment before. Some of the items looked more like what would go on someone's foot, or maybe even on their elbows or knees. To the amazement of the skeptics in the group, Manuel began very calmly explaining his thinking.

"Found these in the ditch out on the Cape road. I drive the Cape road sometimes to clear my head and listen to the ocean with the engine turned off. There are only two types of vehicles using that road; the Coast Guard coming, and the Coast Guard going. What I can't figure out though, is why the Coast Guard would need to have this stuff. We need two people to go and check this out. If they're up to something shady, then they're probably deliberately avoiding vehicle travel until the hours of darkness."

The room fell silent, as Special Vic looked around the table to quickly survey the level of surprise on the faces of the others. Nobody present could believe they just heard this guy get serious about something for the first time in memory. Maybe at last, it was because there was a situation materializing that was worthy of Manuel's lofty participation criteria. His voice was so calm, and genuine sounding...*was he playing some kind of game with everyone all this time?* Before anyone could form any sarcastic innuendos and put them into words, Manuel made a slight adjustment to his stance and began speaking again.

"I know that you people think I'm psychotic, but I just think sometimes you all get cabin fever in here, and you start thinking too much about things that aren't real. I hope you all realize that when that kind of sickness starts creeping into your head, it will happen so gradually that you won't even notice it. By the time you start recognizing a pattern that all leads back to you...it'll already be too late. Don't spend your life in a soap opera people. Spend your life in the now and stop sweatin' me. Food for thought anyway."

Everyone just looked at one another without saying a word. They all knew a part of Manuel's psychosis was that he had practiced the art of mimicking healthy mental states for self-entertainment and perhaps for some unknown future utility that might have to do with his need to manipulate people. He had perfected the art of passive-aggressive rage. True to form, Manuel was exceedingly hard to predict. Understanding his actions and his general demeanor were a challenging problem that the rest of the crew still had yet to figure out. But they were all quite curious now about how the entanglement equipment came to be out on the Cape road, and had started to forget about the enigma of Specialist Manuel as their focus shifted back onto the mission.

There were no problems finding volunteers to go check things out. But eventually the group's chatter settled on sending Leonard "Trigger" Quire and Paul "Hound-dog" Monty to complete the task. Together they were occasionally known as "Triggerhound", which they were glad to embrace as a badge of honor. Everyone agreed they were the perfect duo to go out and check on the Cape road. They were born for this work. There are those who force themselves to settle into trades that are naturally unbefitting the self. But then there are those like Monty and Quire, both of whom wasted precious little time from a young age discovering the right combination of job aptitudes and willingness to fully commit to a singular life path. Growing up together from the age of seven in sector ID-10 had taught them how to work together. As young lads, they learned how to hunt and stalk together. They moved as one instrument of sudden execution, and they could strike anywhere without warning. That was *before* they joined the Marine Corps together in Coeur d'Alene. The infinitely variable nature of the tactical problems faced by reconnaissance artists was its own reward for these two. They thrived on the new challenge of each mission, and this would be no different. They were the perfect improvising two-person fire team. Kahmay's only regret about the two was that they had yet to teach the others in the group about how to exercise these same skills. But they would learn to be teachers in time. If they weren't going to teach the other members of the team, then maybe they would teach their children out in space one day on some other planet.

It was recently rumored that Edo-00010011 had areas that were almost identical to the places on Earth where the people go to hunt for food. Hunting on Edo-00010011 was one of Quire and Monty's favorite topics to speculate on. But so far, the only two things to substantiate the rumor of Earth-like ecology were the somewhat inadequate images of the James Webb Deep Space Telescope and a few pieces of highly believable conjecture. The James Webb images were thus far the most highly resolved images of the exoplanet. But they were still not resolved enough for the decision makers to decide with absolute certainty that a deep-space journey to go and see it up close could be justified. So far as the Det. IV crew was concerned, Edo could end up being a lifeless moon and they still wouldn't care. They were prepared to settle on an asteroid if necessary.

Hound disengaged the primary vehicle power and control umbilical cables that connected to the bunker complex, and the two specialists climbed into B-2 to head out onto the back roads toward the Cape road. With nothing more than active night vision and the onboard heads-up-display (HUD) systems to guide them, they rolled off into the night toward the target with the noise discipline of a tree snake. The B-2 vehicle was a specially modified forest green Geo Tracker from the year 1994 that had been converted into full electric. During the day at the training bunker, B-2 sat seven meters underground in an old 6.2-meter storage container. She was plugged into a bidirectional charge controller assembly that allowed her to either feed her own battery energy into the bunker-complex array, or receive energy collected from a high-efficiency solar collection grid on the surface. The voltage thresholds of the onboard parallel monitoring circuits were set to bias-on a drain from the vehicle auxiliary battery array into the bunker controller at night, and then take a 20% trickle from the array during the day while the bunker was running steady on the other 80% of the available solar. In the autumn and winter periods, which were high-use periods for B-2, she relied more heavily on the finely resolved gyroscopically controlled kinetic energy collection assemblies. Any inclination or declination of the chassis that was more pronounced than 2.1 degrees, and for more than a constant 1 second, and the appropriate assembly deployed from under the B-2 chassis. Forward coasting triggered the rear collection assembly, and reverse coasting triggered the forward collection assembly. Inertia and fundamental gravitational acceleration were the only other things required for the collection assemblies to begin winding up the tensioners. Only a few good hills were required to wind the tensioners to their maximums. Once fully wound up, the tensioners did not begin releasing their mechanical energy into the micro-gen until after the aggregate parallel battery level in the array had dropped below 18.7 VDC. When used in conjunction with the regenerative braking system, B-2 was always under the impression that she had received a full charge from a long sunny day. In the spring and summer periods, in order to offset the cost of powering the bunker-complex during heavy-use periods, she collected so much energy from multiple sources that she fed it back into the territorial prime-grid for money. She was the ultimate improvised vehicle for the two masters of adaptation as they made their way to the last curve on the fire break trail before the beach front. Monty was the first one to break the silence.

"Range to target 0.6. Stand by for TRS deploy. Initializing in 3...2...1..."

The rear cargo compartment hydraulics of the B-2 began tilting toward Y on the aft Z-axis as the Tactical Recon Scout (TRS) drone props began silently whirring in preparation for liftoff from inside the B-2 rear entrapment. Just as the canopy locked into the fully open position, Quire flipped his ultralight video-feed display panel down into his field of view and began viewing a live feed of the TRS night vision camera. He was in Trigger mode now and deep into his routine. He stared at the targeting alignment decal on the inside wall of the rear entrapment and imagined his own eyes attached to the outer surface of the TRS.

The B-2 was obscured from view in case any of the personnel at the old Coast Guard complex were outside. Posted sentries on the outside of the facility would be the biggest threat to the element of surprise as the TRS approached. But Hound Dog somehow always managed to get close without being noticed.

The standard software package for the TRS was programmed to ascend the scout vertically to 100 meters and then surrender vector and targeting input to either a preprogrammed course sequence, or a Manual Human Operator (MHO) via static digital loop interrupt. Battery-interrupt resulted in Bingo return protocol, and MHO-interrupt enabled real time tri-axial vectoring. Quire was one of the finest human MHOs in the business. He was truly married to his work, and even nicknamed B-2's TRS unit "BITO", which was assumed by the others on the team to mean "Bun in the Oven". The truth was that none of the crew really knew why he named it BITO. They all thought it was strange that Quire could sometimes be seen talking to BITO during the slow times, as if angry at it. He had even been seen on many occasions shaking his finger at it whilst verbally scorning its recent performances. Of course, this caused concern in the group that he was not mentally stable. It was no mystery why he left his engineering position for reconnaissance operations while he was still on active duty. The phenomenon known as "ground fever" was creeping into his mind several years back after a long underground assignment on graveyard shift. Typical symptoms of the fever included acute paranoia, insomnia, and hypervigilance. In Quire's case, he was suffering the worst of the symptoms and was keeping it to himself. He loved his work in applied engineering and did not want to lose his profession. But once the physical symptoms of the fever started, he had no other practical choice but to switch his primary duty position to something with more sunshine and vitamin D3.

Quire's results spoke for themselves. There were so few humans left that met the universally accepted criteria for the title of "stable" anymore that the crew just dismissed Quire's behavior as a case of "that's just life in all of its vast and interesting flavors".

Quire was not a danger to anyone or anything unless he was trying to feed his family and you were the one standing in his way of doing that. Those who knew him best figured out that leaving him alone was the best policy, and would ultimately work fine in space. His buddy Monty was the only system of checks and balances he needed for the most part. Everyone knew there would be plenty of time to learn more about the mystery of Quire's obsessions and compulsions. But for now, they just needed BITO to find out what was going on inside the Coast Guard station. After powering up the scout to 60% rpms, Quire calmly relayed his intentions through the headset and settled in with the control panel.

"BITO launch on my mark. Two...One...launch."

The miniaturized launch pad's clasping relays disengaged with a pull of the trigger and opened the clasps releasing the TRS up to 100 meters. Quire quickly scanned the immediate area through the view panel for any possible threat before diving down to just five meters off the deck to head for the tree line. Hound, now in the "spare set of eyes" role, slowly blinked his eyes to prepare himself for handling the visuals of a high speed course through the wind stripped Cape trees. He could often see things that Quire couldn't focus on while avoiding obstacles.

Quire was heading for the darkest spot of the complex to observe at close range from beyond the trees and wasted no time getting there. He swerved through the trees and followed the terrain in perfect contour as he made his way to the opposite side of the courtyard. It was an ideal night to fly BITO because it was dark, and the slight breeze created a lot of distracting movement in the trees for any unseen sentries who may have been observing the general insertion area. Some dead leaves were blowing around in the area, and completed the favorable distractive camouflage effect perfectly. The high-rpm blades of the BITO easily chewed through the occasional leafy collision.

There were no signs of any outside guards, but flickers of interior lighting could be seen coming from the south window of the wall facing the courtyard. Quire knew he had to come in high and dark so he could zoom in on any observable activity. On approach to the sweet spot he began to notice gigantic cylindrical objects coming into focus on his view panel. Neither man could believe himself when the full magnitude of what they were seeing struck them all at once. The objects were modular cross-section assemblies for the old VANGUARD system! The two had no idea why some no name element was inside the Coast Guard building with giant sections of an obsolete near-Earth cargo delivery platform. Quire attempted to move in closer with BITO, but knew the risks were elevated. Foul activities flourished in this dark time, and most people had finally given in to apathy concerning the rule of law. Whatever was going on inside the facility, it reeked of an illicit nature. Just as Quire had achieved a motionless hover in the sweet spot, both he and Monty spotted a woman through the window in a white lab coat carrying a clipboard. It appeared as though she was making a visual inventory of the contents inside one of the cargo modules. Just as she began walking down the steps leading back down from the top of the container, a man dressed in static dissipative scrubs walked up the steps to place a small object into the container. Obviously these people were using the VANGUARD system to make a delivery into space. Hound broke the silence and whispered to Quire.

"Did you get 'em Trigger?"

"Affirmative," replied Quire. "Pics in the bag. Comin' up on Bingbat...she's runnin' out of juice already. Buggin' out."

Quire's tiny Heads-Up Display had been flashing the words "Bingo Battery" in tiny bold red letters to indicate that 45% of the scout's battery had been used, and that the return leg should commence immediately.

"Copy Trig. Prep for TRS receive en route," said Hound with a steady voice.

"Roger, go for receive en route," Quire replied, as Hound engaged the Vector Oriented Radar and Instrument Landing Systems (VOR/ILS).

Quire began swerving his way back through the trees while the B-2 was already quietly making her silent backtrack out of the area. BITO emerged from the trees with Quire's eyes aboard, now searching through the view panel for his best approach to recapture. Hound found the turnout they had passed earlier on the way in and quietly turned the B-2 around to begin heading back to the bunker complex. The B-2 launch bay was still open and the VOR/ILS antenna was still pulsing the vector beacon signal at the rate of 182.1 Hertz. Quire easily locked the signal and began increasing speed to make sure he caught up with the B-2 for recapture before the TRS battery was depleted. BITO gently hovered into position over the mobile launch pad and gradually came to rest into the clasp handles triggering the lock relays. Quire flipped his view panel up and took a deep breath with his eyes closed as the hydraulics gently brought the canopy back down. Hound increased B-2's speed from the recapture speed of 38 klicks up to full extraction speed and the two specialists disappeared quietly as phantoms in the night. They had to make sure TSgt Kahmay got the word right away.

Meeting of the Minds

Earth
Sector CO-0001
December 05, 2025 C.E.
Saturday
0642 HRS

The view of the Denver airport from 8,000 feet was slightly obscured by giant blobs of scattered clouds, as Doctors Jared and Shannon Foyle began to stow their notepads and personal effects back into their cases in preparation for landing. They knew this was going to be an important meeting, and they knew that their expertise in the fields of Psychology and Anthropology were needed. But they had no real idea why, or to what degree. It was strange for DSECC to be meeting in Denver, and even stranger for the meeting to be held at an airport. Their instructions were to deplane, proceed to the baggage carousel area, and then look for a man with a sign by the arrivals exit. They would then be led to a meeting hall where a gathering of experts from all over the world would be held to discuss something that had to do with the future of space exploration. Beyond that, all they knew was that they were to be prepared to answer any and all questions pertaining to Operation *Kaminari*.

The Foyles had written peer-reviewed papers on such specialized topics as *Space Humans: Group Dynamics and the Need to Control the Present*, and *Population Zero: Translating Human Culture into Extraterrestrial Application and Practice*. Their work was well known in select circles, and to the space exploration community. But they knew that their respective fields of expertise scored high on the "Why the heck should I care about that" scale of human existence. Suffice to say, they were nervous about meeting in the same room as a hundred physicists, multi-disciplinary engineers, astrobiologists, and an assortment of administrators.

The couple slowly made their way down the aisle and quietly walked closely abreast through the masses of deplaning passengers on their way to the baggage carousel area to look for the man with the sign. Sector CO-0001 felt dramatically different than the fast-paced rivers of civilization back home in New York. They enjoyed being home in Greenwich Village, but the lower population density of the western part of the country was a welcome change from what they were used to. Jared was the first to spot the man with a sign that displayed the word "FOYLE" in large black capital letters.

"There he is love...right where they said he would be," said Jared cheerfully.

After a brief exchange, the three were immediately headed to the far western end of the arrivals level toward an array of elevators. The man they were with depressed the "up" button of the very last elevator closest to the exterior window of the building and the three were soon inside waiting for the door to close. Rather unexpectedly, the man reached out to the control panel and used a small key to open up a hatch next to the numbered floor buttons. The hatch revealed a dimly lit retinal scanner, which the man leaned his face toward to confirm his identity. All of the floor indicator buttons flashed from white to pale blue, and suddenly the numbers appeared different. They no longer indicated the former selection of vertical destinations. It was an entirely different set of numbers being displayed in a weird looking font. After observing the man press the bottom button, which now indicated "SB09", the Foyles began to notice that they were rapidly going down to a deep sub-basement level. They nervously looked at one another with an uneasy exchange of moderate nonverbal panic. Shannon could not help but speak in order to try and ascertain the degree of panic that would be needed to get them through the next hours.

"Excuse me, uh...what was your name sir?"

Without averting his eyes away from the double-doors, the man replied with a rather incongruent response to the question being asked of him.

"Everything will be explained soon ma'am. There's no need to worry," he said calmly in his naturally deep voice.

"Ohhhh...,"replied Shannon with a lightly enunciated whisper and a hint of subtle sarcasm. "One of *thooose* names...I get it now."

The time for conversation expired just in time for everyone to be spared further awkwardness as the elevator car came to a smooth stop. The door opened to reveal an oversized tubular corridor curving back in the direction of the area underneath the airport. The faint sound of a hundred chatting voices could be heard getting louder as the mysterious escort led the two uneasy scientists to an open double doorway. Inside was a large amphitheater-style auditorium with a 270-degree audience area. There were 40 or 50 rows of cascading fold-down seating available and a little over half of the seats were already filled with strangers.

"I have always dreamed of seeing a top secret sumo wrestling tournament, but I never imagined a podium and armed guards in the dream...is this what they've been hiding under here all these years?" asked Jared rhetorically, now struggling to conceal his concern for the unexpectedly secretive looking appearance of the whole event.

"What is this Jared?" asked Shannon. "What is so important that DSECC would need a cloak and dagger approach?"

"Well it makes sense actually...they wouldn't have gone to the trouble of flying us here if it were something 'normal' as it were. Do you think they are going to..."

Jared was interrupted by feedback coming from the public address system, which had obviously just been switched on by someone preparing the podium for a speaker.

"Excuse me, excuse me everyone...could we all just take our seats please? We'd like to go ahead and get started here. Yes...thank you, thank you very much for coming here today" said the man with his right arm raised high to direct everyone's attention to the podium area. "For those of you who have not already had the pleasure, I would like to introduce you to the Secretary of the Deep Space Expeditionary Command Council, Madame Nancy Alon.

The attendees were all a little confused as to whether to applaud or not. It felt more like a "just pay attention in silence" kind of event. The collective conscience of the audience had indeed chosen to remain quiet without conferring, and the stern-faced, darkly clad appearance of the Secretary seemed to confirm without words that this was not the kind of gathering where people applauded. This was a gathering of people who were about to be told something sensitive.

"Good morning to you all. I am inspired to see that most of the individuals whose presence was requested made it here safe and sound. For those of you who arrived this morning on red-eye flights, please feel free to consume your morning caffeine tonics without regard for formality. Those of you in the 'elixir' category may want to take notes and eat some crackers. We had to bring you here today with an impromptu approach, to an unlikely place, because we needed to keep you safe. Any known affiliation with DSEF places you all at elevated risk, as I am sure you were well aware of before coming here today."

The Secretary turned to her right with her slide-advance control as the extra-large presentation screen lit up and the auditorium lights were dimmed. The first slide was just a bulleted text line entitled "*Operation Kibo*". The Secretary looked away from the screen back toward the crowd of scattered people and adjusted her microphone angle one last time before clearing her throat and beginning to speak. The screen behind her changed to video mode and began showing familiar footage of all the photos and videos that were being shown in the mainstream media at the time of the *Kibo* disaster. She deliberately allowed the spectating group to observe the images and media recordings in silence for about 12 to 15 seconds. It was just about the amount of time it took for her anger to boil over when she was viewing it the previous night in her lodging pod. She decided it would be the appropriate primer material for what she knew would later come as a shock to all those in attendance.

"Five summers ago on the afternoon of August 6th, I was sitting on the back porch of my house with my children and grandchildren in Colorado Springs drinking iced tea and enjoying a mild summer day with a cool breeze. We were all together filled with hope and optimism about the future of space exploration. The *ESS Earth 1* crew audio was live, and Commander Xu had just issued the order to send the first shuttle down to the surface of Mars to begin the long-anticipated process of human colonization on the planet's surface. Their first order of business was to conduct an intense search for life in the *Valles Marineris*; specifically, the *Noctis Labyrinthus* region in the western end of the canyon system. It was the first step of the Martian planetary protection protocol. But while we were all enjoying the smell of grilled picnic food and feeling good about life, these 16 individuals were scattered across the planet anticipating the imminent hour of their cowardly attacks on the *Earth 1*, and against our ground control stations across the country." The Secretary advanced through successive video surveillance footage clips of the nine men and seven women sneaking into various DSEF facilities with backpacks that were presumably full of high-explosives. She continued moving through the background segment of her speech, which by now was straining the ability of those present to continue listening.

"Nobody knows exactly what transpired on the *Earth 1* that day. All we know for certain is that its destruction was perfectly synchronized with the attacks here on the ground, and that the attackers were part of a larger terrorist network with an ideological doctrine that permits them to commit mass murder. Now, I can speak for myself and tell you that by late evening on the 6th, I had already decided hours earlier that these soulless people were not going to get in the way of our mission. But not everyone in the UGC agreed with me. In fact, this graphic here summarizes the extent to which the world's leaders were divided by early September." The Secretary advanced the slide to show a slowly rotating three-dimensional earth model against the backdrop of space with various landmasses throbbing red to indicate reactive defunding of global space initiatives.

"The Command Council worked tirelessly behind the scenes attempting to convince the UGC that going forward on the supercruiser contracts was the right thing to do. We reasoned that, until such time as the world once again regained its ability to hope, we could not simply press the pause button on such a grand economic scale. We tried to appeal to their practical sensibilities. By the spring of 22', we had convinced them to allow the public contracts to mature. Later that year by summer's end, after showing them in confidence that we could still achieve the goals of *Kibo*, they were willing to begin privately funding Operation *Kaminari*. Publicly however, they demanded secrecy. We have steadfastly complied with their every request until today."

Secretary Alon advanced a series of three blank slides, and then revealed a photo with the fourth click that drew various gasps and sounds of verbal shock from many within the gathering of increasingly anxious onlookers. It was a vertically panoramic high-definition photo of an obviously gigantic structure extending upward into the sky from the surface of a large body of water. The thick structure was shown with a proportionally oversized base structure and was observed to be disappearing up into an enormous array of dark nimbostratus clouds.

"This photo was taken in the summer of 2017. It was never shown to the public. There are still only 8,217 people on planet Earth who even *know* that this project ever made it this far along. The rest of humanity is still under the impression that the project never made it past the initial fanfare."

The Secretary advanced the next slide and quickly revealed its nature. "This is HEIWA last month. It is one of the two primary fruits of all the 'fuzzy math' of the last decade and a half."

This time, those in attendance could only examine the photo in silent, awestruck bewilderment, as they carefully searched the huge image in vain for signs of hoax or imperfection. There were seven separate tether lines trailing off into the sky, with an incomplete eighth line sticking up out of its individual base structure like a giant lightning-damaged tree trunk. The incomplete line was actually HEIWA-1. The ocean surface at the HEIWA site was now depicted with seemingly endless fields of windmill arrays and heavy-duty dark-blue buoys interspersed between them. Two of the tethers had extraordinarily large container-looking objects built onto them so as to be curvilinear and adjoining horizontally along a circuitous octagonal perimeter of the base complex. There were giant ships and barges shown going in and out of the primary gateway to the interior of the octagon.

"The HEIWA complex is fully operational, with the obvious exception of HEIWA-1 here. You might have noticed it has not been completed, nor does anyone expect it to be anytime soon. Southern supply lines to the complex were cut off four days ago by an exceedingly large fleet of Hammerhead-35 and Dimsho-38 hunter-killer attack subs. With our present nano-production capacity, it will take our robotic friends four months to grow enough nanotubes to replace that which has been lost off of the barges in the past 96 hours. Even if we had time to complete the final tether, it is simply not practical to do so. The supercruiser that was supposed to have been moored above HEIWA-1 would still need to be constructed after the tether is completed. But we are out of time. We and the UGC are unanimously agreed that now is the time to initiate the operational phases of Operation *Kaminari*. We need all of you...along with all of your families, pets, coffee machines, pillows, photo albums, friends, and heirloom wedding rings...to leave the planet immediately."

Everyone present was stunned and sent back into their seats with few exceptions. This was not at all what they were expecting. Usually these so-called important meetings were consultations and short-term solicitations of expertise. The secretary began talking again before a chain-reaction flurry of questions was allowed to take hold.

"Every friendly Navy in the Pacific is working to reopen the domestically connected shipping lanes. We are counting on them to deliver you and everything you own...up to 32,000 kilograms per household...to the HEIWA complex and up into geosynchronous orbit, where you will board one of seven supercruisers and detach into space untethered. The losses of both vital freight and human life have been staggering. In addition to sunken barges loaded with nanotubes, tactically significant defensive capabilities have been heavily degraded by the Hammerhead and Dimsho packs. If we cannot open the shipping lanes, then we will fly you to the complex. If we cannot fly you there, then we will hitchhike, commandeer, swim, row, slingshot, catapult, or airdrop you from the stratosphere if it should become necessary. We need you *out there*!" The Secretary pointed up toward space and held her static non-verbal gesture until she perceived that all those present had understood the urgency.

      Jared and Shannon finally dared to look one another in the eye as Secretary Alon reached down for her water bottle. Their minds were filled with all of the implications of what they had just heard. Jared noticed that the beginning of Chopin's Marcha Fúnebre had started to creep subtly into his mind's background audio system. His sense of dread about what would happen to all of them had dramatically intensified. The reality of their probable future painted a picture of broken interpersonal relationships, manifestations of depressive anxiety, and untreated guilt. Shannon was in shock at the realization that they were all entering the "interplanetary systems of civilization" era on such short notice. She could not stop thinking about everything she had to do before they left; the cleaning, the packing, the persuading of reluctant loved ones...the boxes of old vinyl records in the attic? She could not get over the dramatic difference between merely *believing* that this would happen eventually, versus the *real* experience of going through it. It was mind-numbing for any human to think in these terms without more specific knowledge of the changes that were to be applied to the many small processes of human life. Their trances were quietly interrupted by the Secretary beginning to speak again; this time in a comparatively quieter voice than before.

"We have mechanized packing crews on standby prepared to seal and cube your entire material life...and they are very thorough. If you could only see fit to address the human issues this dire request has brought upon you, then it is my solemn promise to you that every material article of your life will be safeguarded, loaded, and placed in the respective section of your designated ship. Your cube will be accessible to you at any time unless the ship is experiencing an emergency that requires you to remain in your quarters for safety. All you need to do for now is prepare a 300 kilo express baggage shipment of things you and your immediate family deem necessary for your first two weeks. That is our best estimate of how long it might take for the utterly disorienting experience of being cast into space to begin resembling something more routine to the uninitiated. You will be in a one-g environment once aboard. But you will be in microgravity from shortly after beginning your HEIWA ascent until you reach the corridor leading to the one-g area of your ship. Please review the ship assignments before leaving here this morning. You will need to come up here closer to see it. For operational security reasons, the text has been made intentionally small. Please leave any digital devices in the seat you currently occupy before coming down closer. We cannot afford for this information to fall into the wrong hands."

The Secretary advanced the slide to a comprehensive listing of all the personnel present for this session and their respective ship assignments. Relatively few of the many who were present felt the need to immediately go and check the listing. But over the course of several minutes, more and more of the attendees were making their way down the aisles to view the list. The ambient conversation volume was gradually increasing when Shannon turned to Jared and asked him, "Do you have any antacids on you?"

"Yes, as a matter of fact, I have been in the habit of keeping a small pouch full of sodium bicarbonate in the inside zipper pouch of my attaché for several years now.

I find it to be more convenient than flavored chewable vitamin-enhanced chalk pellets," Jared replied with a nervously cheerful laugh. It was endearing to him that his delicate Shannon-flower required regular pH adjustments like an unruly aqueous solution when she became acutely overwhelmed. He was pretty sure they would get along famously in space. But he had no idea how he was going to convince his great grandmother Beatrice that she would still be able to get extra-stout beer and Friday night boxing videos in space. *Maybe if I just tell her the truth she'll surprise me and want to go*, he thought. Jared marveled at himself for not being more concerned with the prospect of dying a horrific death aboard a spaceship. Mastery of personal fear hinged on understanding where the fear comes from, and he wasn't entirely sure yet if there was anything beyond the obvious to be truly fearful of in the first place.

Opportunity Knocks

Earth
Sector AK-0006
December 11, 2025 C.E.
Thursday
1352 HRS

    The Detachment IV crew was sitting around the holo-projector trying to occupy themselves with something besides worry and anxiety. But it did not come naturally to the normally busy crew to just linger and loiter. There was always something that needed to be done somewhere. Today they were needed in the common area of the bunker complex to receive a message that was sure to contain important information. They had specific instructions to be present and to be on time. Still, they could not sit still. They sensed that the pace of life was accelerating, and that soon there would be precious little time to do anything but work and maintain high focus for long periods of time in a high-intensity test of mental and physical agility. Just as the subdued chatter of the room was gradually becoming louder and full of the more relaxed sounds of human life like laughter, the holo-projector beam turned on and the audio channel began beeping to prepare the listener to listen. Sergeant Kahmay's image popped up as a one-sixth scale projection standing on top of the water cooler.

"Hey...where is Rufus?" asked Kahmay's scaled down image. "Rufus! Where are you?"

Everyone began looking around the room for Specialist Rufus Mayfield at his three favorite hangout spots; the table-tennis station, the dartboard, and the refrigerator. Then the familiar sound of the high-powered government toilet flushing in the background broke the silence as the bathroom door flew open and Rufus replied, "Right here! Right here!"

"I wanted you to be front and center when you heard it man! They scored the package at 97.4! We could change major aspects of the original and it would still fly with room to spare so..."

The room erupted with expressions of happiness and rhetorical questions, and some who were sitting now sprung up out of their chairs with animated arm-waving, and shouts of "YES" and "YEEEEEEEEEEEUHHH". Specialist Mayfield was the first one to bring in a draft copy of the kind of ops-plan DSECC would approve back in early 22'. He had been sitting in front of a projection screen for many days and nights drafting the first copy of the ops-plan at a time when nobody believed such work would bear any fruit at all. The concept of DSECC outsourcing the supercruiser missions was flimsy speculation, and most people had no inclination to believe it would ever happen. Mayfield really made an impression on Kahmay at the time, because the ebb of the tide of optimism in 22' was so dramatic that only an innocent, fresh kind of soul like his was capable of bringing new optimism to the table.

Kahmay was not yet finished with the conference call and was ready to continue hitting the key points. She tried to get the crew to calm down a little bit and listen up for the next important piece of her delivery.

"HEY, HEY, HEY...SHHHH...LISTEN UP...SHHHH!" Several long moments went by until everyone was finally quieted down and once again looking back in the direction of the NCOIC's projected image. Once again Kahmay began explaining the approval in more detail as everyone sat riveted to news of the confirmed reality that they would be leaving the planet soon.

"Our first destination cannot be discussed over unsecure channels like this. But I can tell you that the *X-Tensai* will be our next stop on the long road to Edo-00010011. Do whatever you want for the rest of the night because I plan on going out of my way to make you all suffer after the holidays. You've earned the night off. Please don't go anywhere alone, and use the buddy system at all times. I consider *all* of you to be the most important assets of our shared future out there. If you insist on leaving the complex tonight, please leave your comm-units on. There's a lot to do and I might need you to come back in a hurry...so don't go far, and don't...," suddenly Kahmay was interrupted by none other than Specialist Rufus Mayfield himself.

"Yes, yes mom...we get it. We're your family, and you don't want your family getting hurt right before 'go time'. It's two o'clock in the afternoon, minus 37 centigrade, nearly pitch black outside, and we may as well be on Mars. Now, who wants to stay in and order pizza and just chill at home tonight?"

"DART TOURNAMENT!" shouted Specialist Lenihan.

"Can we get pineapple? I love pineapple," said Hutch with a lick of his lips.

"Yeah, and Canadian bacon would be nice...and incidentally, what's the difference between Canadian bacon and say...California bacon?" asked Specialist Penelope Gordon to anyone who might have had the answer.

Specialist Tamara Levi pushed her glasses back up onto her nose and decided to try and address the question as she did all questions that were asked rhetorically.

"More than likely, you are referring to 'back bacon' since you are what is colloquially considered to be one-hundred percent "Yank". But I do not wish to commit to that as my final response because, the ongoing development of bacon, along with its many evolutions of constitution and nomenclature, are changing too rapidly to be accurately accounted for at any one moment in time. You may be referring to 'peameal' bacon, or one of the lesser known varieties of 'bacourcky'...which can be an indication of a potential cultural exclusion of any manner of pork or bovine derivation not listed in the more frequently queried repositories of recipes and exhaustive and/or abridged culinary references. I can tell you where to look for the answers to questions like that and other such trivial matters of...oh, you weren't really looking for an answer...okay, okay that's alright. My bad, I thought...I guess I just..."

Specialist Levi's dear friend Penelope interjected to relieve the social awkwardness that was developing as Tamara's speech became increasingly more jammed up by uncertainty.

"It's okay Tam...it's okay. It's comforting to know that your encyclopedia module is working while the rest of us fall victim to the fleeting mortal euphoria of long-awaited, life-altering news from a holographic projection. It instills a certain feeling of safety in my heart that I can't quite explain...but that I can recognize when it happens. I'm so glad you are you" said Penelope with a sincere smile.

"Well...yes, I am glad *you* are *you*...as well," said Specialist Levi, folding her hands behind her back to disguise her personal reservations about such vagaries as gladness and sadness.

Tamara Levi volunteered to enlist with DSEF on the afternoon of her graduation from the school of "stay in your room and master these 700 reference books before you come out". Her adoptive family had lived in sector CA-0033 going back three generations to the early 20th century. In the mid-1990s when she was a toddler, she spent a lot of time alone as an only child. Her parents were descended from a family culture of extraordinary dedication, and rarely ever spared the rod of discipline when it came to school work and household chores. In the summer times of her young life, Tamara's family brought her into the agriculturally rich central valley of the California territory. The three of them worked in the fruit and nut orchards for fun, and to get away from the stifling noises of the big city for a while. It was there in the orchards that Tamara discovered her passion for dried apricots and smoked almonds.

It was very difficult socially for Specialist Levi in her youth. Endless confrontation with ignorant people about her African-American parents rarely ever yielded anything more than hateful slander and disappointment.

In the absence of meaningful interpersonal connection to others, she forced herself to become academically better than her peers, and drove herself to near madness in the pursuit of knowledge, skills, and abilities. The net result of her life had transformed her into a master of facts and machine-like decision-making. She was tough, had a strong work ethic, and would go out of her way to help her teammates. Besides her adoptive parents, her teammates were the only other family she knew.

"Whatever you say guys" said Kahmay. "I gotta go back and rejoin the others now. The C-330 from sector JP-0046E finally arrived over at HEIWA this morning after playing chicken for two and a half weeks since leaving sector 46. Travel time to HEIWA from here in sector 99 and from there in sector 6 is expected to be pretty slow-going so it's time to move now people. Every boat leaving the coast could end up being the last one before everything is closed off. They're having a hard time keeping the lanes open."

Locked and Loaded

Earth
Sector OR-0042
December 20, 2025 A.D.
Saturday
2317 HRS

The late evening darkness made everything feel a little more difficult for Church and Marie, as they worked past sunset to get the GEMINI 2050 and the single box trailer loaded and secured for the long journey north into the Alaska-Canadian territory. Marie would be driving their little 4-cylinder hybrid compact car as a chase vehicle. Neither of them had ever been to the northern territories in all of their years. But they had always wanted to go and see the untainted beauty of the far northern sectors of the United States since a young age. They never imagined their grand northern adventure would commence at the beginning of winter, nor did they foresee that it would be their last stop on the road to outer space.

The McGradys had decided weeks ago after Kahmay's visit that they would both take a paid month off to seal up the homestead, function-test the security system upgrades, and micromanage the freight configuration. They had to leave room in the back of the GEMINI's box-trailer for the precious cargo pick-up at kilometer-marker 3,916 in the Yukon province of the Canada territory. All Kahmay could tell them nine days ago were the grid coordinates and the dimensions of the extra space that would be required to accommodate the four pallets they would be picking up from a man codenamed "Reaper". Kahmay was also careful to specify that there was nothing to be afraid of, and that "Reaper" was actually quite friendly once you understood what he was reaping.

In all of their years of working full time hours, Church and Marie had never taken more than a week off work at a time, save the one time back in 97' when a triple-jeopardy combo-punch scenario involving death, sickness, and catastrophic mechanical failure of their vital privately-owned vehicles hit them all at once and required both of them to take 59.57 hours of paid-time-off in conjunction with a weekend. It was awkward for them to be at home and still be paid for their daytime minutes. But they knew they needed extra time to methodically address the many small decisions they were still faced with making before their departure.

They sought to extract the value of their remaining paper currency by converting 70 percent of their life savings into nutritious food, equipment to freeze-dry and preserve nutritious food, and special EMP-shielded ground radio equipment systems. Something in Church's gut told him he needed to purchase a satellite phone system with uniform replacement parts kits and triple redundant back-up units. He wondered if some of the more technology-oriented people onboard the ship might be able to find a way to make early use of the phones in the near-Earth region of space. It made sense to the multi-talented McGrady that tapping into the satellite systems already in orbit around the Earth would be both practical and possible. He suspected future satellite systems might be deployed around other planets, and a dedicated back-up comm-gear stash would be mighty welcome in the event of an untimely coup or mutiny. *But how reliable is this so-called software-based 3-D printing plan gonna really play out though...really*, he thought. He wondered whether the "thing-printing" infrastructure would be able to handle the production of so many "things"; especially large "things". He was only slightly reassured by his recollection of Kahmay mentioning to him that the first things produced were going to be the machines required to produce *other* machines. Church remembered how he and his older brother Presto used to joke as children back in the 1960s about how the '*blah-blah-blah*' technology had a funny way of going '*bing-bong-bang*' when you most needed it to go '*ying-yong-yang*'. Church had a notoriously close relationship with the philosophy of William of Ockham, and he just knew that somehow the phones would come in handy for a prolonged layover period after all the so-called "advanced" equipment had given out.

Each physical object on the homestead was identified with a color-coded destination tag. The red tags were reserved for scrap, rubbish, and giveaways. Not that they had a plan for every red tag. But once an item qualified for a red tag, the decision about its future would not need to be discussed further from that point on. The time saved by only needing to make one decision about the future of a terra cotta planter pot was priceless. Both the mister and the misses agreed that they could definitely do without terra cotta. Having the composition and known facts about terra cotta stored in triplicate on supercomputers would be good enough for now. Those kinds of files included, but were not limited to; production techniques, substitute materials, and special considerations. That would be enough.

Yellow tags identified the highest priority items, and each had a number to indicate the order in which the items were to be loaded into the front of the main trailer cube. Green tags indicated items that could be left alone entirely. Church placed green tags on a few of the derelict pick-up truck carcasses. The carcasses were originally dragged over by the tractor to strategic points along the homestead perimeter to provide fortified high-ground firing positions over-watching the canyon to the east, and the river valley below to the west. He found himself wondering if the day may yet come when the tribe would need to rely on such measures.

One of the McGradys' biggest concerns in life was that humans would unwittingly end up in an oppressive dark age. Of course, they couldn't have been more right about that. Their fears were based on hard truth. Ever since the spring of 2011, the media had become flooded with a vast number of stories about ongoing civil wars, military escalations, terrorist provocations, mass murders, and any number of other glaringly obvious signs that the deterioration of modern human civilization was well under way. By 2019, even the most pacifist humans felt they needed to take *some* action to defend their lives from this now inevitable-looking onslaught. The scourge that now threatened the free world was formless and unpredictable. It was pure evil flowing through the path of least resistance like electricity. It seemed the only goal of the evil was to place itself in the face of those who would dare pretend it did not exist.

Perhaps the most annoying evil for the McGradys as midnight on the eve of the solstice approached was the cruelty of knowing that they would be heading out onto a remote foreign highway at night, driving into the dead of the Northern Hemisphere winter, and with a load of stuff they would be taking to outer space. Somehow even that scenario didn't feel so bad to the couple after a nice strong cup of coffee.

"Hey babe" Marie called out. She peeked her head around the shop bay door from outside. "You in here?" she asked.

"Yeah, yeah...over here sweetie," replied Church, mildly surprised by Marie's abrupt presence. Fatigue and late evening silence in the dimly-lit vehicle maintenance bay had hypnotized him into a standing slumber.

Marie squeezed her way into the maintenance bay through the space between the bay door threshold and the passenger side of the truck. "What you doin' in here?" she asked.

"Well, I'm just wondering whether or not to deflate some of these spares so that if we run into any uphill ice we might have a better shot at crawling up the mountains before having to get out and put chains on. My brain is fried though hon. I don't think it's safe for us to leave tonight. Honestly...we'll get out there and have a good hundred miles or so behind us, and then I'll start seeing phantoms run across the road that aren't really there. Know what I'm sayin'? White-line fever type of stuff ya know?"

"I know...I was thinking the same thing a little while ago. I was up at the double-sink watering my African violets, and for the life of me, I couldn't remember why I should even bother," said Marie, lowering her head in tired relaxation.

"Kahmay said it's alright to bring those violets babe. You remember her sayin' that? You're not going into space without those violets Mare...just ain't gonna happen. They're a part of you, and they're comin' with us...end of story. I'm just about done here. Why don't you bring those down to me so I can stash 'em away in this little cubbyhole down under the bed?" Church opened the truck sleeper's driver's side suicide door and pointed down underneath the mattress platform to a small empty cavity with white glossy side panels. "Now check this out." he said, reaching up to turn on a small switch. Small tubular lights lit up the cavity with enough blue-spectrum 6500-degree color temperature light to grow a small bonsai almond orchard. "See, there's no need to say goodbye to the violets babe..."

"Oh my God...is that what you have been doing down here all this time?" asked Marie, shocked and surprised that her beloved husband would still go to so much effort to safeguard her happiness over the "little-big things" in life.

"Yeah, but like I said, I was also contemplating letting some of the air out of a few of these spares, and wondering whether or not to red tag your dad's old magnehelic gauge. That old gauge reminds me of how important patience and humility are in life. I always loved your dad Mare...I respected him in ways...that I can't even describe. He was like a dad to me in so many ways" said Church.

Church was a mess inside. He knew they had to leave during the hours of darkness. Kahmay would not have specified as much if there were not an important reason. But in his overtired state, he felt helpless letting go of so much history. He and Marie had poured their full hearts into the homestead, and the thought of meandering strangers urinating all over his sword ferns and salmonberries was hard for him to accept.

"Kahmay left this for you last month. She told me not to give it to you until the day we left," said Marie. She produced a small envelope with the word, "Dad" written on the outside. Church did not want to grab it with his greasy hands, but he was immediately curious about the contents of the envelope. "You want me to take it out and show it to you?" asked Marie.

"Yeah, yeah...could ya? My hands are all screwed up," he said.

Marie carefully pulled the small slip of folded paper out of the envelope and opened it up to begin reading it.

"It says, *'Hey man. I left you a surprise inside the back part of the cinder block wall where that little piece of rebar is sticking out. Hope you like it. Please don't leave sector 42 without it. Love you always, Kahmay XOXO P.S. You guys please be so careful out there.'* What do you think it is babe?"

"I couldn't even begin to guess at this hour. But I know we're not leaving without it" said Church. "Wanna come with?" he asked. Church grabbed his flashlight and took Marie by the hand. They walked slowly up the steep driveway incline to the cinder block wall behind their house. Church shined the light onto the spot on the back of the wall where he remembered a small piece of rebar sticking out. He placed his hand on it and tried to wiggle it like he thought it was going to open up the whole wall, but there were no signs of any automated mechanisms. He reached down inside the hollow section of the wall under the rebar and touched what felt like a bundle of plastic lying diagonally down inside the crumbling hollow interior of the wall. Pulling the bundle up and out of the wall, he handed the light to Marie so that he could take the plastic wrapping off of the mysterious object. It was an old M-50M multi-weapon that looked like it had never even been used at all.

"Wow" said Marie with a smile and a laugh. "She remembered! You were nagging her for years about that. She kept telling you she would get it at the auction, and you kept pushing her buttons to make her think you didn't believe her so she would hurry. I swear...that girl...will only go slower when you tell her to go faster. HA! Cool! Okay, let's go. No time to test it out. Put it on the back of the truck so it will be the first thing off. Deal?"

"Sounds good honey. I'm too tired to function test it anyway" said Church, slightly disappointed that he didn't have the energy or the time to acquaint himself with the M-50M. But he was consoled by the recollection that he had been saving small crates of the different kinds of specialized ammo for the M-50M for years in anticipation of finally procuring the end-item weapon. He tried not to let his mind wander about which function of the weapon was best to use in a given situation. He knew they had to get going. "Let's have one more look at the checklist so we can at least make it over to the next county before sunrise" he said.

"I have it right here," said Marie, "Nothing has changed in hours. Doff your anxiety and don your gear McGrady. All we have to do now is drive down to the bottom of the canyon and set the briar system. If they lose power in this sector, the briar grid is still going to be set to give the collection cells access to the sun during the longest three non-transitory enemy satellite surveillance periods. I'm setting the consumption rate at level 2 for the hours of darkness, and less-than-or-equal to +7% of nominal-natural during the daytime so the batteries can charge and still blend in thermally on the spectrum. All other periods will show a formless briar stand with no unusual thermals or angular characteristics. Should last on autopilot for about...12 to 15 years...but anything could happen. We just won't know until we get back here to see it someday."

"Okay then. I'm ready to kick the tires if you are. I'm glad you're on top of this Mare. I had no idea you knew so much about all that. Sounds like you got it set exactly how you guys talked about. Do me a favor and flash your high-beams at me if you see me starting to ride the line too much" said Church. He finished securing the M-50M in the very back of the trailer being careful not to deny himself access to the weapon system from the front hatch. Church designed the access system so the trailer was joined to the sleeper with a flexible conduit system and a cypher lock to gain entry from either side. The anchors for the flexible conduit were thick solid aluminum elbow pieces that he selected for universal compatibility with the various load-mating configurations on the list Kahmay had given him a while back.

The McGradys started the truck engine and held one another in a prolonged embrace, as the unique sounding whistle of the turbo diesel filled the background ambience with the sounds of progress, and the smell of victory. The workshop's wood-pellet stove creaked intermittently as it cooled off in the back corner of the workshop and struggled to keep the last of the dying maple pellets glowing orange. Church rather enjoyed the feeling of wood-fired warmth in the workshop over the winters. Sector OR-0042 was known for its high humidity and menacing storms in the winter. It had always been medicine for his soul to be warm while he was rebuilding a tractor transmission, or fixing yet another broken household appliance.

It seemed the powers that be had smiled upon them with great favor as they prepared to test their security upgrades and head out into calm conditions and unseasonably mild temperatures. Church placed a gentle kiss on the cheek of his beloved Marie, and the two of them grabbed their coffees with a resolute firmness. Marie took one last look into the outer zipper compartment of her shoulder bag to make sure her little pouch of loose-leaf green tea for their first pit stop was tucked safely inside. Church locked the workshop one last time and looked at the keys in his hand with the faith of a man who knew he was coming back someday. He decided then and there that he would keep the keys on his person for a while as a reminder of all the reasons why their plight was indeed worthwhile.

Both the truck and the hybrid crept quietly down the long, steep twisting driveway without betraying anything beyond the idle rpms of the truck to the ears of the rainforest. The hybrid would be all but completely silent until they had sufficiently drained the battery enough to kick on its hydrogen cell. They got out of their vehicles, which were now parked and running with no lights on at the bottom of the canyon. The security system upgrade was basically a remote-enabled fatal-retribution system. Kahmay had rigged it so the homestead satellite uplink could be received aboard the *X-Tensai* for as long as the closed loop power system at the homestead still functioned. The McGradys were unsure of whether it could withstand the test of time and looters. They nonetheless carefully rolled aside the natural feature that concealed the control pad and entered in their arming code. They moved away from the front gate and slowly stepped backwards toward their vehicles waiting for the tiny green pin-diode indicators that were nestled back into the evergreens to light up. The diodes lit up gradually one-by-one and then extinguished. It was visually seamless the way they looked exactly like some kind of near-undetectable firefly that was so naturally green that a person would surely come to the conclusion it was a species native to the forest if they were not local. The briars up the hill that were concealing the power collection panels were drawn over the hardware like curtains. Everything was working exactly as they had hoped.

The range of the remote command and control part of the system was limited. But Kahmay seemed hopeful that the system would communicate as far away as Pluto and beyond. Of course, watching a video of someone breaking the windows out of the cabin and setting fire to it from hundreds of millions of miles away would make immediate response impractical. Any response would be significantly delayed by the limitations of light speed across the solar system. The idea was to make the homestead an inviting place, where people would take care not to destroy that which might sustain them through a cold night. There would be plenty of time to remotely trigger the booby traps after a thorough study of the invaders could be made from the ship. Murderers and rapists would have to be summarily killed by one of several static fully-automatic crossbow bolt delivery systems. Foreign ideological invaders would be killed slowly with extreme prejudice, and with the national anthem playing over the public address system in the background. Allied troops and Beaver militia would be granted access to the armory, ammo dump, and vehicle fleet. Church felt the need to leave notes inside the nicer trucks he couldn't bring with him, asking the potential user of the vehicles to, "Please take care of my truck, and bring her back when you're finished, and I won't hurt you when I return". Church packed most of the McGradys' nicer weapons onto the big rig for use off-planet. But he left a few shotguns in plain sight and some old archery equipment under the floorboards in the guest bathroom. His bread and butter truck was an old 10-wheel drive Yankee-900, or as Church preferred to call it, the "Tote Goat". The packing drones had completely disassembled her and wrapped her up with hermeti-seal for inclusion into the McGradys' main household goods shipment. Church could not believe all of that truck could fit into such a tiny cube when it was packed by a machine. He was mostly just ecstatic that he was allowed to bring it at all. It was terminally distracting for him to think about driving the "Tote Goat" on a different planet.

   Survival rations for unaffiliated civilian non-combatants were stored in large sealed shipping containers and buried at locations known only to the members of the family for the time being. If allied survivors had managed to make it into the safety of the cabin, then the McGradys would be able to unlock the cellar remotely from inside the ship. The rations in the cellar would provide enough supplies to keep a large group alive through the longest of winters. Marie placed blankets and small stuffed animals on the children-sized bunk beds so that well-meaning travelers would be comforted by the unspoken gestures of empathy.

The McGradys made their way out into the night as quietly as possible, and tried not to look back. They knew the secret to happiness did not dwell exclusively in one physical place. Happiness would be where their hearts were, and that was out there in space with Lacey, Kahmay, Rebecca, and all of the grandchildren. That simple realization alone carried them out of sector OR-0042 and placed them firmly into their new urgent reality.

E.S.S. X-Tensai

Earth
En route to Sector HI-0007
December 24, 2025 C.E.

It was quite unexpected to have so many calls coming in during the initial days following the official announcements of December 11th. Kahmay was not in the mood to be answering phones, but knew it would be necessary to address the interested contractors with immediate urgency. For the sake of everyone that would be aboard the *X-Tensai,* they had to get the best deal possible. Specialist Conway had already taken five messages from five different corporations and Kahmay was exceedingly thankful that she did not have to listen to strangers over the phone just yet. She was not ready to bring her mind to that special place where only accountants and comptrollers could dwell for very long. Planning strategies for *Kaminari* was one thing the Sergeant knew how to do well. However, to participate in the microeconomic discussions of it all without becoming bored to tears was always a challenge for her. The outside inquiries were not yet about numbers. But in Kahmay's eyes, all outside relations were sure to morph into something related to money eventually. All but one of the calls were general inquiries from mining companies. It was that fifth call that had Kahmay's predictive mind tied up for the moment.

"Please tell me about that last call one more time Conway. It seemed strange when you explained it to me the first time. You said he sounded different? Like, maybe he wasn't an ordinary profiteer?"

"Yeah, said he owned some hotel-casino resorts and thought maybe we could establish a dialogue about how we might be able to establish a 'flourishing synergy' with one another. But he didn't sound as eager as the mining companies. He was calling from sector DU-0003...didn't have an accent either...which I thought was a little out of place...I mean, *besides* the use of the word 'flourishing' of course." said Conway.

"Out of place how? In what way precisely?" asked Kahmay.

"Well, I don't think he was from Dubai. Didn't hear one revealing diphthong...which probably means he's either American or Canadian. Think about it...how many people have *you* ever talked to who sound exactly like...nobody...and everybody...all at once? But even the Canadians have little clues and nuances in their enunciations compared to us...so I'm guessing he's a worldly lower 48 Yankee, maybe...an ex-pat from the pirate or mercenary ilk."

Kahmay shook her head side to side in disbelief of the fact that they were even spending time talking about these things in the first place.

"Hotels and slot machines in space...wow, that sounds farfetched even to me! But that's the way it's going to go I guess...people are going to need a place to stay, and the ones providing the beds, showers, and entertainment are going to need all the capital they can get their hands on to build the next one and the next one so...maybe we should call him back...in a few days."

"Maybe" said Conway with her head intentionally leaned in, and her left eyebrow dramatically tilted up in sharp contrast to the right one. "You know, we have an opportunity here to avoid trouble and make a good choice. I would prefer spacious capsules like the ones in those hyper-efficient Japanese hotels. I heard about this one guy over in Eastern Europe...Slovakia maybe...or...was it Armenia? I don't quite remember but, he invented those ultrasimple, spacious, all-amenities capsules that are supposed to be almost impervious to cosmic radiation and ultra-high-energy subatomic field-fluctuations. I think he named them 'Planck-Pods'. You just plug them into the ship when the occupant needs to travel and voilà; that's their passenger berth while they're aboard. You know what I'm sayin'? Make the future of humans in space something practical and... modular I guess? Do you think mercenary-man has anything in his proposal repertoire that resembles these notions? We can wire-up say...a hundred or so...of those universal power interconnects to one of the four auxiliary power substations on the *X-Tensai*, then float the capsules over at the request of the 'guest'. We'll plug them into our grid and immediately afford them a sense of agency as they go about the process of say...applying their expertise toward the goal of everyone becoming self-sustaining and mobile? Perhaps we could even offer them a discount if they donated a fraction of their time and expertise to the long-term sustainability and improvement of the *X-Tensai*?"

Kahmay just didn't have the mind for business at the moment, and all of A.J.'s brainstorming was making her a little tired. Overly-utopian notions of "going green" in space were making her sick to her stomach for unexplained reasons. She worried that it was because she knew that business deals meant interacting with strangers and all of the problems that usually come with those strangers. There was entirely too much work to do before the profiteers could be allowed to prematurely commandeer the dialogue. Her mind began to drift toward more clearly defined concepts like mathematics-specifically trigonometry and astrophysics. She was calculating absolute acceleration and deceleration outcomes to avoid talking about business, and found it soothing to change the mass and velocity variables to give herself a representative sample curve of various outcomes for her mental drawing board. She had to know how to do those things if something were to incapacitate members of the crew, or otherwise degrade their human capability. More importantly; a life in space *demanded* a mastery of the knowledge and practices involved. She imagined a three-dimensional modeling frame in Earth's solar system and began placing the planets into their respective orbits with a slow-moving mental animation. She could not decide what strategy would be implemented, and the apparently infinite number of navigational choices clouded the more important issues like propulsion, intercept, and starvation. But one thing the Sergeant could not dismiss was the opportune coincidence that Mars would be in close opposition to Earth by the mid-terrestrial-winter of 27'. The *X-Tensai* and her escort would need to leave Earth's gravitational Hill Sphere no later than early autumn of 26' just to be safe. The distance between the two planets would be a larger fraction of the astronomical unit than what occurs over on the Capricorn side of the sun, when Mars would be in perihelion if opposition occurred on that side. Mars was unfortunately going to be near its *aphelion* in 27'. Additionally, even with the *X-Tensai's* unprecedented speed, the ship might still need to use Earth's perihelion advantage to slingshot around the sun over to the other side of the inner solar system in time to catch Mars if they missed their window. But the prospect of becoming mechanically disabled within the grasp of the sun was enough to discourage further thought on the subject. *No. Better to stay away from the sun if possible*, she thought.

More specific thoughts about the course for Mars were going to have to wait until a definite departure date from Earth's orbital path around the sun could be more accurately known. Kahmay felt relief in knowing that they had months remaining before they needed to leave Earth's orbit and that there was no reason to panic just yet about *that* part of the mission. She had not yet informed the crew that they needed to go to Mars and set up an elaborate base camp for Earth refugees. Most of them were only just now starting to fully realize that their initial stay in Earth orbit was going to be several months.

There were only a few hundred people within DSEF who had ever seen the data feeds from the final moments of Operation *Kibo*. The data would have shown the empirical reality that occurs when the initial impulse within the mostly unloaded supercruiser chassis is applied from a stationary Mars orbit. The *E.S.S. Earth 1* failed to complete proper transmission footer protocols for the last data packets of their final moments of transmission. The last packets would have contained the final aggregate Sigma error results. The propulsion to load calculations required final variables to continually reproof the move toward efficiency for the ideal course-curve limits. There was a built-in five-second delay before relaying new data to give the supercruiser mainframe time to duplicate and triplicate every piece of raw "delta-x" and "delta-t" data collected. Five seconds meant that the supercruiser mainframe was as slow as a slug on sedatives if it needed all that time to transmit. The name "supercruiser" was obviously *not* necessarily indicative of a commensurate "supercomputing" capability. It was mild false advertisement, and laughable to Kahmay that an enormous space cruiser would have such a basic computer for a mainframe. But then she felt immediately ashamed and humbled by the fact that so many humans had died breaking the trail for them all. There was a lot of really important non-compiled data in that last five-seconds besides just basic telemetry. But none of the non-compiled stuff was critical enough that it couldn't be carefully put to the test again. It was the obvious evacuation of archival data that concerned Kahmay the most. DSEF was still claiming they did not have any archival *Earth 1* data for things like hull degradation and real-world reactor efficiency curves. But Kahmay was trying to build a lower risk, longer-duration intercept to buy time for all of the things she knew would need to be worked out before they left Earth's universally accepted legal proximity zone. The navigational efficiency curves presently required at least basic supercomputers, and none were installed on any of the supercruisers because it was always assumed before Operation *Kaminari* that Earth would be the *X-Tensai's* return base. Now more than ever, the RIKEN exemplars Colonel Kleen had placed into the Operation *Oblivion* file jacket did indeed seem to be meant for supplementing the *X-Tensai's* mainframe. Operation *Oblivion* wasn't really an operation at all; it was turning out to be more of an idea-repository with a built-in Earth-egress contingency that assumed zero outside collaboration. They were going to upgrade the *X-Tensai* mainframe whether they needed to or not.

By now the Sergeant was drifting into an avalanche breakdown cycle of endless neurosis, and knew she needed to stand up and burn some calories. The psychiatric consequences of an overactive mind with no physiological baselines were dangerous. Without healthy fitness baselines, there would be no ground-reference from which to cull the over-rationalizations out of the "forest of hard and simple realities" in life. One could have a heart attack from something that was only in their mind. Kahmay was no stranger to the kind of physically-debilitating anxiety that leads to long-term chronic problems in the mind. In the Sergeant's case, she had been forced to fight against the urge to exact unilateral revenge against a deserving target outside of the law. But summary execution of a human pestilence without due process was a gross violation of the global capital code. Spending a lifetime in prison or being executed for premeditated murder would have defeated the whole purpose of carrying a justified grudge. Kahmay had not done the *right* thing, because it would have been the *wrong* thing.

"*Approaching Sector HI-0007,*" said the feminine-sounding voice of the shuttle computer. "*All personnel prepare to disembark. ETA seven minutes.*"

"Look at that…absolutely surreal…" said Conway, marveling at the sheer size and scale of the HEIWA complex, as their surface shuttle brought them closer to the landing zone. Kahmay looked out the small window on the starboard side of the shuttle and noticed the endless fields of wind turbines and dark-blue buoys that coated the ocean surface. She failed to notice the enormous stand of tethers that made up HEIWA-2 through 8 off in the distance at one o'clock. She brought her gaze back inside the shuttle and looked at Specialist Conway in an attempt to determine whether A.J. was impressed with the power farm, or if she was just admiring the vast beauty of the ocean from a high-speed, low-altitude vantage. Conway was instead staring off toward the horizon. Kahmay looked back out the window into the direction Conway was looking and saw the tethers trailing up into the sky for the first time.

"No way..." said Kahmay." You have got to be shitting me" she exclaimed with a whisper. "How in the *hell* did they do that?" she asked rhetorically.

"They didn't," said Conway, bringing her interpersonal presence back into the shuttle for the first time since initially spotting the monstrous structure. "Look" she said, pointing down to the windmills at a swarm of small-sized maintenance drones. The drones were moving like enormous schools of airborne minnows from grid to grid identifying areas within the power farm that required either preventive maintenance attention, or planarity position readjustment.

"Okay, now I'm starting to understand why the price of non-ferrous scrap in the Pacific Northwest has been so high for the past 20 years. I was really hoping they were going to solve at least part of this problem with the plastic onsite. Could have killed two birds but oh well" said Kahmay. She was feeling better now that she was slowly snapping out of her celestial mechanics trance and back into surface-reality.

"Yeah, they did...actually use the plastic...for boron-nitride reinforced carbon nanotubes I think" said Conway.

The shuttle gently placed them down on the landing pad and opened the starboard-side gull-wing door. After trotting over to the Heiwa-1 ground-complex arrival terrace, and finding refuge from the gusty wind underneath a protected breezeway, Kahmay and A.J. could see that they were surrounded by a very busy-looking scene. All seven operational tethers appeared to be in various modes of usage. The ascension pod for HEIWA-2 could be seen on final approach as it crawled the final 500 meters down to the ground platform at a slower speed than the standard descent speed for an empty pod. The words "Inuk'sik" were painted in black along the side of the dark gray pod. The human load crew at pier 2 stood by in anticipation of touchdown and was positioned so the individual workers could immediately begin transferring cargo from off of the freight barge that was moored at the adjacent pier. Kahmay panned her view clockwise toward HEIWA-7 and 8 just in time to notice that pods 6 and 7 were joined together and were departing upward, slowly ascending along two tethers at the same time. Pod 6 had a black scorpion painted onto its side with emphasized blue dots indicating the stars of the constellation Scorpius. Pod 7 was adorned with the image of an angry-looking feline creature standing amid an aura of fire and what looked to be an artist's depiction of several quasars or pulsars.

"Would that be for the *Scorpius* and the *Hell Cat*?" asked Conway.

"Yeah, looks that way. Much of the stuff needed on board the *Hell Cat* is common to the *Scorpius*. They have similar mission parameters. The *Scorpius* is a short-range Jackrabbit-class infiltration ship with special weapons and stealth capability. The *Hell Cat* is a long-range warrior class, and she's to be our escort to Mars. I think the tiny fuzzy hairs on my arms and legs just stood up" said Kahmay. "I must be...emotional...or something."

"I knew it. You know more but haven't said anything to the others yet, right?" Conway was eager to find out more specifics. The whole team wanted to know all the details. But they would not be briefed until later.

"Welcome to HEIWA," said a voice from behind the two newcomers. It was Lieutenant Colonel Norris gesturing forward with his outstretched arm pointed toward HEIWA-8. He had snuck up behind them unnoticed to hear their candid first impressions of the vast complex. Kahmay and A.J. were quick to come to attention and pop their salutes.

"At ease, at ease. We better get going. There's a lot to cover before you head back over to AK-0099. Shall we?" he said. He was leading them to HEIWA-8, which appeared to be filling up with old VANGUARD rocket cargo sections and civilians. Even using the much closer counterclockwise approach, they still had to walk the overhead footbridge from the HEIWA-1 platform over to Pier 8 where the pod for the *X-Tensai* was.

"Sir, wouldn't it have been easier to ferry across?" asked Conway. A.J. was an expert trained in multiple skill sets; most of which involved heights. But ever since her youth she had experienced problems with high-altitude pedestrian and vehicular bridges. "This is *bullshit*," she said as the three of them were elevated by a rapid escalation stairway. Vibrations from the surface water surging against the structure were not making anyone feel better.

"Only if you're afraid of heights Conway. You're not afraid of heights are you?" asked Norris with a mocking laugh. He knew that once a human fear was identified it had to be exorcised immediately or many people could end up being needlessly put at risk.

"It's not the heights Colonel. It's the long horrific uncontrolled free-fall towards the center of the planet that I haven't quite figured out yet. I'm working on it though. Let's not talk about this anymore" said Conway. Her anxiety about being so high up was only slightly eased by the presence of another barge beneath them coming in through the main gate. The giant reflective placard on the port side of the barge with the number 4 stenciled onto it suggested it was headed for Pier 4. But it looked like it was headed for Pier 5.

"Is that for one of the supercruisers sir?" asked Kahmay as they approached the Pier 8 staging area.

"Affirmative Sergeant...it's for the *E.S.S. Terrawatt*. She's parked up in Bay 5. They just started pressurization this morning early...so they're a little behind. Pier 4 and the assigned cargo barges were for the *E.S.S. Dark Star*. Now those resources are being used to load additional raw materials onto the *Terrawatt*. She's our only heavy freighter and she's going with the *X-Tensai* and the *Hell Cat* for phase 2. The *Dark Star* has been loaded and ready for days...same as the *Hell Cat*. In fact, while I'm on the subject, the *Hell Cat* doesn't even *have* a full crew yet. Here, this is our stop. Climb in and make yourselves comfortable. It'll be a while" said Norris.

Pod 8 had been sitting empty and had not been up to mooring Bay 8 in several days. The ops-plan for the *X-Tensai* did not require as much freight on the manifest as for the other supercruisers. Fewer people meant less cargo and less logistical consideration. Specialist Mayfield had originally prescribed a more comprehensive capital equipment list. But when section 7 of the plan was peer-reviewed, the freight list was curtailed in favor of a more aggressive extraterrestrial procurement strategy. The vast unused empty spaces that resulted from the abbreviated freight list were to be used and reused for other things depending on need. The greatest value of the empty space was the flexibility of use it would provide when the time came. The *Terrawatt* on the other hand, was chalked all the way full with all of the spare Class-B reactors, giant drill assemblies, freeze-dried food, vehicles, steel beams, and a huge swarm of irradiated construction drones bound for the planet Mars. It would all have to be off-loaded onto the red planet before the Ice-haul segment of the *Kaminari* mission.

Anarchy

The New Solar Year of 2026 C.E.A.D. had come and gone without a combined global celebration, as had been the case for so many consecutive solar years going back to 2012. But the humans came to see the year 2001 as the year the dusk really settled into view for Earth. The Twentieth century had seen many wars between good and evil, and 2001 was the grotesque closing argument to a century-long case for change. Many of the people from those generations were drawn unwittingly into a time-sensitive choice between lesser evils at the time. But the hope of a peaceful future thrived in those days. Honorable people put themselves in harm's way with the special vigor of those who knew they were on the side of good. One could actually feel *good* about dying for such a worthy future as the one proposed by the humans of the era. But something had changed since then. People from all cultures could sense that the core evil of humanity was only just now being stirred awake from its most restful sleep. All the horrific episodes of the past were merely the first bubbles of scorching steam boiling off the surface water of a vast cauldron of the darkest energy in the galaxy. The evil that was coming would make all that humanity had seen before 2001 look like the devil's symbiotic bacteria-eating parasite buddies. The blood-sacrifice of so many hundreds of millions of humans had stirred the full might of the beast into its absolute ugly, wakeful form. The beast was apparently still under the hopeless, sad impression that darkness and suffering could possibly prevail against the power of so much human light.

Those who celebrated the start of another year in 26' did so privately in doomsday bunkers and fallout shelters that were prepared many years ago. This year, people of Earth who bothered to celebrate were not celebrating the beginning of another year, but rather, they were celebrating the end of another year-long test of willpower. They reveled not with spirits and dancing, but with milliliters of apple cider and cheap tobacco sweets over quiet games of gin rummy and blackjack. The black-flag insurgents were attracted like hyenas to merrymaking and overtly loud celebrations.

Sleeper-cells with murder in their hearts waited throughout the peaceful lands for years, just to have one glorious opportunity to blow themselves up at midnight from within a group of "infidels". They were like rotten, blighted tomatoes splatting themselves like so much fertilizer. It was premium cowardly excrement that was decomposed and fully composted long ago in what was left of the dead human shells of the black-flag humans.

Sentient cognition with the soul was no longer possible for them.

The last time the world was under the collective impression that the Earth would soon cease to exist, an unnamed survivalist renascent period was born. The era of "prepping" as it would eventually come to be called, was recharged by new impetus. The movement had begun during the Cold War period, and involved the construction of "fallout shelters" to protect people from nuclear fallout radiation. The basic homebrew designs of the shelters changed with the times to become natural, sensibly upgraded versions of the original concept. The survivalist movement led to the randomly-scattered worldwide construction of an entirely new mode of human existence that had not yet come to full maturity.

The peak of the survivalist movement was likely drawing near as 2025 came to an end. But it was not really predicted to be a peak, which implies a sort of camel's hump on a two-dimensional line graph chart. On the contrary, the more likely outcome was proposed to be something more akin to a sustained threshold of hunter-gatherer, post-apocalyptic kinds of societies with unknown longevity potential. On January 11, 2026, the world awoke to unprecedented anarchy. Hypothetical conversations about the future of humanity took a back seat to the news that a coordinated worldwide coup d'état had taken place on four separate continents.

The hostile takeover of moderate governments by hardliners, extremists, radical fundamentalists, and aspiring dictators with large followings had sent the world into an unmistakable collapse. Throughout the day, broadcasted on what remained of the global media, video clips depicted the worst of humanity coming to life, or death as it were. Fires were started with Molotov cocktails, or a burning tire that could still roll. Journalists and reporters could not warn the reading and viewing public of graphic depictions of executions as fast as they kept happening.

In London, embassy row now appeared to be something more like the running of the bulls, or a reenactment of a well-produced movie about zombies. One video showed a camerawoman being knocked down while she filmed a monologue of a self-declared black-flag leader. The media outlets were in a determined hurry to get the word out to people who were not yet being directly affected by the chaos. They couldn't edit everything in time to get it out there, and the result was a gory end for the camerawoman after she had already been incapacitated by kicks to the stomach. People all over the world watched that poor woman being stomped to death by the brand new combat boots of a marauding band of thugs. It was utterly sickening. The

British Prime Minister managed to get a video message out to the masses imploring the innocent to do what they could to find safety and shelter long enough for rescue to come. It was nothing short of creepy that he could not promise said rescue.

In Moscow, the shit had really hit the fan hard. The old Soviet guard had finally risen back to power, and no longer had to convince the world that they were interested in a peaceful Kumbaya sort of world. By 1630 hours local Moscow time, they boldly announced on state television that the "figurehead" president was to be publicly executed later in the evening. Publicly executed he was. But nobody expected to see drunken Russians reveling in the streets as they played a game of kick-ball with the president's severed head. That spectacle was over the top for most, as the world struggled to understand why all of this madness was happening at once. Even if they swore they saw it coming, the denial instinct was powerful for most.

Only Australia, the Americas, and the sparsely populated areas of the Arctic and Antarctic were spared the massacre. In the Far East region, Japan and most of Southeast Asia were also still holding their own. Countries that were isolated on all sides with bodies of water fared better than areas that were connected contiguously to the larger of the enemy land masses.

In the United States, which had nearly achieved the perfect police-state by the time everything came crashing down, all of the states and protectorates had managed to deploy their Homeland Defense Forces in time before sunrise to quell anything that had been planned. But there were roaming tactical squads hunting down leads in every state. Dogs, drones, and closed-circuit video surveillance systems were working in overdrive trying to catch just one glimpse of the cowards that thought they could use chaos to their advantage.

The world had gone mad, and none of the things thus far being heard on the radio or seen on net-vision came close to the real danger unfolding behind the scenes. The "New Leaders" who emerged on the Day of Anarchy had been quite busy accomplishing the work of darkness in the chaotic in-between of the last 24 years. The cancerous spread of evil had trained up an entire multi-generational group of soulless predators; piss-ants, who had procured the authentication codes for over half of the world's most advanced weapons of mass destruction. Nuclear, Biological, and Chemical weapons were now off the reservation, and nobody could predict where the altered targeting coordinates were going to point in this "New World". But in the meantime, functional allied assets and resources had to be safeguarded and deployed (or re-deployed) where appropriate. Anything and everything was being done to minimize further losses.

In the Pacific, the full might of the United States military was called to action. Their primary goal was to safeguard the HEIWA complex and defend the lines of resistance and the Allied supply lines however they could. But hundreds of nuclear-armed submarines were out there now, swimming around like schools of confused fish looking for clues to their next prescribed course. Nobody really wanted to think about what that course would be, because those still hiding out safe somewhere *knew* that the scourge was coming eventually. There was something terminally incurable about the bloodthirst of a divinely-inspired self-righteous enemy.

By the middle of the first week following the collapse, losses from skirmishes and fire fights were being reported from the field of battle. Thousands and hundreds were being lost at a time in many places. Western Europe was a blood bath. Everything friendly south of Edinburgh and west of the Russian border was moving into position to defend or evacuate. The sea ports became clogged with refugees attempting to flee Europe and come across the North Atlantic into North America. Despite warnings from public officials to avoid the airports, panicked crowds jammed themselves through lines of riot police to get into the terminals in the desperate hope that the governments would rethink their decision to ground air passenger traffic. In the case of Europe, the skies were now being patrolled by *Shiite Empire in the Arabian Region* (SETAR) and Russian fighter-scout aircraft. Before the Day of Anarchy, some sovereign nation-states in the Middle East had managed to secure certain concessions from the West that had long been withheld from them as a result of their belligerent behavior. Within months after the world decided to place their trust in the suspect nations, the Mediterranean had become infested with hostile nuclear submarines just lying in wait for their day of attack. Their crews subsisted on rice cakes and the inspiring nationalistic songs of their homeland until "The Day" arrived. When they finally surfaced on that fateful day, they unleashed old 20th century Sarin nerve agents with single-shot medium range PUDD missiles and advanced tactical MIRVs. No Southern European targets were spared. Rome, Naples, Florence, Athens, Madrid, Aviano Field, Lajes spaceport, and the classified unmarked short-range anti-ship missile silos in Eastern France were all hit with either Sarin or 1500 kilogram payloads of extended-radius (X-Range) implosion rounds, the latter being the smoking gun connection with Mother-Russia herself.

      The West knew beyond a doubt that the Russians were working directly with nation-states like Yemen, and borderless amorphous nations like SETAR. But there was nothing overtly implicating them that could be shown to the public. One of the known constants in the complex equation of war was that Russia was the only potential foe on the planet with X-Range implosion technology. For as arrogant as the Iranian hardliners were, nothing could save them from the ridiculous truth that all they had up their sleeves were some old, obsolete ballistic missiles that had to be photo-enhanced for propaganda videos so the news would not get out that all they had were antique firecrackers and a couple of nuclear power plants. It was not until the X-Range implosion rounds hit Southern Europe that the world really believed the Russians had gone beyond Crimea and Eastern Ukraine in their territorial aspirations.

The Ring of Fire over in the Pacific had become the de facto green zone back in the fall of 25', as land grabs and political brinksmanship had already succeeded in accomplishing the expulsion of most Allied garrisons outside the Ring. All of the friendly humans still outside the green zone needed to be brought to safety quickly.

The one small glimmer of hope that shone through Europe on The Day was an incident that occurred on the northwest coast of Ireland. Allied militia and DOD regulars had adopted the custom of paying homage to the inspiring memory of the incident by shouting "Long live O'Connor", so spoken in recognition of Marcas O'Connor, who led a team of seven seaweed farmers in a revolt against a Russian submarine crew. The Russian crew had come ashore and managed to take all of the farmers as hostages inside of their own harvest-processing facility. Marcas and his crew of seven seaweed farmers managed to use seaweed-cutting knives and brass knuckles to subdue the unsuspecting Russians before putting on the Russian naval uniforms and formulating a plan. All but one of the officers were executed and mulched. The remaining officer was taken with them at gunpoint to the inflatable rafts and sped out to the Akula-class nuclear hunter-killer submarine. Each farmer had four kilos of C-4 tucked into his ruck. The Russian hostage had managed to get a duress word into his sentences during forced communication with the sub's third in command, and there was subsequently a gang of Russians waiting for Marcas and the guys once they were unsafely inside. But miraculously, Marcas himself came over the radio to inform the Irish Coast Guard that he and his partners-in-defiance had decided to go ahead and scuttle the sub since they couldn't get access to the launch codes. They didn't want to chance the sub getting off the hook again so it could go launch its missiles at allied targets. But they didn't want to die either. The way Marcas told the story was that they forced the crew to strip and abandon ship with no floatation equipment while they placed the

C-4 in various locations throughout the reactor room. They all then sat patiently smoking up the abandoned Russian cig-rations while they attempted to extract more information from the officer that they had spared back on land. The hostage craved death, and asked to be killed, but death eluded them. The seaweed farmers wanted to know where the other subs were, so they could go about the process of sinking them all. They did eventually go on to sink two enemy subs in the region that were sitting parked right next to one another down on the seafloor at 500 meters. Apparently, the subs were awaiting orders to launch Sarin warheads at the U.K. from the west side of Ireland.

The eight crazy family men from just outside Donegal had drafted themselves into the allied navy by lunchtime, and drove around patrolling Donegal Bay in a Russian sub for many hours before the allied naval command was able to talk them down and get them to the surface. It took almost two hours for Allied Command in the North Atlantic to convince the guy with the dead man's switch for the C-4 to come out of the reactor room. Those were indeed some bad-ass seaweed farmers.

The farmers had bought the allies enough time to get an escort force into the area so that surface vessels could at least concentrate on getting the refugees that were in the most immediate danger to the safety of

Iceland, and into the remote Inuit lands of Greenland. Allied forces still had a strong line of defense in those regions, but were ill-prepared to look after hundreds of thousands of refugees in the middle of winter in such naturally hostile areas of the Northern Hemisphere. Shipments of extreme cold weather clothing had to be sent to Nuuk and Reykjavik on short notice. Some of the refugees embarking out of European ports were given arctic clothing kits as they boarded large ferry ships bound for the distant North. About half of the refugees leaving out of places like Normandy, Lisbon, Hamburg, and Copenhagen had originally come from Africa and Asia, where the enemy had gained untold strength, and had begun slaughtering and torturing the innocent.

    The abrupt human-induced warming of the planet, combined with the regular fluctuating historical patterns of Earth climate had profoundly changed the strategic situation in the Northern seas. For at least the third time in 26,000 years, the interglacial period on the planet had become one of glacial retreat. If one wanted to try and predict what phase of the interglacial period Earth was in, there were now enormous correction factors that had to be applied to account for the human-generated portion of the greenhouse gas cycle. But for practical purposes, there was no need to calculate anything in January of 26'. Even in the dead of winter, the waters of the Arctic Bowl remained mostly liquid.

The effect was most noticeable near the continental land masses. That was all that mattered in the war effort.

Scandinavian Forces sent everything they had to the Russian border and began the perilous task of evacuating civilians across the North Atlantic into Eastern Canada. Safe passage through the North and Baltic Seas was becoming increasingly difficult with the passing of weeks and months. The allied naval blockade just offshore from the Baltic nation-states was meant to buy enough time for refugees leaving the area to head south toward Poland and northern Germany so they could be evacuated from one of the more southerly ports. The more east one traveled through northern Europe, the higher the probability that safe haven could be reached. For now, the Allies had created a passage out of Eastern Europe that was narrowing from both the Black Sea and Baltic Sea sides at a rapid rate.

The preliminary execution phase of *Kaminari* had already begun nearly two months prior to the Day of Anarchy. Some of the DSEF supercruiser teams and their associated remaining freight were still stuck on the other side of the world from HEIWA, and were desperately trying to get over to the Pacific, which by now was being transformed into a war zone itself.

Part of the group selected to be the active duty crew of the *E.S.S. Hell Cat* had gone missing back in late November. Their whereabouts remained an indefinite mystery. The search for a replacement crew finally began three weeks after their disappearance; just eleven days *after* the announcement to the public by DSECC that the mothballed supercruisers were being loaded with "appropriately trained" crews, and would be departing from an elaborate space elevator system known as "HEIWA". That announcement by DSECC would prove to be a monumentally gross error in judgement, for now HEIWA was the enemy's new prime target.

We Need You

Earth
Approaching Sector AK-0099
December 22, 2025 C.E.
1450 HRS

Colonel Kleen was just finishing her second REM cycle when she was awoken by a rapid knocking on the door of her quarters aboard the *Connie*. She had just been dreaming of a walk in her outdoor rose garden back in the states, when the knock awkwardly sounded in the garden. Her subconscious recognized the impossibility of such an occurrence and sent a wave of adrenaline through her body, which woke her up immediately.

"Enter!" said the Colonel, adjusting her voice so as not to sound like someone who had just awoken from a utopian garden scene. The door opened to reveal a young junior enlisted guy with a serious look on his face.

"Ma'am, they're requesting your presence up top. Something about a volcano in the Aleutians" said the young man.

"Outstanding. Please let them know I'll be right over Seaman" said Tabitha.

"Yes ma'am!" said the junior enlisted troop.

The Colonel was excited to hear about what happened out a Kanaga, and hastily donned her uniform and grabbed a cup of coffee before departing the peace and quiet of her quarters. She took a quick glance at her nav-screen on her way out the door and noticed that they were approaching sector AK-0099. She made her way through the twisting labyrinth of hallways and stairwells to the corridor that led above decks and was almost to the control room when she noticed one of the Air Corps' Serpent aircraft sitting on the deck. The idle-cooling turbines were still blowing cool ocean air into the intakes to cool the exhaust assemblies, which meant the Serpent had not been on deck longer than ten or fifteen minutes. One of the shift officers, Ensign Edwards, approached the Colonel as she crested the stairwell. The Colonel's glare was still transfixed on the Serpent. She had no idea what it was doing there.

"Colonel," said Edwards popping up her salute, "Sergeant Rahiko Bakuhatsu from the 7th Devil Dogs says he has instructions to bring these civilians and all of their equipment onboard. I checked it before granting permission to land. They're for real. Additionally, DSECC requests you interview the crew of the Serpent as candidates for the incomplete crew of the *Hell Cat*."

"Thank-you Ensign...I'll take it from here."

The Colonel hastily marched her way out to where the Serpent was parked. The Devil crew was busily going through the preflight checks on the Serpent in preparation for return-to-base.

"Good afternoon Sergeant Bakuhatsu" said the Colonel. "You have important cargo for us?"

"Ma'am, yes ma'am" said the Sergeant as he and the other Devils came to attention and afforded their courtesies to the Colonel.

"As you were folks, as you were. Pleasure to meet you all. Who are these civilians with you Sergeant?"

"Ma'am they're contractors...courtesy of DSECC. Our orders were to bring them to you...I guess you guys were the nearest fortified ride to their final destination ma'am."

"Thank you Sergeant. I take it your crew is the team that was sent to go investigate their activities...is that correct?"

"Yes ma'am. They were out at Kanaga of all places. Turns out they are the interim caretakers of all that is knowable...on the planet."

"Yes, okay, now I know who they are. Were your people able to decrypt and or demodulate the information contained in their transmission Sergeant?"

"Yes ma'am...that would be Senior Airman Madrone here." The Sergeant directed the Colonel's attention toward Raven, who was under the belly of the Serpent visually inspecting the EHF antenna array.

"Outstanding work over there Senior Airman. What are you doing for the next 30 years?"

"Ma'am?" Raven was confused by the Colonel's unexpected question.

"I've been authorized to recruit you and the rest of the crew for duty on board the *E.S.S. Hell Cat*. I'm guessing you are qualified and well-suited to perform the duties of an Electronic Warfare Officer (EWO) on an Interstellar supercruiser?"

"Uh...supercruiser? Like..."

"Yeah, like...a big giant space warship...presently without a full crew. We're running really short on time here, and we would be honored to have you escort us out there. Just say the word and we'll read you into the mission. That goes for the lot of you."

Sergeant Rahiko and the rest of the crew looked back and forth at one another trying to see who was going to bust out laughing first. Something inside them told them they shouldn't laugh, as the Colonel was dead serious when she made her proposal. Sra Madrone was the first one to take the offer seriously enough to formulate a serious question.

"Ma'am, you can count me in...but if we're going to be out there for 30 years, I need to ask if it's okay for me to bring my father with me."

"Yes, this will be a dependent-authorized mission with a household goods allowance of 32,000 kilos" said the Colonel.

"In that case, I'm definitely in" said Raven.

"Count me in too Colonel" said Rahiko. "Everything I own is back at the unit in my locker and out in the parking lot inside my car. I have no dependents."

"Alright then, take your craft back to sector 99 while we're still here in the area and get yourselves ready. But we need you to off-load the auxiliary Mech-dog and any of its associated on-equipment out of the Serpent before you go back to cut ties. We're going to start disassembling it and scanning it for reproduction off-planet. I'll be clearing all of this with your home unit while you're en route to base. We will be holding our position here until you return from sector 99 with the Serpent. But don't take too long. The mission has been underway for a couple weeks now, and we are ready to rock and roll. We have to get you all up there with your equipment and get you oriented into your new assignments...like *yesterday* folks. We need you for this!"

"MA'AM YES MA'AM" said Rahiko as the entire Serpent crew came to attention once again.

"Dismissed" said the Colonel with her own reciprocal salute.

Real Men Smoke Fish and Chew Cabbage.

Earth
Sector AK-0003
December 24, 2025 A.D.
1544 HRS

    Driving along the narrow two lane highway in an 18-wheeler with a load of vacuum-sealed seeds was not exactly the heist that Church McGrady had imagined in his younger days of trucking. In his youth, he often imagined that if he were doing something illegal in a big rig, it was probably going to be grand theft auto, or grand theft computers and solar energy collection equipment. But there was something altogether different about preparing for a trip to a far out destination in outer space and driving around with illicit agro-contraband. Although he was cruising toward remote Southern Alaska with a truck load of household goods and future space food, he could not get over how surreal it all felt.

"Hey, ya gotta try and keep a little more space hon... I can't see you when you move in close like that...over..."

Marie heard the love of her life over the radio and was excited to engage him in conversation again for the first time since their last bathroom break.

"Copy that cutie pie...I was just trying to get a closer look at your rear...sorry about that...over...," said Marie with a youthful laugh. She was getting tired of staring at the back of the trailer, and desperately wished to be in the cab with her beloved Mr. McGrady. The decision to follow in the hybrid was not her idea. But there just wasn't anyone else to do it on this day, so she was resigned to spending the many hours alone in the little front wheel drive. Settling for the occasional brief conversation over the radio was a small temporary sacrifice that would be made right the next time she wrapped her arms around Church and rested the side of her face against his neck.

The sight of the rapidly setting sun was getting worrisome for Church because he knew his Marie would have trouble driving in the fading light of dusk. They couldn't just stop and rest, and even if they wanted to pull over, there were no pullouts large enough on the tiny two lane remote highway to accommodate the tractor-trailer and the hybrid. He decided to keep her talking so that her mind would not try to go into that anxious place where the human mind tends to wander when it feels vulnerable.

"Hey...you there?"

"Yes sir... I sure am... you want some fresh coffee or some food?"

"No, no, babe...that's okay...I'm okay. Just wanted to touch bases with you and find out how you're doin'...you still seein' alright outta those shades?"

"Yeah...I'm okay for now. But I'm gonna pull a switcheroo and put my real ones on once the sun stops hittin' me in the face every time we clear the tree line. You gotta pee or anything?", asked Marie, knowing full well that Church could hold it for hours, and that she was likely going to be the one who needed to pee before they cleared the winding mountain highway.

"I'm alright. Don't worry 'bout me baby. Let's just concentrate on gettin' there in one piece okay? I'm mostly worried about you and this darkness...we still have almost a hundred kilometers to go before we get to the junction...you gonna make it?"

"Oh yeah...I'm gonna make it. We've come too far to *NOT* make it...right?"

"There ya go...that attitude is gonna get us there with no sweat. If I see a place to pull over I'm going to do it okay? Hey, cheer up! You just survived an encounter with a dude named 'Reaper'!" said Church with his unique three-part laugh.

The McGradys had traveled hundreds of miles since receiving their "illicit" cargo from the reclusive Canadian man back across the border. Marie agreed with Church that it would be a good time to pull over because there were so few wide places to pull their mini convoy over. Sometimes getting out of the vehicle for a few minutes and stretching was all it took to push the rest of the way to the destination. But after so many hours of driving and stopping, it was hard to remind oneself that the darkness was just an illusion. It was actually still quite early in the day, and although the sun was setting, it was still the middle of the afternoon. The McGradys struggled to ignore the conflicting messages of the mind and the clock, and were gradually degrading into a state of irrational fatigue-induced panic that caused them both to feel a sense of familiar dread. So many times in their youth, they had taken to the road thinking they could conquer any white-line fever or inclement weather challenges along the way. But, as Marie was fond of saying in such circumstances these days; they were "no spring chickens" anymore at their age. Despite being within striking distance of their destination, they both knew they were going to have to set the heaters in the truck's sleeper and get a few hours of rest before taking to the road again.

"Alright babe, I think I see a good place to stop up ahead. You think we oughtta go ahead and just sleep it off for a while?" asked Church.

"Yeah, I think so. That junction may or may not be open, and if it's not, then we have way more than 60 or 70 miles left babe. It's gonna be more like hundreds of miles of detour. I don't think my psyche could handle news like that right now. We'd do better with a little shut-eye, even though it's going to be dark by the time we wake up. I'd say we're still better off rested in the dark than delirious in the dusk."

"Okay...why don't ya back off a little in case I have to mash the brakes hard okay?"

"Yes sir...and fire up those heaters trucker-man...it's too cold out here to mess around."

"Copy that Commander...firing up the heaters. Stay in the car and leave it running until I get the hot water going and the warning markers out alright?" said Church in his most chivalrous tone. He hated the idea that his Marie was out in this bitter frozen forest. He wanted the journey to be completely painless for her, and it frustrated him that he could not protect her from every unpleasant detail of their unscripted covert adventure.

Church switched the truck's right blinker signal on as soon as he spotted the ideal pullout. He had a feeling that this was going to be the last place for them to get a tangible rest before continuing on the rest of the way to the destination. It was a large third-lane expansion meant to allow large slow-moving vehicles the chance to move over and crawl their heavy loads up the mountainside. The third lane connected to a generously large gravel landing near the top of the mountain, which was an ideal selection for those worried about the speed of an oncoming vehicle.

After Mr. McGrady was confident that everything was as it should be, he gave Marie the all-clear and climbed up into the cab. It was time to sit back in the sleeper on the edge of the bunk to enjoy some together time with her. They sat in silence and enjoyed hot mugs full of Marie's homemade clam chowder. It was truly enough that they were still alive and together. After dinner, they sipped lightly-sweetened decaffeinated coffee from little cups and were both content to just lay there staring at the glow-in-the-dark stars that Church had glued to the ceiling above the bunk for his youngest daughter Lacey so many years ago. They fell asleep with fragmented thoughts of the future stubbornly lingering in their tired heads. They wondered how all the years of their past had ultimately led to such a surrealistic reality. Lastly, they wondered why it sounded like someone was suddenly knocking on the driver's side door of the GEMINI.

"Scuze me folks!" the trooper shouted as he knocked on the tractor door a little harder each time the McGradys were unresponsive. "Anybody home? This is trooper Werner! Is anyone in there?"

Church gave a gentle shake to Marie's shoulder to let her know that he was going into the cab to see what was going on. He hurriedly made his way through the privacy curtain to see what was happening. He couldn't help but think to himself about where the firearms and ammunition were inside the sleeper underneath the rear fire extinguisher mounting bracket.

"Yeah, yeah...here, here..."said Church, rolling down the window a tad below the halfway point so that he could keep the heat in and still allow the trooper visual access to the immediate area around the driver's seat. "What's going on? What's wrong?"

"Oh no, there's nothing wrong sir. Everything is alright. Just checking on you and making sure you're alright and have everything you need to be safe here. You have plenty of fuel and blankets and food and stuff like that?"

Church was flabbergasted at how strange it was for a law enforcement officer to be checking in on his welfare out there in the middle of nowhere. It was not entirely unheard of in the lower 48 for things like this to happen. But the news and media reports had become exceedingly flooded with stories of all the horrible injustices that had been committed during unexpected random encounters for so long that people had really started to forget there was such a thing as a human being that cared about a stranger's well-being. The only safe assumption was to assume *nothing*.

"Is that how you guys do it up here on the frontier? You all look out for one another and check in on each other?" asked Church half rhetorically, and with a nervous laugh.

"Yes sir, that's really the best way to hedge your risk against the retribution of nature up here, and plus...it's the right thing ya know. Did I wake you up? I'm sorry 'bout that. Lotta times I check in on people and they're just lying there frozen to death. That has happened before, a number of times. Or sometimes you can interrupt criminal activities that were taking place under the cover of all this darkness ya know...and we don't have back-up troopers most of the time so."

"Sounds like you guys need more people up here." said Church.

"Yeah...but who in their right mind would choose this over fast food and crowded freeways?" joked the trooper. "Population has been steadily falling for about 20 years now. But we make do with what we have up here ya know. Sometimes it ain't pretty, but we do alright. This time of year is especially dangerous though.

It's a little under minus 30 out here at the moment...was on my way home and saw ya here."

"Right...yeah, we're just owner-operators bringing this agro-load to the port down there in Anchorage. I guess they're going to do something with it out on some little island somewhere. We just need a few hours to rest and then we're gonna get going again."

By now the initial anxiety of having a stranger knock at his door in the middle of the night had started to wear off and Church was gaining more situational awareness than when the knock first came. He noticed that the trooper's appearance looked a little different than what he would have guessed. But his conscious mind kept trying to dismiss what his subconscious mind was telling him about the overall demeanor of the trooper. Something wasn't right with this guy. *Why would his sidearm holster be unfastened? That's not normal is it?* Church could no longer ignore the voice in his instinctive mind that was yelling at him to figure out what was going on with this guy.

"Alrighty then sir." said trooper Werner. "Name's Karl by the way," he said, extending his left hand toward the partially open driver's window.

Church's heart skipped a beat when he saw the passenger door of the trooper's patrol vehicle opening out of the corner of his eye. The second man was smoking a cigarette and had the look of somebody angry and impatient. Church tried not to betray any surprise as he shook the trooper's hand and began snapping the fingers of his free hand behind the seat to get Marie's attention. "Pleasure to meet you Karl, I'm Church and my wife Marie is in here with me too. Yeah, we just pulled over after driving all day. Don't want to keep ya out here in this cold sir. Appreciate you lookin' in on us." Church heard the familiar sound of the snub-nosed 12 gauge quietly cocking behind him and kept his face as straight as possible as the trooper withdrew his hand and quickly went for his sidearm.

"You bet Church...now I'm gonna have to ask you folks to slowly exit the truck and turn around with your back to me."

The veteran truck driver's fight or flight instinct was now pounding his body with adrenaline and he could feel his breathing trying to change. He knew if he could shield Marie from view and then move out of the way, she had a chance to ventilate this coward and jack another round into the pipe before this other punk showed up. Without thinking about it any longer than necessary, he began to open the door and slowly turn his body as the man's accomplice was running around the front bumper of the truck cussing something inaudible. Without hesitation Marie produced the barrel of the 12 gauge over Church's right shoulder and squeezed the trigger. BOOM! The man flew backward about five feet and crumpled down on the gravel holding his hands over the gaping hole in his chest with a choking gasp and a look of final bewilderment on his face. The second man came whirling around the driver's door where Church was still standing sideways with his body halfway out of the cab. Church put the full might of his hips into a sideways kick to disorient the man while Marie was jacking another round into the chamber of the shotgun. She had already swung the barrel over top of Church's right shoulder blade, then BOOM! She had blasted a slug into the second man, launching him almost directly on top of the first man. Church quickly threw himself and Marie back into the cab and slammed the door shut. He looked out the window for a moment to make sure the men were still motionless, and to take in the full magnitude of what had just happened. They were roadside armed robbers who had done an exceptional job of pretending to be the good guys...for about three minutes...in the dark.

"We gotta get 'em off the road and roll that car over the cliff. Come on, let's put some clothes on and get this mess cleaned up so we can get the hell out of here. I'd say the chances of us getting to the destination without falling asleep at the wheel just went up to 100 percent." said Marie, still tightly clutching the shotgun in preparation for another unexpected visitor.

"You can say that again...hell with this, we're outta here. Please forgive me Lord," said Church aloud.

The McGradys dragged each body to the edge of the steep shoulder and rolled them down into the snowbank one by one. Marie grabbed the warning indicators while Church drove the still-running dark sedan to the edge of the road. The McGradys' concerns about whether these guys were *actual* outlaws was confirmed by the presence of high-velocity blood spatter on the inside passenger window of the patrol cruiser. Church expected to find an actual body in the back seat of the cruiser, but there was no body. There was however a large, body-sized blood stain on the back seat that looked fresh.

After turning the cruiser's ignition off, he got out and turned the key back to the "ON" position and put the floor shifter into the "D" position. He fought the now argumentative transmission with just enough success to get the car to start rolling down on top of the two lifeless bodies. The McGradys knew the investigation would lead back to them. But they did not fear the consequences of their actions. Everything they had done to get out of the difficult situation was justified and necessary. The long arm of justice would not have arrived on scene in time to save them from these foul animals. They had too much to live for, and these dime-a-dozen thugs weren't going to get in the way of that.

Irons in the Fire

Earth
Geostationary Orbit
Sector HI-0007
December 27, 2025 C.E.
1517 HRS

All civilian personnel assigned to the *X-Tensai* were gathered in a section of the ship's forward fuselage. Some of the group members were talking with family members through the courtesy-comm terminals provided in many of the common areas of the ship. Others were gathered in small handfuls here and there discussing all of the details related to the immediate and not-so immediate future of their impending journey. The wide open area they presently occupied made them all look small compared to the previously held ideas of what the scale-ratios had historically been between human bodies and spacecraft interiors. The ship was so spacious inside that one could actually become lost inside of it. There would be plenty of time for them to explore the deepest caverns of the ship, as their journey aboard would be a prolonged one.

The area deemed most practical for the civilians was in the pressurized, environmentally-controlled microgravity environment of the central fuselage. Everyone was getting used to it in their own way. The majority of the civilians were not allowed into the one-g areas yet because their household belongings were still being floated in from the mooring terminals by DSEF ground crews currently assigned to the HEIWA complex. The ground crews were also still setting up their own one-g quarters and moving their families in while the civilians waited. It was the same courtesy afforded active-duty members of the armed forces since the creation of organized military and peace-keeping forces.

Jared and Shannon Foyle were off by themselves studying a detailed three-dimensional map of the ship while they waited for word from their DSEF sponsor about what would come next.

"Do you think Beatrice is looking a bit pale Shannon?" asked Jared. His great grandmother was sitting comfortably strapped to an anchored, orthopedically-enhanced chair watching a real-time news broadcast from Reykjavik looking like she had just stuck her finger into a light socket. Her hair floated freely above her scalp, and may possibly have been adding to a visual illusion that made her look extra surprised by her present circumstances. Jared began pulling himself over to Beatrice to inquire about how she was feeling while Shannon was reading her old copy of *Lord of the Flies* wondering whether the present group of humans would be reduced to primitive violent behaviors by the time the mission grew long enough to manifest such latent human instincts. She found it hard to imagine that the future reality off-planet would happen in the way of the horror movies and worst-case-scenario studies. She thought about how different things would be with a community of hundreds of thousands, versus the kinds of numbers in most of the case studies of isolated humans she was familiar with. She had primarily studied groups that tended towards the several hundred individuals at most. But the circumstances of this exodus, coupled with the advances in technology, would likely lead humans into a period of rapid change and adaptation. This was only the beginning of a period in human history that was sure to signal the start of something that would ultimately bloom into an infinite number of possible sociological outcomes. Shannon wondered which adaptations would benefit the survival of one individual the most as months turned into years, and years turned into decades. She looked up at the crowd of floating experts with their children of all ages in tow. They were all getting along fine for now, steeping in their various behaviors and making light of the crisis-like situation the best they could. Shannon marveled at how flexible the spirits of the many had been through all of this change. Most of the individuals aboard had no idea as recently as one month ago that they would be leaving the planet Earth.

Over in sector AK-0006, the crew of Detachment IV were busily packing the last of their personal effects and monitoring the ongoing situation both inside and outside of the Green Zone. Orders from Sergeant Kahmay were for Specialists Hutchinson, Monty, Quire, and Doyle to wait at the Homer port while the rest of the Det. IV crew escorted the last of the express bags to the HEIWA complex as quickly as possible. The window of opportunity for surface travel to the main HEIWA complex could not be relied upon to remain open indefinitely. The group of four in Homer was to make sure that the final phases of ground operations in the Alaska territory were completed. That meant waiting for the McGradys and their seedy precious cargo, and ensuring their safe passage in the event Kahmay could not meet them in sector AK-0099. The Sergeant was still holding out hope that she was going to be able to make it to sector AK-0099 to meet up with the McGradys, and to make in-person contact with the 7th Devil Dogs concerning the future of the *E.S.S. Hell Cat*. The *Hell Cat* would be escorting the *X-Tensai* to Mars at some point for the initial phases of the Mars segment of the mission. But Kahmay needed to know the crew was aboard and prepared to act once the time came. She clung to her faith that mom and papa Church would understand if she did not travel to Alaska to meet them.

Meanwhile, the McGradys were still steadily making their way through the Alaskan highways one mile at a time. The trip and all of the work that preceded their departure from sector OR-0042 had completely exhausted them. They had been reduced to making frequent stops for horizontal resting and recuperating.

By the time the Det. IV crew left their teammates in Homer bound for sector AK-0099, the McGradys had a little over a day or so left to drive if they could just keep their current pace of progress. The drunken spruce forests of the lower interior portion of sector AK-0066 had really cast an ominous shadow over their continued progress through the interior of the territory. The drunken spruce appeared dead, and frozen in time in their leanings. Frost heaves underground going back millennia had twisted and contorted their root systems into a less efficient symbiotic-entanglement with the soil. Only the individual trees with the most adaptive root systems would be allowed to procreate in future generations.

Ordinarily the McGradys would have been allowed to take a road south of the interior toward the southcentral region of the territory into sector AK-0006. But the highways and byways connecting the lower interior to the southcentral territory had been poorly maintained over the years, and would not allow the safe passage of large vehicles through the connecting shortcut to the southern sectors. The entire passage between Tok and Glennallen had been cut off by enormous swaths of broken road. Giant sections of asphaltic coral roadways had their foundation grades evacuated by unexpected geological phenomenon like sinkholes and liquefaction. Survey drones were used to identify the trouble spots before anyone could be caught unwittingly falling to their death into gigantic trenches and deep holes. The drone crew had no choice but to close the road for the winter.

Both Church and Marie found it frustratingly slow traveling through the interior at the rate of 31 statute miles per hour. They had unwittingly pinned their hopes on being able to take the east-west shortcut through Tok into the Matanuska Valley. It was a serious blow to their morale when they discovered they were going to have to go further north before they could come back toward the south. It felt like the closer they progressed toward the center of sector AK-0066, the more they sensed a pervasive darkness lurking about the region. It was an uncomfortable feeling having to drive so far north away from their destination to the south, just to get where they were headed. They complained with increasing frequency to one another that they were "…getting too old for this shit."

Sergeant Kahmay was back at the command bridge of the *X-Tensai* with Lieutenant Colonel Norris and Specialist Conway going over the details of what would happen once they were no longer tethered to the mooring platform. Conway could not help but notice the uncharacteristically distracted appearance of Kahmay's face as the Lieutenant Colonel carried on discussing duty assignments and proposed civilian involvements.

"The only way I can see the sterilization room being adequate is if we limit its use in its current form to accommodate only scheduled entrances and exits. If we're going to end up in an extended rescue situation before we leave the near-Earth region, which appears extremely likely now, we have to establish an alternate receiving room. Think of it like a triage area with a positive pressure decontamination layer." said Norris, looking alternately into the eyes of Conway and Kahmay. "Sergeant, what say you?" Without skipping a beat, Kahmay spoke her mind.

"Sir, I say we don't need to be checking rocket-evacuees for microorganisms on the way in. We're too low on power to be using so much of our capability before the reactor is up. Everybody has a little bacterium on 'em somewhere. We'll examine them in the entrapment with the bio-kits. Some of them might have been exposed to CAT-V agents on the surface before they blasted off. If they pass contagion analysis, we'll send 'em to med-bay for observation. We'll have weeks and months to check 'em at the other end on the way out for whatever else they might be afflicted with. The end of phase 2 calls for 'gradual introduction SOP'. There will be lots of time to shower and disinfect ourselves one-by-one during that time frame. The *X-Tensai* is one of Earth's new petri dishes. Extremophile research has shown those little buggers are going to last millions of years out there in the vacuum all dressed up in ice with no place to go. Load her up with Earth-stew and worry about decontamination next year or the year after, once the robo-horde has accomplished enough for us to even bother with extravehicular activity on the Martian surface."

Conway looked at the Sergeant in awe of how gross her previous miscalculation of Kahmay's mood was.

"Is that really what you were thinking sarge?" asked Conway.

"Yes and no, well, not entirely. I was also thinking that this might be a good time to address that one thing sir" said Kahmay, answering Conway's question, but with her response directed at Lieutenant Colonel Norris.

"Agreed," said Norris, reaching into his pocket. He produced a set of subdued Sergeant's stripes. "Specialist Conway, it's time for you to have the rank that is most commensurate with your responsibility and your achievements. Congratulations Sergeant Conway. You've earned these. The next time I see you, I expect these to be sewn on or else."

"A.J., we don't have time for sunshine," said Kahmay. "You know how I feel about it. You earned those back in Edo as far as I'm concerned. The bureaucracy slows down like a lead balloon when the world speeds up. But you already knew that. I'm glad we can move on with our newest NCO now. What news from aft Colonel?" asked Kahmay. She was ready for the conversation to be about something else because she knew how embarrassed and shy A.J. became when the attention was on her.

"HEIWA ground crews are loading the last of their dependents and freight into the port side one-g as we speak. Some of them are over with the civilians in the main corridor coaching their undecided loved ones into safe havens down on the planet. Civilians are lollygagging in the dayrooms. We need to green light the anxious ones into their needed positions as soon as possible." said Norris.

"My daughter Visna is ready to start setting up in Bio-10 sir." said Conway. "Her husband Fyn and her son Hauk were with her last I knew. Fyn should be reporting in over at engineering within the next hour or so. He wanted to make sure Visna and Hauk were okay before leaving them there.

"Visna...she's the snake charmer right?" asked Norris, unsure of whether he had it correct or not.

"Negative sir, she is the one who has a special way with reptiles and amphibians. She also happens to be a Zoologist. The snakes are naturally charmed, but not because she purposely set out to do so sir. It is something she was born with" said Sergeant Conway.

"Copy that Conway." said Norris. "I didn't mean to sound demeaning. I know Fyn is a qualified interdisciplinary engineer, and that Visna is a master of Zoology who happens to specialize in herpetology and entomology. They are going to be valuable assets to our team. Go ahead and show her to Bio-10 and make sure she feels at home back there. That's *starboard* one-g, section 10; where most of the other work sections are. The whole starboard hemisphere has been spinning up here for two weeks. It had to be thoroughly tested before the live specimens could be brought aboard. The longer it takes us to get both hemispheres spinning, the less energy we have available to counter the unreciprocated friction and torque effects of the starboard side. The less time you spend up here in microgravity the better. Go get some heavy exercise. If you see any other natural-sciences types in the common areas on your way back, go ahead and invite them to come along with you and your family. The sooner we can make this place functional the better. They won't get their room assignments over on the port side until after the ground crews are finished in there. What about your people Sergeant Kahmay?"

"Coming through sector AK-0066 last I heard." said Kahmay.

"Do they know what's happening in the Gulf of Alaska?" asked the Colonel.

"It's doubtful sir. I believe the last reliable report they have in their possession probably showed everything north and east of the Hawaii territory to be all clear. But that was *before* the Canadians found the Hammerhead off Prince Rupert. God only knows what has found its way into the Gulf by now." said Kahmay. "I trust that Hutch, Doyle, and Triggerhound will get them here sir."

"Good. Do you trust them enough to turn your attention toward something besides worrying about your family?" asked the Colonel.

"Yes sir, I'd like to go and have a look at the status of our defensive capabilities and reprogram the search drones to look for anything on the exterior that does not match up with the blueprints. We can't afford an attack with so many people concentrated in just a few areas. The sooner we get the civilians settled and dispersed throughout the ship the better. Plus, we need to run diagnostics on the ship-to-ship shuttles. We won't be permanently housing unposted civilians and will need to transfer them to their semi-permanent homes as quickly as possible to get out in front of Mars. Have you heard anything from the ground recently sir?" asked Kahmay.

"Negative Sergeant. I'll let you go ahead and do that while I touch bases with the folks in the central corridors." said Norris. "Do me a favor and meet me in Operations in thirty minutes. We gotta see a man about a Rectenna."

"Copy that sir. See you down there in thirty then." said Kahmay.

Kahmay spent some time acquainting herself with all the instrumentation in the command section. One by one, she acknowledged each instrument for its intended purpose, reviewed the key points of the use of each instrument, and took herself through ground radio acquisition as if it were her first time attempting to make contact with individuals on the surface of *any* celestial body. Everything was arranged just as it was in the simulators in Edo. Asteroids and other objects with no ionosphere were pretty straight forward. Things became a little tricky when an object had atmosphere and a charged ionosphere. Denser point mass objects could be hacked for communication purposes quicker than the calculations for exotic orbital dynamics. Much of the navigational calculations for an intended destination would need to be accomplished while underway as more data about the destination became available. The course trajectory information would become more reliable with additional data and proximity to target. But there would be plenty of time much later to deal with destinations beyond Mars. The real initial work of phase 2 was going to be right there at Mars from stationary orbit, and then eventually on the surface. Mars and all of its legitimate, essential micro-analysis would feel like a second home by the time the *X-Tensai* had to leave on its way to a tertiary destination. For now, plugging 3.72 meters per second squared into the basic orbital formula for F-sub-G still felt a little strange.

Kahmay was supposed to be contacting the ground, but she had left the planet for a moment in her mind. She was thinking about what lies *beyond*, and failed to control the automatic tendency to forget about what lies *below and in front*. But the ground was not something that would ever be forgotten. No matter where they went in the universe, there would always be a "ground" of some qualification, and a "space" that appeared far away on any given day. Back there, right here, over there, everywhere and nowhere. Every day would be different, and would come to resemble whatever one made of it over the course of many days, weeks, and years. Kahmay spied the tuner and standby transmission controls for the aft transmitter array and switched the standby oscillator output to "I", which turned on the carrier for the S-Band transmitter signal and synchronized the output carrier frequency-stability with the thermally-controlled stable oscillation clock. It felt natural in her hands, like something she had done a million times over the course of many decades. Before keying up, she remembered they were doing all of this for the people "down there". Adrenaline began flowing normally once again through her circulatory system. Gradually, her moment of rest was starting to feel more like the familiar step 27 in a 50-step process.

"HEIWA-8, this is Sergeant Kahmay O'Conaill on the *X-Tensai,* can you hear me? Over…"

There was no response on the S-Band, so Kahmay switched over to the X-Band and tried once again to raise someone on the ground.

"HEIWA-8, this is the *X-Tensai*, how copy? Over…"

"Copy *X-Tensai*, this is Airgun-5. We hear you, go ahead."

The transmission had to come from a pilot of an allied fighter aircraft. But Kahmay did not know exactly where they were at. She was on their tactical channel feeling around in the dark for the HEIWA ground station. But she realized the *X-Tensai* was definitely going to need to be able to stay in contact with *any* Allied channels available, and so she engaged the pilot in conversation.

"Copy Airgun-5, was wondering if you had heard from any humans at the HEIWA tower...over" said Kahmay.

"That's negative *X-Tensai*. They should be on the S-Band...try 3.1415 niner golf hotel Zulu...over."

Kahmay looked at the S-Band center frequency setting and saw that it was set at its default of 2.000 gigahertz from after its successful completion of the start-up initialization self-test.

"Copy that Airgun...looks like someone reset the porch light up here. God speed sir...thanks again...*X-Tensai* out."

"Roger *X-Tensai*, very welcome...excuse me while I land this ole' lawn dart and call it a day. Airgun out."

Kahmay smiled as she adjusted the S-Band transceiver to 3.14159 gigahertz and thought about the pilot she had just spoken to. There was no readily available way to know exactly which base he had flown out of, or landed at for that matter. But Kahmay didn't need to go ascertain his position with the other instruments. All she needed to know was that he was on the good side, and that he knew the command operational frequency for the HEIWA ground station. Everyone in theater had the need to know. The fact that he was at the conclusion of his mission and was flying a fighter jet made her smile even wider as she thought about the miracle of one of their own coming home alive from another exceedingly bad day at work. The Northern Pacific front was the only semi-quiet front of the entire green zone, and that was only because of the stormy conditions and divine winter's grace. All other fronts were a raging conventional battle front. Kahmay keyed the ground station and hurriedly solicited a reliable human response.

"HEIWA-8, this is the *X-Tensai*, come in over."

"We read you *X-Tensai*. This is HEIWA control. Recommend adjust to plus 10 Meg for HEIWA-8 over."

"Copy control...adjusting to plus 10 Meg. Thank you" Kahmay said.

Kahmay fine-tuned to the number 8 tether communications center where someone with an update would hopefully be waiting at 3.15159 GHz.

"HEIWA-8, this is *X-Tensai* control requesting sit-rep over" said Kahmay.

"Copy X, no change since 1500 local. Still four active outstanding, 294 civilians Uncle November Kilo. Looks like your missing actives are Hutchinson, Doyle, Monty, and Quire. Does that sound right?" asked the ground sentry.

"Yup, that's them alright. I wish they would hurry their asses up man. We're about to light this candle. Thank you 8...you see McGradys and O'Conaills on there?"

"Copy that...McGradys last known 20 was Alpha, Kilo, Zero, Zero, Six, Six...with two inbound...O'Conaills' last known 20 was Hotel, India, Three Zeros, seven...with four inbound plus two canine...and uh, wait, just now received additional information regarding a separate McGrady...alternate 20 is...Oscar, Romeo, Zero, Five, with three inbound. Would that be two separate arms of the McGrady family?"

"Yes sir" said Kahmay. "That's my younger sister Lacey in Oregon with her husband and daughter. The O'Conaill party is my older sister arriving at the base complex here with my three nieces and their two dogs. That first McGrady contingent is mom and dad up in Alaska. There's a third McGrady contingent, but we've been out of contact for many years. Are you showing manifested lading for everyone else though?"

"Yes ma'am, well...almost everyone. The Alaska McGradys are showing incomplete logistics. Do they have the rest of their cargo with them as they travel?" asked the HEIWA-8 sentry.

"Yes sir. They'll get it here...one way or another" said Kahmay. "Should be...about 12 to 14 pallets of miscellaneous and a few oddball items. Plus, there should be one high priority item divided into four discrete units that are tagged for the mission."

"Copy that sarge" said the sentry. "That's what I'm showing. That, and I'm showing a 1988 GEMINI-2050 model semi-tractor with custom multi-trailer? Does that sound right to you? They're bringing their old semi-truck too?"

"Yeah" said Kahmay with an abrupt laugh. "It was the only way I could get them to come. It's not that old though. The chassis is from 1988, but it was comprehensively upgraded back in 19'. Hey one last thing and then I'll let you go man. Did you say the Alaska McGradys last check-in was sector 66 up there?" asked Kahmay.

"Yeah, that's your folks right? Are they overdue Sergeant?"

"No, no...not yet. But if you hear anything coming out of that neck of the woods, can you send word to *X-Tensai* control here?" asked Kahmay.

"Solid copy Sergeant Kahmay. HEIWA-8 out" said the sentry.

Rebecca and the girls, with Bingo the Border collie and Bullseye the Pug in tow, were now somewhere on the HEIWA-8 tether. Kahmay imagined they were on their way up and would soon be safely aboard. But Lacey had not yet checked in, and the folks were still held up somewhere between the Alaskan interior and the awaiting escort down in Homer. That was hundreds of miles of really rough traveling, and a lot could still go wrong.

Sacred Rendezvous

Earth
HEIWA-8 Tether
December 27, 2025 C.E.
1530 HRS

The pieces of the puzzle were finally starting to come together for the crew and passengers of the *X-Tensai*. Most of the civilians who were expected on board were already aboard and settling into the routines of the cavernous ship one day at a time. There were a number of civilians suffering from the despair of what was still happening down on the surface. Cold feet about what was about to happen was expected, and loading the civilians aboard early was part of a larger strategy that involved providing them the opportunity to back out if they wanted. But for all of the children, elderly, and sick aboard, it was clear that most families had chosen to live out their last days in space with the rest of their loved ones. They took their time saying "see ya later" to the ones on the surface, and then tried to put it all in the rearview mirror. That was really the best way to do it for most. But what a lot of the folks aboard the ship did not realize was that the larger mission would likely provide them a future opportunity to return to Earth if things weren't "working out" for them. Furthermore, still relatively unbeknownst to them all, was the fact that they were soon going to be headed to Mars as part of the initial wave of humans meant to establish a safe, well-equipped waypoint for vessels and humans bound for still more distant outposts both within and beyond the solar system. The full, clear perspective of their new reality would not hit them until they began to see other places throughout space as locations on a map, albeit with special circumstances. Critical features of new worlds would be defined in the addendum sections of new atlases. Somebody would need to ensure the maps and waypoints of the new world were accurately drafted and published.

Establishing a thriving catalyst-colony on Mars would open the doors to others on Earth who were innocent and in need of refuge. Operation *Kaminari* would necessarily begin as a time-sensitive humanitarian relief operation; one that was likely to continue indefinitely for many years until a new balance among humans could emerge from the chaos of war.

"We're almost to the top" said Specialist Gordon with an optimistic look on her face. "Sure hope we remembered everything."

The incomplete DET. IV crew had been sitting inside Pod 8 crawling up the HEIWA-8 tether for the better part of three hours. They were jammed inside the pod with over 200 express cubes full of DET. IV vital equipment and two large VANGUARD rocket sections full of DSEF ground crew household goods. True to form, Specialist Tamara Levi could not resist the temptation to answer her long time teammate.

"If by 'everything' you mean, 'all of the itemized contents on the express bags packing list', then, I would say you have nothing to worry about Penelope.

Specialists Manuel, Mayfield, and Lenihan were sitting across the pod playing draw poker to take their attention off of the fact that they were miles above the surface of the Earth. The three had spent the first hour staring out of the tiny pod window observing the Earth's surface like children on their first plane ride. But, like so many humans; once the first plane ride started to feel like the 119th plane ride, they lost their interest in the novelty and pulled out the playing cards.

"Pod-8, Pod-8, this is *X-Tensai* control. We have your ETR at 6 minutes. How copy over?" came the voice of Sergeant Kahmay over the pod's internal public address system.

"Solid copy control" said Specialist Manuel. "See you shortly."

"Be prepared to get offloaded as quickly as possible. We have people inbound and moving into position down on the surface who need this ride ASAP.

Get it done people." The Sergeant was starting to become noticeably concerned that some of her family members were not going to make it to the complex on time.

"Hey, that sounded like my younger sister. Was that Sergeant O'Conaill?" asked Rebecca O'Conaill.

"Yup, that was her alright" said Penelope Gordon. "I'd recognize that voice anywhere. She's your sister?"

"Sure enough" said Rebecca. "Does she know we are here and that we are safe?"

"Yeah, you checked in down at the surface before we climbed aboard?"

"Yes, all six of us."

"No worries then" said Gordon. "She knows."

Rebecca had been sitting down reading the news stories of the past several days. She wondered about the implications of each revelation as she flipped from story to story with her fingertips on the surface of her personal comm-device. Her normal news feeds were not showing up properly in the display. But instead of the normal error 404, she was noticing that many of the news outlets had gone to the trouble of posting special messages on their feed servers. The Basic News Headlines(BNH) site had a message that read, *"We will be off the air indefinitely through this crisis. We are sorry for any inconvenience this may be causing you. We have safeguarded our vital broadcast resources in a secure location and will commence broadcasting once this crisis has passed. Again, we apologize for this service interruption."*

Page after page, the results were similar but basically identical; the grid was shutting down.

Rebecca, together with her three daughters and two canines, looked at each member of her group as they all simultaneously felt the pod's climb rate slow down. This was the part she had been feeling the most apprehension about. They could all feel themselves straining against the seat harnesses as their momentum sought to carry them through the harness and still further into space as the pod decelerated. Bullseye, the smaller of the two dogs, was floating weightless inside of his travel kennel. He was periodically twisting his body in a futile attempt to right himself against the effect. But he did not seem to be in any pain. Bingo the border collie was bracing himself against the walls of his comparatively larger kennel gently whining at the uncertainty of being weightless inside of a ventilated composite-plastic cube.

They were all soon going to be making their way through a pressurized conduit that was connected to the *X-Tensai*. Because of the immense time pressures to get everyone aboard, they were going to have to make the crossing *without* the reassurance of a self-propelled spacesuit.

The pod's ascension-rate control mechanisms gave a slight whine as they brought the structure to a halt at the entrance to the conduit. Thyra was the first of the O'Conaill daughters to notice the flashing red light near the control panel that opened up the bay door into the conduit."

"Uh-oh, do you see that? It's a flashing red light. That can't be good can it?"

"I wouldn't worry about it girl" said Rebecca. "I think it's flashing because they have to wait and make sure the pressures are equalized before they can open the doors."

The flashing red panel light changed to a steady green light that was continuously on. The sounds of the differential pressure remainder could be heard transferring into a storage plenum behind layers of plating inside the pod. The double doors were silently opened and revealed an oversized tube connected to an enormous spacecraft at the other end. It all looked exactly how Kahmay had described it; "... dangerous, with the look and feel of something that seems far too dangerous to enter."

One by one, the passengers of Pod 8 emptied out into the conduit. The members of Det. IV were helping several ground crew members unlock the cargo lockers to remove the electromechanical freight dollies, while one of the ground crew helped direct the civilians out into the footpath. The freight removal operations and pedestrian transit were designed to occur simultaneously, with the pedestrians forming a line over to the right with their personal items in tow. The freight units floated through the left hand side of the conduit along the generously wide materiel thoroughfare. The thoroughfare connected to a shipboard network of like-designed wide pathways on the *X-Tensai*. The centerline of the thoroughfare was actually more of a trough, with a system of magnetically opposed anchor hoops that utilized magnetic repulsion to in effect, "lubricate" the axis along which vehicles were driven. Vehicles anchored their frames to the hoops and would then be capable of simply rolling all the way to the branched end of the system. The trough and rail union-joints connected seamlessly enough to allow vehicles to simply keep on rolling at 5 miles per hour, with a precisely controlled electric motor anchored and fastened to the thoroughfare surface and mag-ring respectively. The design of the center rail was such that, the cross-sectional depiction of the rail appeared similar in shape to the cross-section of a standard umbrella with rounded corners, or a giant morel mushroom cap.

'Look" said Rebecca pointing to the approaching bay door. "I think I see people behind the door through the window."

Standing on the other side of the hatch preparing to open it was a crew of DSEF personnel and various freight-handling equipment. Unbeknownst to Beck and the girls, Sergeant Kahmay was there with Delmar and Nadia Post, and Dr. Kurt Pittman of the Shooting Star center.

The large hatch door began slowly pulling inward toward the interior of the ship's freight dock. The hatch door moved into its fully recessed position, and then began gently gliding sideways out of the way of the incoming passengers and cargo units.

The butterflies in Rebecca's stomach from being in a microgravity deathtrap were gradually superseded by the thrill of seeing so many familiar faces. She knew the faces of the others floating there in the receiving bay from living in sector OR-0042 for so long. She had met Dr. Kurt a few times while volunteering several years back at the Shooting Star Center. She had also seen the good doctor in passing a number of times while visiting her mother Marie on and off over the years. Delmar and Nadia had been friends of the McGradys and O'Conaills for so long that Rebecca remembered being paid a small cash sum in her adolescent years to water their plants and collect their mail when they went on vacation.

Although, it was a bit confusing to her as she tried to figure out what the Post family was doing aboard the *X-Tensai*. She did not know about Delmar's expert background.

"Glad you could make it stranger" said Kahmay. "We've been expecting you!"

Many hugs were exchanged and then the bottleneck had to be immediately cleared to make way for the onslaught of still more civilians and a parade of giant freight units.

"Did you see mom and papa Church down at the surface?" Kahmay could not resist getting a piece of usable human intel from the field. "I haven't heard from them in two days."

"No, I didn't see them. I'm sure they'll be on the next one sis. Don't worry, I'm sure they're fine. You know they're not going anywhere without a fight."

"I know they're tough. That much is not in question. I just fear this whole thing was a little too much for them. It's turning into a war zone by attrition down there. I did not anticipate so much enemy presence in the eastern Pacific at this time of year. When all of this was being planned there had not yet been any reported enemy contact west of the date line. I know they made it at least as far as sector 66" said Kahmay.

"I tried to convince them to hop the transport with me over in Newport, but they insisted on driving the GEMINI through the northern territories" said Dr. Kurt.

Kahmay smiled at the realization that her folks had done a good job of protecting the covert aspect of their mission from their innermost social circle. Their loyalty to the operational security of the mission would go a long way toward proving to the chain of command that the McGradys could be entrusted to safeguard the most sensitive challenges of their shared future together.

Pay the Boatman

Earth
Sector AK-0006
December 28, 2025 A.D.
0413 HRS

There was a layer of dense fog covering the entire Kenai Peninsula as Church skillfully drove the GEMINI 2050 past the Girdwood outpost on the way to Homer to meet up with the DSEF crew. Neither he nor Marie could understand why the driving conditions were so prohibitive at every turn since leaving sector 42 so many days ago. Of course, the Sterling Highway of Alaska's sector-0006 would be no different from what they had already encountered thus far.

Ever since crossing into the Alaska territory, it had been one painful obstacle after another. Although they were both glad to be out of the gloomy interior, they couldn't get over how they had hit every red light while traveling through Anchorage on their way to the Girdwood junction outpost. The couple was in a mild state of shock over losing Marie's little hybrid chase-vehicle to the extreme sub-zero temperatures of the interior. She had left it turned off on the side of the road near Healy, and nothing either one of them could do to try and start it could overcome the devastating effects of minus 40. They had no choice but to abandon Marie's little fuel-efficient commuter on the shoulder of the highway outside of town.

Church had been driving without rest since the Denali mountain range and had endured more than his eyes and cognition could have possibly allowed him to endure on any other well-rested day from his former reality. Even if it was one of his *better* days, it had been many years since he had pushed himself this hard out on the open road. He didn't even want to go through town while they were back in Anchorage. But the GEMINI was running a little low on fuel. There was something else driving him forward that had been unprecedented in his recent past. He thought perhaps it was the adrenaline rush of knowing that soon, his and Marie's world was to become a neighborhood of planets and stars.

After everything they had been through, Church didn't hesitate to run through some of the red lights and take side roads on the way through the urban and suburban areas of the southcentral region. The entire urban sector looked abandoned. But the abandonment was not the typical middle-of-the-night abandonment. It was like the entire region had collectively realized that military and law enforcement entities were preoccupied with the bigger fish of a foreign military that was preparing to invade the area. There were credit unions and banks on fire, and way too many vehicles sitting on the concrete sidewalks and curbs of the greater metro area. To avoid what was happening at these apparently meaningless red light crossroads, illegal action was unavoidable.

The first red light Church ran through had them sitting there waiting for at least five minutes before they realized that there were humans coming out of the woodwork from the dark shadows of the crossroads. There was nothing the dark strangers could have possibly offered the McGradys at two o'clock in the morning that would have been important enough for them to slow down and engage the strangers in conversation. Church simply down-shifted the transmission and left the area in a hurry.

The second obstacle came at a time when Church thought he was having an optical illusion of a large snake crawling out into the road. He was relieved to see that it was actually a real object. But close inspection with the external directional spotlight revealed that the object was a spike-strip. Somebody had placed it there for them to run over. After more than 3,500 miles of adversity, they'd be damned to come so close and then be murdered for their cargo just a few hundred miles away from their destination. Church again noticed featureless human contours materializing from the darkness as he backed the rig up in preparation to drive the GEMINI through a small field to get around the spike-strip.

"Fuck me man...what the hell is happening here" he asked himself aloud. Marie had been sleeping since Eagle River, and was just then stirred awake from Church's utterings.

"Is everything okay honey?" she asked from the sleeper area. She sat up to clear her blurry, sleepy eyes enough to see the road in front of them.

"Yeah babe, except...I'm trying to get us out of some kind of ambush here. Hold on..."

Church stomped the gas over the curb to gain enough inertia to glide them through the snowy field without getting stuck. The worst thing that could happen would have been for them to be stuck in the snow surrounded by armed thugs. Obviously these people had harmful intentions. But even throughout this high-intensity fight for life, Church couldn't help but think in the back of his mind that it was weird for a major boulevard to be having this problem. He wondered whether Kahmay had known just how bad things were before sending them to this so-called rendezvous point in Homer. But that was his tired mind trying to get him a quick set of conclusions for the questions he had about the hostility of this territory. He knew it was the only paved path to Homer, and that failure to follow that path was not a realistic option.

"You just drive honey, I got these punks" Marie said. She turned on the fog-cutting light array and grabbed the shotgun for the fourth time in four days. The high-powered lights were mounted in the front and on the sides of the tractor and had an average combined total brightness-on-target rating of just under five million candle power. The five darkly clad humans emerging from their separate locations raised their arms across their faces in defense from the blinding light that was now foiling their plans to disable the McGradys' progress under the cover of darkness.

"Roll your window down and lean back" Marie said to Church as one of the men sprinted toward the driver's side of the cab with a lit Molotov cocktail in his hand. Marie unleashed a quick blast at the man's right hand just in time to obliterate the man's hand and explode the volatile cocktail out all over the right side of his body. He fell down onto the snow-covered ground writhing in agony and rolled around trying to extinguish the flames and snuff out the pain of the stump where his right hand was located only a moment prior.

Marie jacked another shell into the breech and quickly switched over to the passenger's side of the cab to start firing at the more distant targets with hopes of suppressing their advance while Church navigated the bumpy path back onto the icy pavement. He noticed another individual running at him from a forty-five degree angle off to his left side and immediately steered the GEMINI directly toward the man, who could not get out of the way quick enough after slipping. He attempted to quickly maneuver out of the way of the giant semi and committed a fatal error. Neither McGrady felt bad for running all nine of the port-side tires over top of the individual, which no doubt resulted in the smashing of the man into a fleshy red mess just next to the curb where he tried to pivot and temporarily lost his footing on the slushy ice-slick. Whatever criminal intentions the individual had towards them, his aspirations for a life of nighttime raiding were abruptly ended with his simple underestimation of how fast a large tractor-trailer combo could capitalize on a two-second human error.

Now more than a hundred miles away from those memories, Church smiled a cautious grin at his recollection of the events that transpired while they were making their way through the city. He was indeed grateful that they were now clear of the urban nightmare and slowly making their way through the soupy-thick fog of the Kenai Peninsula under the cover of darkness. He sipped his cold coffee and shifted his weight back over to his right buttock to ease the numbness of his left cheek. Marie reached up to the AM radio tuner and began scanning the band for news.

"There's only one station peaking the detector in this area. But every time it stops scanning, all that comes through is silence" she said.

"You should just try leaving it there. Maybe there's some kind of loop playing and it hasn't started repeating itself yet."

Marie leaned back in her seat with her arms folded in silent frustration as the dark night wore on. The two of them were so tired that they couldn't even bring themselves to the trough of small-talk anymore. But they were both pretty sure that there was nothing harder in their immediate future than what they had just been through. The roads and death-traps of the Alaska territory made the prospect of drifting off into outer space seem like a vacation in the mind's predictive process.

"Wait, I think I can hear something…it sounds like a human voice…" said Marie, turning the volume of the tuner up just enough to try and make out what was being said. There was a series of equally spaced tones, followed by a voice that once again began talking. It was a looped emergency message coming through at 690 Kilohertz.

"This is an emergency broadcast from the United States Coast Guard. Curfew is in effect for all territories

throughout coastal Alaska, Kodiak Island, and the Aleutian Islands. Please remain indoors between the hours of 2200 and 0600. Foreign military forces have begun what is believed to be a phased infiltration of the coastal sectors of Alaska and British Columbia. If you are contacted by Allied military personnel, please be sure to have your vital identification and birth certificate prepared to show the authorities when requested. Please approach military personnel slowly, with both hands visible. Use an approach speed of no more than three miles per hour if you are traveling in a vehicle. Be advised that Allied Forces are working to secure the evacuation of displaced persons throughout this global crisis. All essential federal and state employees are to report to their immediate supervisors for further instructions. Civilians are urged to seek underground shelter in-place and await contact from authorities."

The message repeated itself in multiple different world languages and many dozens of known Native-indigenous/First-Nation/Athabascan dialects. Twenty-five minutes of repeats played through the noisy crackle of bad AM reception, as the McGradys slowly crept their way through the misty night toward Homer. Several small towns and villages dotted the Sterling Highway as contemporary ghost towns with no power. It was strange to the McGradys to see EV charging stations with no power and small groups of humans milling about in the cold night around barrel-fires. Marie was unexpectedly disturbed by the ones who were alone out in the distance, with only a cigarette cherry to betray their presence. She couldn't reconcile how odd it was that someone would be outside in the below-freezing, sometimes sub-zero temperatures, just leaning against the corner of an abandoned miniature strip-mall smoking a cig.

Ultimately, the root cause of the McGradys' confusion came down to how long the emergency message had been playing, versus the length of time the McGradys had been crawling through the brutal Alaskan interior. It turns out that the initial broadcast had only been playing for a little over 72 hours. It had been at least 96 hours since the McGradys had even bothered to attempt the radio tuner. The reception of any kind of broadcast signal had been so elusive for so long that they had both naturally resisted their urge to obsessively keep checking it over and over again to no avail. No voice ever came on, no music, no sound of any kind beyond the standard electromagnetic noise of ambient reality. The citizen's band was set up to receive anything between 25 and 28 Megahertz, but was tactically risky for anything but listening, or dire emergencies. All they really wanted was a simple weather report or a headline news report so they could at least know the bare minimum about what was happening in the world.

"Geez...are you hearing this Mare? Sounds like martial law out here. We've been truckin' through a damn invasion! So I guess it only takes three days for the world to fall apart then. Man...unreal. I sure hope these jokers are there waiting when we get there, because I don't like our chances just sitting at some ferry terminal waiting to be jumped by rogues, thieves, and, oh yeah I almost forgot, the fuckin' Russians for cryin' out loud...sheesh. Can you grab that middle tackle box out of the cupboard babe? We gotta check the batteries and make sure that puppy is all the way charged. We're supposed to make sure it's tuned to 509.000340 Megahertz hon. It should be on there, taped to the inside of the lid. Can you look at that and make sure all those encryption mode settings and the frequency setting are all what the paper says?"

"Okay, okay, give me a second here. Is it this black brick thing that has 'AN/PRC-152' stenciled on it?"

"Yeah, one-five-two, that's the one. Kahmay said she set it up on the tactical channel and made sure I knew not to change any of the settings, but if they were accidentally changed, they're all right there inside on that piece of paper."

"I'm showing 75% battery. It needs to be plugged into the inverter panel. Here..."

Marie plugged the AC-to-DC charge controller directly into the inverter panel and observed the primary indicator lights flash on and then rapidly dim to indicate the battery-charge was in progress.

"Now I can make sure it's tuned in on the right 'freq.' and make sure the squelch adjustment isn't stomping on the transmission" said Marie. "The more sensitive we have it set, the more likely we are to receive them when they're just starting to come into range."

Church released a sudden burst of pent up laughter as he verbally marveled at how technically proficient his honey was with all the fancy crypto hardware. "Dang woman, you and Kahmay have really been hitting the technical stuff while I'm off in the field eh?"

"Should I try it?" she asked.

"Yeah babe, I think so. We've got less than 20 miles to go. I think that radio was set at that frequency so it could transmit farther on less power. Kahmay was saying something about amplification translators that were put out here for the military. Go ahead and try it. I don't think they accounted for all the moisture in the air tonight, but sometimes I think radios work better in the fog anyway. It all depends...on a bunch of technical factors...I think."

"Delta-4, Delta-4, this is Doghouse 1, how copy over?" said Marie in a clear, concise tone of voice. But there was nothing. Marie immediately tried again to no avail.

"I'll try again in a bit. Why don't you do me a favor and eat some of this tuna and crackers Mr. McGrady. We're going to need our energy for the next couple hours at least."

"Is it alright if I have the deviled ham instead honey?"

The two of them sat quietly consuming their snacks and watching the road in front of them with increasing angst as they approached the outskirts of town. The tactical radio came alive just as they were washing down their middle-of-the-night treats with cold coffee.

"Doghouse 1, Doghouse 1, this is Delta-4, how copy over?"

This time Church picked up the radio and tried to contain his enthusiasm as he gladly delivered their response.

"Copy Delta-4, we read you loud and clear here, please advise over."

"Copy that Doghouse, we're just over here to the south-southwest of your position, recommend you turn off your lights and crawl by moonlight sir. Welcome to the party folks."

"Solid copy Delta-4, how will we know where you are?"

"Uh...just keep crawlin' Doghouse, we'll catch you in a half-mile or so. Look for a wiry, skinny lookin' guy with a dim green flashlight just past checkpoint Lima, over."

The McGradys knew that checkpoint Lima was just before the south end of the pier that extended out into Kachemak Bay. Marie was the first one to spot the flashlight swinging in the distance. Church continued crawling the GEMINI through the darkness until he was close enough to Specialist Hutchinson to roll down the window and find out what came next.

"Hey, how you doin' man? My name is Church. I'm here with my wife Marie to…I guess, drive this truck out onto the ferry and then…go with you guys?"

"Yes sir. Specialist Jimmy Hutchinson, it's an honor to meet you both" said Hutch, extending his hand out to shake hands with Kahmay's dad. "Just follow these little itty-bitty orange markers here and drive 'er all the way out onto the sub and put 'er in park. We'll take care of the rest sir."

"Excuse me; did you say 'the sub'…like, as in submarine?"

"Yes sir. It's a lightly armed underwater transport vehicle for big packages like you. Intelligence reports indicate enemy subs have been spotted between here and the HEIWA complex sir. This one here was built for depth so we can follow the contour of the seafloor. The surface is too dangerous at this time sir. The path is predetermined, and has been heavily mined. It's safe, as long as the enemy doesn't see where the insertion and extraction points are."

Marie and Church looked at one another with alarm as the reality of their new circumstances started sinking in with the force of a mule kick.

"Are you telling me...that boat...right there...is actually a submarine?"

"Yes sir, but she sure looks like an ordinary passenger vehicle ferry at a glance doesn't she?"

Marie was having an exceptionally difficult time keeping her cool.

"Oh my God...no way. There's no way this is safe. No way in *HELL*...we are going to die in a watery grave at the bottom of the ocean with a giant USELESS TRUCK TO KEEP US COMPAN..."

"MARE! MARE! CALM DOWN honey! We're going to be fine...it's the damn state-of-the-art, advanced, ferry-fronting, multi-billion-dollar sub boat ship thing, and I'm sure it's gonna be fine babe. Come on now...let's do this okay?" We have places to be and we are running *LATE*! Are we doing this or not honey?"

Marie frantically searched through her purse to find her little canister of 25 milligram meclizine hydrochloride tablets for the motion sickness that she was convinced she was going to be experiencing as soon as they got underway.

"Fine, yeah...let's do this" Marie said, popping two tablets into her mouth and washing them down with cold coffee. "Move it out McGrady."

Church crawled the rig down to the end of the surface pad and pulled on the parking brake before turning off the GEMINI for the night. They would only be starting her up one more time before being lifted into space to board the *X-Tensai*. Hutch followed on foot and joined up with the others as personal introductions were made and the GEMINI was immediately prepped for dive. Monty and Quire chained the truck chassis to the floor while Doyle placed the sliding anchor-chalks into position so as to fully restrict the forward-to-backward motion of the GEMINI. Hutch helped the McGradys grab some personal effects to take with them out of the cab of the truck for use in their passenger berth. The McGradys watched in awe, as the platform they were all standing on began to sink down into the belly of the sub. The sound of splashing seawater could be heard breaking the night silence as it poured off of the gigantic half-shell cocoon modules that were being lifted up from below the surface. The McGradys stared up at the giant moving walls as they closed in together toward the top center axis to encapsulate the top decks. One final clunking rumble resounded throughout the sub's chassis, and was felt within the bodies of the humans as an uncomfortable high-amplitude, low-frequency mechanical vibration. They were sealed off from the outside and pressurized before finally submerging. It was all too surreal for Church and Marie to even be able to form words.

Specialist Quire approached Church and Marie to give them the latest status report from the HEIWA complex.

"Specialist Leonard Quire," said Trigger, extending his hand to both of the McGradys in succession, "It's a pleasure to meet both of you. We just received word from Sergeant Kahmay that we're not stopping in sector 99 anymore. It's too dangerous. The Sergeant requested we proceed directly to the complex. We must get off the planet immediately. Looks like something big is about to happen. We've done all we can do down here…the rest is gonna have to be up to the Allied Forces that are remaining here to hold the lines."

"Pleasure to meet you too Quire" said Marie. "If that's what you guys think is best…then let's get the hell out of here immediately."

"Ma'am, yes ma'am. We're all over it."

Marie observed Hutch and the others dropping something into a stained wooden box before finally entering the hatch that led down below decks.

"What are they all dropping into that box babe?"

"I don't know. It looks like coins" said Church.

The box was obviously a semi-permanent fixture within the cargo bay. There were some words carved and wood-burned into the side of the box that read:

PAY THE BOATMAN

"It's the ship's custom to place coins in the box for the Boatman" said Hutch. "You guys might want to cough up what ya got...I hear there's really something to it".

The McGradys had not been in the habit of carrying coin on their person for many years. Between the two of them all they could produce was Church's Sacagawea Dollar. He had been carrying the coin on his person inside the secret compartment of his wallet for over 26 years. It was his good luck charm that his youngest daughter Lacey had given him as a gift many years ago. He pulled the coin from its hidden compartment inside his wallet, and held it in his palm staring at it for several moments. He knew his hope and faith that he would be able to bond with his youngest daughter again outweighed the importance of keeping the coin. After all, Church's only wish beyond the joy and happiness he felt in life already was to be there for his children. He wanted to honor the tradition of the Boatman, and to simultaneously deliver his prayer for his beloved Lacey to come back into his life safely from sector OR-0005. He thought about how those two things could be the elusive meanings that were always contained in the coin. He would be glad to part with it, and to consider it his and Marie's joint-contribution to the perilous mission ahead. He looked over at Marie and stared into her travel-weary eyes. She smiled a tired smile at him and closed her eyes. She knew he was struggling with the decision. With her eyes still closed, she bowed her head down just slightly to let him know that the coin would be their fee. Church carefully dropped the coin into the box, and the two weary masters of the open road proceeded hand-in-hand through the hatch.

Solid Copper

Earth
HEIWA, Sector HI-0007
January 4, 2026 C.E.
Just before sunset

The sight of so much hardware climbing its way into space along the HEIWA-7 tether on its way to the *E.S.S. Hell Cat* caused Senior Airman Raven Madrone to reflect on everything she thought she knew up until now. Only in her wildest imagination would she have guessed that she would be performing her duties in space from now on.

The volunteers from the 7th Devil Dogs were to be an armed escort for the *E.S.S. X-Tensai* as part of Operation *Kaminari*. Their mission would be to evacuate refugees and provide sanctuary for any humans that could manage to get off the planet while their survivability remained within the realm of possibility. Additionally, in the event the *E.S.S. Scorpius* were to become disabled at some point during phase 1, they were the number one standby vessel to be called upon to deliver robotic infantry units to the surface in the PMDZ. They were ready to do their part to help keep the Green Zone open long enough to extract as many friendlies off of the surface as possible.

The pervading belief among the crews that were already loaded up and ready to undock from HEIWA was that the armies of evil would have a hard time taking over the Green Zone. But any humans who could not make it *into* the Green Zone, or off the planet entirely, would be hopelessly trapped in the impossible situation of having no immediate way out.

Raven looked upward into the sky with her eyes closed and tried to see what was transpiring in the war between the dark and the light, but her vision of the many dark tentacles of evil was obscured by the confusion of human irrationality and unpredictability. She could see the sharks in her mind's eye. The representatives of the darkness were swimming all around them in frenzied anticipation of the imminent fall of humankind. They were thirsty for the blood of the land. They had been driven to this point, and strained to reach the climax of their revenge. Raven smirked at their predictable nature, for she knew it was their weakness to be careless at the precipice of feeding time. She was looking forward to giving them what they wanted in the form of the blood of the enemy. Mekmech approached her from behind her right shoulder as quietly as a whisper. But she could sense his presence so clearly, that even with her eyes closed she could see everything.

"Can you feel the restless darkness daughter? The surrogates of the will of darkness are growing restless."

"Yes father, I can see them starting to panic. Their numbers are growing. We must leave here now. We cannot stop what is coming...it is too powerful" she said.

"It was not meant to be stopped," said Mekmech, "...it was meant to be prevented...and we have all failed to do that."

"We leave when the pod returns. Now is the time to pray father. We must look to Ellam Cua for the way forward." Their conversation was interrupted by a member of the HEIWA ground crew.

"Y'all should get into the shelter...it's gonna be a about a half-hour until your ride gets here" he said. "There's a fierce rain comin' in from the east-southeast. Wouldn't want to be out here when it hits full force. We have plenty of hot chocolate and ammunition."

Warm beverages and conversation with yet another stranger were far from the minds of father and daughter. They had been taken out of their routine rather abruptly on the day Raven was recruited into service for *Kaminari*. Spending time together without the non-stop vigil of so many other matters was a welcome change to the blur that had defined their lives since leaving sector AK-0099. They remained standing outside on the large receiving platform of HEIWA-1. They were looking out onto the horizon as if they were expecting to see something beyond the angry swells and hovering gulls of the Pacific. Raven was still on duty in her mind, and sought to conduct herself accordingly. It was true that her instincts were telling her something about the larger picture; something that did not *feel* right. The most recent reconnaissance report from inside the Green Zone indicated an increased presence of the enemy in waters that were previously believed to be secure. Her attention was temporarily drawn to an old group of F/A-18 Hornet fighters that came screaming across the airspace headed west.

"What kind of planes are those ma'am?"

Raven looked over her left shoulder to see a civilian woman standing just slightly over 5 feet tall with her hand raised to her brow to shield her eyes from the intermittent sun. "I believe those are F/A-18 Hornets ma'am. They're not usually quite so low to the surface."

"Do you think they're on their way to go deliver a special message of high explosives?" the woman asked.

"It's really hard to know what their exact mission is. But I know it's not going to work out well for whoever is on the receiving end of it. Excuse me ma'am, I'm

Raven Madrone. Are you family with one of the crew of the *Hell Cat*?"

"Nice to meet you Senior Airman Madrone. My name is Marie McGrady. I am family with one of the crew of the *X-Tensai*. But I didn't even know that latter bit until they briefed me several days ago on that fancy submarine over there. We've been stuck in the deep sea minefield for the last week."

Marie pointed over to Pier 8 where Church and the remaining DET. IV crew were still carefully maneuvering the GEMINI 2050 into position to be loaded into Pod 8 when it arrived.

"It's a pleasure to meet you Marie. May I call you Marie?

"You can call me whatever you like Raven. 'Marie' would be fine if that's what you prefer honey. With that uniform on, I'm gonna respect you regardless. My Kahmay is part of the crew of the *X-Tensai*. She's already up there on board. Are you part of one of these ships Raven?"

"Yes ma'am. Me and my father are on the *Hell Cat*. We are going to be your heavily armed escort for phase 2 of this mission. Have they briefed you on phase 2 yet ma'am?"

"No, they just told us we were gonna be floating up there close to Earth for several months. Then, I guess we are going to be departing for a different destination. They didn't say where, but I'm sure I could guess."

"It's our duty to keep you safe Marie. You surprised me when you called me 'Senior Airman'. I never told you my rank. You must be familiar with the Zoom ranking system?"

"Yes, my Kahmay started off as a Zoom. But back in her day they were still using a slightly altered version of the post-1947 rank structure. I guess they finally wised-up and forced the Army and the Air Corps to get remarried! Some couples were never meant to be apart. They should have left well-enough alone. I guess everybody went a little crazy during the Red Scare. It didn't help with all those UFOs flying around complicating the matter either."

"You are a very interesting woman to talk to Marie. Maybe we will run into one another someday up there in all that space."

"That would be just fine with me honey. You seem like someone who would be easy to get along with and float around out there in space with. Maybe we can do lunch on the moon someday."

"It's a date Marie!"

Marie left and walked back toward Pier 8 to go and see if it was time to load up and leave skyward yet. She felt proud to meet one of Kahmay's potential future colleagues. She stopped just short of the footbridge and wondered how much pain she would feel in the morning going back over it again. Normally the footbridge functioned as an escalator-type pedestrian walk. But the hour was late, and all available power was now being shunted into the tether system to fully charge the solid-state power-storage matrices inside the supercruisers. Allied Forces had to make the decision to shut down all of the unnecessary systems while the fleet still had access to ground-power sources. The pain in Marie's hips was so punishing that she wondered whether or not it was wise to have walked across the bridge in the first place. But one step at a time, Marie did climb the mountain of steps. With each step, one isolated battle was fought against the pull of Earth's gravity. With one equal and opposite exercise of the will of a single human being, the step could be neutralized. Marie's courageous refusal to be held captive by the *fear* of a thing in her life had brought her the necessary bravery to confront whatever would come thereafter.

"Hey Mrs. McGrady!"

"Hello there Paul. Excuse me while I catch my breath. It was a mistake to cross it."

Specialist Paul Monty smiled in awe of the 76-year-old mother to Sergeant Kahmay. He wanted to ask her who she was talking with over at the receiving platform. But he did not have the heart to force her to begin speaking before she had regained all of her oxygen saturation.

"I was just over talking to a member of the *Hell Cat* crew. I probably should not have pushed myself so hard. But I wanted to do something that forced me to remember the unique feeling of what it is like to experience the aches and pains of planet Earth. Pain can be a powerful memory device."

"I concur with that sentiment one-hundred percent ma'am. Looks like those *Hell Cat* people are catching a ride over to Pier 7 on that tug boat" said Monty.

A large tug boat with the number seven stencil-painted onto the side of it had just returned to the HEIWA-1 receiving platform. Raven and several others climbed aboard to get a ride over to Pier 7. The tug had just finished helping to guide an empty freight barge out of the mooring station octagon and back out into the open ocean. Once the freight barge was through the mouth of the complex and back out into the open ocean, the tug returned to the HEIWA-1 receiving area to stay out of the way, or to transport passengers when there was an opening at the mouth of the octagon.

"Well that just stinks" said Marie. "I wonder if they would have dropped me off here on their way over to Pier 7. Oh well, I guess the exercise was a good thing."

"C'mon baby, we're getting ready to button it up here and go to outer space now" said Church with his signature laugh. "We have to leave at the same time as the number 7...something about shared power resources...I guess they have onboard battery-assist modules and when they leave together they connect these circuitous jumper harnesses and..."

"Okay! Okay! I'm coming...Mr. impatient!"

The McGradys found their seats inside Pod 8 and watched the ascension preparations with nervous intensity while the last of the Det. IV crew and a handful of DSEF ground crew went around the inside of the pod checking the tightness of the many cargo nets and the floor anchors.

Simultaneously, the same scene was playing out aboard Pod 7, as Raven and Mekmech sat quietly looking out of the small window inside the pod. Raven was the first to bring her attention to the inside of the pod to begin thinking about something besides the distracting disturbance she had been sensing. She looked inward toward the center of the pod and noticed that the VANGUARD cargo sections had the words "Precious Metals" stenciled onto the sides. She leaned in to see the fine print of the detailed inventory listing just below the stencil. It was a detailed listing of the contents of a circuit fabrication kit with large quantities of various precious metals like platinum, gold, and copper. She was mildly surprised at herself, because she had not previously considered how important it would be to have such resources aboard a multi-capability military escort ship. The *Hell Cat* would always need exotic communications and electromagnetic countermeasures capabilities as long as the ship's mission-role never changed. To remain fully capable, the crew had to have sustainable processes of fabrication and recycling on board. Precious metals would likely be just as difficult to procure on other worlds as on Earth. Many of the tools of her trade were fabricated with elements that were currently believed to be *universally* rare, regardless of what planet one looked for them on. *It doesn't matter where we go in this universe, people will always place a higher value on this shit,* she thought. *We are changing.*

"Look daughter, isn't the sunset so beautiful?" said Mekmech.

The western horizon of the mighty Pacific appeared to be temporarily frozen into a solid copper lake by the touch of the sun to its distant edge. It was a surreal scene of calmness against a foreground of unprecedented human engineering and technological enormity.

The scene of earthly beauty was abruptly interrupted by a loud, piercing alarm buzzer that was being used at the pier to signal the beginning of an ascension. Raven felt their pod shake ever so slightly as the electrically powered transmission engaged the tether. She and Mekmech shared a glance as they both felt the pod begin climbing smoothly skyward.

The McGradys sat stunned in Pod 8, as they felt the pod and all of its heavy contents being lifted up off the Earth's surface. Specialist Hutchinson sprang up from his seat and began walking toward them from the far end of the pod with his comm-unit in hand.

"Hey Mr. and Mrs. McGrady, are all of your people up in the ship already?"

"We have no idea man" said Church. "We haven't had enough contact yet to be able to know what happened to the others in our group. Our orders were to just keep on going and get here safe. Is everything alright?"

"Not exactly sir. The enemy just delivered a unified threat across the entire planet. They claim they're going to quote 'finish off the remainder of the allied heathen once and for all with one mighty blow'…unquote. That crazy dictator woman from North Korea had a projection screen set up right next to her and showed an authentic-looking video of a mass execution. Looks really bad out there."

"Don't you worry Jimmy" said Marie. "Those little cockroaches are going to get what's coming to them. And any allied troops or civilians that are being executed at this point deserve to be honored as war heroes. That little woman is not going to understand what hit her when her whole delusion comes crumbling down on top of her. I hope she gets a painful, slow death for what she has done to the people of this planet."

"Look at all those ships" said Doyle. The pod had climbed far enough up the tether so that an enormous panoramic view of the surrounding waters revealed a large convoy of Allied drone destroyers off in the distance to the north.

"Looks like they're escorting a line of ferry-subs" said Quire. "Those are probably all people headed for the HEIWA-5 pier."

"What's at HEIWA-5" asked Church.

"That's where the *Terrawatt* is sir. Most of the refugees and raw materials are being loaded into the *Terrawatt* because of her size" said Quire. "Basic phase 1 strategy. She's gonna linger here in geostationary until the majority of refugees off the surface are loaded in. I don't think I'd wanna share company with a bunch of nuclear reactors, but I guess there was no other way."

Payback, Then Punch It

Earth
E.S.S. X-Tensai, Geostationary Orbit
January 5, 2026 C.E.
0600 HRS

The "normal daytime hours" effect was still in play aboard the *X-Tensai*. The civilian and active-duty occupants were all either floating around in one of the many microgravity regions, or they were busily walking throughout the one-g section they had been assigned to. It was determined that there was enough power available to keep at least one hemisphere of the ship's two aft hemisphere assemblies spinning with adequate revolutions to be able to place a force precisely equivalent to the Earth's gravity on everyone and everything contained within the hemisphere. Once the giant hemisphere was spinning at the proper revolutions per minute, the energy requirements to maintain the spin-rate was comparatively small. The hemispheres were each greater than 93% regenerative in microgravity.

For the first time since everyone came aboard, civilians and active-duty personnel were seen eating in the communal mess hall together. Kahmay sat with the others at the booth-style table in the back corner of the dining area in port side one-g. She was with all of the people in the world she loved...and that included both her biological family *and* her crew-family. There was no time to linger. But for a brief while they all sat forcing themselves to eat and go over some of the things that were pressing.

"So, I know most of you have been here for less than 48 hours...there are no windows in here because most people get sick to their stomach when they realize they're spinning in a giant circle...it comes with the territory unfortunately. If you want a good view of the outside that won't cause nausea and vomiting, you'll have to head for the fuselage. Did you all get your room assignments yet?" asked Kahmay to her family while she wolfed down a bite of ham and cheese scramble. Thus far, the rehydrated ham and cheese scramble entrée was one of the only two non-liquid things on the menu for the day.

"Yeah, they got us in D-Block" said Church. Mr. McGrady's eyes were still exceedingly bloodshot from the journey to HEIWA. He sipped espresso with a satisfied-sounding "ahh" after each sip.

"What about you guys Beck?" asked Kahmay.

"We decided that C-Block would be best. It's close to the gym, and just far enough away from the production areas so it will be a little quieter during sleep hours. Plus, it's close to Lacey" said Rebecca. "We have a lot to catch up on."

"What about you guys?" asked Kahmay in the direction of Delmar and Nadia Post.

"I think we're going to be up here close to the crew quarters area. The more distance I put between me and that nuclear reactor during off-duty hours, the better. If one of those field-generators fails...I just don't trust the cold shut-down fail-safes yet. That plasma will wreck your whole day if it gets loose" said Delmar. Seated next to him on his left was Nadia leaning on his shoulder to support herself. She was still receiving I.V. medication and was seen throughout the morning dragging her I.V.-stand around the mess area trying to get one of her six daily recommended 500-foot rehabilitation-walks logged in for the day. The gene-targeting drugs she had received after coming aboard were significantly easier to tolerate than what she had been receiving on the surface. But she was tired and fighting the urge to go to sleep back in their room.

Kahmay wanted very badly to be able to talk to everyone longer and enjoy their company longer. Visitation with family was a pleasure that had been exceptionally fleeting for all of them over the decades. But her utopian breakfast was due to be cut short. Somehow the sarge knew that seeing A.J. walking toward her at high-speed was going to be the abrupt end of the long-awaited visitation.

Sergeant Conway arrived to the table with a tense demeanour and a moderately pained look on her face. She leaned in to very softly whisper into Kahmay's ear.

"It's about your uncle Prescott. He's over on the *Hell Cat*. The Devils picked him up out on the Aleutians with his children. He was out there doing something for DSECC."

"Presto? Prescott McGrady is on the *Hell Cat*?" asked Kahmay in shocked surprise. "No way, really?"

"Yeah, he's over there being debriefed about his experimental transceiver. There's a hundred micro-drones over at the volcano creating a detailed high-resolution 3-D model of the interior and exterior of Kanaga Island. Full GPR and geodetics...is your uncle some kind of whiz?" asked Conway.

"Oh yeah...you could say that" said Kahmay, lifting her eyebrows to stave off the physical response induced by the "understatement effect". "Did he damage the volcano?" Kahmay asked.

"What? Damage the volcano? Uh...no...but, I mean...is he the kind of person that is capable of damaging a volcano? That...was just a weird question to be asking. I'm a little alarmed that your first question was something so..."

"A.J....," interrupted Kahmay, "...uncle was born in the MKUltra era. But he's fine. Save your questions; there's no threat...but there *is* an unbelievable true story behind it. I'll tell you all about it on a rainy day while we're en route for phase 2."

"Alright...anyway, the Colonel wants you up on the bridge as soon as possible. She wants to talk with you about him."

"Alright, thanks A.J.. I'll be right up."

The breakfast visit was over, and now everyone present at the table seemed to be scattering all at once. The feeling of purpose and meaning was overwhelming, as everyone was excited to continue doing their part for phase 1 of *Kaminari*. It was time to put the hurt on the enemy.

"Det. IV...go back to your duty positions and continue familiarizing yourselves with your new environments until later. I need everybody rested and sharp. We're going to brief Phase 1 at 0900 back here by the espresso machine. I'll be here early if you have questions" said Kahmay. She gave her hugs to her family and everyone went their separate ways temporarily. Kahmay was on her way to go see the Colonel, while the McGradys took the opportunity to go grab a short nap. Church and Marie had not seen Lacey for several years prior to now and spent most of the previous night talking, fuelled only by their love and excitement to finally be realizing the dream of reconnecting with Lacey and meeting her family.

Kahmay made her way through the corridors and passageways of the port-side one-g hemisphere into the fuselage. She latched herself to the bidirectional sled that led up to the front of the ship and switched on the high-speed winch that would pull her all the way there. Moving around in microgravity felt painfully slow to her compared to the traction and maneuverability of walking in one-g. But humans had not yet figured out how to recreate gravity without the assistance of "artificial" reactive centripetal acceleration. The inconvenience of microgravity was simply going to have to be tolerated until they could set foot on an object massive enough and dense enough to accelerate them toward its center with significant naturally-occurring fundamental force.

"Ma'am?"

"Good morning Sergeant. You shouldn't sneak up on people like that. At ease" said the Colonel so the Sergeant would drop her salute. "Would your dad have a problem being in close quarters with your uncle?"

"I really don't think so…but they are brothers, and you know how complicated sibling rivalry can be. Is he requesting to come over here?"

"Well, he's on the hook to spend some time with the *Hell Cat* crew going over some things that we think will be very helpful to the mission. After that, we need him to come over here to work on some things, and then, I'm hoping he'll help get the final package ready on the *Blackfoot*. He will be assisted by Yasunaga Atamagawa and Mizuki Kurohaisha, and then the three of them will be permanently assigned here on the *X-Tensai*. The *Blackfoot* is leaving as soon as the package requirements in the *Oblivion* jacket are complied with. And yes, he does seem enthusiastic about the prospect of coming over here. But he can still choose to stay down on the surface if that is what he wishes. Like I said though, he seemed enthusiastic about coming over here and staying."

"I'd say no significant worries ma'am. They both know the stakes, and I'm sure brawling and grudges are pretty low on their list of hopes for their near-term futures. All things considered, the risk is tolerably low."

"Copy that then Kahmay. We want to get him over here as soon as possible. He's partially in charge of safeguarding Earth's intellectual property. The *Hell Cat* is preparing to deliver their offensive payload, but I don't want Presto on that ship when they start their run. I'm marking him down on the mission critical personnel roster so he and his children won't be arbitrarily displaced by a bullshit technicality."

"I appreciate that ma'am. I'm willing to put significant money on it that his contributions to the mission and to the *X-Tensai* herself will be uniquely and immeasurably valuable."

"Very well then. Go brief your crew. It's time to get busy."

"Copy that Colonel...or...I mean...is it Commander now ma'am? asked Kahmay.

"That would be correct Sergeant."

Kahmay had made the double-mistake of initiating her departure without the compulsory military bearing required while in uniform, and had forgotten that the Colonel's new job was to command the *X-Tensai*. But she was not officially bound to that requirement until after she had donned her BDUs and had commenced her briefing at 0900. It was only moderately uncomfortable for her to be discussing mission-related issues in her civi-clothes.

The ninth hour of the local Earth morning had arrived, and with it came the Det. IV crew piling into the mess hall at the booth table in the back; right next to the espresso machine as requested. Kahmay had been there for over half an hour slamming the high-caffeine shots down like she was expecting Armageddon. She waited for the natural quiet of the gathering to settle in, and then gave it to her crew head-on.

"Welcome back to the cause everybody. I have several key points I need to hit with you all this morning, and then we're going to get right to it and get 'er done.

I'm going to say it once, and I'm going to say it fast, so pay attention. Here's the situation" said Kahmay, moving herself into position next to a map of the Earth she had taped to the wall. "Allied Global Forces in the Pacific report the current unbroken perimeter to be here along this red line."

Kahmay drew a line counter-clockwise on the Ring of Fire from Prince Rupert, BC all the way over to the southern tip of Kyushu, Japan, and then continued the line from Port Moresby down around the entire Australian coast and New Zealand.

"The seas between southern Kyushu and Papua New Guinea are no longer secure. The Philippine government has been taken over by unpredictable radicals, and has now begun collaborating with the Chinese and North Korean Navies. Indonesia has helped the Shiites by allowing SETAR to establish bases throughout Java, and over here in select remote areas east of Bali. You can thank the Australian Navy for denying the enemy access to the southern passages. They are currently heavily engaged with SETAR off the western Australian coast over here to the northwest. They and the New Zealanders have lost a lot of people in that location. Intelligence at JTF believes this giant gaping hole is where the majority of enemy forces have been leaking through into the North Pacific for the past couple months. There's just too much ocean between

Hawaii and Edo for the JMSDF and the U.S. navy to catch 'em all. The radicals in Manila had been working behind the scenes with Abu Sayyaf and other militants in the south of the country for weeks to allow for the safe passage of Chinese naval forces out into the Pacific through Mindanao and Leyte. The area here formerly known as 'Okinawa Prefecture' or, 'Sector JP-0047R' as it is also called, is believed to be occupied by a large North Korean contingent. Hence, the Dimsho-38s that keep popping up out in the open ocean. Totally unacceptable. We have no contact with any friendlies along this entire line here."

The crew was quiet, but they were all deeply engaged with what was being said. Their eyes were filled with questions, which for now were being held back in anticipation of more answers.

"Now...number one...we are tasked with focusing all of our surveillance resources on the integrated battlespace in the southwestern quadrant here. We're to report to the JTF in sector 7, and to the operational PMDZ commanders on the surface. There are a number of other Allied enclaves that have been entrusted with operational coordination, and we will be interacting with any number of these folks as things come up. If you have an idea that will help our forces on the ground, bring it forward immediately so that we can consider putting it into play. Number two...we have work to do up here in orbit. This morning, as we are gathered here, the other ships in this fleet are all having meetings of their own. Two ships over, in between the *Hell Cat* and the *Terrawatt*, is the *E.S.S. Scorpius*. Crews on board the *Scorpius* and the *Jackrabbit* are preparing to accept delivery of ten-thousand robotic infantry that have not been produced yet. The infantry units will be produced both here, and over on the *Dark Star*. We are the only two ships currently equipped with 3-D fabrication units, so surprise, we're it! But you guys already knew that, because it was your idea in the first place. Our five-thousand units will be delivered to the *Scorpius*, and the five-thousand produced on the *Dark Star* will be transferred into the *Jackrabbit*. It's time to make good on our promise to DSECC, and to the people who are down there on the surface counting on us, and dying for us. The longer it takes us, the more innocent people of Earth will continue dying. Each shuttle-barge is capable of safely transporting up to four tons of raw material from the *Terrawatt* over here to the aft fuselage receiving docks. It's all about the fuel people. So it might take many trips to get those units out the door. Welcome to your crash course in real world orbital logistics. The sooner we get the raw material intended for this part of the mission, the sooner we'll be able to fit more people into the *Terrawatt*. Her mission, as she is emptying out all of her phase 1 materiel, is to fill up with refugees and then travel out to a more distant orbit in the interplanetary space between here and Mars. There is where she will wait for four to six months until the Mars insertion-window rolls around. Between now and then, we are going to be working around the clock producing. We must help turn the tide down on the surface before the insertion window comes to pass. Our departure from here with the *Hell Cat* as our escort will signal the start of phase-2 operations. We are to rendezvous with the *Terrawatt* and proceed to Mars as planned."

"Sarge," said Quire, "what about the *Dark Star*?" he asked.

"The *Dark Star* and the *Jackrabbit* are going to begin moving into position to support the other side of the planet. The North Atlantic Forces are holding the lines at Edinburgh, Reykjavík, Nuuk, and Halifax. But the lines extending south from Halifax are heavily perforated. Evacuees from the south are being led into Canada to join the others and proceed west toward British Columbia. But all of that is going to be moot if we can't keep the ocean open" said Kahmay.

Throughout the next several days, evacuees from all over Earth were pouring into the HEIWA complex and were being frantically situated into temporary living arrangements aboard the *X-Tensai* and a number of the other cruisers in the fleet as well. Passenger ferries transporting civilians from continental land masses to the HEIWA complex were not all making it to the destination. Several ferries had been forced to cross through open water without being able to utilize the deep sea minefields for safety. Many of the ferries were targeted and sunk at depth. Others that managed to squeak through enemy patrols did so using nerve-racking cat-and-mouse tactics, and took a lot longer to complete the journey than those that had come through the minefields. By the tenth of the month, the flow of refugees had dropped down to a trickle.

Down on the surface, Allied Forces at HEIWA were receiving word from the JTF that the VOTRR beacons in Autonomous Zone 3 were sporadically reporting errors that could not be explained. The beacon line in Zone 3 was one of the last autonomous warning systems the Allies could rely on to give them advanced warning of a large-scale attack coming out of the Okhotsk region. StratoRaven scout-craft confirmed the worst-case scenario was indeed unfolding on all fronts. Remote Allied early warning bases were reporting short and medium range ballistic missile profiles all over the planet.

"Attention, attention" said Colonel Kleen addressing the entire *Kaminari* fleet. "All ships initiate forced separation immediately! Repeat, all ships initiate forced separation immediately! Scorpion, Scorpion!

This is not a drill! Repeat, this is not a drill! Assume defensive posture! Repeat, assume defensive posture. Possible enemy missiles incoming! We have possible enemy missiles incoming! Prepare to defend yourselves! How copy over?"

Severing the Umbilical

Earth
Asynchronous Earth-Freefall
January 11, 2026 C.E.
0017 HRS

The entire crew looked down in horror upon the dark Earth from one of the many starboard observation windows, while a scene of unreal carnage unfolded right before their eyes. Ballistic missiles could be seen detonating in several locations along the distant horizon. Together with the added tiny flashes of various artillery pieces, the scene on Earth appeared like a volcanically-active moon. The fact that the ship was drifting away from the planet temporarily took a back seat to the dumbfounding effect of watching the home planet succumb to full-scale war. In the static microgravity of the *X-Tensai's* gigantic fuselage, the quietness of the gently floating team was a starkly contrasting image against the backdrop of an Earth crust that was literally burning and exploding. The Multiple Independently Targeted Re-entry Vehicles had finally done the job they were intended to do so many decades ago. Each individual was in shock from their own respective nightmare about what they left behind on the surface. Several were in the paralyzing clutches of spontaneous near-outbursts. Awestruck and unaware of all else, the hypnotized crew was effectively paralyzed by the appearance of so much death. Technical Sergeant Kahmay began to feel her airway tightening up, and her body began to feel like it was being electrocuted by a gradually intensifying electrical current. She could hear a screaming sound in the deep reaches of her mind that was so real it clashed with conflicting sensory inputs that sought to debunk the possibility that anyone could hear a human voice so far away and attenuated by distance and atmosphere. Kahmay's heart began to pound faster and harder as the voice began to sound more like someone she knew-someone human. She was confused by what she was hearing, and then suddenly she felt herself being grabbed by the arm and gently shaken. She looked into the eyes of the person who now stared directly into her face. It was Sergeant Conway...but what was she saying? *Oh crap I'm passing out*, thought Kahmay as she noticed the familiar black curtain of unconsciousness falling from her brow toward her lower extremities. It was disorienting passing out in microgravity. It felt more like narcolepsy accompanied by intense nausea.

    Kahmay temporarily lost consciousness while Sergeant Conway began checking her vitals and assessing the best immediate medical response. Her training kicked in and she began instinctively barking orders to the others.

"Somebody help me float her to the med bay... Hey! Hutch! HUTCH!" shouted A.J. to snap him out of his trance.

Specialist Hutchinson tore his head away from the observation window and came to life all at once when he saw the two down on the floor. "Whoa...what the...what happened?" he asked.

"She passed out and went cold, and her pulse is thready," said A.J. with a rapid, intense whisper. Suddenly Sergeant Conway heard a weak voice coming from Kahmay.

"Keep a safe distance and track all the chemical rockets...some of them will be filled with people...we need to get those people before they get too far away from us...they're probably all freaked out...I was stupid and didn't eat...sorry Sarge...won't happen again," said Kahmay with a forced half-smile before drifting off into unconsciousness once again.

"Hey, stay with us O'Conaill...come on, wake up" said Conway.

"How hard would it be to find some orange juice around here?" asked Kahmay, before once again lifting her eyelids open to check if she could see anything more than a multi-colored blur yet.

"Grab her legs," said Conway, as she grabbed Kahmay's shoulders to steer her floating teammate into the med-bay and get her strapped into a gurney for a few minutes of nourishment and low-flow oxygen. Hutch followed with synchronized motion until the two had brought her all the way to the ship's central torsion tube area. The torsion tube area would normally be the quickest way to the med-bay from the observation corridor. But the *X-Tensai* was not yet fully powered up. The scant power presently being consumed was being trickled out of the solid state storage matrix and had to be used sparingly until a period of relative calm could allow them to run through the reactor initialization sequence. The tubes drew power from the reactor, and sometimes delivered regenerative power into the secondary solid state power storage grids, depending on gravitational circumstances. But the ship was too far away from anything remotely resembling gravity for the regenerative power functions to be helpful. A.J. knew she was going to have to bring Kahmay up the stairs.

"I don't need to go all the way up there...I just need some damn orange juice," said Kahmay, this time with the vocal grit of someone who was quickly coming back to the land of the living.

"Hutch, go check in with Norris and Kleen. Do what you can to help. I'm taking her to the galley," said Conway.

Lieutenant Colonel Norris and Colonel Kleen were busy in the control room studying the orbital trajectories of no less than 34 separate chemical rockets and a number of large pieces from the HEIWA that had been flung from the counterweight area into the mooring structure after the other cruisers were free and away. For now, these were the only 34 objects that did not appear to be either debris, or enemy missiles headed for a distant terrestrial target.

Something about the forced separation sequence had obliterated large areas of the mooring structures. But the counterweight itself appeared to be holding its position. The positioning boosters for the counterweight system were apparently still functioning. Ramping up the secondary propulsion system was the only option available to the *X-Tensai* if they were going to pluck human beings out of their crew capsules. The more time that passed, the grimmer the prospects became for those cooped up in the "bottle rocket" lifeboats with their waning oxygen and supplies. All 34 of the rockets being tracked were squawking the proper IFF codes and were high probability rescue candidates. The IFF was the only thing keeping the fleet from blowing them out of the sky. But they wouldn't be allowed within 2000 kilometers of any of the supercruisers until they successfully communicated the proper response to the challenge word. There was still a chance that some of the crews were forced to launch under duress. Additionally, there was still a chance that enemy ICBM targeting profiles could be redirected to their position in orbit.

In addition to the 34 identified life boats, there were a small number of other *unidentified* chemical rockets being tracked by the *X-Tensai's* short-range tracking system that had just popped up on-screen. Kleen fixed her eyes on the UFO tagged by the short-range RADAR as "Unk-00002". She noticed it was on a trajectory that would bring it to within about 514 klicks of the ship and immediately sought to hail the craft on the emergency band. She didn't want to give the order to kill them, as their trajectory was not going to bring them into contact with any of the supercruisers. She finger-swiped the tracking tag for the craft onto the main screen so she could see a magnified view of the craft once it came into clear visual range of the *X-Tensai's* telescopic cameras. Once the images became available from the forward SR-1 feed, the Colonel hoped they might provide a clue as to the craft's origin.

"Attention unknown vehicle bearing 172 decimal 4, this is the *E.S.S. X-Tensai*. Are you in need of rescue?

She squinted slightly as the initial images started showing up on the main screen as red and white tones with some blue mixed in. Gradually the image came into focus as the unknown vehicle sped toward its closest approach to the *X-Tensai's* aft starboard corner.

"Attention unidentified vehicle bearing 172 decimal 4 equatorial, what are your intentions? SCORPION, SCORPION, how copy over…" asked the Colonel. "Are you in trouble, over?" The Colonel switched the nav-computer from geocentric over to heliocentric hoping the unidentified craft would respond to the adjusted identifier.

There was no "TARANTULA" response from the vehicle, and the Colonel could not think of any other immediate way to hail the craft before it would be past its closest approach to the ship, apparently on its way to an unknown destination. The signals room directly below the command deck was not yet up and operational, but was being feverishly brought online by what was temporarily Sergeant Conway's new crew. They were attempting to rapidly give the ship its expanded operational signals capability. The key to tracking vehicles that were headed out of the near-Earth space was down in that room, and only the long-distance laser tracking and RADAR would allow them to keep tabs on any potentially friendly craft that were now headed into oblivion because they jacked up their trajectory free-fall calculations, or experienced some other systems malfunctions. The fact that the signals room was not fully operational at the time of forced separation would go down as a monumental screw-up for sure. People at all organizational levels knew the clock was ticking, but nothing sobers up and calibrates the mind more than a rude upper-cut from crisis in the reality of real time. It was inexcusable that such a crucial element of the ship's capability was absent when it was most needed. It was common knowledge that a hasty evacuation would, in all likelihood, be accompanied by the need for expanded signals capability. Somewhere along the line, somebody thought the *X-Tensai* and her crew would be just fine with a basic operational test-launch package.

C'mon Kahmay...where the fuck are you? thought Colonel Tabitha Kleen. The Colonel was starting to panic about how far they were drifting, and why the ship's third in command was not there to help stabilize their orbit.

As a matter of fact, where in the HELL is ANYONE AT ALL? she thought. Kleen tightened her squint on the image of the unidentified craft as it crossed its closest approach point of 513.7 kilometers. The craft turned out to be an old Russian-flagged rocket of some kind. It was really moving; traveling at over 14.1 kilometers per second with no propulsion plume. Their telemetry profile was stable, but they were not answering the Colonel's challenges and hails. Obviously, judging by the craft's tangential acceleration, they had already used a lot of propellant for their size, and had no intention of remaining close-by in perpendicular equilibrium with local gravitational acceleration. Such a hair-on-fire number had to be meant for some other region of the interplanetary neighborhood. She knew there was no way they got going that fast without a secondary burn *after* local air density had reached near-zero conditions outside the Earth's atmosphere. The maximum dynamic pressure ratings for chemical rockets had come a long way in the past ten years. But not *that* far long. She couldn't help but wonder if she'd ever see them again as they streaked past the area into the darkness of interplanetary space. The rocket did not look like an offensive missile. But there was too much other stuff going on to pay too much attention to it. As long as it wasn't an immediate threat, she could let go of her preoccupation with it and focus on more important matters that they actually still had some degree of control over. There were more survivors to collect, and the *X-Tensai* had only just begun the near-Earth phase of Operation *Kaminari*.

The Colonel's worry about righting the ship's orbit was exacerbated by the fact that she was only getting intermittent reciprocation from members of the crew that were scattered elsewhere about the *X-Tensai*. Lieutenant Colonel Norris was hopelessly busy delivering instructions to the chemical rocket crews. They had to be coached in one at a time on how to position themselves in such a manner so as to ensure that they ended up in position to afford the best opportunity to be quickly intercepted and rescued. But all he could really do was place them into an orbit that he believed the *X-Tensai* or the *Hell Cat* could reach before things snowballed out of control.

"Sergeant O'Conaill reporting ma'am" said Kahmay with a quick, crisp salute. The Sergeant came gently floating to the command console where the Colonel had been glued for the past two hours. "Conway just made her way down to signals to try and keep track of everyone in danger of wandering outside the Hill Sphere."

"Geez...you look like shit Sergeant. Why the hell is your face so white? Oh yeah that's right, you've been running around here like a chicken with its head cut off for the past week...without eating. Well look Kahmay, if you're all finished with your hunger strike, we need retro-return back to geostationary like NOW! And from now on I think I'm going to demand that you carry a damn energy bar or something in your BDU pocket at all times."

"Yes ma'am...will comply. Does your screen show those long range transceivers up and running yet? Disregard, disregard...I see the long-range array coming up now...here comes the data points for all the runaways...whoa, I'll let you look at that while I hit the gas."

Kahmay opened up the propulsion menu and brought up the orbital positioning sub-menu. She initiated the pre-checks for the ion system and selected "equal and opposite" from the retro menu. Within two minutes all of the ion systems were reporting "standby", which actually translated to "go ahead and light the fire". The retro menu showed two choices: "Go" and "No Go". Kahmay hit "Go" to allow the positioning boosters to angle thrust in the direction necessary to decelerate the *X-Tensai* in precisely the opposite direction of the original forced-separation blast that sent them drifting out of their stationary position.

"Where is Norris guiding the LEO rockets to ma'am?"

"So far he has managed to line up two of them in stable orbits around their original parallels. But they're all still too far away to just reach out and touch. Plus, we're in the blind here from the other cruisers. The entire fleet has been told to widen interval spacing out to 20 degrees longitudinal and to be prepared to execute evasive maneuvers. The last thing we need is to be crashing into one another while we're trying to evade and destroy an ICBM. But we don't know if they've received the message, or if they are trying to guide the other rockets somewhere else...after we've already told 'em to stay put...or what! Why don't you try and see if you can raise the *Hell Cat*...we at least need to know where our neighbor up here is."

"Copy that. Retro-return to geostationary in-progress. In the meantime, I'd say let's just stop this beast and go from there."

With the touch of a finger, and a physical push of the shielded "Thrust" plunger, Kahmay engaged the ion drives and began slowing the ship back down to a stationary position. Everything seemed to be alright for the time being considering the circumstances.

Uncomfortably Numb

Earth
Untethered Geosynchronous Orbit
E.S.S. X-Tensai
January 12, 2026 C.E.
0300 HRS

The day that followed "The Day of Anarchy" was indeed the darkest hour for the fleet. Most of the crew of the *X-Tensai* remained quietly and frantically busy in starboard one-g, or in the signals room below the bridge. A.J. and Kahmay carefully monitored the onboard navigational systems from the control room section of the bridge, and periodically checked in with med-bay to see about the status of the recovered survivors. Thus far, the crew had managed to bring 51 daring souls onto the *X-Tensai* through cargo bay three on the starboard fuselage. That was a victory, and would be helpful in adding strength to the ranks of tired survivors, most of whom were still struggling to get oriented into their new surrealistic environment. The ship needed more humans; especially the ones that were "crazy" enough to launch themselves into space without a guarantee of being rescued by one of the supercruisers. Those people building rockets in their barns were going to become part of the crew and they didn't even know it yet.

Some time had to pass to give everyone the opportunity to come to the realization that there was a lot of work left to do at their present location. Were there more survivors? Were some people encapsulated underground on what remained of the broken Earth...surviving as the first mammals did so many millions of years ago? Why hadn't they heard from any of the other supercruisers in the fleet since the attacks began?

The large volume of new variables to assimilate was initially stifling. There was so much to do, and so very little time to do it. The crew was still significantly more vulnerable than they realized. But they had trained for this, and were all rapidly processing the changes. Several major issues confronted them in the hours following the surface attacks.

The primary propulsion system was not yet functioning. But in order to get it going, the crew was going to have to act fast. The longer they used available power intended for the reactor's ignition lasers, the less power would be available for the lasers once the initialization sequence began. The ship's oversized ion thrusters were currently being tested in offset mode, and were not providing any discernable impulse for the purpose of flight. Kahmay had set the power level to 5%

since returning the ship to geostationary orientation. The low setting was chosen so a period of break-in could occur while they all contemplated their new situation with the utmost caution. She did not measure any discernable position-drift over a precise time interval, which meant that the offsetting functions of the secondary propulsion system were still working properly. Kahmay put the thrusters into station-keeping mode once the offset test passed so that the ship would now periodically correct itself, burning thrusters only when there was a discernable position drift to correct. But what the *X-Tensai* and the other supercruisers really needed was full functionality of the fusion-powered capabilities of the cruisers. Expedient travel and significant offensive and defensive capabilities simply could not be operationally tested until the Class-B fusion reactor system was brought online. The list of things that required the full power of the reactor system was growing by the hour.

The enemy would have a turkey shoot if they could figure out how to reprogram Earth's long-range ballistic missiles to target the fleet in orbit. Every ship in the fleet was equipped with extreme-high-power(EHP) multi-role lasers. But without the reactor to draw power from, the range and effective neutralization rating of the lasers was limited. The lasers were originally meant for obliterating small asteroids and other potentially hazardous objects in the flight paths of the cruisers. But the two-part system was 50 to 80% degraded without the fusion reactor to power the variable EHP side of the system. If ICBMs were indeed launched offensively against the fleet, the fleet would have to use the low-power side of the system, which was still arguably powerful enough to take the "smart" out of the incoming missiles. But there was no guarantee; such a scenario had never been tested, even if it had been predicted long ago.

The preset laser was capable of firing a variety of focused, fixed-power output levels, accompanied by inversely shortening burst-time intervals. Effective incineration and disintegration distances varied predictably with homogenous target density, the target's relative angular velocity, and total target matter. Exhaustive variation in the crucial control variables during surface-testing likely meant that the device was probably originally going to be used for military applications. It was often true that only the power of a governmental purse could afford such copious reassurances for the kinds of dark projects required to destroy asteroids, or supersonic ICBMS; whichever came first.

The larger of the two laser systems was fundamentally similar to the low-powered preset. The maximum output power of the high-range was set to one-quadrillion watts. But the burst interval at that power level could only be sustained for a handful of microseconds without the reactor. Longer burst intervals would be needed to achieve the amounts of energy requirements needed for the destruction of large massive objects at longer distances. Only a ship's reactor could provide such energy levels.

The high-end leg of the dual-system was also equipped with a variable power output; selectable down to as little as 10 kilowatts. With such a wide range of wavelengths and power levels, the system could utilize the capability of a variety of different user-selected power curves depending on target specificity. In the case of the high-end laser, its likely applications would most definitely include the destruction of asteroids, as long as the asteroid wasn't disproportionately large like a planetoid or a small moon. Most common-encounter materials could be easily neutralized energetically with the proper coherence and collimation settings.

"Tarantula, tarantula..." came the long-awaited voice over the encrypted tactical channel. "Tarantula, tarantula...this is the *E.S.S. Dark Star*. How copy over?"

"Go ahead *Dark Star*. This is Sergeant Kahmay O'Conaill of the *X-Tensai*."

"Oh, helloooooo *X-Tensai*...we were starting to get worried we lost you out here."

"We may be a little disoriented, but we're still here. We've been watching you and the others for quite a while *Dark Star*...but this is the first voice contact we've had from anyone since forced-separation" said Kahmay. "Have you heard from any of the others?"

"That affirmative Sergeant...you guys were the last holdouts. We isolated the communication problem early this morning. But we didn't have a way to let the others know, so we sent one of our shuttles out to go around and visually signal everyone about the fix. How the hell did you guys fix it without knowing?"

"Her name is Specialist Penelope Gordon. She realized a few hours ago that when forced separation occurred, it placed the ship-to-ship comms into standby. We think it was a last minute change that was never written into the technical literature."

"Outstanding! If you see our guy zooming by in a bobtail flashing a big flashlight at you, he's on channel 4A. Could you please tell him to return to the ship?"

"Copy that *Dark Star*..." said Kahmay. Glad to know you guys are okay. Who am I speaking with?" Kahmay asked.

"This is Master Sergeant Derrick Sanders...yes, the same one you served with over at the RADERS girl! Who put you in charge?" asked Sanders, laughing at the improbability of the run-in.

"I knew I recognized that voice. I was always in charge dude…I thought you knew better! But no, seriously, I'm just here because our starters finally had to get some sleep…and because I swore to give my life in defense of the Republic for which it stands. Nice to hear your voice Master Sergeant. Something about familiar voices never gets old. Did you guys get your production line up and running yet?"

"Negative, uh…we're really just getting started over here. The first load of materials from the *Terrawatt* is on its way over as we speak. We only had nine survivors from the lifeboats. So they caught a ride with the first shuttle and got dropped off over there at the *Terrawatt*. They're waiting on all of us to get that stuff emptied out so they can plant the garden and focus on not starving before the completion of phase 2. Even if they take on several thousand more passengers by the time phase two rolls around, they still have enough in there to last 13 or 14 years. Nobody's trying to let it come to that though. Report from command over there is that she's up and running and the dormant reactors are all secure and stable. They've been adding small handfuls of refugees over there all night. For our part, we're down to just crew and operational civilians with all the families tucked in safe and sound over in one-g. No HEIWA refugees onboard here at the moment."

"You guys have us at a disadvantage Sanders...we're still pretty far away from the *Terrawatt*. But give us a little time and we'll make it right sir. They need these ten-thousand units down there more than ever. I better let you go so we can start making contact with the others. Please give our regards to the *Jackrabbit* my friend."

"Will do Kahmay...you guys ready to get to work?"

"We're all over it man. I think we're having a little trouble coming up with enough stimulation power to get the reactor going. It's kinda like owning a big fancy motorhome and trying to start it with a 9-volt battery. Our solid-state matrix is running low. We're all pretty tired...but we've only just begun to show what we're made of...*X-Tensai* out..."

"Copy that Kahmay...we've got your back...let us know if you need a jump...*Dark Star* out..."

"Did I just hear you talking to someone? Was that the *Dark Star*?" asked Lieutenant Colonel Norris as he walked over to Kahmay from across the bridge. He seemed decidedly alert for a man in his late fifties who had just woken up from an hour-long nap.

"Yes sir. They've already been in contact with everyone else. Their first load of materials is on its way over to them from the *Terrawatt* as we speak."

"We need to get our process going immediately" said Norris. "The *Scorpius* and the *Jackrabbit* need to leave on their deliveries at the same time. We are going to need two shuttles to keep pace with the productivity of the *Dark Star*. We'll load the completed infantry units onto the *Scorpius* as each individual unit is completed. We're going to randomly sample the outgoing units with a 10% selection rate for functional verification testing. Who wants to volunteer to be the first two inter-ship cargo shuttle pilots?"

"Hell with it, I'll go Colonel" said Quire floating forward out of the port-side union passage that connected the bridge to the signals room.

"Yeah, we'll go" said Monty, coming in with Specialist Lenihan right behind Quire. Monty was quick to take the second spot so that he could have the honor of joining his brother-in-arms with the full Triggerhound advantage. If anybody could get it done, they could.

"It's settled then; get over there quick and safe gentlemen" said Norris, shaking each of their hands in succession. "Don't think about the big picture of it guys; just take it one load at a time. We're going to be firing up the fabrication systems while you're gone. And maybe, just maybe...we might be able to get our hands on some serious power by the time you get back. Delmar Post is down there right now getting set up for reactor initialization. Lenihan, you are our most knowledgeable propulsion guy, hands down. You are the one Del needs with him right now...he has been studying the system for several months and has been here acquainting himself with the system in-person for about two weeks already. He can bring you up to speed and he has a lot of knowledge...so learn everything you possibly can from him as soon as possible Zeke. Special knowledge is a rare commodity these days; we gotta keep the knowledge train going. I trust every last one of you guys" said the Lieutenant Colonel to those present in the immediate vicinity. "Let's get it done."

  Monty and Quire floated themselves over to the winch-sled and launched themselves at high-speed down to the aft end of the *X-Tensai's* port-side fuselage where the shuttle barges were located. They unhooked themselves after stopping the sled and gave each other one last handshake and a brotherly hug before entering their respective doors that led into their shuttles. They busied themselves setting the flight and HUD controls and were rapidly initializing all of the critical life-support systems while small groups of refugees entered the shuttles and began the process of strapping themselves into the restraint harnesses. Moments later the shuttle bay was depressurized and the large launch doors began slowly retracting sideways from the middle. The mooring clamps gently pushed the shuttles through the bay openings and the two small craft slowly floated out into the port-side space. Monty and Quire carefully maneuvered away from one another initially in order to provide themselves with a more generous space allotment as they turned around and set their course for the *Terrawatt*. Kahmay watched their departure through one of the *X-Tensai's* starboard observation cupolas with hope in her heart, as she thought of the fate of those still on the Earth's surface.

Meanwhile, Delmar Post and Specialist Lenihan were down in the reactor control area faced with the problem of how to steal enough energy from the solid state storage matrix to excite the ultra-dense deuterium contained in the reactor's core without depleting the available stored power in the matrix. The available power in the solid-state matrix was already becoming too low for comfort.

The stable fusion of deuterium had been designed in such a way so as to be maintained in a geometrically perfect, extremely low-leakage closed system for near-indefinite periods while in storage. The humans proved in 16' that previously unpredicted quiescent states within reactor tokamak structures could be achieved through the use of phase-tuned positive-feedback adjustments. Plasma states with unusually high stability were useful, because they afforded the kind of reliability required for long-term performance and accurate control of the fusion energy. Certain amplitude-quadruplicating points were identified within the revised deuterium-tritium torus, and as luck and the laws of physics would have it, the energy requirements to overcome the coulomb force normally *preventing* "D to D" fusion was just about four times of that required in the "D to T" models. Thus, the first pure D-D fusion products were the result of the earlier D-T reactions. That being said, the fusion energy process for space propulsion became one that eliminated the need for dangerous tritium on board the cruisers. Enormous amounts of energy were there for the taking. But the energy levels required to give the reactor core its initial boost to its stable operational output had to come from the solid-state storage matrix. Feedback loops taken from the reactor's output were used to inform the intensity of the stimulation lasers that kept the deuterium core sustainably excited enough for practical safe use. But one burst from the stimulation laser would probably degrade the ship's other capabilities so far that it was not value-added to use up the remaining stored power without first taking certain precautions.

"I'm tellin' you man...it's not going to work without more power. We gotta get that solar collection array deployed *right now* if we're gonna have a hope of getting this thing going in the next 24 to 48 hours" said Delmar, scratching his head and wiping the sweat from his forehead.

"Copy that sir" said Lenihan. "I agree...there's not enough in the matrix to jump this thing. Where did all of our power go?"

"It can't be created or destroyed Zeke...it had to go somewhere. Do me a favor and see which systems are in use right now. We need to shut down everything that isn't critical. That way we can have a look-see about whether we have enough to excite this thing into action."

"Hey man...look at this...it's the usage log...see right here where the two shuttles took off...we used up 3.27% of the solid state power just opening up the launch bay doors for crying out loud. The good news is that they haven't shut 'em yet, so there's still time to make sure they stay open until all the materiel is on board and the shuttles get parked back in there" said Lenihan.

"*THAT'S* what I'm talkin' about right there man. Keep doing that...save as much as possible. We're gonna need it to get this big ole' heap up and running."

Down on the bridge, Kahmay keyed up the ship-to-ship comms to see if she could get ahold of the *Hell Cat* now that she knew everyone else had their communications up and running.

"Scorpion, scorpion...this is the *X-Tensai*. Attention *Hell Cat* control, does anybody over there read me?"

"Tarantula, tarantula…this is Sergeant Bakuhatsu of the *Hell Cat*. Nice to have you guys back online Sergeant!"

"Damn good to hear from you Rahiko! I think we're gonna need your help over here pretty soon man. You guys get your Class-B initialized yet?"

"Oh hell yeah we did Kahmay…it took everything we had left in our solid state matrix…but we were able to get it on the first try after we shut everything down first."

"Yeah…we're just now figuring that one out over here. We're going to try that and see what happens. Stick close to the comms Sergeant…we might need a jump" said Kahmay, laughing at the irony of the flagship requiring a jump from the escort.

"Solid copy Kahmay…it might not be too late for you guys if you shut everything down immediately. We'll be here standing by…good luck."

Delmar and Lenihan remained busy shutting down unneeded subsystems while Kahmay and A.J. methodically checked in with each of the other ships in the fleet.

"Okay Del…that's it man. We've got a little over 62% to work with. If that's not enough, then…I guess we'll need to move on to the next solution" said Lenihan.

"This isn't guesswork Zeke" said Del. "The laws of physics are clearly defined, and will reveal the absolute truth every time as long as we get the calculations right. Prepare to prime the laser."

"Roger that...priming ignition laser...cavitation less than 2%...aberrational field-flux negligible...standby for ignition...in...5...4...3...2...1...and...firing laser..."

The gain-medium cylinders lit up the reactor room with a bright blue, as the ignition laser fired into the reactor core and began the chain-reaction energy-release within the primary power system. The low throbbing sound of the increasing energy-level within the deuterium core caused both men to clinch their jaws tightly as they waited for the available output metering to show that the nominal operational threshold had been achieved. One by one, the feedback loop indicators turned green, and then the moment they had all been waiting for came to pass; the propulsion control monitor flashed the message indicating full power was available.

"HELL YEAH! We did it! WE ROLLIN'! WE ROLLIN'!" said Del. He and Specialist Lenihan slapped a hard "five" and began the rewarding process of carefully bringing all of the subsystems back online one at a time. Throughout the ship, equipment and lighting began coming to life and the crescendo of activity began filling every nook and passageway of the gigantic supercruiser. Cheers could be heard everywhere, as everyone on board took notice of an entirely new ship; one filled with the sound of progress and purpose. The dream of *Kaminari* was real.

By the end of the month of January, the interstellar fleet had come into its own with an irregular, rare kind of speed. The hearts and minds of the *Kaminari* forces were more determined than ever to keep the enemy at bay, and to preserve the human way of life. Sustainability of operations heading into phase 2 still looked challenging. But there were new reasons to be hopeful every day. Mass production of the robotic infantry units was fully ramped up. Contact with the HEIWA complex had been reestablished, and updated situation reports from the surface of Earth were flowing into the planning rooms of the entire *Kaminari* fleet. It was the exact vision that was born so many decades ago, and was the realization of a long-awaited dream.

Allied forces on the surface celebrated the *Kaminari* fleet's arrival to full operational capability with giant bonfires, and uninhibited revelry. It was the first significant piece of positive news the forces of good had received in many weeks. Troop morale was taking a turn for the better, as everyone fighting the dark armies took a brief moment to be thankful for one another, and for the promise of a brighter future.

On February 5th, 2026, the fleet's two short-range infiltration ships, the *Scorpius* and the *Jackrabbit,* each delivered their first of several robotic infantry payloads from orbit to the Allied commanders on the surface. In their first week of battle, the infantry units were consistently achieving kill-ratios in the range of 500 to 1 with skilled MHOs at the controls. The enemy did not yet know how to neutralize this small sampling of the Allies' most secretive weapon-systems. More time for the refugees had now been secured. Evacuees and additional raw materials were once again making their way up the HEIWA tethers and out into the fleet. Humans everywhere had new reason to be hopeful.

"This is Commander Tabitha Kleen" said the Colonel, addressing the entire *Kaminari* fleet over the radio. "I am very proud of all of you for how far you've come, and for what you've all had to sacrifice to get here. The tide is turning on the ground, and we are now on-schedule to transition into phase 2. At 1800 hours local HEIWA, the *E.S.S. Terrawatt* will begin her careful drift into position for Mars insertion. She will be joined later this coming spring by us here on the *X-Tensai*...and by the *E.S.S. Hell Cat*. We will be preparing a place for all of you in the dark western labyrinth of *Valles Marineris*. You are all in our thoughts, meditations, and prayers, as we fight for our right to exist in this galaxy...without fear of retribution for our beliefs or for who we are, and without hindrance by the darkness that has tried so desperately to subdue us. I ask you only for your continuing courage...and for your will to keep fighting in the face of whatever may come. Prepare yourselves...and take care of one another. *We*...are all that we have. *We*...are the Exosapiens. *X-Tensai* out."

To Be Continued…

Made in the USA
Charleston, SC
22 November 2016